JUST SAY YES

"There's no such thing. A girl always expects to be kissed. It's only the where and the when she doesn't know," Tisha answered.

"We must answer those two questions, then." Warmly and briefly his mouth touched hers; then he was once again looking down at her, watching the hot color steal over her cheeks.

"Was that the best you could do?" she asked, surprised to find her breathing was shallow and uneven.

The glinting humor in his eyes took in the other dancers around them. "Under these circumstances, yeah," Roarke answered smoothly.

"I didn't realize discretion was one of your virtues."

"I didn't know you thought I had any."

Right now, if she had to be absolutely honest, virtue was the last thing on her mind.

from "Valley of the Vapors"

BOOK YOUR PLACE ON OUR WEBSITE AND MAKE THE READING CONNECTION!

We've created a customized website just for our very special readers, where you can get the inside scoop on everything that's going on with Zebra, Pinnacle and Kensington books.

When you come online, you'll have the exciting opportunity to:

- View covers of upcoming books

- Read sample chapters

- Learn about our future publishing schedule (listed by publication month *and author*)

- Find out when your favorite authors will be visiting a city near you

- Search for and order backlist books from our online catalog

- Check out author bios and background information

- Send e-mail to your favorite authors

- Meet the Kensington staff online

- Join us in weekly chats with authors, readers and other guests

- Get writing guidelines

- AND MUCH MORE!

Visit our website at
http://www.kensingtonbooks.com

JANET DAILEY

Bring The Ring

ZEBRA BOOKS
KENSINGTON PUBLISHING CORP.
http://www.kensingtonbooks.com

ZEBRA BOOKS are published by

Kensington Publishing Corp.
850 Third Avenue
New York, NY 10022

All Kensington titles, imprints and distributed lines are available at special quantity discounts for bulk purchases for sales promotion, premiums, fund-raising, educational or institutional use.

Special book excerpts or customized printings can also be created to fit specific needs. For details, write or phone the office of the Kensington Special Sales Manager: Kensington Publishing Corp., 850 Third Avenue, New York, NY 10022. Attn. Special Sales Department. Phone: 1-800-221-2647.

First Printing: July 2006
10 9 8 7 6 5 4 3 2 1

Printed in the United States of America

CONTENTS

SUMMER MAHOGANY   7

VALLEY OF THE VAPORS   165

SUMMER MAHOGANY

Chapter One

Gina stared in shocked disbelief. After all these years . . . there was Rhyder. It seemed impossible. But those were his blue eyes, startling and clear. Did he recognize her? Reflexively, she touched the gold band of her grandmother's wedding ring. It burned like ice around her finger.

She turned away swiftly before he could see her and kneeled in front of a shallow trough of stainless steel, raised by short legs above the firewood. The tough material of her scarlet jumpsuit didn't protect her knees from the gritty sand beneath them, but Gina was oblivious to the discomfort.

Her heart was pounding like a frightened rabbit's. She was hot and cold all at the same time. It was a mistake, an illusion. But she couldn't make herself look again. The one glimpse of his tall, muscular frame was enough. Not once in nine years had she ever mistaken anyone else for him, not for a second. There was no reason to think she might have done so now.

No, it was Rhyder, his jet dark hair ruffling a little in the sea breeze. Maturity had made his aquiline features even sexier and intensified the aloof bearing that bordered on arrogance. His sun-browned skin was a startling contrast to his blue eyes.

Gina didn't exactly want to remember her response to her grandfather's question the first time he had seen Rhyder, but it came back to her. He'd wanted to know who the man was that his young granddaughter was staring at.

"He's from away, summer mahogany," she'd answered, using a phrase her grandfather understood instantly.

Anyone not born and raised in Maine was referred to, amiably enough, as being "from away," and "summer mahogany" had once meant the yachting set and the distinguished families who'd summered in Maine for generations.

In other words, a cut above the regular "summer complaints," an affectionate term for not-so-rich tourists who rented cottages and took all the parking spaces at the beaches.

In recent years, the "summer mahogany" category had broadened to include brash hedge fund millionaires and tech types who'd made even bigger fortunes in the computer business. Some of them never even set foot on the decks of their expensive toys and looked like they rarely saw the sun either, even if they were rich enough to own their very own islands, and many were. But Rhyder's deep tan was real, and the term described him well.

To the impressionable eighteen-year-old that Gina had been nine years ago, he'd seemed as glamorous as a movie star. Rhyder personified summer mahogany, with his features appearing chiseled in hardwood and browned by time spent outdoors and on the water. There had been a raw virility about him, something she hadn't encountered before then, not to that degree— or since.

Gina trembled visibly. She wanted to run before another meeting with Rhyder was forced upon her, but she couldn't. Now that she was here, she had to stay. Inventing a plausible excuse to leave the party wasn't going to happen.

"I know the breeze is brisk, Gina, but you can't be cold," a female voice chided. "Shivering is not allowed."

Gina turned her head to reply to the woman who'd spoken to her, trying to mask her emotional turmoil. Katherine Trent, Justin's sister, was looking at her.

"I was thinking of winter, I guess," Gina lied.

"It isn't even officially autumn yet. Don't be rushing the seasons." The admonishment was offered laughingly. "Want to give me a hand packing this?" Katherine pulled a large plastic bag toward the shallow trough, three-quarters full of water. "Justin's succeeded in getting detained by the late arrivals. He manages to do that at every clambake."

Gina smiled stiffly, but didn't comment. "I don't mind helping. Part of the fun of a clambake is the preparation." But her hands were still trembling as she reached into the bag containing the seaweed. Fortunately Katherine didn't seem to notice. They added seaweed to the water in the trough.

"Most people think the eating is the fun part." Katherine closed the plastic bag and turned to remove the burlap top, saturated with water, that covered the large drum filled with live lobsters.

Stacked on top of each other in the metal drum, the lobsters crawled around with difficulty. Their hard shells glistened dark green against the seaweed scattered among them. Avoiding the waving claws, although each had been rubber banded, Gina and Katherine lifted the lobsters individually and set them in the trough.

"Prepare to meet your Maker," Katherine intoned. "Would you like to say a few solemn words, Gina?"

"Oh, stop it," Gina said. "It's not any different than

eating shrimp. They don't jump into the supermarket package on their own accord."

"I guess not."

When the bottom was covered with lobsters, they added more seaweed, followed by another layer of lobster and more seaweed. The barrel drum was emptied, and Katherine turned to the clams, already wrapped in cheesecloth sacks.

"Do they get a farewell speech, too?" Gina asked.

"No. I never know what to say to the clams."

Gina had to smile. A few of the guests drifted over to observe the preparations. Their casual interest heightened her hidden tension. The moment was approaching when she would have to face Rhyder. There were nearly thirty guests at the clambake, and she couldn't hope to avoid him indefinitely.

Mentally she tried to brace herself for the meeting, telling herself there was a slim chance he wouldn't recognize her. After all, she had been eighteen the last time he had seen her. Nine years would have altered her appearance more than they had altered his.

True, her hair was still dark, as midnight black as his, but it didn't fall in long silken strands past her shoulders. It was cut short, waving about her ears to add a touch of sophistication to her appearance. Her eyes were the same ocean green, outlined by thick lashes, but were no longer trusting and innocent. Her curves were more womanly now, but her figure hadn't changed that much.

Gina sincerely doubted that he had forgotten her, any more than she had succeeded in forgetting him. No matter what, she resented his second intrusion in her life, and she guessed Rhyder would feel the same when he recognized her.

"Gina!"

She stiffened at the sound of Justin Trent's voice calling her. A sixth sense warned her before she even looked his way that Rhyder was with him. A forced smile curved her mouth as she turned around, carefully avoiding any glance at the man walking beside Justin. But she could feel the sensation of narrowed blue eyes sweeping over her body.

Her fingers closed tightly over the cheesecloth bag of clams as she fought the waves of panic rising inside her. If she had been given a year, she still wouldn't have been prepared for this moment. Her composure was eggshell brittle, threatening to crack at the slightest jar.

"I've been looking for you." Justin slid an arm around the back of her waist. His hand tightened slightly on her hip in a faint caress.

"I've been right here all along." Her husky laughter sounded fake to her ears, but the men didn't seem to notice. She tipped her head back to gaze into Justin's handsome face. "What do you want?"

His brown gaze lingered briefly on her curved lips, then shifted to the man watching them. "There's someone I want you to meet. Rhyder, this is—"

"There's no need to introduce us." His voice was smooth and low as Gina was forced to acknowledge Rhyder with a look. The hard blue eyes sent a cold shiver of fear to her toes. "We know each other, don't we, Mrs. O—"

"The name is Gaynes," Gina broke in with a rush. "Gina Gaynes."

A dark eyebrow flicked upward in sardonic mockery. "My mistake."

"We all make them." She shrugged in an attempt at lightness. But Gina and Rhyder both knew secretly how accurate her response was, even though it was ambiguous.

"Who did you think Gina was?" A half smile of curiosity was in Justin's expression.

"It doesn't matter." Rhyder let his gaze swing blandly

to Justin. "I think you were going to offer me a drink before we were sidetracked."

"Sure." Justin nodded, removing his arm from around Gina, suppressing his curiosity for the time being. "What'll you have, Rhyder?"

"A beer."

"Wait here. I'll get it," Justin said, and moved toward the opposite side of the crowd.

Gina stood uncertainly for a moment in front of Rhyder, her fingers clenching and unclenching the bag of clams. His alert gaze picked up the nervous movement, and she immediately stilled the betraying motion. It wasn't as if she could say the clams were trying to escape . . . something she wanted more than anything to do herself.

"Excuse me," she murmured, then turned away, taking the few steps necessary to carry the clams to the trough. Rhyder followed leisurely. Gina tried to pretend he wasn't there as she again began to help Katherine, but she was disturbingly conscious of him. He stood apart, watching the preparations with absentminded interest.

Despite the best efforts of the breeze, there was little color in her cheeks as she spread another layer of seaweed over the clams while Katherine went to fetch the sweet corn. When she returned with an armload of foil-wrapped ears, Gina took them from her and began distributing them atop the seaweed-covered clams. Katherine left again to get more corn.

An ear of corn rolled to the ground. Gina moved to retrieve it, but it was Rhyder's sun-browned hand that reached it first as he bent beside her. He didn't immediately offer it to her, forcing her to extend a hand. She kept her gaze averted from his chiseled features.

"I wasn't aware you'd changed your name." Rhyder placed the ear of corn in her outstretched palm, speaking so softly only she could hear.

"I wasn't aware that it was any of your business," Gina retorted bitterly.

The creases around his mouth tightened. His intelligent gaze moved to the gold ring on her left hand. "What about that?" he challenged coldly.

She lifted her hand, letting the precious metal flash in the sunlight. "That's my grandmother's wedding ring, the only thing I have that was hers. I have to wear it on my left hand because it's a little too small for my right."

Gina straightened, feeling a glow of malicious satisfaction at his inability to dispute the truth. Before she could replace the ear of corn, his hand closed over her elbow. Anger smoldered in his gaze.

His fingers dug into her skin, but Gina didn't try to pull away. Her eyes were as cold and green as the sea when she lifted her contemptuous gaze to his.

"Let go of me." She issued the order in an I-mean-it undertone. "Or would you rather I called for help?" They were brave words, considering the hammering of her heart at the way he towered beside her.

But they had the desired effect as Rhyder abruptly released her, his mouth twisting with emotion. "Can't come up with anything more original than that after all these years, huh?"

Inwardly Gina flinched, but she turned away before Rhyder could see that his pointed question had hit its target. Then Justin and his sister arrived almost simultaneously, with someone else Justin wanted Rhyder to meet. After handing him a cold bottle of Sam Adams, Justin led Rhyder away, pausing to suggest that Gina accompany them. She refused, insisting she wanted to help Katherine, who, fortunately, was too preoccupied with the arranging of the sweet corn, potatoes, onions, sausage and hot dogs to comment on Gina's silence.

Finally the moistened burlap bags were tucked around the heaping mound of food, and canvas covered the burlap. Gina didn't stay for the lighting of the fire beneath the shallow trough, hurrying to the beachside house with the excuse of washing her hands.

Almost the very instant she stepped inside the quiet house, reaction set in. The man was worse than a migraine. She collapsed in the nearest chair, feeling nauseated, pain throbbing in her temples. Her mind reeled as she tried to take in the implications of this second meeting.

Rhyder had been invited to the clambake by Justin. The two men were obviously on a first-name basis. Rationally, Gina knew that didn't necessarily mean the men were friends. Justin's gatherings were generally business and pleasure.

Since she couldn't recall Justin's ever mentioning Rhyder's name in the past—and that was certainly something that wouldn't have escaped her notice—it was possible that Justin was only now attempting to cultivate Rhyder's friendship for business purposes.

Seemed like a logical explanation and it also provided a reason for Rhyder to be in Maine in September instead of summer. But that was cold comfort. Gina didn't want him involved even in the remotest sense with her life. She ran a shaky hand across her damp forehead and down one cheek, wondering how long he would be staying.

The irony of the thought brought a humorless smile to her lips. Nine years ago she had been concerned about the same thing for an entirely different reason. Nine years ago she had dreaded the day he would leave. Now it couldn't be soon enough.

Where was her sense of humor? Gina wondered. She ought to be laughing at the situation instead of being unnerved by it. Nine years ago was a long time, part of the past, her first crush an experience to be filed away as part of growing up.

Summer mahogany. He had seemed like a god to her. The sea wind and sun had chiseled the masculine planes of his face in smooth and powerful lines. If Gina had been given to romantic flights of fantasy, she might have regarded him as a knight in shining armor. Perhaps in her subconscious, he had been.

At the time, Rhyder had simply been the most compelling man she had ever met, just about the first man she had ever been aware of in a physical sense. His grown-up masculinity had thrilled her, unlike the unwelcome attentions of the goofy local boys her own age. Rhyder had been twenty-six that summer. His lifestyle alone set him apart from everyone else.

Within a few days after seeing him for the first time, Gina began subtly trying to attract his attention. Sometimes she was conscious of what she was doing, but mostly she was guided by instinct. Fate and a malfunctioning engine in his sleek sailing yacht had put him into the port where her grandfather trapped lobsters. Gina had dozens of ready-made excuses for being around at any hour of the day.

From being a nodding acquaintance, she graduated into passing the time of day and from there to brief conversations. At eighteen, Gina had thought herself pretty enough—she had a mirror, after all, and spent a fair amount of time in front of it, like any other teenage girl. But she really hadn't known that guys thought of her as incredibly alluring. The combination of long black hair and green eyes was something men noticed. Rhyder was no exception.

Gina had often seen his veiled gaze running over her face and figure in silent admiration. But he was also aware of her youth and the nearly ten-year difference in their ages.

She remembered the afternoon she had gone to the beach for a swim, knowing beforehand that Rhyder

would be there. Wanting to get to know him better
seemed innocent enough, but she'd discovered a streak
of guile within herself that she hadn't known existed.

It helped her to pretend to be surprised when she
saw him in the water, send him a friendly wave, and
swim alone as if she didn't mind sharing the secluded
cove with him. Later, when she waded ashore, he was
sunning himself on the sand, his muscled chest and
legs looking very, very good.

The sandy beach area of the cove was small, so it was
perfectly natural that she had to sit within a few yards of
him to dry herself off. His gaze flicked to her briefly,
faint amusement in the blue depths, as she toweled the
excess water from her skin.

"It's a beautiful summer day, isn't it?" she declared
artlessly.

"Mmm," was his sound of agreement. Then Rhyder
closed his eyes.

For a while Gina said nothing, willing to settle for a
companionable silence. Then she asked, oh-so-casually,
"Is your motor repaired yet?"

"I'll find out tomorrow," Rhyder answered. "We're
taking it out for a test run."

"We?" Gina repeated blankly, then nodded understanding. "Oh, you mean Pete."

She hadn't figured out just exactly what relationship
the man had to Rhyder. At times she thought he might
be an employee, a deckhand or something. Other times
they seemed like the best of friends.

Yet bookish Pete didn't strike Gina as the outdoor
type, so if he was a friend, she couldn't imagine him vol-
unteering to crew on a sailboat. He would be more at
home in a library than on a yacht.

Rhyder was lying on his back, arms raised to rest his
head on his hands. He shifted slightly to allow his alert
gaze to sweep over her, taking in the jutting firmness of

her breasts beneath the one-piece, canary yellow swim-suit. He smiled slightly before he spoke.

"How old are you, Gina?"

"Eighteen. I'll be nineteen in August." She felt compelled to add that, wanting to sound a little older.

The lines around his mouth had deepened. "At least you're legal. Sometimes you barely look sixteen."

"Sweet sixteen and never been kissed, you mean." Gina managed an awkward laugh. "That's so not me."

"Hm. You look amazingly untouched by all your experiences."

Gina's heart beat faster. She knew Rhyder was out of her league. But she was enjoying the exhilarating sensation of flirting with him.

"I never said anyone had taken me into the bushes." She met his gaze levelly, her eyes as clear and as bright as the ocean's green depths. "I was only talking about kissing." She'd decided it was best to ignore his reference to other experiences. He obviously knew a great deal more about all that than she did. Firsthand.

"Done a lot of kissing, eh?" He had made it a question, a dancing light in his eyes.

Gina leaned back on her hands, a smug half smile curving her mouth as she lifted her face to the sun. "Oh, once or twice at least."

"Are you good at it?" There was a suggestion of amusement in his low voice.

"I'm learning." She darted him a laughing glance, fielding his teasing questions with lighthearted abandon. Gina had never traded words like this before, not about making love. It made her feel daring and gloriously wicked.

"Why don't you come over here and show me what you've learned?" Rhyder hadn't shifted from his position—flat on his back, hands under his head, only the blue of his gaze turned to her.

Gina's breath caught in her throat at the suggestion. There was nothing in the world she wanted more than to find out what it would be like to have Rhyder kiss her. Luckily, before she submitted to his invitation, she realized that he was only making fun of her. It hurt, but not as much as it might have if she had taken him seriously.

So she laughed, a forced sound, not quite natural, but she didn't think he'd noticed. "No, thank you, Rhyder."

She had rolled gracefully to her feet, holding an end of the beach towel in her hand and letting part of it trail in the sand. She shook her head and smiled, her refusal as adult as her just-graduated-from-high-school self could make it.

"What's the matter? Are you afraid?" The taunt had been gentle and not really argumentative.

"Mmm. Maybe the word is wary." There was a lot of truth in that statement. "That's how I've managed to stay out of the bushes."

"Quaint way of putting it."

Gina blushed, feeling awfully unsophisticated. She covered her embarrassment by flicking a wayward strand of blue-black hair away from her cheek. "I'd better be getting back so I can start supper for Gramps."

To get to the path leading from the beach, Gina had to walk past Rhyder. He had levered himself onto one elbow at her last remark. As she walked past him, his hand reached out and caught the trailing end of the towel. He pretended to use it to pull himself to his feet. Once upright, though, he didn't let go of the towel.

Something elemental seemed to hover in the air, charging it with an unknown tension. Gina was aware of her pulse beating wildly, but she wasn't able to move.

The laughing glint left his blue eyes as they darkened with purpose, and the strong angles of his face hardened slightly. His grip tightened on the towel, pulling her toward him. Gina didn't resist, drawn by a magnetic force that somehow emanated from him.

With one hand, Rhyder kept a hold on the towel while his other hand settled on the naked curve of her shoulder and arm. As his dark head bent toward hers, she closed her eyes.

At the touch of his mouth, her lips quivered. In seconds, the exploring expertise of his kiss had coaxed a response from her that was all about natural instinct. Thrilled, Gina let her hand rest on the bare hardness of his abs, not willing to fight her desire to actually caress him.

When Rhyder lifted his head, she felt dazed. Her equilibrium was slow to return under his methodical study of her. "I can't make up my mind about you," Rhyder muttered.

She said nothing in reply, just gazed up at him wide-eyed.

"Uh-oh." He smiled. "Don't look at me like that, okay? I'm only human and you're only eighteen. Now run along home and fix that supper for your grandfather."

He gave her a playful push in the direction of the path, and Gina didn't mind letting it end there. She wanted to savor the sensations, remember every one in detail. Rhyder had kissed her, and it'd been wonderful . . .

The memory made Gina draw in a soft, sighing breath. Why hadn't it ended there with just a romantic dream? If Rhyder had left the following day when his engine tested out, she wouldn't be going through all this anguish over seeing him again. He would've been just a sexy stranger who'd captured a young girl's heart on a summer day—and then faded into unreality.

But it hadn't happened that way.

The nervousness she'd felt nine years ago walking down to the harbor the next day came flooding back. Gina's heart had leapt at the sight of Rhyder's yacht, the *Sea Witch II*, coming in to dock. The repaired engines were humming, not missing a stroke. That done, there wasn't any reason for Rhyder to remain in this uneventful port.

Since it was likely to be the last time she'd see him, Gina stood at the dockside, fighting the lump in her throat as Pete clambered awkwardly from the deck to the dock to tie up, trying not to drop the lines in the water. Gina couldn't help wishing Rhyder was doing the honors and not Pete.

"Everything sounded smooth when you came in," she said to Pete after he had self-consciously returned her smile. "Guess the problem's fixed, whatever it was."

"Rhyder says so."

"Um, will you be heading out tomorrow?" She hated asking the question.

"No, we're going to stay here and explore the Washington County area. It's too crowded farther along the coast."

That sounded more like Rhyder's opinion than Pete's to Gina's intuitive ears. But she wanted to jump for joy. If they were staying in the area, that meant she had a good chance of seeing him again.

"There are a lot of dogfish there," she agreed, hardly able to contain her excitement.

"Dogfish?" Pete stared at her blankly, then smiled. "Oh, that must be another one of those terms for tourists, like 'summer complaints.'"

"You know tourists," Gina said hastily. "Can't live with them, can't live without them. Wait a minute—that sounded bad, but we don't mean anything bad by it."

"You sure? Dogfish is a kind of shark. Hardly complimentary." He hummed the theme from *Jaws*.

"Yeah," Gina protested with a laugh. "Handliners—fishermen—almost hate the dogfish because when the haddock should be taken, along comes the dogfish. Tourists start arriving at almost the same time."

"Even the way you say tourist sounds bad. Can we call

them seasonal visitors? Or is there some other term I don't know?"

Gina didn't mention "summer mahogany." That was special, reserved for Rhyder. Pete gave her a grin, wiping the sweat from his brow and flipping back a wayward lock of sandy hair.

"Hey, Pete. Getting a lesson in Maine-iac expressions?"

With a startled, quarter-turn spin, Gina turned to face Rhyder. Her heart skipped a beat at the sight of him, his black hair ruffled and tangled by the salty ocean breeze. A cream-colored polo shirt showed off his broad shoulders and leanly muscled chest.

He swung down from the water-splashed deck, his blue gaze skimming over her, making her aware of the way she was staring. She looked quickly away as Pete replied, "I certainly am."

A crony of her grandfather's walked by at that moment, peering at the trio before he nodded to Gina. "How's Nate?" he asked, referring to her grandfather.

"Nicely, thanks." She slipped her hands into the slanted pockets of her jeans. "They crawlin' good?"

"Daow!" he answered emphatically.

"Gramps changed water in his traps today, too," Gina agreed, as the old man continued on his way.

"Would you mind translating that conversation?" Pete's face wore a bewildered frown.

Her sideways glance caught Rhyder's amused and interested look. Gina obligingly launched into an explanation of what had been said, aware that she was the object of Rhyder's attention and determined to acquit herself intelligently.

"Clyde Simms asked how my grandfather was, and I told him he was doing nicely as opposed to poorly—or in poor health. Then I asked him if the lobsters were crawling—or moving along the ocean floor and with luck into the lobster traps. His reply was 'daow'—a negative just about as definite as you can get." Gina grinned. "He would've said that whether it was true or not."

"What did you mean about changing water in the traps?" Pete asked.

"When a lobsterman goes out to haul and comes up with empty traps that he has to rebait and reset, it's called changing water in the pots. In other words, an unproductive task, since he didn't catch anything."

"Got it. Really picturesque," Pete declared, addressing the comment to Rhyder. "If we stay up here much longer, we're going to sound like that, too. Holy seagulls, Rhyder Man."

"A lot of it is nautical talk or logger lingo," Gina pointed out, a little annoyed with him.

"Well, Maine is pretty isolated up here in the corner all by itself, practically," he conceded. Rhyder didn't attempt to contribute to the conversation, but stood to one side, listening and watching Gina.

"We're not all that isolated. Look at all the, um, seasonal visitors we get from all parts of the country and the world," Gina argued. "And Mainers are real individuals." A bright twinkle entered her eyes. "People come from away, hear how we talk, and go back to tell all their friends what quaint things we said. Everyone knows word of mouth is the best advertisement. There's no better way to encourage even more tourists to come here and bother us."

Rhyder laughed, joined almost immediately by Pete, then Gina. It was a magic moment, knowing she'd made him laugh with her and not at her.

"Good point." Rhyder smiled at her. "But you didn't think I was complaining about Maine, did you?"

"No, I didn't think that."

Maybe her reply hadn't sounded as friendly as she'd meant it to. At that moment, he seemed to withdraw, his smile becoming indulgent instead of sharing amusement.

"Well"—she scuffed her sneaker along one of the dock's weathered two-by-fours, not understanding his sudden aloofness—"I gotta go. See you around." She took a hand out of her pocket to wave goodbye to the two men.

When she moved away, Gina sensed Rhyder watching her leave. There was satisfaction in that, and in the knowledge that he was sticking around for a while. She would see him again, and maybe things would work out better the next time.

After all, he had kissed her once. She lifted a finger to her lips in memory of the thrilling sensation. He would hardly be reluctant to kiss her again if the opportunity presented itself. Gina hoped that there would be an opportunity, or that she would be able to create one. Yes, she would see him again . . . and soon.

That was nine years ago, she reminded herself as she snapped out of her reverie. Nine years.

Chapter Two

Gina buried her face in her hands, but the haunting memories of that long-ago summer wouldn't stop. Any moment now she would be missed, and someone from the clambake party would come looking for her. Rhyder would guess immediately that he was the reason she was hiding.

Well, she wasn't hiding exactly, but that was what he would think. She would rejoin the others, she promised herself, in a minute. Only a minute more in the peace and quiet of the house.

But there wasn't any peace and quiet, not in her mind. It was noisy with thoughts, especially of another day, that same summer, on a serene beach . . .

Gina poked a toe at the regular row of seaweed, the high-water mark of the tide. She hadn't seen Rhyder for three days, not since the day they'd all met on the dock. A short piece of driftwood rested above the seaweed, smoothed and whitened by the salt water and sun. Burnished gold grass grew in sturdy clumps, accented by the lavender purple blossom of the beach pea.

But Gina didn't notice any of it, or the pale pink of the bindweed flower, or the colorful shells tangled in the seaweed. Rhyder had left and hadn't come back. Foolishly she'd believed that because Pete said they'd be staying in the area, it meant they would be using her small port as a base.

"See you around," she'd said confidently, not realizing that she'd actually been saying goodbye to him.

With a dispirited sigh she turned away from the beach, toward the headland cliffs and the jumble of rocks, some smooth and some jagged, but all spectacular. Gulls screeched overhead, swooping and gliding in graceful acrobatic acts. Tenacious blue flowers grew out of the rocky cliffs, supple stems bending with the wind.

Although Gina was planning to go home, she took a roundabout route by the harbor, unwilling to admit that Rhyder would never return. She didn't really expect to see the yacht, *Sea Witch II*. In fact, she was so sure she wouldn't see it that she nearly didn't. When she recognized it, she took two racing steps toward it before she could control her exultation and saunter casually forward.

Rhyder was on deck, the white of a billowing nylon sail spread across his lap. Gina could see he was patching a tear and doing a skillful job of it. She was pleased to see that he would take the time for a minor but necessary repair like mending a sail himself. Obviously he knew his way around boats, unlike a lot of the summer people. She paused on the dock where the *Sea Witch* was tied up.

"Hello, sailor," she said mockingly.

He glanced up at her briefly. "Hi, Gina. Come aboard." He bent his dark head again to his task.

She wished his welcome had been a little more enthusiastic. But she was much too glad to see him again to let herself worry about that for long. She stepped aboard with alacrity.

"Where's Pete?" Gina glanced around.

"Ashore buying some groceries so we can eat dinner tonight."

For a second she considered inviting them to eat with her and her grandfather, but she sensed that would be going too far, too soon. She leaned a shoulder against a mast and watched him work.

"I was beginning to think you wouldn't be coming back here," she said at last.

He looked up, a mischievous gleam in his blue eyes. "Did you really think I wouldn't come back to see my girl one last time?"

His gaze slid over the golden length of her bare legs, then darted up to her face to leave her in little doubt that he was referring to her as his girl. She knew he was only joking, too.

"Come on, Rhyder." She laughed, but tightly. "I bet you have a girl in every port."

A flash of jealousy hot as summer lightning shot through her. She suddenly imagined all the girls he probably had held in his arms. She was only eighteen. What chance did she have of attracting a man like him?

"Yeah, right." His eyes crinkled at the corners, but his mouth didn't curve into a smile as he teased her. "Too many to remember. But I couldn't forget you."

Gina straightened away from the mast and tossed her head in proud defiance of the truth. "Well, I'm not your girl. One kiss doesn't make you belong to someone."

"Depends on the kiss."

She blushed and looked away. "It was nice, but it wasn't that big of a deal."

"I keep forgetting how experienced you are." His voice was low. "Hey, want to help me out for a second?" He pulled off the leather palm and set down the needle and patching material. "My fingers are getting stiff. A cup of something hot would help, and I could use a break."

"Okay."

"There's a jar of instant coffee in the galley and a propane stove. Think you could manage to boil water without blowing up the boat?"

"I think so," Gina declared, trying to think of a fast, equally obnoxious comeback. Nothing came to mind. She liked poking around in boats anyway, and she was curious to see if the inside of this one was as shipshape as the decks and rigging.

She went below and found that it was. Everything she needed was right at hand and immaculately clean. Gina cranked the little stove, lighting it on the first try. She dumped brown coffee crystals into the two mugs she set on the small counter in front of her, heating the water in a pan on the stove and watching absentmindedly as the bubbles clinging to the bottom and sides rose. She shifted impatiently, then turned with a start as Rhyder entered the small galley.

"It's almost ready," she said quickly, turning back to the stove.

"No hurry." He slid onto a bench seat behind her. "So where did you learn to be so handy in a galley kitchen, Gina? Did your parents sail?"

"Yes. But they were lost at sea when I was only two," she replied unemotionally. She had never really known them, so it didn't bother her to talk about them.

"Was your father a lobsterman like your grandfather?"

"No, he was an attorney, specializing in maritime law, but Gramps said he loved the sea. My mother did, too, I guess. They went out whenever they could. One time they got caught in a storm and never came back," she explained.

"So your grandparents raised you," Rhyder concluded.

"They've been wonderful to me." Her voice carried the warmth of deep affection. "Of course, we lost Grandma two years ago. The doctors said her heart just stopped. Gramps and I have been on our own ever since. He's a sweetie."

The water was nearly boiling. Gina lifted the pan from the flames and deftly filled the cups. She set down the pan at the back of the range, turned off the burner, then handed a mug to Rhyder. She started to offer him the sugar and canned milk she had set out, but he waved them away.

"I take it straight," he told her, and motioned her toward the bench seat opposite him. "What have you been doing these last three days?"

"Nothing special." Gina shrugged. *Except waiting for you to come back*, she added silently.

"No heavy dates?" He was mocking her again.

"None." She sipped at her coffee, knowing it was too hot, and nearly burned her tongue.

His gaze ran over her face, blue and glinting. "You're a great-looking girl. You must have a boyfriend or two somewhere around. The local guys can't be that clueless."

Sensitive about what he seemed to regard as her lack of sophistication, Gina tried not to let her irritation show. And he didn't care whether she had any boyfriends or not. Rhyder was teasing again.

"There are one or two," she agreed with forced calm. There probably were, but Rhyder was the only male who interested her. "But no one special." There was a flash of green fire in the look she gave him, but she veiled it quickly with her black, curling lashes. "How about you?"

"You must have forgotten," he said. "I'm supposed to have a girl in every port. You said so yourself. So how could I have a special one with so many to choose from?"

"That might have been a slight exaggeration," Gina conceded. "But I'm sure you get around. A lot of girls must be crazy about you." And she hated every unknown one of them with the violent emotion of youth.

"Maybe." His tongue was very definitely in cheek; he was amused by her answer and probably guessing that she was one of the girls who was crazy about him.

Gina lifted her chin, thrusting it slightly forward, determined to be adult and womanly. "Do you get what you want from them? The girls you take out?"

The mockery left the clear blue of his eyes as a dark brow arched at her prying question. "Do you mean, do I kiss them or—how did you put it the other day—do I take them into the bushes?"

The subtle inflection of eroticism in his voice brought a pink glow to her cheeks. Gina bent over her coffee mug, hoping he would blame her rising color on the heat from the coffee.

"I guess I wondered if you were the kind that thought a girl owed you something just because you asked her out," Gina hedged.

"Huh?" Without pausing Rhyder demanded, "Exactly where is this conversation leading?"

"Nowhere in particular." The forbidding line of his mouth made her more uncomfortable. "We're just talking, that's all."

"That's all?" He gave her a look of cool disbelief, but it made her feel warm all over. The tiny galley was a little too close for her comfort. Fortunately, Rhyder pushed himself from the bench and got up to pour the coffee from his mug down the drain. "Someone should tell your grandfather how dangerous it is to let you run loose," he said amiably. "He should keep you under lock and key. You're still wet behind the ears yet."

"How would you know?" Gina challenged, stung by his patronizing comment.

She got up, too, and dumped her own coffee into the sink. When she would have turned away, Rhyder took her by the wrist and pulled her around.

"Quit it," she protested tightly. He released her, but she didn't move away, just stood there glowering at him. "What do you want?"

"A kiss," he growled, and pulled her against him.

His mouth closed tenderly over hers as his arms

crushed her against his muscular length. But the pliant softness of her almost womanly curves molding against the hard contours of his body seemed to immediately intensify the sexy shock of his unexpected kiss.

The mobile pressure of his mouth became sensual and arousing. Gina wound her arms around his neck, surrendering with innocent abandon to his embrace.

Abruptly Rhyder took his lips away from hers, and she pressed closer to him, trying to force his head down. "Rhyder, please," she invited.

A tense muscle in his jaw worked as he gently pulled her arms from around his neck. "I think we're playing with fire. And as the designated grown-up, I have to stop this."

"Then why did you start it?"

The expression in his eyes turned cold, and he didn't answer. Realizing she'd just been rejected, she gave a sobbing gasp, and then put both hands on his chest and shoved him hard. Rhyder stumbled back, and she raced past him up the steps to the deck, nearly knocking a returning Pete down in the process.

Once ashore, she slowed her pace to a measured walk, trying to bring her emotions into line step by step. Her hurt feelings were only feelings, she reminded herself. This moment would pass—but she hated the way she'd let Rhyder get to her. So much for her pride. The humiliation she felt was magnified by the force of her desire for him. In his arms, in only seconds, she'd been transported to a different world of intense sensation, but the real, boring, same old world was right where she'd left it. Here. She kicked a small stone off the dock into the water and watched it sink with a dispirited sigh.

For two days she avoided the harbor as fiercely as she had once sought it. The harbor and any place where she might run into Rhyder. Considering the smallness of the community, it meant Gina practically had to restrict herself to the house.

The third day her grandfather mentioned that the *Sea Witch II* wasn't at its moorings when he had gone out to haul. And Gina felt free to wander to some of her childhood haunts without encountering Rhyder.

After washing up the noon dinner dishes, she slipped out of the house. Her grandfather was busy repairing some damaged lobster pots and probably wouldn't miss her until nearly supper. She walked, her pace fast as if she were trying to race to escape the thoughts that her freedom aroused. By three o'clock the summer sun and her exertions had made her hot and sticky. The prospect of an ocean swim became decidedly inviting.

She made a brief stop at home to change into her halter-top swimsuit and grab a towel, then set out for the small beach where she always swam. She was picking her way along the rocky path down the headland when a movement near the beach caught her eye. She looked, then stopped short as she recognized Pete wading ashore. Her searching gaze found Rhyder swimming toward the shallow water.

Common sense told her to run before she was seen, but pride insisted that she had to show Rhyder that he meant nothing to her. She sure as hell wouldn't let him know that he had hurt her with his rejection. With a determined toss of her raven hair, she continued along the rocky path to the beach.

"Man, that beer's going to taste good when we get back to the boat," Pete declared, a breathlessness in his voice from swimming.

Rhyder didn't respond to the comment, and Gina glanced up as she took her first step onto the sand. He was staring at her, a little grimly, and she immediately looked away with a haughty lift of her nose. Pete turned to see what had captured Rhyder's attention.

"Hello, Gina," Pete offered quickly.

"Hi, Pete," she replied, but she deliberately avoided greeting Rhyder, and he did the same. Out of the corner of her eye, she saw Pete glancing from one to the other and knew he felt the crackling tension in the air. She dropped her towel on the sand and started slipping off her sandals. "How's the water?"

"Fine," Pete answered uneasily. "Look, er, we were just leaving. If I stay in the sun much longer, I'll turn into a boiled lobster." He laughed uncomfortably at his own lame joke.

Gina knew he was only trying to cover up Rhyder's pointed silence. "I couldn't care less whether you leave or not." She shrugged, and pushed her sandals under her beach towel.

"Are you meeting someone?" Rhyder suddenly asked. His tone was curt.

She glanced at him, her expression cool and disdainful. "I don't see that it's any of your business, but no, I'm not."

"You shouldn't swim alone."

"You're right. But nothing's happened to me yet. I've been here hundreds of times on my own, and I'm a very strong swimmer," Gina declared.

"Ability has nothing to do with it," he growled.

"Really?" she answered mockingly. "Well, for your information, I never get out of my depth."

"Uh-huh. You seem to know everything, as usual." His steel-blue eyes touched her mouth and the rounded swell of her breasts in a suggestive look that sent the blood rushing to her cheeks. "You could very easily get into trouble."

"I certainly wouldn't call to you for help if I did," Gina muttered. "Go drink your beer and leave me alone. What might or might not happen to me has nothing to do with you." Impatiently she moved away toward the waves lapping the hard-packed sand of the beach.

"Pete, go on back to the boat," Rhyder said. "I'll stay here and keep an eye on her."

As if I was a child, Gina thought wretchedly, and raced toward the waves, diving straight into the breakers to hide the mortification he made her feel. She swam hard for several minutes, needing the exertion, and had to force herself to settle into a less vigorous stroke and edge closer to shore.

After her rash boast, she didn't want to get tired before she reached shallow water. No way was she going to look like she needed rescuing, especially by Rhyder. Only once did she glance toward the beach to see if he had stayed. He was there and Pete had gone. She remained in the water for as long as she could, wanting Rhyder to have a long watch.

Eventually her muscles began to tremble in protest, and she turned toward shore. When her toe scraped the bottom, she stood up and waded in. Her gaze slid over him where he stood out of reach of the lapping waves. The wait seemed to have set his features into chiseled harshness.

Ignoring him as best she could, Gina walked to where she'd spread out her towel in the sun. Exhausted, she wanted nothing more than to collapse on the sand, but doing that would reveal a weakness that she would rather Rhyder didn't see. She picked up the towel and began briskly rubbing her arms, aware that Rhyder hadn't moved, only half turned to watch her.

"You can leave now." Nervousness caused her voice to tremble slightly. "As you can see, I survived the solitary swim. And I would have whether you had been on watch or not."

"At least I know you're safe," he snapped.

"No one appointed you my guardian, certainly not me." Gina glared, her eyes flashing a stormy green. "There's no reason for you to stay, so why don't you go?"

He came striding toward her. "Brat."

"Look who's talking."

He held up his hands, palms out. "Whoa. I'm not going to take the bait. You're acting like a child."

"Am I? What's next, a spanking?"

His eyes flashed. Gina knew the remark was provocative in more ways than one, but she didn't care. An unbidden fantasy of him putting her over his knees for a few stimulating smacks came to mind, and she quickly pushed it away. Instead she shook out her towel, making sure that the prevailing wind carried the sand his way. Even that provocation failed to anger him. He just stood there, and Gina realized with chagrin that he was right about her being childish.

But Rhyder grabbed the towel on its final flick, yanked it from her hand, balled it up, and tossed it as far as he could.

She sent him a baleful look and spun away, running and stumbling, as if the stupid towel were something precious to her. She reached to pick it up where it lay crumpled in the sand, losing her balance and dropping to her knees beside it.

A shadow fell across her, long at first, then shortening as Rhyder knelt beside her. She wanted to cry, she wanted to smack him, she wanted to—oh, hell. His hand touched the curve of her shoulder, and she didn't know what she wanted anymore.

"I'm sorry, Gina," he murmured in a low voice.

"Leave me alone," she demanded through gritted teeth, and drew away from his hand.

"Dammit, Gina, I shouldn't have kissed you."

"I wanted you to."

"But all the same, I shouldn't have." His hand settled again on her shoulder, but this time in a grip she couldn't elude. Rhyder turned her around and drew her against his chest. He smoothed her wet hair with his fingers, nestling her head near the curve of his throat. "I'm sorry, Gina. I'm sorry." His mouth moved against her hair.

Her emotions got the better of her, and Gina relaxed

into the soothing comfort of his embrace. She lifted her head slightly as his mouth touched her temples, his breath warm against her skin. His lips encountered a trace of seawater along her cheekbone.

"Salty," he murmured. He seemed to find her tasty and pressed his lips to her skin. His hand curved along her slender throat, turning her face toward him. She seemed to stop breathing, not needing air as long as he continued exploring every inch of her face. When his mouth closed over her parted lips, she could taste the tang of the ocean in his kiss. The pressure of his hand near the small of her back arched her toward him.

Through the wetness of her swimsuit she could feel the solid beat of his heart. The mahogany hardness of his chest felt delicious against the softness of her breasts. A sensual warmth began to spread through her body.

Gina stopped passively accepting his kiss and began to return it. Her response deepened the kiss, and the pressure of his mouth intensified, demanding possession.

Rhyder lifted his head a fraction of an inch, their breaths mingling. "Open your lips, Gina," he instructed huskily.

She did, and his hard male lips claimed hers again, showing her the sensual fullness of a kiss between a man and a woman. Wildfire raced through her veins at his exploration. Her bones seemed to melt with the heat he was generating inside of her.

His weight was pressing her backward. It didn't ease, not even when gritty sand was beneath her shoulder blades. The heat of his sun-warmed body seemed to induce a languor that lifted her to a dreamlike state.

Fine white streaks of seawater clung to his skin, mixing with his musky male scent to make an intoxicating aroma. Her hands spread over the rippling muscles of his back and shoulders, trying to evoke the same pleasure his stroking caress was giving her.

The knot of her halter top was digging into the back of her neck, an uncomfortable lump in an otherwise satisfying bed. She moved against Rhyder in relief when his exploring fingers encountered it and loosened it, pulling the straps away.

When Rhyder dragged his mouth from hers to explore the slender column of her throat, she felt a giddiness she had never previously experienced. She tipped her head back to expose every inch for his inspection.

Delicious shivers danced over her skin as he roughly nibbled at the lobe of her ear, then trailed over the sensitive cord to investigate the pulsing vein in her neck.

A thousand sensations assaulted her mind when he pushed the top of her swimsuit away and his hand glided over the curve of her breast. Fleetingly it occurred to Gina to protest against this liberty, but the firm, yet gentle caress of his hand erased her momentary apprehensions.

His warm mouth left the hollow of her throat, drawn to the pointed tip of her breast. Instinct and desire exploded within her when his lips touched her nipple. The fierceness of the sensation nearly overwhelmed her, but Gina fought her way back to the reality of what was happening, stiffening in fear at the wanton longings his fiery touch was arousing.

Immediately Rhyder shifted his attention to her lips. His burning kiss reassured her she had nothing to fear from his passion. Again her flesh became pliant to his touch, her body almost limp. The moment of resistance had been conquered masterfully.

As her fingers started to curl into the wavy thickness of his black hair, Rhyder ripped himself from her, rolling away, turning his back to her as he knelt sitting on his heels. For a stunned moment, Gina lay where he had left her, staring dazedly at his slumped shoulders and bent head. She could see the effort he was making to try to control his erratic breathing.

"Rhyder?" She murmured his name in confusion and scooted into a half-sitting position. Her trembling legs were curled to the side. She drew the top of her swimsuit over her nakedness, holding it in place with a shaking hand, and started to move toward him.

He either sensed her intention or heard her movement. "Don't come near me." His taut voice trembled huskily, but the tone was unmistakably commanding.

"Why?" she whispered.

He raked a hand through his hair and answered roughly, "If you have any sense, you'll leave me alone for a minute."

"But—"

"Fix your top," ordered Rhyder, as if giving her something to do.

Shakily Gina did as she was told. Her gaze never left the point between his shoulder blades. The wet straps of her swimsuit weren't cooperating with her efforts to tie them together, but Gina didn't really care.

"Did I . . . did I do something wrong?" she asked hesitantly. She couldn't think of anything else to say. Even with her lack of experience she could figure out why Rhyder had ended the embrace.

There was a slight movement of his head in a negative answer. "*You* didn't do anything wrong," he said with a sigh.

"Then what is it?"

"Never mind." Rhyder turned all the way around at last. He stared at her for a long moment. Gina didn't realize that the effects of his lovemaking still showed on her face. Her lips were parted and sensually swollen by his possessive kisses. In the bewildered green of her eyes, there was still a fiery glow of desire. The softness of surrender seemed to radiate from her.

His eyes darkened to a midnight blue. For a moment Gina thought he was going to take her into his arms again, and he almost did.

He rose to his feet, his hands gripping her arms to draw her with him. She would have swayed against him, but iron muscles kept her an arm's length away.

"Don't you want me, Rhyder?" she asked, not meaning the question in the obvious way.

A muscle twitched in his jaw. He released her and bent to retrieve her towel from the sand. "Don't ask me that, Gina," he growled with taut control.

A crimson heat stained her cheeks as she realized what she had asked. Then, crazily, she knew she had to hear him say that she did attract him sexually, man to woman. She lowered her head, ignoring the towel he held out to her.

"Do you?" she persisted quietly in a strained voice.

"Dammit!" He reached out to jerk her a foot closer to him.

Her face lifted to gaze at the impatient anger in his expression. Rhyder's attention became focused on her mouth. The parted softness of her lips was an irresistible lure. He pulled her within an inch of his own.

"Yes . . . yes, I do," Rhyder muttered brokenly, and claimed her lips once more as his personal possession.

His powerful arms circled her and brought her against the naked wall of his chest. The sun-bleached hair on his legs chafed the smooth skin of her thighs as he molded her to his length. Arched roughly against him, Gina felt the thrust of his male hardness and, for the first time in her young life, knew the answering, instinctive ache within herself.

With a muffled groan, Rhyder pushed her away, shoving the beach towel into her hands. Gina didn't protest this time. She was shaken by the discovery that his touch could completely make her lose control, something she thought happened only in romance novels. The realization was sobering.

"Go home, Gina," Rhyder ordered tersely. "Go home

to your grandfather before—" He clamped his mouth shut without completing the sentence.

"I . . ." She wanted to say something. She didn't know what. She didn't need any pictures drawn for her.

Rhyder turned away, massaging the back of his neck. "For God's sake, don't say any more," he said thickly.

Bowing her head, raven hair falling across her cheek in a silken tangle, Gina took a step toward the rocky path leading from the beach, then hesitated.

She glanced back at him. "I'm sorry," she murmured, without really understanding for what.

"Are you?" Rhyder asked the question softly but didn't wait for her answer. "I'm not," was all he said.

A cold chill ran down her spine. Her knuckles were white from gripping on the beach towel. An emotional chasm seemed to be widening between them, and it frightened her. "Will I . . . see you again?" she whispered.

"Not if I can help it," he muttered.

"Rhyder." Her pleading tone didn't seem to move him.

"Don't you realize what's happening?" The line of his mouth was uncompromising and grim. "C'mon, Gina. No one's that innocent anymore."

"I don't care." The tortured words were torn from her throat.

"You damned well should," snapped Rhyder.

Gina flinched. "Are you leaving?"

A heavy sigh broke from him, and he paused before answering. "Not right away," he admitted grudgingly.

"Then I will see you again?" she persisted in breathless hope.

"I suppose it's inevitable."

Rhyder walked away toward the ocean waves. He didn't look back as Gina slipped on her sandals and took the narrow path up the headlands. She put one foot in front of the other, making her way carefully but feeling caught between boundless love and despair.

Chapter Three

"One of your friends left today," Nate Gaynes announced blandly.

"Really?" Without much interest in eating, Gina stabbed at a pea on her plate. It rolled away. She stabbed at it again and got it this time.

"Aye." Her grandfather nodded. His hair had once been as dark as hers, but age had liberally streaked it with iron gray. The years hadn't dimmed the perception of his eyes, which gleamed at Gina. "The Coast Guard got ahold of him this mornin'. There was some emergency in his family, and he flew home."

"He?" Until that moment Gina hadn't been paying attention to what her grandfather was saying. Now it was undivided. Initially she had thought he was talking about a school friend going off on vacation, but that wasn't whom he had meant.

"That's what I said." He bent over his plate.

"From the *Sea Witch*?"

"Aye."

"Which one left?" Gina held her breath.

"The sunny-haired one."

Relief washed through her. "That's Pete."

"That could have been his name," he conceded.

Gina fell silent, the possible implication of her grandfather's announcement racing through her mind. Since the afternoon on the beach, she had seen Rhyder on three different occasions. Each time Pete had been present, unknowingly acting as a chaperon. Rhyder had said little to her. Most of the conversation had been between Gina and Pete.

The meetings hadn't been all that satisfying, although a couple of times Gina had caught Rhyder watching her as she talked to Pete. Naked desire had burned in his eyes, only to be quickly veiled when he became aware that she had noticed. Not once had he attempted to be alone with her or indicated that he wanted to be.

But Pete had left. He wouldn't be there anymore to keep them apart. Hope flamed with new vigor. Another thought occurred to her before the renewed fire got out of control.

"What about Rhyder?" she asked suddenly. "Will he be leaving?"

"I shouldn't think he'd be goin' anytime soon, unless he's a fool. Strikes me he'd be smart enough to hire him another deckhand before headin' back to Boston. Either that or wait for this Pete to come back, if he's comin' back." Nate Gaynes leaned back in his chair and took a pipe out of his pocket.

Silently Gina agreed that Rhyder wasn't a fool. It wouldn't be easy for him to find a deckhand, either. Most of the men around here were already employed. It would take at least a couple of days, if he got lucky, to find someone to replace Pete.

Gina exulted silently in the knowledge that she'd be able to see Rhyder again—alone. There wasn't any way he could prevent it. And she believed that secretly he didn't want to, not really.

"You're sure lookin' happy as a clam about somethin'," her grandfather observed, holding a match to his pipe and puffing until the bowl of tobacco glowed.

She flushed slightly and began stacking the supper dishes. "Really, Gramps, I don't know what you're talking about."

"Harrumph!" He gave her a disbelieving but affectionate glare. "You've been moonin' around this house for the better part of a week. The last person I remember behavin' that way was your daddy, back when he was seein' your mother before they was married. Trouble was, she was seein' the Wilkes boy, too. He was actin' about the same way you been."

"I'm surprised you can remember back that far, Gramps." Gina kept her face averted as she teased him in an attempt to change the subject.

"I do." The pipe was clamped between his teeth, the fragrant aroma filling the kitchen. "I notice you ain't denyin' it."

"Denying what?" She tried to sound blank and indifferent.

"That you like this Rhyder feller."

"What are you talking about?" Gina carried the dishes to the sink and turned on the faucets to soak them for a little while. Her grandfather didn't see any point in buying a dishwasher, so she did them in the evenings, and he did them in the day.

But Nate Gaynes ignored her question. "He's a good bit older than you. You realize that, don't you?"

"You were eleven years older than Grandma," she pointed out, adding the dish soap.

He ignored that comment, too. "And you don't know how he is with women. With his money and pedigree, females probably fall all over him, for what it's worth. Rumor has it that his mother was married three times before his father ditched his second wife and went after her."

"I wouldn't know."

Her grandfather puffed on his pipe. "My point is that summa those rich blue bloods divorce like other people sneeze. Growing up with that attitude can make a man afraid of commitment."

Gina gave him a long look. "Have you been watching TV talk shows, Gramps?"

"That's neither here nor there. What I'm saying is he probably feels entitled to takin' what he wants and just as entitled to throw it away when he don't care about it anymore."

"You don't know that for sure," Gina protested lamely.

"You have to admit he isn't a please-and-thank-you man." Gina didn't respond to that observation. More pipe smoke filled the air as her grandfather paused before continuing. "There's another thing. He'll be leavin' soon. Chances are he won't be comin' back this way, maybe never."

"What are you trying to say, Gramps?" His reasoning was calm but disheartening. "Are you trying to tell me I shouldn't see him again?"

"No," he drawled slowly. "I ain't a-tellin' you what to do nor what not to do. I just don't want you to go gettin' carried away by somethin' that probably don't have a snowball's chance in hell of lastin'."

"Yes, Gramps," Gina said. His well-meaning words only filled her with a sense of desperation. She simply had to see Rhyder. Everything would be all right if only she could talk to him again. Then her grandfather's warnings would prove empty.

But she didn't get a chance until the following day. He was on the deck of his boat polishing the brass fittings when she approached. At the sound of her footsteps on the wooden dock, he glanced up, nodded, and returned his attention to his work.

"Hello, Gina," Rhyder greeted her smoothly.

"Hi. You're working hard, I see."

"Trying to." He smiled at her briefly, but continued with his task.

"I heard Pete had to fly home yesterday," Gina said.

"That's right." Rhyder straightened. "His sister was in a pretty bad car crash."

"I hope she wasn't hurt."

"Banged up but not too badly. Air bag, seat belt, reinforced chassis. Everything worked the way it was supposed to, but the car was totaled," he answered, glancing at the gold watch on his wrist. "He called me late last night to let me know."

"Is he coming back?" she asked, trying to conceal how interested she was in his answer.

His mouth tightened. "Unless Jill develops complications, he'll be back at the end of the week."

"You're on your own until then, huh?" She smiled with difficulty, crossing her fingers that he might say something about spending time with her.

Rhyder shrugged and turned away. "I don't mind."

She bit her lip, nibbling briefly at its softness. "If you get tired of your own cooking, you can come have supper with Gramps and me one night," she offered tentatively.

"Maybe." But he made it sound as if it were unlikely he would take her up on the invitation.

"Want some help with the polishing?" She wanted to kick herself for sounding like a tagalong little sister, but she couldn't help it.

"I can manage."

The corners of her mouth sagged downward with disappointment. Rhyder couldn't have made it plainer that he didn't want her around. She'd sounded pathetically eager, that was for sure, but she summoned up a few shreds of pride at last.

"I won't keep you from your work, then," she declared, and turned to leave.

Rhyder muttered some reply, then got her attention again with a loud, "Gina!"

She gave him a resentful glance.

"If you want to make yourself useful, you can fix some coffee," he stated, looking angry with himself for making the suggestion.

Did he have any idea how obnoxious he was being? Gina hesitated. Obviously not. She was beginning to think her grandfather was right about rich blue bloods and their sense of entitlement. "You're very self-sufficient, Rhyder. I'm sure you can fix it yourself."

He got a smudge of brass polish on his hand and swiped at it, then glowered at her. "I asked you." He turned his back to her and resumed his polishing, making long strokes over the already gleaming rail.

He wasn't the type to beg her. The decision was hers, and she would be a fool to pass up the chance for his company. There might not be another. Swallowing her pride, Gina stepped aboard.

Rhyder didn't turn around to look at her as he said, "You know where everything is. Bring it on deck when it's ready."

Sure, Gina thought resentfully as she descended the steps to the galley, bring it on deck where they would be in full view of everyone at the harbor. Instead of one chaperon, Pete, they would have a dozen or more.

She boiled the water, dumped teaspoons of crystallized instant into the mugs, and successfully fought the temptation to add a dash of dishwashing liquid to his. Would have been fun to see his face on the first sip, she thought as she dutifully carried the mugs on deck. Gina had half expected Rhyder to continue his work and ignore her. It was a pleasant surprise when he set down his polishing rag to take the coffee.

While it cooled to a drinkable temperature, they talked about sailing, the coast of Maine, the weather, and various other inconsequential things. His air of friendliness enveloped Gina in a warm feeling of pleasure. All her earlier resentment was gone.

"It's going to be a warm night tonight," Rhyder commented.

She gazed skyward, noting the high cirrus clouds moving in. Mare's tails, she thought, meant rain tomorrow, but she didn't say that.

"Yes," she agreed with his remark, redirecting her gaze to his strong, carved profile. "Perfect for a moonlight swim."

His gaze sliced to her, then shifted to his brown mug. There was a subtle change in his manner. "Yeah, probably will be," he said noncommittally.

"Doing anything special tonight?" Gina asked boldly.

"Nope, nothing special." There was a visible hardness to the line of his jaw.

"Well?" Gina tipped her head to one side in a flash of impatience. "Do I have to ask you to take me on a moonlight swim?"

"Gina," Rhyder began, saying her name with vague irritation, "why don't you invite some kid your own age? Someone who'll stroll along the beach with you and hold your hand, maybe steal a kiss or two while he shows you the stars. What you want is a harmless little flirtation." He looked at her long and hard. "You're kind of innocent, if you don't mind my saying so. You should be seeing someone who doesn't want to have sex with you every time he takes you in his arms." He stopped and shook his head. "What am I saying? That's all teenage boys want to do. But I can't take advantage of you."

"Maybe that's what I want you to do," she breathed in helpless longing.

"Don't be deliberately provocative, Gina," Rhyder said sharply, but the smoldering look in his eyes seemed to mean something very different. "If you had any brains in that beautiful head of yours, you'd listen to me—oh, geez. No, don't listen. I can't believe I just said that. Being around you confuses me."

"Do you really think I'm beautiful?" Gina murmured. Only his backhanded compliment registered in her mind.

"You know you are." His gaze locked onto hers, almost unwillingly, as if compelled by a force he fiercely resented. "What do you want me to say? That your eyes are like the emerald depths of the ocean or something? Grow up."

"Nice start. Go on," she said tightly.

He took a step away from her toward the railing. He stood there with his legs slightly apart, braced to the gentle roll of the boat, and gazed at the limitless stretch of ocean.

Rhyder's words, awkward as they were, thrilled Gina to the core because they were so reluctantly issued and had ended the instant he realized what he was revealing.

Confident now of her attraction, Gina moved to his side. She stood at a right angle to him. "No one has ever said anything like that to me before," she commented artlessly.

Nothing in the set of his features indicated he had heard her. Gina was overwhelmed by an urge to touch him and make sure he was flesh and blood.

Her hand moved to his sun-browned arm. The muscles contracted at the touch of her fingers, rippling in reaction. His head jerked downward to stare at the hand lightly resting on his arm. Finally his gaze lifted to her face.

The blazing passion in his eyes jolted through her. Rhyder turned slowly to face her, and Gina's hand dropped to her side. He towered above her, totally masculine, so close that she had to tip her head back to see his face. Only inches apart . . . but neither of them attempted to bridge the short distance. Rhyder seemed to strive for control.

"Gina." His voice was low and charged with emotion. "I don't suppose you can read my mind . . ."

"Actually, I think I can," she answered weakly.

The spell that gripped them was broken by the long breath Rhyder exhaled, a sound of soft frustration. Then he widened the distance between them.

"I think you'd better leave," he told her levelly.

Gina was stung. "Oh. Well, sure. Let me take care of the mugs, though." She took his mug with the hand that held her own, touching them together with a faint clink.

"Don't bother. I'll take care of them after you've gone," responded Rhyder in the same calm tone he had used before.

"Not a problem." She dropped both mugs over the side of the boat and watched them sink, then turned back to him. "You always seem to be telling me to leave," she sighed.

His mouth was open with surprise, she noted with satisfaction. Then he seemed to decide not to get angry over her deep-sixing the mugs. "I'm just trying to do what's right," he said tautly.

"Right for whom?" Gina challenged. "For me? I think I'm a better judge of that."

He controlled the impatience that flashed across his face and spoke firmly, but gently. "Gina, I don't want to argue with you. Just go, Okay? We're both on edge,"—he took a deep breath—"and it isn't going to get any easier."

"All right," Gina said reluctantly and left with a simple goodbye.

That evening a rising, lopsided moon found Gina wandering along the quiet beach. Although Rhyder had more or less nixed the idea of meeting for a moon-light swim, Gina had come on the chance he'd be there.

But the sands were deserted. There was only the soft rustle of the beach grass and the subdued rush of waves onto the beach. For nearly an hour she waited, staring at the moon. It was almost full, looking as if someone had chiseled a silvery arc from its circle. Finally she returned home.

By the following afternoon, the portent of yesterday's clouds had come true. It was raining steadily, without any sign of letup. The weather kept her grandfather at home. Gina was trapped there as well, restlessly prowling the house trying to think of a valid excuse to leave.

She wanted to see Rhyder, but she didn't want her grandfather to know. It was the first time in her eighteen years that she could ever remember wanting to keep something from him and she felt guilty about it, which made her all the more tense.

The slow-moving storm system meant darkness came early. At half-past eight Nate Gaynes was dozing in his big armchair. Gina knew he would probably sleep there until after midnight before rousing to go to his bed.

Yesterday's events and Rhyder's comments kept running through her mind. She'd made a decision, one that Gina didn't want to think about in case she lost her courage. With her grandfather sleeping in the chair, she had the chance to put it into action.

Quietly she slipped out of the house and ran through the steadily falling rain to the harbor. Her heart was hammering madly against her ribs when she reached the dock. A light gleamed in the darkness from the port window of the *Sea Witch*. Rhyder was there.

Pausing only for an instant, she hopped aboard and darted down the steps to knock at the galley door. It was opened almost instantly by Rhyder, who had probably risen at the sound of footsteps on deck. He stared at her for a stunned moment before becoming aware of the falling rain. He took hold of a wet wrist and drew her inside.

"What are you doing out in this downpour?" he muttered as he shut the door behind her.

"I wanted to see you." There was a lilt of urgency in her voice.

He stared at her for another second, taking in the cotton blouse and jeans that were plastered against her skin, water dripping on the galley floor. More water trickled down her forehead from her rain-soaked hair.

"You're drenched to the skin," he accused her in irritation. "You should have worn a raincoat."

His words made her feel like a straggly kitten half drowned by a downpour. "I know I should have," she admitted, shivering more from her cool reception than from the damp. "I forgot all about the rain when I made up my mind to come."

His mouth was compressed grimly for a minute. "Wait here," he ordered. "I'll get a towel or something to dry you off."

As he disappeared down the narrow corridor, Gina hesitated for a split second, then started stripping off the wet clothes until they lay in a damp heap on the floor. She left on her bra and panties, but self-consciously she crossed her arms in front of her at the sound of Rhyder's return.

Ducking his head to enter the galley area, he came to an abrupt halt at the sight of her. A folded blanket was in his hand. Gina's teeth began to chatter uncontrollably. It wasn't from cold. She was frightened by the shamelessness of her own behavior where Rhyder was concerned.

His features were half in shadow, the angular planes revealing nothing. She sought the clear blue of his eyes. They mirrored the image of a slender girl—herself. But she didn't want to see herself as he saw her. Vulnerable. Wanting him. Willing to do anything, no matter how foolish, how impulsive, to have him.

"I want you to make love to me, Rhyder." The words tumbled out. Her voice was thin, betraying the taut state of her nerves. "That's why I came. No one has ever made me feel the way you do when you kiss me. And I remember what you said yesterday about my being innocent—and how you didn't want to take advantage—"

"Gina—" he began, looking directly into her eyes and not anywhere else.

"No, let me finish. I know you'll be leaving sometime, probably before the summer is over. I might not ever see you again." She breathed in shakily, the blood roaring in her ears. "But I think I love you, Rhyder, and I want to belong to you completely, even if it's only for a little while. I swear I won't ask any more than that from you. I just want you to love me."

Her voice trailed off as he walked slowly toward her. The shadowy light from the single lamp didn't illuminate his expression. She searched with pathetic eagerness for some indication of his answer. When he stopped in front of her, his mouth was curved in a tender smile, but it told her nothing.

His unreadable gaze never left her upturned face as he unfolded the blanket and drew it gently around her shoulders. Gina trembled at the touch of the soft material against her naked skin. He crossed the ends securely in front of her, tucking it under her chin and holding it shut with one hand.

"Oh, Gina . . ." He murmured her name in a sigh that almost sounded sad.

Her chin quivered. "Please, Rhyder, don't send me away," she begged. "I couldn't stand it."

"Someday"—he tenderly brushed a damp strand of hair from her cheek—"a nice guy will come along, and you'll marry him in a big church wedding, walking down the aisle in a lace gown with your grandfather to give you away. And eventually you'll have a houseful of kids with green eyes and dark hair. And when they're all making a happy racket upstairs on a rainy night just like this, you'll curl up next to your husband with a glass of wine and look back on this moment and be glad that I told you to go home."

"No," Gina protested.

"Don't tell him you ever did anything like this, okay? Now go home, Gina," Rhyder insisted quietly. "Go home and wait until you're grown up. Save all that love for the right man when he comes along."

"But I want you," she pleaded desperately.

"No." He shook his head. "Right now you want to experiment, to discover what it's all about. You picked me because I was at the right place at the right time in your life, but I'm the wrong man."

Just why he had to be so damn noble was beyond her. "You're just saying that to get rid of me!" she hurled at him through her tears. "You couldn't kiss me the way you did unless you cared about me! And while we're on the subject, yes, I do want to find out what it's all about— or I did—with you . . . but right now"—she choked back a sob—"I guess loving you was a really unbelievably stupid idea. Right now I hate you! Do you hear?" she screamed hoarsely. "I hate you!"

His fingers released the blanket, and she pivoted away, clutching the ends with one hand and grabbing for the door with the other. As she pulled it open, his hand gripped her shoulder to stop her.

"Gina, for God's sake, don't—"

She twisted away from his hand and dashed up the steps. Tears were streaming so rapidly from her eyes that she didn't even notice the rain. She was aware only of Rhyder mounting the steps behind her, and she ran as if fleeing from the devil.

At some point in her headlong flight, Gina realized

that he was no longer behind her, but she didn't slow her racing strides. She was too numbed with pain to feel the slippery sharpness of the gravel beneath her bare feet or the sharp whip of the wet blanket against her legs.

There seemed to be no air left in her lungs, but still she ran, pursued by shame and humiliation at the fool she had made of herself.

The lights of her home gleamed ahead, and she used the last of her strength to reach the door, flinging it open and stumbling inside. Heaving sobs shook her shoulders as she pushed the door closed. She leaned weakly against it, needing its solid support.

"Gina!" Her grandfather's astonished voice startled her. "What happened to you, child?"

Still gasping with uncontrolled sobs, she tried to focus her tear-blurred gaze on the spare figure standing near the entryway. Then she realized the blanket had slipped from one shoulder, exposing the bare curve of her breasts in the bra.

Quickly she covered herself, but it was too late. Fresh waves of humiliation swamped her as she remembered the wet pile of her clothes on the galley floor.

"Where have you been?" Nate Gaynes demanded in a steely voice that sent a shaft of fear through Gina. "Who were you with?"

She opened her mouth, but no words would come out, only more wretched sobs. Her grandfather's face was gray and pale with shock.

"You were with that Rhyder feller, weren't you?" he said stiffly.

Gina nodded. Bowing her head, she cried harder. "I'm s-so ashamed," she sobbed.

He walked to her, a weathered hand reaching out, but Gina couldn't accept his offer of comfort. Not after what she'd done. When it came right down to it, she had no one to blame but herself.

With a broken cry of pain she ran past him to the stairs, racing up them to her room. She slammed the door behind her and threw herself across the quilted spread on her bed. She heard his footsteps on the stairs, but someone pounded on the front door. Her grandfather hesitated before turning back to answer it.

The walls of the old house were hardly soundproof. Gina's heart stopped beating when she heard Rhyder's voice below. He had followed her!

"Did Gina come back here?" he demanded.

Her grandfather must have nodded his answer. "You're just the man I wanted to see," he said ominously.

"Here's your granddaughter's shoes and clothes. I know how it must look to you, but I believe I can explain." Rhyder's tone was respectful, but he didn't sound intimidated by the situation or her grandfather.

There was a pause during which, Gina guessed, her grandfather was sizing up the stranger. In a slow, drawling voice, he said, "We'll go through to the kitchen and have our talk there."

Chapter Four

The kitchen was directly below Gina's bedroom, and the floor register permitted her to hear what was being said. She was shivering again and threw off the wet blanket to slip beneath the covers of her bed.

Shutting her eyes tightly, she tried to block out the whole miserable scene, but she couldn't shut her ears to the voices below. More slow, hot tears squeezed through her wet lashes.

"I could do with a shot of whiskey," her grandfather said. "You?"

For a while there was only the drumming rain on the roof. Glasses clinked as they were set on the kitchen table, followed by the thud of a bottle, the one kept for "medicinal purposes" on the top shelf of the cupboard. Good old Dr. Jack Daniels always made house calls.

"I knew she took a fancy to you. I probably should have forbidden her to go down to the boat and all, but I was afraid of sweetenin' the excitement." There was a thread of weariness in her grandfather's sigh that made Gina feel all the more wretched, but there was no sign of it when he added sharply, "You knew she was only eighteen, didn't you?"

Rhyder's yes was almost inaudible.

"Now that's the age of consent, son, but even so," Nate Gaynes harrumphed. "She's too young for you."

"I tried to tell her that."

"Mebbe you did, but she's not real good at listening to things she doesn't want to hear," her grandfather pointed out.

"I noticed," Rhyder said grimly.

"So mebbe you'd just better tell me what did happen tonight and how my granddaughter's clothes came to be in your possession while she was running through the streets practically stark naked except for a blanket flappin' in the wind."

Clearly and concisely Rhyder sketched the night's happenings, not dwelling long on Gina's impassioned plea for him to make love to her. Gina wished she could fall asleep and never wake up again.

When he had concluded his explanation, there was a long pause. The bottle thudded again on the table, no doubt after her grandfather refilled the glasses.

"And you expect me to believe this was all her idea?" Nate's quiet voice was quavering. "It couldn't be that you suggested it, and she got cold feet at the last minute and ran away?"

"I swear I didn't lay a hand on her." Rhyder's tone didn't vary in its pitch, conviction running firmly through his words.

Gina turned her face into the pillow, shame scorching through her veins. Her grandfather must despise her. He had trusted her, and she had let him down.

"And I don't suppose you ever did anything to make Gina think that you might be wantin' to bed her?" came the inevitable challenge.

This time Rhyder hesitated. "I might have, yes," he said finally.

"You *might* have?"

"All right, I did," he admitted grudgingly.

"A sensible girl like her"—Gina cringed under the covers—"well, she wouldn't get ideas like that about a man who's only stolen a kiss or two," her grandfather stated.

"I . . . did step out of line a couple of times." At least Rhyder was honest. Despite her misery, Gina was pleased by his reluctant response. But it didn't ease her humiliation to hear him concede that he was partially to blame for her behavior that night. She simply buried her head deeper in the pillow, trying to muffle their voices.

"I'm glad to hear you admit that," Nate Gaynes declared, faintly triumphant. "Now maybe we can get down to some serious talking."

The bottle thudded on the tabletop for the third time. Gina pulled the pillow over her head and began sobbing into its fluffy depths. She couldn't bear to listen to them discussing her as if she were a child. The tears couldn't begin to ease the agony of recriminations, but they flowed from a bottomless well.

Time was measureless. Seconds seemed minutes, minutes seemed hours. And Gina cried for an eternity. Several times she heard raised voices from the kitchen below, but they only served to increase her torment.

And Gina was no longer curious to know specifically what they were discussing. Obviously it concerned her, but more than that she didn't want to know. At last her sobs were reduced to dry, hacking sounds. Emotional exhaustion carried her into sleep.

A knock on the door wakened her. Gina rolled over, fighting through the stupor that made her feel leaden and lifeless. She blinked her heavy lids and became immediately conscious of her near nakedness beneath the covers. A moan of remembrance broke from her lips.

The sound prompted another knock at her door.

Gina stared at the wooden door, wanting to order who-ever was on the other side to go away, but no sound could get through the constricted muscles in her throat. She wished there was a lock on the door so no one could ever enter. She didn't want to see anybody ever again.

The door was opened without her permission, and the gently smiling face of her grandfather greeted her from the hallway. Gina turned her head away as he walked into the room, carrying a tray. The covers were up around her neck, and she didn't move when he stopped beside the bed.

"Sit up, Gina," he told her with forced cheerfulness. "I'm treatin' you to breakfast in bed."

She couldn't sit up, feeling too self-conscious of her unclothed state. She should've at least put on some pa-jamas for last night's pity party, she thought bitterly. Then she wouldn't be embarrassing herself in this way.

"I don't want anything," she mumbled, refusing to look at him.

"There's some hot chocolate here, toast and jelly."

He was trying to tempt her with her favorite comfort food, but it wouldn't work. Gina didn't want to be com-forted. She turned her face deeper into the pillow. "Please, I don't want anything," she repeated hoarsely.

Her grandfather set the tray on the stand beside her bed and turned to her huddled figure. He sat down on the edge of the bed, a weathered hand smoothing the tangle of black hair from her cheek.

"I know you feel badly, Gina." His voice cracked with emotion.

She squeezed her eyes tightly closed. "I wish I could die," she whispered.

He smiled. "That's a bit drastic, don't you think?"

"I don't care." Gina caught back a sob.

"Now, you know you don't mean that," he insisted gently. "Everything will work out all right. You'll see."

"How can it? You must be so ashamed of me."

"Last night"—his gnarled hand rested on her hair—"when you went to him, you went because you loved him, didn't you?" her grandfather questioned.

"Y-yes." That's what she had thought. Now she hated him and she hated herself.

"Love, and things done in love, are not something to be ashamed of, child. I'm not condoning what you did, but I understand," he told her.

"You don't understand." Her head moved restively beneath his touch. "I don't see how I can face him again. Or anyone again."

"You'll soon change your mind about that. He doesn't hate you."

"Oh. How nice to know that. But I hate him."

"Now, Gina. He's right outside that door. You and I both know he did the right thing by you. He's a decent young feller. You got him awful confused for a few minutes."

"Sounds like you two finished the whiskey," she snapped. "Now what? Is Rhyder Owens your new best friend?" She sat up and grabbed a piece of toast, energized by renewed anger. If she was going to be mad, she was going to need fuel. The toast disappeared in three fast bites.

Nate sighed. "He isn't your enemy, I can say that much."

She took another piece of toast and stuffed it into her mouth, then watched with round eyes as the doorknob turned and Rhyder's head came around the edge of the door.

"Good morning."

Nate got up slowly, favoring his arthritic knee, then covered up his granddaughter with the blanket that had slipped down when she sat up. "I'm turning this over to you, Rhyder."

"Mmf!" She almost choked on the toast in her mouth.

"Guess you can make your apologies now. She's almost decent."

Gina swallowed and spluttered on the crumbs as she watched her grandfather leave and Rhyder enter.

"Calm down, Gina," he said wearily. "I promised him I'd apologize to you. It means a lot to him. Cut the old guy some slack, okay? He really cares about you."

"Unlike you, you son-of-a—" She paused to make sure her grandfather was heading down the stairs. Judging by his careful creaks, he was.

"Go ahead and curse. Get it out of your system."

She huddled under the blanket, not trusting him for one single second.

"No."

"Why not? Mind if I have that last piece of toast? I know you hate me; I heard you through the door. Call me any name you want to."

"Because you're giving me permission to and you're doing it in that smug way. Like last night was some big joke. Maybe it was to you, but not to me."

He shook his head and helped himself to the toast, taking a spindle chair with his other hand and turning it around so he was sitting in it backward. He rested his forearms on the top, but she could see his shirt-clad chest through the spindles. The memory of how good it had felt to touch him there when he was kissing her made her extremely uncomfortable.

"I didn't think of it as a joke. You scared the hell out of me for a minute or two, though." He ate the toast and brushed a few remaining crumbs from his fingertips.

She quivered with indignation. What was she supposed to say? She'd been scared, too, but that hadn't stopped her from setting a world record in impulsive idiocy. If only she'd had the presence of mind to drop him overboard the way she'd dropped the coffee mugs.

All I wanted was for you to make love to me, and you wrapped me up in a blanket and said no.

"Hey, I have to say I was flattered that you, uh, offered yourself to me the way you did. But like I told Nate—and yes, we did finish the whiskey—there was no way in hell I was going to take advantage of you."

"Well, well. Somehow you managed to give him the impression you're a hero, huh?"

Rhyder only shrugged.

"You're not my hero."

"Okay, I can live with that. Drink that hot chocolate. Your grandfather went to a lot of trouble to make it just the way he said you liked it."

"I'm sure he did." She picked up the cup and took a small sip, then another. The sugary warmth of the hot drink was irresistible, but it didn't do anything to sweeten her temper. If Rhyder thought for one minute that she was going to accept his apology—well, she wasn't going to.

He drew in a deep breath and looked into her eyes. "Gina, I'm sorry if I gave you the idea—"

She wouldn't let him finish. "Never apologize. Never explain. It only makes things worse."

"But—" He broke off and studied her for a long minute. "Right now you seem a lot older than eighteen."

"Yeah, well, I cried myself to sleep. I don't suppose it did anything great for my looks." Her eyes had to be red and puffy, and she couldn't even get a hand through the tangles in her hair. She wanted him to go, but he showed no inclination to leave.

Oh, right, he'd bonded with her grandfather, who seemed to have forgotten his dislike of blue bloods, thanks to Dr. Jack Daniels. She couldn't yell and scream and upset Nate. They sat in silence for a minute or more, as wild plans for revenge raced through her mind. If only there was some way he could feel the humiliation she had experienced—but there wasn't. She looked at him, self-assured and sexy and looking right back at her.

How richly he deserved a comeuppance. How powerless she was to give him one.

"Can't we be friends, Gina?"

"No."

"Why not?"

"Because I don't feel friendly toward you." His presence in this small room was definitely affecting her, though, and she tried to figure out what she did feel. Passion—but that was over, after last night's fiasco. Loathing—that would last. Her body trembled, and her temples throbbed. Maybe what she was feeling was a headachy mixture of both passion and loathing, with a pinch of stupid mixed in.

He raked a hand through his black hair, which didn't look too great after last night's stormy weather. "You know, by the time we'd finished the whiskey, I actually told your grandfather I'd marry you someday. How crazy is that?"

She stared at him. "Not crazy at all."

Rhyder rocked back in the chair, then remembered he was sitting in it backward to begin with, and set the legs down on the pegged hardwood floor with a thunk. "You didn't say that."

"Yes, I did. You won't marry me, though."

"How do you know?" His tone was level, but the look in his eyes was intense.

"Because you were just trying to get on Nate's good side. You didn't mean it. And you were drunk."

He clasped his hands together. "Yeah, we got a little bombed, but I think I did mean it. Even though you and I hardly know each other."

"Let me get something straight," she began, an edge in her voice. "I understand that your mother was married three times—"

He didn't stop to ask her where she'd learned that interesting information but corrected her all the same. "Four, counting my father. And he was married twice before her."

"Gramps was right," Gina murmured.

"What?"

"Nothing. Just pointing out that you don't come from the kind of family that takes wedding vows seriously. You're more the I-do-I-do-oops-no-I-don't type. Telling my grandfather that you'd marry me meant less than nothing."

He shook his head. "You're wrong about that."

"Prove it."

"How?"

"Marry me, Rhyder."

He looked at her steadily as if he were actually considering it, while Gina contemplated how much fun it would be to ditch him at the altar.

"Married?" Her grandfather gaped at her, his coarse, iron gray brows lifting up almost to his receding hairline.

"You heard right. I'm going to marry Rhyder," she said when it seemed like he could breathe again.

"Gina, we live in a very small town, but this ain't the 1950s. You don't have to worry about your reputation when half the girls in U.S. high schools have been fooling around since sophomore year."

"Where the hell did you get that statistic?" she asked, taken aback.

"I heard it somewhere. Anyway, nobody has to get married anymore."

"I don't have to marry him, Gramps. But I'm going to all the same."

"That's plumb crazy," the old man said slowly. "Now, Rhyder may have said something like that last night somewhere around the bottom of the bottle, but you can't hold a man to that."

"But I realized that you were right about Rhyder being a decent guy. I can't let a good one get away."

"You're only eighteen."

"So everyone keeps telling me. Guess what? I'm of age and I can do what I want."

Her grandfather shook his head. "Never could stop you once you'd made up your mind, Gina. You might be making a big mistake, but mebbe not. And . . ."

"And what?" She softened her tone, not wanting her animosity toward Rhyder to spill over into an argument with her grandfather.

"It's your mistake to make. Some people have to learn things the hard way." He gave her a rueful smile and didn't say anything more.

What with one thing and another as the next few weeks went by, Gina managed to see very little of Rhyder until their wedding day. The ceremony was going to be small, and the necessary arrangements had been made easily enough. She kept telling herself it was going to be a breeze to ditch him at the altar, especially since he seemed so casual about the whole business. He hadn't even kissed her more than once or twice, and they were kind of husbandy kisses. As in not passionate.

She guessed that he was playing along to get what he wanted—sex from her. She hadn't been wrong about the look in his eyes, even if he stopped himself before, that one time on the beach, and the memorably miserable night on his boat. Not that she had cared, she tried to tell herself.

And her grandfather would probably be relieved. Nate had kept on dutifully trying to talk her out of it, while saying that he did think Rhyder was an okay kind of feller for offering and all.

If, for some reason she couldn't anticipate, she actually got through the ceremony with a straight face, the marriage could always be annulled. Compared to a divorce, an annulment was a piece of cake, according to the information she'd found on the Internet. As long as there was no arguing over money or property or things that people really cared about. Love couldn't be legislated, and that was that.

Rhyder's expression was bland as he stood beside her in front of the minister. He spoke the vows clearly and without emotion. Nothing in his eyes revealed his inner opinion of the marriage; he barely glanced at her except when he'd caught a glimpse of her before she came down the aisle with Gramps, as she tugged at the crooked bodice of her bridal warehouse dress, an inexpensive, short A-line of white satin with matching shoes. He'd smiled at her, and she'd almost rushed out of the church then and there. When they were pronounced man and wife, he brushed her lips with genuine tenderness.

Scary.

The scene Gina had rehearsed in her head hadn't happened. With her grandfather there, beaming as he glad-handed the few guests, she just couldn't set down her bouquet and walk out.

A token amount of rice marked their departure from the church. Rhyder brushed the few grains from the shoulder of his jacket before sliding behind the wheel of the car. Gina plucked one from her hair and began rolling it between her thumb and forefinger.

They drove for nearly twenty minutes and not once had he spoken to her. The silence was stretching like a rubber band, each minute increasing its tautness. She wanted to tell him off, was waiting for that big so-hah moment, but she just couldn't. His hands on the wheel, strong and sliding over the smooth leather with each curve in the road, were a distraction. A sexy one, she had to admit, if only to herself. Maybe she should wait until she was down to bra and panties to reject him, just the way he had rejected her that night on the boat.

Gina tossed the grain of rice to the floor. "Are you sorry yet?"

His gaze slid to her, but briefly. "No."

Her mouth was compressed tightly, her nerves on edge. "Where are we going?"

"To a hotel. The honeymoon suite, with deluxe everything. Isn't that what newlyweds usually do?"

"Oh." Her breath felt tight, or maybe it was just the white satin dress. She hadn't changed after the ceremony, and he still wore the same dark, well-cut suit. They looked like newlyweds, something she hadn't thought of. "We could just as easily have gone to your boat instead of this."

"Your grandfather wanted you to have a real wedding." A corner of his mouth lifted in a half smile.

"I don't particularly care," Gina retorted.

"Neither do I."

"Then why are you going through with it?" she demanded, throwing him a cold look.

His profile was chiseled against a golden sunset, its lines hard and sensual. This indomitable person was now her husband, however easy it might be to get an annulment. The thought unsettled her.

"I want you," was his noncommittal answer.

Cool blue eyes held her gaze for an instant before Rhyder returned his attention to the highway.

Gina tipped her head to one side, her green eyes narrowing. "Why did you say that?" She studied him warily.

"You're my wife. Isn't that how it's supposed to be?" He added, "*Mrs.* Owens."

Suddenly Gina realized that her grandfather was

right. She had made a mistake, but not for the reason Gramps had thought of. Staying angry, wanting revenge, she'd set up this charade to get back at a man who was fundamentally decent and actually liked her enough to marry her. Yeah, okay, he'd promised to love and cherish her for a lifetime only an hour ago, but that was how the marriage vows were written.

She was going to learn a lesson, and she'd learn it the hard way. Gina sat back in her seat, trembling, and stared straight ahead.

"Y-your parents," she faltered, "do they know about me?"

"Not yet," he answered. "You know they don't give a damn about marriages, mine or theirs."

Discreet but dramatic, the sign for the hotel blinked just ahead of them. Rhyder slowed the car to make the turn into the circular drive. The night air was warm as he opened her car door, but Gina felt unaccountably cold.

A young valet in a red vest accepted the keys, looking thrilled with the chance to drive such an expensive car. Rhyder didn't even look back as the kid sped off. *Money to burn,* Gina thought uncomfortably.

The hand directing her into the lobby was definitely in charge—and there was a sexual undercurrent to his touch that made her even more nervous. It wouldn't look good if she pulled free. She had no wish to embarrass him in public that way. Oh, hell. What had she gotten herself into? The explanation—and it was going to be a doozy—would have to wait until they were safely behind the doors of the honeymoon suite.

It occurred to her that she wasn't going to be exactly safe in a room like that with him. Try as she might to hate him, her sexual attraction to Rhyder was getting the upper hand. Just being alone with him for the ride to the hotel in the confined but luxurious interior of his gorgeous car had proved that.

Glancing around the richly furnished reception area, she tried to ignore the speculating look of the desk clerk. Vaguely she heard Rhyder mention something about reservations. Nausea gripped her stomach as her downcast gaze saw him write Mr. and Mrs. Rhyder Owens on the registration slip.

"We've been expecting you. The honeymoon suite is ready, sir." It was a simple statement of fact from the clerk, not meant to be suggestive, but Gina blushed in miserable embarrassment.

Rhyder flicked an unreadable glance in her direction. "Excellent."

Her ears were burning as the bellboy escorted them to their suite, carrying their few pieces of luggage. Gina discovered the polite attention of total strangers was more unendurable. They thought she was a happy new bride. Well, she wasn't. She didn't look at the bellboy when Rhyder gave him his tip and he left them in the room.

A scarlet-covered bed dominated the room. Gina walked stiffly to the window, wanting to ignore it. Her forehead felt clammy, and she knew she was just about as pale as her white satin dress. Rhyder's gaze was on her. She could feel it prickling her spine.

"Have you eaten anything today?" He sounded like a parent, and Gina gritted her teeth.

"No. Bridal nerves, I guess."

"Would you like to go to the restaurant, or shall I order something from room service?" Rhyder asked politely and indifferently.

Her first instinct was to choose the restaurant, but the prospect of getting knowing looks from the hotel staff quickly made her reject it.

"Room service, please," she answered. Not that she had ever enjoyed that particular luxury in her life. She knew it came on a trolley and a nice person with a black bowtie and black vest rolled it in and disappeared. She had seen that much in the movies. "And order lots of champagne. I feel like getting drunk."

"Don't try to be sophisticated, Gina," Rhyder said. "You can't carry it off."

"Aren't you sweet."

"I don't want you getting sick."

Tension gnawed at her stomach. She turned around to confront him, but made no reply for a moment, somewhat unnerved by the look in his eyes. She managed a haughty glance in return, but deep down inside, she felt more than a little ashamed of what she had done and what she planned to do: walk out on him.

"Afraid someone will talk if I do? Are you ashamed of me?" Despite her bold challenge, she felt intimidated by the raw masculinity emanating from the dark-suited man standing only a few feet away. Her heart began beating in sharp, uneven thuds.

"What makes you ask that?" The bland question was not what she had been prepared for.

"Uh, because you haven't told your parents about our marriage. So I figured you might be having second thoughts by now." Gina held her breath, hoping that would do.

His eyes narrowed. "I'll tell them when I'm ready to tell them, put it that way. We're married—which is, after all, what you wanted."

Gina wanted to cry. She felt like a stupid kid who'd tripped up in the middle of a huge lie. And—she had to admit it, because the deception was becoming unbearable—that was exactly what was happening. "It isn't what I wanted," she said in a choked whisper.

A long moment passed. Excruciatingly long. Gina hung her head and studied the pattern of the carpet, unable to explain her actions to him.

"Ah," Rhyder said at last. His voice held an acid touch of irony. "So much for love and honor and cherish. I get it. This is your revenge, because I said no to your attempt at seduction. You're going to yell for help or some damn thing next."

Tears stung her eyelids. She'd only intended to hurt him back by walking out with a little more dignity this time. Surprised when he'd seemed so serious and so real about getting married, Gina had wondered in the last weeks if the sight of her in a wet bra and sheer panties was really enough to drive men crazy. In the last weeks, she'd braced herself for the possibility that he would snap out of it. However, he hadn't, and she'd stuck to her plan to get back at him.

Yell for help? Accuse him of something? That hadn't occurred to her. But he seemed to think she was capable of really ingenious malice. Nothing she could do about that now, Gina thought ruefully.

Rhyder took a deep breath and started in on her again. "You only wanted to conduct a sexual experiment, huh? See what kind of a reaction you could get with that little striptease? And when you didn't get what you wanted, you came up with Plan A: make me believe you cared about me. Hey, maybe there was a Plan B, just in case I didn't believe you. Guess not. You even get your gramps involved."

Hot tears rolled down her face, remembering how happy the old man had been, despite his obligatory cautions on the subject of early marriage.

"He's the one who's really going to be hurt, Gina. Pity you didn't think about that before you went through with that bogus wedding ceremony, or neither of us would be in this mess."

She turned back to the window so he wouldn't see her cry. She couldn't argue with his harsh reminder that her foolishness was to blame for the present situation. The scarlet carpet partially muffled his footsteps, but she was aware of him walking toward her and stiffened.

"Here's the room service menu." He thrust a printed

paper toward her. "You can choose what you like," he said, curt and indifferent.

"It doesn't matter." Gina shifted her position to keep her back to him. "Order anything—I don't care." She didn't want to eat, but she had a feeling she'd faint if she didn't, and despite what Rhyder had said, she had no wish to get him in trouble.

"Okay, be childish." His patience was being stretched. She could hear it in his clipped tone. Rhyder turned away, muscles rippling tautly beneath the neatly tailored suit. "I'll order for you. Will milk and cookies do it?"

Incensed by his patronizing inflection, Gina spun around. Emerald fire blazed in her eyes, made even brighter by a shimmer of tears.

"Why don't you just tell me to go wash my hands like a good little girl?"

"That's enough, Gina!"

"What's the matter?" she taunted, without the slightest regard to his admonition. "Are you afraid I'll get hysterical?"

"I wouldn't be surprised," Rhyder said with quiet grimness, his temper severely checked. "You've used nearly every trick but that one."

"I'm sorry—you don't know how sorry I am!" Gina cried.

He exhaled a hissing breath and turned away from her, anger charging the air around him.

"I am not going to argue with you, Gina," he declared roughly.

"Well, good for you." She couldn't hold back her sarcasm. "Take the moral high ground. How's the view from your horse?"

"You were the one who played Lady Godiva. Quite a scene. Gave the whole damn town something to talk about." He cast her a furious look over his shoulder.

"So what?"

"So nothing."

Gina shook her head. "You didn't have to follow me or talk to my grandfather or even apologize. And you sure as hell didn't have to tell him you would marry me, no matter how drunk you were."

He held up a hand. "Wait a minute. Are you going to say I shouldn't have married you next?"

"You insisted. So chivalrous of you," she shot back at him, only to see something flash across his sun-browned features. That glimpse made her stiffen warily.

"Thanks," Rhyder said dryly.

Gina swallowed, pride keeping her head erect. "Did you, um, really want to?" she demanded in a low voice, afraid to hear his answer.

"Is this part two of your experiment?" There wasn't a trace of emotion in his voice. "Now I know how a lab rat feels waiting for the next shock." His flat gaze gave away no emotion whatsoever. He shook his head and walked to the telephone. "I'll order your dinner."

A shiver of apprehension raced over her skin. Gina crossed her arms, rubbing them to rid herself of the foreboding chill, but she seemed only to push it deeper inside. Her knees trembled. She felt weak and vulnerable and—worst of all—fully responsible for her failed scheme.

Numbly she went into the bathroom, wishing she could sink into the depths of a hot bath and think things over, instead of acting like the child that she kept insisting she wasn't. Gina had learned something that she didn't think she wanted to know: revenge wasn't worth it.

She felt guilty. She felt stupid—phenomenally stupid. And to save her life, she couldn't think of a way to explain any of this to her grandfather. She looked in the mirror and wiped away what little makeup she had on, wondering if she should call a cab and just leave quietly. Then she remembered that she had no money . . .

and she didn't exactly feel like asking Rhyder for it. Even though he'd probably hand it over, no questions asked. She wasn't a prisoner of anything except her own troubled conscience.

No, she would have to get through this awful night somehow and just not make things worse. No small task. When she returned to the bedroom, intending to explain Plan B, the inevitable annulment, her doubts dogged her, nipping and snapping until her nerves were raw. The frayed ends became sensitive to Rhyder's silence. She jumped visibly when a knock at the door announced the arrival of room service and her dinner. Rhyder hadn't ordered anything for himself, and Gina had to pick at exquisitely prepared food that had no taste at all.

He'd taken off his jacket and tie, turned back the cuffs of his white shirt, and unfastened the top three buttons. A brandy he'd poured from the portable bar was in his hands as he reclined almost indolently in an armchair. The expression on his hard, tanned features was a study of remoteness.

Gina stared at the food remaining on her plate. With a jerky movement she let the silverware clatter to the tray and pushed herself away from it, rising in agitation. She was conscious of drawing his attention.

"Finished?" Rhyder inquired evenly.

"Yes." Gina flashed him a nervous look.

"I wasn't going to tell you to clean your plate," he snapped, and downed the swallow of brandy in his glass.

"That's good," she said sharply, "because I wouldn't have done it."

"I was hoping food would improve your disposition." He rose impatiently and walked to the small bar to refill his glass. "But obviously it hasn't."

"So what are you going to do? Drown your sorrow in

drink?" Gina immediately wished she hadn't tried to be funny.

Rhyder took a healthy swig, not exactly savoring the brandy the way you were supposed to, Gina noticed. He refilled the glass before he moved away from the bar.

"Maybe you were right earlier," Rhyder commented with a sardonic lift of an eyebrow. "Getting drunk could be a good idea."

Her pulse throbbed as he lazily approached her. Minus jacket and tie, and with the open front of his white shirt revealing his leanly muscled chest, he looked more like the man her heart remembered, virile and strong. Pain splintered through her nerves.

"I'll join you," she said tightly.

She started to walk past him to the bar, but his hand shot out to halt her, his fingers closing around the soft flesh of her upper arm. His firm grip made something snap inside.

"Don't touch me!" she hissed.

"Don't touch you?" repeated Rhyder, tightening his hold. "That's how this whole situation happened, because you begged me to touch you and I refused."

Scorching waves of shame seared through her, bringing high color to her face and neck. She struggled to twist free of his grip—he wouldn't release her. She clawed at his hand, trying to make him ease the pressure.

"Let me go!" She lacked the strength to make him obey.

Low, harsh laughter came from his throat. "That's not what you wanted me to do before," he mocked her.

Gina made a backhanded swing at his chin, missed, and knocked the brandy glass from his other hand. It fell harmlessly to the thickly carpeted floor, liquid splashing out in a wet stain.

His free hand got hold of her other arm, and he

yanked her against him. The anger in his eyes frightened her, and she struggled wildly.

"Let me go! I can't stand you!" she declared, breathing heavily with her efforts.

He kept her pressed to his chest while his hard fingers seized her chin and lifted it upward. "But we're married now, my love," he jeered. "It's all perfectly legal. In fact, it's my conjugal right."

"Screw y—"

He didn't wait to hear her curse him out but brought his mouth down on her quivering lips. His kiss, passionate and furious and somehow tender, stole her breath and left her limp in his arms.

Did he assume she had surrendered? Had she? Gina was intoxicated by the sensuality of his kiss. Her trembling response made little impression on Rhyder. Not until her fingers were curling weakly into his shirt did he ease the pressure of his mouth to masterful possession. His male attraction was something she couldn't fight, nor did she want to resist the wild sensations his lovemaking aroused.

Desire flamed as he plundered the softness of her throat. Her hands fumbled with the buttons of his shirt, but she got the rest of them undone, letting her fingers glide freely over his hard flesh, smooth as leather.

A gasp of heady pleasure caught in her throat at the touch of his hand sliding open the zipper of her dress. As it fell around her feet, Rhyder lifted her out of it and into his arms.

Without a word, he carried her to the bed and settled her on the scarlet coverlet. A knee rested on the edge of the bed as he towered above her, something primitive and conquering in his stance.

Gina's lashes fluttered. In the next second, his shirt was discarded, and the muscled brown of his naked torso was bending toward her.

Chapter Five

The muffled sound of voices wakened Gina the next morning. The pillow was damp beneath her cheek, and she remembered sobbing into it last night.

After that amazing kiss, all she'd wanted was sex with him, but she'd known in her heart of hearts that it wasn't a good idea. He'd asked, though, and she'd said yes, and he'd asked again if she was absolutely sure. Same answer. Yes. So she had no one to blame but herself if she felt awful afterward, even though the sex itself had been fantastic, a bewilderingly erotic fantasy come true.

Thanks to his sensual expertise, she'd reached the ultimate fulfillment of desire, despite her nervousness—and then burst into tears.

Rhyder had attempted to comfort her, but it had soon become evident that he intended to ease her pain with the same tactics that had caused it in the first place. Gina had poured out her side of the story, not even asking him to understand, and he'd listened in stony silence. Then he had left her alone with her tears.

Very slowly she lifted her head from the pillow and glanced over her shoulder. A shudder of relief quaked through her at the empty pillow beside hers. Warily she

looked around the room, but there was no sign of
Rhyder. Then she heard his voice coming from the terrace outside their suite. She listened, unable to figure
out whom he could be talking to—until she heard a familiar voice.

"You married her?" was Pete's astonished question.
"I mean, some guy at the dock told me you did, but I
thought he was pulling my leg. But you actually did it?"

"Yeah," Rhyder replied, his low voice on edge. "But
she decided she didn't want to be married to me about
three seconds after we walked into the honeymoon
suite last night."

Gina tensed, her muscles protesting as she slipped
from beneath the covers. Her clothes were still scattered on the floor. She sidestepped them, wanting to
forget how they had come to be there, and hurried to
her suitcase on the luggage stand.

"But why? How?" she heard Pete's puzzled voice ask.
"Begin at the beginning. I have a feeling this is going to
be really interesting."

Gina pulled a pair of jeans and a top from the folded
clothes. She was just stepping into the jeans when she
heard Rhyder finally answer, "The beginning? I saw her
with nothing on. Almost nothing," he corrected himself.

"Yeah, so? You've seen a hundred girls with nothing
on," Pete said breezily.

"More than a hundred," was Rhyder's reply.

Gina wanted to kick him. Hard.

"Rhyder, my man—are you losing your mind?" Pete
went on. "What happened while I was gone?"

With careful movements, Gina finished dressing. She
now strained to hear the voice she had tried to ignore.
She had to know what Rhyder's answer would be to that
question.

"She came to the boat late one evening. It was raining, and she was soaked to the skin," Rhyder began his

explanation tersely. "I went to get a blanket to wrap her in. When I came back with it, she had taken off her clothes and was begging me to make love to her."

"Oh, God," Pete said. "But she's eighteen, right? Did you—"

"I told her to go home and grow up!" Rhyder snapped. "She went out of there, crying through the streets, half-naked. Nearly the whole damned town saw her leave the *Sea Witch*."

Gina was furious. There was no arguing with the stark truth of his words, but she hated him for telling Pete about her impulsive behavior. It was just demeaning—there was no other word for it.

"What did you do then?" Pete wanted to know, incredulity running through his low voice.

"I decided I'd better tell my side of the story before the uproar got so loud nobody would listen, so I went to her house to talk to her grandfather."

"And he didn't believe you?"

"Unfortunately, he did." Rhyder gave a mirthless laugh. "I mean, he started off with a lecture, but once I'd explained things, he decided I wasn't such a bad guy after all. I made it clear that I liked Gina and respected her, and that nothing had happened."

"If he believed that, you must have gotten him drunk." Pete chuckled.

"Actually, it was the other way around. He brought out a bottle of whiskey, and it was empty by the time we were done talking."

Gina blanched as she remembered the thud of the bottle on the table at least three times before she had buried her head under the pillow.

"At first I thought it was some kind of, you know, test of my manhood. I didn't really care, because I was walking back to the boat anyway. But I got kinda bombed, and what with one thing and another, the old man got me to agree that maybe I'd given his darling granddaughter the wrong idea, and then—and then I told Nate that I'd marry her."

"Were you joking?"

There was a long pause. "No," Rhyder finally said. "Anyway, I showed up the next day to apologize, just because I felt sorry for her."

"Never explain. Never apologize. How many times have I told you that?"

"Once or twice," Rhyder said. "Anyway, no Monday morning quarterbacking, please. You weren't there."

"I almost wish I was."

"Pete, I have to say it—I wanted her. Bad. She looked so good in just a wet bra and panties, you should have seen her—"

"Too much information." Gina could practically see Pete holding up his hand to make Rhyder shut up.

"She even looked good the next morning all curled up in a big, miserable, embarrassed ball, crying her eyes out because she'd done something so crazy."

"Uh-huh," Pete said knowingly. "Then what happened?"

"I, uh, talked to her for a little while. Then it kind of came out."

"What came out? What you told her grandfather about marrying her?" Pete asked.

"Yeah. I don't remember how we got on the subject. She said something like 'marry me,' and—"

"And you said sure. Idiot."

"Thanks, Pete. You're a good friend."

Gina heard Rhyder slap his "good friend" on the back hard enough to make him cough.

"You didn't have to marry her just because you looked at her. Gina's a nice girl, but what are you going to do with a child bride?" Pete declared in confusion. "I just can't see you giving in to pressure just because of small-town gossip, Rhyder."

"She said she wanted to marry me. And I wanted to

believe her." Cynicism deepened his voice to a rough sound. "But I got her to tell me everything late last night, after several shots of brandy and"—he hesitated for a fraction of a second—"amazing, absolutely amazing sex. God, she's hot—"

"Too much information," Pete said again.

"I wasn't going to go into the details. Anyway, she didn't really want to marry me, just get back at me for not playing her game the way she wanted it. But we're definitely married. Entirely legal. She's eighteen."

"Got it," Pete said sharply. "Otherwise known as barely legal."

"That was and is a consideration," Rhyder continued. "The newspapers would have a field day with the whole story, honorable intentions on my part or not. Especially considering the ongoing investigation of the political contributions made by my father's firm."

"Talk about barely legal," Pete muttered.

"Hey, whose side are you on?" Rhyder said indignantly. "Any negative publicity would be damning for my father. But get one thing straight: I married Gina because I wanted to. It's just my tough luck that she was playing bitchy games with me. But it's not as if I can plead innocence."

"I'm afraid you're right," Pete agreed in a reluctant tone.

Closing her eyes, Gina remembered how easily she had allowed his sensual kisses to change her attitude. The faster her impulsive plan for revenge had unraveled, the more she had realized that she actually had wanted him. Last night had proved just how much.

But she couldn't hold him to a promise she hadn't meant. And right now his words didn't sound exactly understanding or loving or anything at all like what he'd said last night in the throes of passion.

"What are you going to do now?" Pete asked, not

pursuing the former topic. "Just don't take her home to meet your family. Geez, can you imagine her meeting some of your sister's friends? They'll tear her apart! Not to mention the catty remarks from some of the girls who planned on catching you themselves. Are you going to tell your family the truth? About how she tricked you into marrying her?"

"I don't know," Rhyder said, then paused before adding, "They'd never believe that I could fall in love with a teenager. I would be insulting their intelligence by trying to convince them."

"Your sister would never be able to keep quiet about it," Pete warned. "In a month, Clarise would see that everyone knew. It'll be hard on you and Gina."

"How do you think I feel right now, Pete? She just played me for a fool, and I never saw it coming. Didn't think that someone that innocent could be so underhanded, I guess."

"You still want her?" Peter's question was blunt.

Rhyder didn't reply right away. "I don't trust her."

"Hey, you've got a thick skin; you can take the heat you're going to get. But the kid . . . ?"

"Maybe she deserves it," was the impatient reply, and Gina's temperature rose.

"Come on, Rhyder. She's young yet."

"Maybe I should make her so miserable she'll settle for a quickie divorce and some get-lost cash," Rhyder growled. "I just hope she doesn't get pregnant."

It was Pete's turn to be quiet. "Don't tell me you didn't take care of that," he said at last. "You know where babies come from, Rhyder. And there's no getting around a paternity test. The Owens DNA is solid gold, and child support is expensive."

"We were tired, we were angry, we were confused, we'd had too much brandy—"

"Hey," Pete interrupted. "Mind if I point out that

those things don't usually inspire amazing sex? Just the opposite, in fact, especially in combination. You two wanted each other in a big way."

"Oh, shut up. I don't want her. Not anymore. I'd write out a check now, for any sum she'd care to name, if I thought it would get rid of her," Rhyder declared irritably.

Gina stood up straight and tall. Cold rage stiffened her shoulders as she walked toward the sliding glass door that opened to the terrace. At the pressure of her hand it glided open, the sound immediately drawing both men's attention.

"How much?" she demanded before either could speak.

A dull, embarrassed red flooded Pete's fair skin. The forbidding look on Rhyder's face didn't change at the sight of her, expressing no surprise at her appearance or her question.

"You said a moment ago you'd be willing to pay to get rid of me. How much?" Gina repeated her question.

"How much do you want?" Rhyder countered smoothly.

Gina named the first large sum that came to mind. Something flickered in his steel blue eyes, and she realized immediately that he had expected her to ask for more. But it didn't matter to her that she could have asked for more and received it.

"I'm surprised, Gina. I would have thought you'd want more." Rhyder studied her for a long moment, resting one shoulder against a wrought-iron pole supporting the terrace roof.

He was dressed only in dark blue jeans, the morning sun glistening over the bareness of his chest. Gina found the virile show annoying, really annoying, and a too vivid reminder of last night's sensual intimacy.

"You're getting a discount," she retorted.

"But a divorce so soon?" Rhyder commented mockingly. "Don't you want to wait and hold me up for some serious money?"

Gina shrugged. "I think we should both get out while we're still ahead. Of course, I could still find a reporter and tell the world what a pig you are. Haven't decided yet."

The line of his mouth thinned harshly. "Sweet."

"You and I agree on one thing at this point," she continued. "This marriage never should have happened."

"Right. And I agree to your settlement request. Of course, you'll have to go over everything with your own attorney so you can't renege and say I coerced you. Keep in mind that you'll have your money the minute the divorce papers are signed." The contempt in his eyes chilled her to the bone.

"An annulment would be much less complicated," Pete said hesitantly.

"Yeah. And faster." Rhyder's steel gaze narrowed thoughtfully on Gina.

"That settles it, then," she declared.

The annulment was obtained, but it took Gina a while to overcome her grandfather's initial objections. It wasn't exactly easy to live it down, not in a community this small.

Although the adults were forgiving of her impetuous and failed marriage, the boys looked at her with different eyes. They got a whiff of experience that interested them, and she had to put up with a lot of comments that she never responded to.

Her grandfather's pride was offended by the money Rhyder had given her. Nate Gaynes had deposited it in the bank, refusing to touch a penny of it. Gina, too, had felt it was somehow tainted. The bank's mailed statements of the account and its accumulating interest arrived monthly, but she rarely opened them.

Each time she saw the envelopes she was tempted to throw them away. Her grandfather became quiet whenever he saw them. Gina sensed that he felt he had failed her by encouraging her to marry, and she had tried in subtle ways to make him understand that she was more at fault than Rhyder—although she couldn't bring herself to explain that she'd only married the man out of childish spite.

In the months that immediately followed the annulled marriage, her grandfather had grown morose and introspective. The next summer he'd died in his sleep. Grieving deeply and no longer caring where the money came from, Gina finally drew upon the settlement account for his funeral and medical bills.

Then she sold the house. That last year had erased many of the happy memories that had once been associated with it. . . .

Nine years later, with her twenty-seventh birthday just celebrated last month, she was a woman with a career and a brilliant future. So why, Gina moaned silently, did such an unwelcome person from the past have to reenter her life now? All the violent emotions she had thought were buried were surfacing.

Her skin felt hot to the touch. She walked to the sink of the beach cottage kitchen where she'd retreated from the clambake and turned on the cold water to let it run over the inside of her wrists. The outside door opened, and she stiffened at the sound, breathing shallowly.

"Gina!" Justin Trent let out a mock sigh. "What are you doing in here? The party's outside."

"Oh, I don't know. Just needed a little downtime, I guess." She turned off the cold water tap and dawdled over finding a towel to dry her hands. "So I came in here."

"Party pooper." He walked to her side, took the towel from her hands and tossed it on the counter before taking both her hands in his. "Here I want to show you off to all my friends, and you're hiding inside the house."

"I wasn't hiding." Gina forced a smile, unable to meet the warm glow of his brown eyes.

He carried her left hand to his lips, brushing the tips of her fingers with a kiss. Through the concealing veil of her lashes, she saw the wry twist of his sensual mouth as he gazed at her hand.

"I wish you wouldn't wear that ring. It always makes me feel as if I'm fooling around with someone's wife," Justin mused.

An uncontrollable shiver raced down her spine. Gina quickly removed her fingers from his light hold and turned away, guiltily covering the gold ring with her other hand. "I told you—it's my grandmother's ring."

In fact, it was the "something old" that her grandfather had sentimentally presented for her long-ago wedding to Rhyder, accompanying it with a wish that their marriage would be as long and happy.

"You amaze me, honey. Sometimes you're so cool and career-oriented. Then other times you're deliciously old-fashioned and feminine." His finger traced the curve of her cheek. "When I first met you, I thought you wore that ring to keep guys like me away."

"It works for that, too." Gina smiled.

His light caress made her uncomfortable. It came too soon after the memory of another man's touch. But she couldn't draw away from it; Justin wouldn't understand the rejection when she had been allowing him similar little liberties for the last few months. And Gina didn't want to explain or lie.

"It works—unless you want a guy to get closer, mmm?" Justin's finger tilted her chin upward.

Her lashes closed as his face moved closer. Beneath the warm possession of his lips, hers were stiff and faintly resistant. She tried to relax under his kiss, but the attempt didn't succeed, and Justin lifted his head.

Regret trembled through her, regret that she had ever had the misfortune to meet Rhyder and regret that he had suddenly reappeared after nine years.

"Much as I'd like to ravish you at the moment"—his mouth hovered near her temple, his moist breath stirring the short black waves of her hair—"I think we'd better return to the clambake, since I'm the host."

"Yes, we should," Gina agreed quickly, anxious to bring an end to the embrace, especially when she was reacting so unnaturally to it.

"You don't need to sound so eager." Justin laughed, and curved an arm possessively around her shoulders.

"Hunger pangs," she lied brightly, walking at his side to the door.

"We'll cure those." Justin ushered her through and slid his arm back to its former position around her shoulders as he escorted her to the gathering of people.

Amid the crowd was Rhyder, magnetically drawing Gina's gaze against her will. His raw masculinity and rough vitality set him apart from the others. His attraction was powerful. Even while she despised him, Gina felt its strength.

His gaze drifted through the crowd, caught Gina's look and stopped. She glanced quickly away, her gaze skittering in every direction except where Rhyder stood.

Breathing in deeply, she resolved not to let his presence disturb her. The shock of seeing him again was over. As much as she disliked him, she refused to let him spoil her enjoyment of the clambake.

"You got back just in time," Katherine Trent spoke up as her brother approached with Gina under his arm. In an aside, she joked to another couple standing near the steaming trough, "Trust my brother to turn up when the food is ready!"

"I've never been accused of bad timing," Justin responded good-naturedly.

Gina slid a surprised glance at her watch. She'd been in the house nearly an hour on a mental walk down memory lane, trying to make sense of the events of nine summers ago.

Justin turned to the guests and called, "Come on, everybody. We're ready for the unveiling!"

There were plenty of volunteers to help draw back the layers of canvas and burlap. A mouthwatering aroma rose from the mound of seafood and vegetables, wafting through the air as an appreciative murmur ran through the guests.

"It's been years since I've been to a clambake," someone declared, "but that's an aroma I'll never forget!"

Gina glanced in the direction of the voice, an understanding smile curving her lips. Rhyder blocked her view, his eyes on her, alert and blue. The smile faded as her heart skipped a beat.

She was forced to acknowledge that there were many memories that time couldn't dim. Not all of them were angry; intense desire could blaze in the mind, too. She paled, wanting to remember only her bitter dislike of Rhyder and her vow never to be vulnerable again to humiliation from him.

"Dig in!" Katherine waved the guests over as the bulk of the food was set on a long table, leaving the lobster on the bottom, bright red-pink against the seaweed bed.

With Justin at her elbow, Gina joined the line of people piling food on their plates. She lost sight of Rhyder in the milling group and hoped the separation would be permanent.

"Take our plates to that table over there," Justin said, pointing, as he handed her his plate. "I'll get our lobsters and the drawn butter."

As Gina turned to comply, she saw Rhyder seated at

the picnic table Justin had indicated. She hesitated, but Justin pushed her forward playfully. Other tables were filling up. She couldn't tell Justin that she didn't want to sit at the same table with Rhyder, and there was no other objection she could make to the choice.

Reluctantly she walked toward it. His blue gaze swept uninterestedly over her as she set the plates on the table on the opposite side from where he was sitting. His attention was directed to the couple seated beside him. In seconds Justin returned, balancing two plates while holding on to a cheesecloth bag of clams.

"I don't know what to eat first," the woman across from Gina declared with a laugh.

"Take a bite of everything," the man who was evidently her husband suggested. "Here," he added, reaching for the small bag of clams between their plates, "I'll shuck you a clam."

"That's wrong, Henry," Justin spoke up as Gina helped him set the lobster plates on the table. "A Maine-iac shucks corn, but he 'shocks' clams!"

A discussion followed of other unusual expressions typical of the state. Stories were traded between the couple and Justin of funny incidents they'd heard of or experienced themselves. Neither Gina nor Rhyder took part.

Once, when Justin was explaining how a term had originated, she had felt Rhyder's gaze touch her. She couldn't help wondering if he was remembering when she'd instructed Pete on the origins of various phrases.

"What about the expression 'happy as a clam'?" The woman frowned.

"Now, that one I don't know," Justin admitted.

"Maybe Gina does," Rhyder stated. "She's from down east."

In the middle of breaking a lobster claw, Gina glanced up, momentarily startled by the sound of her name on his lips. The mocking, faintly satirical light in his eyes said he remembered.

"Do you?" the woman prompted.

"'Happy as a clam' is the short version," Gina recovered swiftly to explain. "The whole expression is 'happy as a clam at high tide,' for the obvious reason that no one goes digging for clams at high tide."

The trio laughed appreciatively. "Down east?" The man called Henry repeated the phrase Rhyder had used. "I always get confused about that. It has something to do with the wind, I know, but would you mind explaining it again?"

"The prevailing wind along the coast of Maine is from the southwest. In the days of the clipper ships and other sailing vessels, a ship that left the Boston harbor for some point in Maine would sail downwind in an easterly direction or 'down east.' It's a bit confusing, but if you're traveling up the coast of Maine, you're going down east," Gina concluded.

"That's fascinating, isn't it?" the woman declared. "I remember when we were in . . ." and the conversation shifted to places they had traveled.

Again Gina didn't take part in the discussion, nor did Rhyder. Several times she sensed his gaze on her, and it made her uneasy. The food seemed to stick in her throat as her tension grew, but she kept eating, swallowing hard and refusing to let him see that his presence had destroyed her appetite.

Her long silence got Justin's attention, and he leaned near her ear. "You're withdrawing again," he whispered.

Gina shook her head. "I'm eating."

Justin's face was very near hers. Gina knew she had to turn her head only slightly to invite his kiss, but she was too conscious of Rhyder's watching eyes. The other couple rose from the table to refill their plates.

"You've picked your lobster clean," Justin observed after a few seconds. "I'll get you another."

"No. Really, I—" But her protest was wasted as Justin left the table.

"Does he always wait on you?" Rhyder asked dryly.

"Justin is very considerate." Avoiding his gaze, Gina picked up a clam and made a project out of shocking it.

"Of course," he said. Several seconds ticked away in taut silence, then Rhyder began, "Your grandfather—"

"—is dead," she interrupted harshly.

"I'm sorry."

"No, you're not." The flash of her stormy green eyes challenged him to deny it.

He studied her face before he conceded the point. "Do you need to be right? Then you're right. Excuse me." And he rose from the table.

Strangely, Gina didn't feel any relief when he didn't return, but drifted among the other guests, some still eating, some replete and leaning back to chat. Eventually he was one of the first to leave, but the ghost of his presence remained to haunt her.

It was late in the evening when the last of the guests left and Justin was free to take her home. She sat silently in the passenger seat, staring into the night as he drove her to her apartment in the city.

"Good party, wasn't it?" he commented, finally breaking the silence.

"Yes, it was," she said. "Did Rhyder Owens ask any questions about me?" Immediately after the question was out, Gina could have bitten her tongue. Why had she brought up his name, anyway? All she really wanted was to forget that he'd been there.

"No." His gaze left the highway for a second to glance at her. "You two know each other, don't you?"

Gina hesitated, then decided on the truth. "I met him a long time ago."

"And?" Justin prompted.

"And nothing." She couldn't tell him the rest, not yet.

"How long ago was it?" he persisted, sensing there was more to be told.

"Nine years."

"You were what? Eighteen?" Gina nodded curtly when Justin glanced at her again. "If you remember him after all that much time, he must have been more than a stranger in the crowd. Is he an old flame?"

"Hardly."

"Okay. So after nine years, what do you think of him now?"

"That he's still arrogant and self-centered. Let's talk about something more pleasant," she suggested.

Justin complied, a satisfied half smile curving his mouth. He talked about the clambake in generalities for the rest of the ride, not once referring to Rhyder in even the most casual way. In front of her apartment he stopped the car, switching off the engine, and turned in his seat.

"Now that we've gotten the small talk out of the way, let's discuss the moon and the stars and"—he reached out to draw her gently toward him—"the beautiful woman in my arms."

With inner reluctance, Gina allowed herself to be curved against his side. "But there isn't any moon," she pointed out.

"Never mind," Justin murmured as he lowered his head toward hers. "There's a streetlamp."

His kiss was both commanding and tender. Gina's reponse was totally pretense. The strong circle of his arms didn't generate the warm feeling it usually aroused. She blamed herself for his failure to kindle her desire.

A familiar mental barrier got in the way, something that made her indifferent to a man's caress. It was a defense mechanism to protect her inner feelings.

When the embrace reached the stage where it had to grow or die, Gina ended it. His arms tightened in protest at her withdrawal, but she pressed her hands firmly against his chest, wedging a distance between them. Sighing, Justin released her, and she smiled an apology.

"Unless you've changed the time of our nine o'clock morning meeting," she said gently, "I'm going to have to be up early in order to get to my office and look over the proposals again before meeting you. Which means I need some sleep tonight."

"I don't suppose you're going to invite me in for a fabulous cup of decaf, are you?" He eyed her ruefully.

"No."

"Why?" Although lightly asked, his question seemed to require a serious answer.

"Because if I asked you in, you would interpret the invitation to mean something a lot more stimulating than decaf."

Justin laughed softly at the accuracy of her observation, then studied her quietly for a second. "What's that old line? Are you just playing hard to get with me?"

"I am hard to get." The line of her mouth curved into a smile to take the edge off her words.

"Somebody must have hurt you really badly once." His brown eyes darkened at her startled glance in his direction. "I guessed it some months ago. Which probably explains why I've been more patient with you than it's my nature to be. Don't worry," he added as a closed expression stole over her features, "I won't ask you to tell me about him as long as you don't ask me about the women I've known before you."

"That's a deal." Gina leaned over and lightly brushed a kiss on his lips. "Good night, Justin. And thank you." There was a magnitude of meaning in the last.

Chapter Six

The three-piece black suit, consisting of a skirt, fitted vest and jacket, was tailored to the max, but the ruffled jabot of her white blouse was distinctly feminine. The overall effect was crisply professional, even with the raven sheen of her hair and the contrasting ocean green of her eyes.

A smooth leather briefcase in her hand, Gina breezed into Justin's outer office. His secretary glanced up from her keyboard and smiled a greeting.

"Mr. Trent's expecting you. Please go right in, Ms. Gaynes." The woman nodded toward the inner office door.

"Thank you." Not bothering to knock, Gina opened the door and walked into the plush executive office.

"Here's my attorney now," Justin declared, rising from the chair behind his desk to greet Gina. "She's the secret to my success. Everyone forgets the terms they were negotiating when they deal with her, Mr. Arneson."

Gina's cool, businesslike smile froze on her face as a pair of steel blue eyes bored into hers. Seated in a leather wing chair in front of the massive walnut desk was Rhyder. A movement near him finally attracted her stunned gaze.

A third man sat in the other leather chair. He rose automatically to his feet at the sight of her. Receding sandy hair crowned a high forehead, and dark-rimmed glasses nearly hid his hazel eyes. The years had matured the features of the boyish face inclined to freckles, but Gina recognized Pete instantly.

His recognition of her was slower, as if he were unable to believe it was possible. He glanced at Rhyder's hardening look for confirmation.

Gina recovered first, walking forward to extend a hand to an astonished Pete. "Hello, Mr. Arneson."

"It *is* you, Gina," he said. Disbelieving wonder gleamed through the lenses of his glasses as he held her hand for a long moment without shaking it. Abruptly his mind registered the formal way she had addressed him, coolly and politely. "I'm sorry, I . . . I should have said Mrs. O——"

"Ms. Gaynes," she supplied instantly, a husky tremor in her voice.

"Oh!" His sandy head jerked slightly. "You had it legally changed back after——"

"Yes, that's right," Gina interrupted a second time, and withdrew her hand from Pete's, noticing the frown on Justin's handsome face.

"I think I missed something here." Irritation blocked Justin's attempt to make it a laughing declaration.

"It's——" Gina began, but this time she was the one interrupted by Rhyder.

"Justin, Gina has unfortunately chosen to keep a secret from you. The fact is, she's my wife." Sardonic amusement glittered in his eyes as he met the killing look she threw him.

"Ex-wife," she corrected sharply.

"You were married to him?" Justin's eyes narrowed at Gina. His surprise seemed to be equally divided between finding out that she had been married and that Rhyder had been her husband.

Feeling like the accused, Gina stood before the walnut desk, hoping her inner trembling wasn't too obvious. Her heart was beating against her ribs like a trapped animal.

Pete was standing to the side, shifting uncomfortably at the situation his astonished words had precipitated. Justin was plainly confused and looked almost angry. Only Rhyder seemed to be blessed with self-control as he sat in his chair, relaxed and insouciant.

"I have no idea why Gina changed her name or why she failed to tell you of our marriage," Rhyder said. "Unless, perhaps, she was ashamed of her actions during the brief time we were together."

"I was not!" Gina wished for a fraction of a second that she could slap that smug look from his face. "I didn't want to remember you, for obvious reasons. My name is Gina Gaynes, personally and professionally, and it has been for years. I removed all traces of you from my life."

"Not quite all," Justin said dryly, his gaze sliding to her wedding band.

Her cheeks crimsoned. "It's my grandmother's wedding ring." But she knew and Rhyder knew that he had been the one to slip it on her finger.

"I wish you'd told me all this yesterday," Justin said grudgingly, as if unwilling to admit as much in front of the other two men.

"I hoped I'd never see him again after yesterday," Gina replied heatedly. "I didn't expect to walk into your office this morning and see him sitting . . ." The legal proposals in her briefcase seemed to burn through the leather to scorch her fingers. Her gaze moved to Rhyder as the significance of his presence registered in her mind. "Oh—I get it. You're the president of Caufield Enterprises, aren't you?"

"That's correct," Rhyder said. The arrogance in his

tone really riled her. "Pete is my attorney, and he'll be advising me during our negotiations for the resort property. Justin's indicated a willingness to sell."

Her grasp tightened on the briefcase. She turned to Justin with every intention of telling him that he would have to find someone else to represent him. The negotiations were likely to be long, because of the difference between the asking price and the offered price and some complex legal entanglements of the property.

Gina sure as hell didn't want to spend the amount of time required to arrive at a satisfactory compromise, since the time would be spent in Rhyder's company. But before she could advise Justin of her decision, Rhyder spoke up.

"I think it would be best if we postponed our meeting for a few days, Justin." He rose leisurely to his feet, his gaze resting briefly on Gina as he stood beside her, towering and masculine, completely in control of his emotions. "I'm sure Gina is as reluctant as I am to sit on opposite sides of a negotiation table. Considering our past association, it will be difficult to be impartial or objective in the discussions needed to reach the various compromises. I quite understand that Gina would prefer that you find another attorney in this matter. Naturally you'll need some time to bring him or her up-to-date on the various issues."

A raging fire seared through her veins. On the surface it sounded as if Rhyder was offering her an easy way out, but underneath she sensed that he was demanding that she be replaced. His mockery or his sarcasm she could have tolerated, but to be virtually ordered to resign under the guise of thoughtfulness was not something she would accept.

"You're mistaken, Mr. Owens." It sounded ludicrous to call him that, yet it seemed like the only way to contain her anger. "I don't prefer to have Justin hire another attorney. I'm well qualified, and I'm acquainted with you and your methods. I'll be better able to protect my client's interest because of it."

Except for the briefest possible glance, there was no indication from Rhyder that he found her decision objectionable. Yet Gina was certain she had scored a hit. Setting her briefcase on a corner of the desk, she opened it and removed a legal-sized folder.

"I've drafted a land contract agreement to use as a starting point." Gina extracted three copies of the document from the folder and distributed one to each of the men. "It will be more constructive to deal first with the items we agree on."

As he was already familiar with much of the language contained in the proposal, since Gina had discussed it with him in some detail, Justin's perusal of the document was merely a formality. Pete read it with concentration, mentally assessing every word and phrase.

With growing irritation, Gina watched Rhyder flip through the multipage agreement, barely skimming the contents. He didn't even glance at the last page as he tossed it on Justin's desk.

"Almost nothing in these documents that I'd agree to," Rhyder stated flatly.

Counting to ten, Gina held her tongue. If he was attempting to bait her into losing her temper by placing an immediate obstacle in the discussions, she was determined he wouldn't succeed.

"I prefer to hear Pete's opinion," she responded with professional crispness.

Rhyder gave a condescending, faintly derogatory nod. Seething inwardly, Gina ignored his rudeness. With negligent ease, Rhyder sat in the chair he had just vacated, relaxing against its winged back.

His hooded gaze made a slow and thorough inspection of her as she waited for Pete to complete his examination of the proposal. Gina pretended to be unaware of Rhyder's eyes on her, but his unwavering gaze was making her edgy.

"Okay, these are competently drawn," Pete concluded when he had finished reading her proposal. He beamed her a friendly smile that turned rueful after a second. "Unfortunately, the language is biased in favor of your client rather than mine. In the points where we are in agreement, I'd like to recommend changes in the wording."

"Let's discuss it," Gina said. Small revisions were to be expected as well as large. She removed a fourth copy from the folder. "Where, specifically?"

As Pete started to turn a page in his copy, Rhyder straightened with undisguised impatience. "Pete and I will look over the proposal, make some notes, and get back to you in the next few days, Justin."

He was already walking toward the door by the time Pete assimilated the information that Rhyder had brought the meeting to an abrupt end. Self-consciously Pete glanced at Gina. The compressed set of her lips no longer concealed her anger. Mumbling a goodbye, he picked up his briefcase, the proposal folded in his hand, and followed Rhyder's retreating back.

Silence descended with the closing of the door. Gina stared at it, wondering how she could have been so foolish as not to resign. It had been what she wanted and what Rhyder had wanted. Why had she sailed straight into danger?

A quiet movement behind her reminded her of Justin's presence in the room, and the explanations he would want. At the moment, she didn't want to give them.

Briskly she turned to the desk and stuffed her copy of the proposal into the folder to slip it into her briefcase. Justin watched, waiting silently. With a slight toss of her head, Gina looked at him and smiled.

"Interesting meeting. We didn't get off to a great

start, but my guess is that Rhyder wants the property or he wouldn't have come all this way." Her businesslike manner didn't encourage any personal questions. "Give me a call whenever he contacts you."

She turned to leave, but was halted by his low, demanding voice. "Gina."

"Yes, Justin?" She glanced over her shoulder, trying not to look too impatient.

"Why didn't you tell me you were married to him?" The strong line of his jaw was thrust forward at an aggressive angle.

"It seemed unnecessary."

"Unnecessary?" He was about to say more, but checked himself with an effort. "How much of what you did tell me was true?"

"All of it," Gina replied stiffly.

"Does that mean you were married to him nine years ago? When you were eighteen?" Justin tipped his head to one side, skepticism in his expression.

"Yes. That's the answer and the explanation," she retorted.

"But you said he wasn't an old flame."

"He's a dead flame as far as I'm concerned." Their chemistry still got explosive results, but that was due to hostility, not passion.

"Dammit, Gina!" His fist slammed against the desktop in anger. "You could have warned me who he was instead of letting me believe that he was someone you had a summer flirtation with years ago!"

"If I'd known he was the president of Caufield Enterprises, I would have told you, believe me!" Gina snapped. "As it was, you didn't bother to tell me."

"I figured you knew," Justin said defensively. "I certainly wasn't trying to keep it a secret from you. You can't say the same."

"I don't appreciate your insinuations!" She unleashed the anger that had been smoldering beneath the surface, kindled by Rhyder. "And I don't like being cross-examined!"

"Can you blame me for feeling as if I've been betrayed?" he demanded.

Breathing in deeply, Gina fought to control her temper. "If you prefer to have another lawyer represent you, you're free to do so, Justin."

He didn't try to stop her as she walked out of his office. The legal firm Gina worked for had offices in a building several blocks from Justin's. The walk in the brisk autumn air cooled most of her anger by the time she entered the reception area.

A pink-pad message to call Justin was awaiting her arrival. In the small cubbyhole that was her office, Gina dialed his number, bracing herself for the news that he was hiring another lawyer. His voice was clipped, but he told Gina that he still wanted her to represent him in the negotiations.

Professionally it was a victory, since she had been slowly building a reputation in real estate dealings. Yet she knew that emotionally it would have been better to have let this one go. Now she would be forced to tolerate Rhyder's company.

Two days later, Gina received a counterproposal in the mail from Pete Arneson on Rhyder's behalf. She had just finished reading it when her extension rang. It was Justin calling to tell her that Rhyder had scheduled a meeting for the following afternoon.

Gina told him about the counterproposal she had received. "If Rhyder thought our proposal was unacceptable, his is ludicrous."

"I don't doubt that we're going to have a fight on our hands to get what we want," Justin replied in a tone that said he wasn't looking forward to it.

"That's what Rhyder's all about," she said.

Her opinion of his counterproposal was repeated the next afternoon to Rhyder's face. Immediately Gina ignored him to discuss some of the minor differences with Pete, choosing ones that could quickly be resolved.

Rhyder stepped in, and they became embroiled in a bitter dispute on a major issue. After nearly an hour of verbal sword clashing, Gina tossed her pencil onto the table beside her long yellow legal pad.

"The guarantees you're asking Justin to give are preposterous!" she declared in exasperation. "From the beginning, you've been aware of the boundary dispute to the south. You can't expect him to guarantee the outcome of that."

"I can and do." There was uncompromising hardness to the line of his jaw.

A long, slow fuse began to burn. "Can you guarantee that after these negotiations are over you and I will never see each other again?" Gina challenged him, meeting the hard steel in his startling blue eyes. "Because if you can, I'll advise Justin to agree to yours."

He didn't back down. "I didn't think you could keep personalities out of these discussions, Ms. Gaynes," he said in a savage undertone.

Gina stiffened, furious at his harsh taunt. The burning fuse nearly reached the dynamite of her temper before she was able to check it. With controlled movements, she began gathering her papers and replacing them in her briefcase, aware of the silence that had suddenly descended on the room.

The briefcase was shut before she looked at any of them. Then it was Pete who got the worst of a glare from her green eyes, as cold as the Atlantic in winter.

"I'm wasting my time. It's pointless to sit here and argue when I have work to do in my office." Gina rose from her chair. "When your client's willing to be reasonable and consider compromises for some of his impossible demands, we can resume these talks." Her gaze sliced to Justin, who was both amazed and uncertain. "I'll talk to you later."

To Rhyder she said nothing, sweeping out of the room without a glance at him. She paused in the outer office long enough to ask Justin's secretary to call her office and let them know she wouldn't be returning that afternoon. Then she walked.

Cold fury propelled her for blocks. Finally she ended up, exhausted and footsore, only a block from her apartment. The problem was, her car was parked in the lot near her office building.

Reluctantly she started to retrace her steps. With a sigh she stopped and walked to her apartment. The car was locked and would be relatively safe until tomorrow. She could take a taxi to the office in the morning. Inside her apartment, her knees began to tremble. A tear slipped from her lashes, trickling down her cheek. It was the first time she could remember crying since her grandfather had died.

The telephone rang. Gina guessed it was Justin or one of her girlfriends and let it ring unanswered, not even glancing at the caller ID. As she started to fill the bathtub, the demanding ringing started again, but she ignored it and added perfumed bath salts to the water. The telephone continued to ring intermittently during her long soak in the bubble bath. The fragrant water soothed her tired muscles and strained nerves.

Wrapped in a short cotton robe, she walked into the kitchen, checked out the meager contents of the refrigerator, and poured a glass of milk. When she stepped into the living room, the ringing started again. Gina stopped, frowning at the telephone and the persistence of her caller. The number was blocked on the caller ID, and she had no idea who it was.

On the sixth ring she answered it, impatient with herself for giving in, yet knowing the caller seemed determined not to give her any peace until she did.

"This is Rhyder," the masculine voice unnecessarily identified itself.

Her first impulse was to slam the receiver down, but she checked herself and asked curtly, "What do you want?"

"If you're over your tantrum and have stopped sulking, I'd like to arrange a meeting for this evening."

"I'm a lawyer, not a doctor. I'm not on call at all hours of the day and night," Gina snapped. "If it's a meeting you want, call Justin and arrange it for tomorrow."

"There is other property I can buy, not quite as ideally located as Justin's, but with the potential for development and minus the hassle I'm getting from you. You either agree to this meeting tonight or the deal is off," Rhyder promised with ominous calm.

"Don't threaten me, Rhyder!"

"But I am. And considering that you were the one to walk out on today's meeting after issuing your ultimatum, you'll have a difficult time convincing Justin that you're acting in his best interests by refusing to meet me tonight," he said complacently. "Justin stands to make a sizable profit from this sale. He isn't going to like losing it, and he won't thank you if that happens."

"And of course you'll make sure he knows that you were willing to make concessions on some of your demands if only I'd met you halfway." Sarcasm honed a sharp edge to her voice. "You'll tell him that even if it's a lie."

"But neither of you would ever be sure it was, would you?" countered Rhyder.

"What time?" Gina had to surrender, but she did so reluctantly.

"Seven-thirty."

She glanced at her wrist, but it was bare. "What time is it now?"

"A few minutes before six," he answered.

There was plenty of time to eat a cold meal, dress, and travel downtown. "Seven-thirty at Justin's office, then," Gina said.

"Since it's after business hours, I thought we'd meet at the apartment I've rented." Rhyder paused. "Unless, of course, you object to that."

Part of her objected strongly. However, to admit that would also mean admitting she was allowing personalities to enter a business negotiation, the very thing Rhyder had accused her of today. She wasn't going to give him a second opportunity.

"Why should I?" Gina returned with false unconcern. "What's the address?"

She set her glass of milk on the telephone stand and reached for the pencil and message pad beside the phone, writing down the address as Rhyder gave it to her. When he hung up she tore the top sheet from the pad and fingered it apprehensively.

An inner sense warned her that she was making a mistake, but it was too late for second thoughts. She had committed herself and now had to follow through.

Returning to the kitchen with her glass of milk, she made a quick salad of cold shrimp, ate half of it before her appetite waned, and stacked the dirty dishes in the sink.

What to wear . . . nothing in her closet appealed to her. Pants seemed too casual without a jacket, and the evening was warm. Finally she decided on a short white skirt and a scarlet tunic that buttoned down the front. The bold color was like a shot of courage, and the white skirt went with everything.

She regretted her choice when the cab driver knocked at her apartment door and gave her a look of admiration, but there wasn't time to change. She took her briefcase, hoping it would keep her from looking too feminine and dressed up. Gina locked her apartment door and followed the driver to his cab.

The man kept up a steady flow of chatter all the way to Rhyder's apartment building. She needed silence to consider her legal strategy for the meeting, but her monosyllabic responses didn't discourage him. Gina couldn't concentrate at all.

Chapter Seven

The drive didn't take as long as Gina had expected. At twenty minutes past seven she knocked on Rhyder's door. When it opened, her senses leapt, reacting to the totally male figure standing before her.

The deep hue of his silk shirt made Rhyder's eyes appear even more blue. Dark pants fit his hips and muscular thighs just right.

"The others haven't arrived yet, have they?" There was a nervous catch to her voice as she tried to sound professional and poised.

"No." He opened the door wide. "Come in." His gaze raked her, a remoteness in his look. Motioning toward the living room behind him, he said, "Make yourself comfortable."

Impossible, Gina thought as she acknowledged his invitation with an automatic smile. The room was decorated in soft sand tones with touches of russet for contrast. Highly impractical but definitely luxurious, she decided. She wondered about the view from the window, but the drapes were closed against the late-day sun.

"I'm having a drink. Would you like one?" Rhyder asked.

"A glass of white wine if you have it," Gina said, sitting down on a plush beige sofa and placing her briefcase on the adjoining sofa cushion.

The palms of her hands were damp with nervous perspiration. She wished Pete or Justin would arrive. The apartment walls seemed to echo the knowledge that she was alone with Rhyder. An office meeting would have been infinitely preferable to this informal situation. It brought the business relationship to a more casual level.

Her nerves tensed as Rhyder approached. He didn't hand her the wineglass, but set it on the end table nearest her instead. Gina was aware that by doing so he had avoided accidentally touching her.

When he sat down in an armchair near the sofa, she knew she was incapable of small talk, especially when she noticed the brandy glass he held in his hands. Instantly her mind flashed back to the night of their wedding. She turned to the briefcase beside her and snapped it open.

"We might as well start—"

"Save it for later." His low voice cut across her sentence, a little harsh but controlled.

Gina hesitated for a split second, then closed the briefcase. Reaching for her wineglass, she leaned against the sofa back, trying to appear relaxed. There was a slight tremor in her hand as it carried the glass to her lips. She sipped the dry chablis quickly and held the glass in both hands. Her nerves vibrated under the watchfulness of Rhyder's gaze.

"I've heard glowing reports about you from your colleagues. You've done well since you passed the bar." He absently swirled the brandy in his glass, his compelling eyes not leaving her.

"Thank you. I've been lucky." She didn't want him to compliment her, if that was what he was doing.

"The fact that you're beautiful didn't hurt. And intelligent." There was a hint of cynicism in his tone. Before Gina could decide if he was being obnoxious, Rhyder continued, shifting his attention to the brandy in his glass. "But with your background, I would have thought you'd go into your father's specialty, marine law. Not real estate and land contracts."

"I seemed to have a natural aptitude for this field and chose it," was her only explanation.

Rhyder drank a swallow of brandy and gave her a considering look. "You mentioned at the clambake that your grandfather was dead. Has it been long?"

His routine questions expressed a polite interest, yet Gina felt agitated. Courtesy demanded that she answer, though. She had to either keep up her part in this tension-charged truce or begin the quarrel that would destroy it.

"Eight years." Made restless by unwelcome memories, she rose from the sofa and wandered to the fireplace, a combination of rust- and sand-colored stone.

Rhyder didn't say anything sympathetic, probably remembering her rejection of his previous attempt at the clambake. "What did you do afterward?"

"I sold the house and went to college, then law school." It was several seconds before Gina realized she had condensed eight years of living into a few short sentences.

Drinking the last of her wine, she held on to the empty glass. It gave her hands something to do. She glanced covertly at her wristwatch, wondering when Justin and Pete would arrive. Soon, she hoped. The atmosphere was already tense.

"More wine?" Rhyder offered, rising from the armchair to walk to the bar to refill his own glass.

"No, thank you," she refused.

"How long have you known Justin?" Something in the cobalt darkness of his look made Gina uneasy. The question didn't sound as politely indifferent as the others, and she hesitated.

"Uh, I met him after I came to Portland to work for my present firm," she answered finally. "I've represented Justin in several land transactions similar to this one."

He nodded, lifting the brandy glass for another sip that he didn't take. "Is your relationship with him all about business?" he asked over the rim of his glass.

She fought the urge to tell him it was none of his business. If she held her temper a little longer, Justin or Pete would come, and the conversation wouldn't center on anything personal.

"I do see Justin socially," she admitted. Rhyder had to have known that. Justin had made it fairly obvious at the clambake.

"Often?" He moved leisurely to where she stood in front of the fireplace.

Her chin lifted to a defiant angle, letting him know he had no right to question her, but she answered him anyway, coolly, concealing her anger.

"Yes. Several times a week."

He held her gaze. "Do you sleep with him?"

The tight rein on her temper snapped. Her hand moved in a swinging arc, her open palm stinging against his hard cheek. When her eyes focused on the slowly reddening white mark near his jawline, she realized what she had done. She took a quick step backward, expecting swift retaliation.

Rhyder didn't move. He was a statue, carved in hardwood, not blinking an eye, yet intimidating Gina until her heart raced in panic.

"Does that mean yes or no?" he asked levelly.

"That means it's none of your business!" she retorted, breathing rapidly.

"It is my business." Rhyder drained the brandy glass and set it on the mantelpiece. "Don't forget, Gina, the basis of any negotiation is trust."

More than ever before, Gina didn't trust him. "What's that supposed to mean?" she asked guardedly.

"It means I'm wondering how far you'll go to get me to agree to Justin's terms," Rhyder explained, his expression hardening in contempt.

"There's no reason you shouldn't trust him." Gina frowned, choosing her next words cautiously. "This deal has been fair and aboveboard all the way. Of course, the precise terms still have to be negotiated."

"Fair and aboveboard? That doesn't exactly describe you, Gina. And you're his attorney."

So he was going to bring up everything that had happened nine long years ago. It was a low blow, but typical of the Rhyder she remembered. He was good at provoking other people's emotions and outwardly controlled his own. Gina got a grip, reminding herself that she was here on Justin's behalf.

"What happened between us has nothing to do with my client or this negotiation."

"Interesting argument. But you'll have a tough time getting me to agree with it."

Gina paled.

"Let me guess. You want to impress Justin. You must be deeply involved with the guy."

"I'm not," Gina said angrily, then caught herself, realizing she'd taken his bait again. "Why are you needling me about it?"

"There's a conflict of interest here. You know exactly what I'm talking about."

"You and I—" She stopped, studying him for a long moment. His expression was unreadable. "That was over long ago. Totally over."

"Really? Don't play innocent, Gina," he jeered. "You were hoping I wouldn't know, but unfortunately I do."

"Know what? You're talking in circles!" But Gina felt she was the one caught in the maelstrom.

"You're a lawyer." Rhyder towered above her, dark and cynical, his powerful maleness almost threatening. "You know as well as I do that our annulment isn't worth the paper it's printed on."

His flat statement hit her with the force of a body blow. "What?" she gasped. She hadn't even read the official decree at the time, just shoved it into a filing cabinet where she later put the bank statements from the settlement. Gina had been almost glad at the time that such a painful episode could be reduced to mere legalese on a few sheets of paper, stamped with a gold seal, filed and forgotten.

"I lied under oath," he said coldly. "At the time both of us wanted out, and that seemed like the easiest and cheapest way to go. But technically the annulment is invalid. Which means, Gina, that you are still my wife."

"No," Gina protested wildly. "It can't be true! How? Why?"

His gaze narrowed. "I swore that our marriage was never consummated."

Gina wondered where the annulment was. Somewhere in one of those cardboard boxes in the back of her closet, no doubt. She wished she could dig out the damn document and make sure that he wasn't lying. But one look at his impassive face convinced her that he wasn't. "Why? Why did you do it?"

"It was the quickest way to end our marriage," Rhyder snapped. "And the cheapest. Divorce can be too complicated and prolonged. You were willing to accept a relatively small settlement, and I didn't want to take the chance you would change your mind and ask for more or decide not to end the marriage at all."

She closed her eyes, trying to pretend it was all a bad dream. If only she could wake up. She reminded herself that this was a technicality that a judge would never take seriously in a million years. Rhyder had lied under oath, not her. A decree of separation would be swiftly granted, and a routine divorce would soon follow. They held no property in common, had no children, hadn't even seen each other for almost a decade—

"Are you trying to convince me that you didn't know this?" Rhyder came nearer but stopped short of actually touching her.

"I didn't know," she insisted, caught between confusion, anger, and fear. "I didn't think. I never read the damn thing." Realization dawned as to the reason behind his question. Indignation surfaced. "You want me to recuse myself as Justin's attorney, is that it?"

"Correct."

"Because you did something—you, not me—that invalidates our annulment and could be seen as a conflict of interest?"

"Also correct," he admitted without a trace of apology in his condemning tone. "You weren't above working me over for money once. Why shouldn't you do it again?"

The emotional storm broke. "I can't believe you just said that!" Gina yelled. "You are totally out of line, Rhyder, legally and in every other way. Because"—her voice shook, but she summoned up her courage, furious at his unwarranted accusation— "all I wanted was to eliminate you from my life. I took your money because you offered it and I wanted you gone!"

Rhyder got a grip on her arm. Yeah, he oughta be afraid that she would smack him again, Gina thought wildly. Her instincts kicked in, and she tried to pull free.

Holding her easily, Rhyder tightened his grip just a little. "So you wanted to be free. You got it. Not that you cared about anybody else. Not me. Not your grandfather."

"I was eighteen, Rhyder. Young and stupid. I paid for

my mistake a thousand times over, emotionally speaking. But I was only eighteen."

"Yeah. The most beautiful girl I'd ever seen. Then and now." He tipped up her chin with one hand, pausing for a tantalizing second or two, his mouth only inches away from hers. Her free arm came up to brace her hand against a muscled shoulder, holding him away. To some degree she succeeded.

"Isn't this romantic," she said through gritted teeth. "Do you want to get slapped with a sexual harassment suit now? Don't tempt me. I despise you." She choked out the words.

Rhyder seemed surprised that she was capable of any resistance. Gina felt it in the rippling muscles of his shoulder. His hand left her chin and shifted to the nape of her neck, which he stroked.

There was infinite gentleness in his touch, very much at odds with his tough words. Gina sensed the emotions so long pent-up in him, and her mind flashed back to that one night of passionate lovemaking, her first night with a man. Their wedding night. It had been an incredible experience.

So was this. Just standing so close to Rhyder, held by him, his eyes looking into hers with a meaning she instinctively understood, was too much. She could have fought him off if he'd been rough, but she couldn't fight his sensual tenderness. Overpowered, she moved her body against his.

The sudden contact with the warm wall of his chest took her breath away. His mouth covered hers, not allowing Gina to think twice.

His shoulders seemed to wrap around her . . . oh, yes. She remembered their breadth. She couldn't stop the hands that molded her curves to fit the hard contours of his male length.

The feel of her soft flesh pressed against him seemed

to have dissolved his wrath. He was no longer ruled by vengeance. The hardness of the arms around her and the sensual pressure of the mouth claiming hers didn't lessen, but subtly changed to mastery.

The years that had passed since their time together seemed to dissolve, too. Embers of desire that she had believed were dead ashes were rekindling. Their glowing heat spread through her veins, making her heart race.

Under the expert persuasion of Rhyder's mouth, she knew in moments she would be lost, completely under his control. But she couldn't let that happen, couldn't ever again be that naïve girl who'd once wanted him so badly. Gathering the last remnants of her pride, she wrenched free of his arms and turned away, nearly stumbling in the shaky steps she took to put distance between them.

Hugging her arms around her waist, she tried to assuage the raw emptiness in her heart. Her back was to him. She couldn't risk looking at him; the rough carving of his dark features was too virile and handsome. A tremor of vulnerability shivered down her spine as she sensed him moving toward her. She had to deal with the way he aroused her, and make sure he understood how things stood now.

"The only thing I want from you is to get out of my life and stay out. It's all I've ever wanted!" she declared hoarsely when Rhyder stopped behind her.

For nine years Gina had convinced herself that she hated him. But if he touched her now, her heart would overrule her mind just as it had before. Closing her eyes tightly, she prayed he wouldn't.

Something brushed the tapering shortness of her dark hair near the back of her neck. Gina flinched, taking a quick step forward to elude his fingertips. Her heart fluttered wildly as she swallowed the soft moan in a faint sigh.

"When did you cut your hair?" Rhyder's musing voice asked—distant yet warm. An underlying hardness in its tone kept it from suggesting a caress.

"A while ago." She tried to sound indifferent, but she couldn't match his remoteness.

"Why?"

Switching to small talk wasn't going to win her over. He couldn't ignore her saying that she wanted him out of her life. But Gina couldn't bring herself to remind him of that. He was standing too close for her to think clearly. An inner radar was sensitized to the scant distance that separated them.

"It was impractical," she answered nervously. "Besides, long hair is out of style."

"No, it isn't," Rhyder said.

"Oh? Who died and made you editor of *Vogue?*"

"Funny girl. Nobody." The inflection of his voice changed as he said softly, "Your hair always reminded me of midnight satin. Sleek and shiny with blue-black lights."

A compliment from him was more than her turbocharged nerves could handle. There was no protection in not facing him, so Gina turned around. His electric blue gaze jolted through her.

For a numbed moment, she could only stare at him. His dark hair grew with wayward thickness, falling carelessly across his tanned forehead. Thick, very masculine brows set off the deep, brilliant blue of his eyes.

Yeah, he was still pretty much perfect, she thought ruefully. Physically speaking, she silently corrected herself. Slanting away from the faintly patrician bridge of his nose were the same chiseled cheekbones, more definite than they'd been in his twenties. But the aggressive thrust of his jaw was softened by smile lines carved on either side of his hard, sensual mouth.

His strength, power and determination were etched in his features for anyone to see. Gina told herself that people just didn't change that much inside, and Rhyder was no exception. When push came to shove, he would allow nothing to stand in his way. She reminded herself that ruthlessness was not high on her list of things she admired in men.

"Why did you have to come to Maine? Why couldn't you buy property someplace else?" Gina protested in angry despair. "I don't want you here! All I want to do is forget!" She'd moved on, succeeded on her own terms, put the past behind her. "Why couldn't you stay away? Why couldn't you forget about me?"

A flash of anger tempered his gaze with the fine edge of cutting steel. The look in his eyes mesmerized her and not in a good way. "That's what you were hoping for?" Rhyder said. "When I met you at the clambake, I got the feeling you didn't want me to recognize you." His tone was contemptuous. Gina only shook her head mutely, unable to admit that he spoke the truth. "Don't bother to lie," he hissed. "I saw it in your eyes that day." A fury seemed to build within him as soon as he said that, but at the last moment he controlled the violence of his emotion.

Gina shuddered, not understanding what had caused it but guessing she was somehow to blame. Her legs felt weak beneath her.

"Do you think I didn't try to forget you, Gina?"

A part of her thrilled to the negative implication of his question. Rhyder had found her as impossible to forget as she had found him. But it seemed unlikely that it could be true when he'd been so eager to get rid of her nine years ago.

"I don't believe you." Gina blinked her widened eyes, trying to armor herself with pride.

He studied her in silence. "My boat could have been named after you," he said at last. "The *Sea Witch*. That's what you were and that's what you are. You cast a very effective spell. Nine years, and it still has the power to dull my reasoning."

"I don't know what you're talking about," she murmured, chilled by the iciness in his voice.

"Don't you?" Rhyder jeered. "True fact—no other woman before or after you came close to making me feel what you did. We didn't have much time, just one night, but I never hit that high again."

"That can't be true," Gina protested in a helpless whisper.

He continued as though he hadn't heard her. "Forget I said it. Not as if you care. And this is a business meeting, right?"

"Right."

"I heard about this property for sale. It was ideal for the diversification we'd planned, but I found myself rejecting it because it was in Maine and that's where you were. I didn't come here to find you or bother you. I came to put your ghost to rest. Just my tough luck that I ran into you a few hours after my arrival."

Gina swallowed. His anger was closer to the surface again, transmitting its changed vibrations to her already sensitive nerve ends. She felt defensive and knew she had no reason to be.

"I was just as stunned to see you," she insisted stiffly.

"Were you? It didn't show." The jab hit its mark. "You greeted me very calmly with another man's arm around your waist, denying that you ever knew me and informing me that your name was Ms. Gina Gaynes. Do you know what my first reaction was?"

"No." Gina shook her head briefly, wanting to stop the acid flow of explanation that was burning her ears.

"That you were trying to conceal from Justin the fact that you'd been married before. I felt sorry for him until you walked into the office the next morning. When I realized you were a lawyer, I expected you to bow out, but you didn't. I can understand why you wouldn't want to explain a conflict of interest like that to your new guy, but that's not my problem. You stood to lose a fat fee if you walked, though. So I took the initiative and explained the situation to Justin," Rhyder said.

"Your side of it, you mean."

"I just didn't want to be set up again," Rhyder said with finality.

"You never were." She took a deep breath and tried to think like a lawyer, talk like a lawyer. "Granted, I did a really stupid thing, Rhyder, but it was a long time ago, and I was really young. And I didn't hold a gun to your head to make you marry me, and I don't see why I should be treated like a criminal now. You're over-reacting, big-time. We settled out of court. Once I got the final decree, I tried not to think about you at all."

"Were you hoping I'd married again? You didn't ask."

"No," she said simply. Gina had never pictured him marrying another woman during their nine years apart. The thought made her uneasy now, but she couldn't say why. "I didn't want to know about you or your life after . . ." She couldn't finish that. "And as far as I knew, the annulment was valid. I should have looked at it, but I didn't. You don't have much of a case if you're going to try to convince Justin otherwise."

Rhyder only shrugged. Gina felt herself bridling at his continued failure to accept her word. He was the one who'd testified falsely, not her.

"So who told you we were still legally married?" She held up a hand before he could answer. "I can guess. Pete, right? And not all that long ago. You two had a few drinks, got into a late-night bull session, and the subject came up. He must not have drafted the request for an annulment or he would've known that right off the bat."

"My father's attorney took care of it," Rhyder said curtly.

"Well, I guess Pete put the fear of God into you. Whatever. You should have contacted me," she said, taking the offensive. "I would've agreed to a divorce."

"For how much?" he said.

The sarcasm lacing his voice startled her. "Money! It always comes down to money with you, doesn't it?"

"You started it." Rhyder towered before her, his hands on his hips as he glared coldly. "That annulment had a price tag. You got what you asked for."

"That's not precisely true," she said quietly. Gina lifted her chin, meeting the blue contempt of his gaze. "I heard you on the terrace talking to Pete the morning after we were married." The humiliating words were branded into her memory. "You basically said you would write a check for any amount to get rid of me. And a lot of other degrading things. Do you honestly think I would have wanted to stay married to you?" she demanded bitterly.

"You didn't hate me so much that you wouldn't take my money," he reminded her.

His arrogance hadn't changed. "Yes, I took it," Gina admitted, breathing with difficulty. "Gramps wasn't comfortable with it, but I guess he thought it was up to me. He was incredibly loving, considering how ashamed he was of the whole thing. And of me, even though he never said so. He was so understanding that it almost made me feel worse. He actually thought he'd failed me. All he wanted was for me to be married and happy, as happy as he was with my grandmother." Anguish made her stop, choked by a sob. "And we had one happy night."

"Yeah." His voice was rough. "I guess we did. Once I got over the news that you'd played me for a fool and we got into the bedroom. What the hell, right? We made the most of it."

"Don't be crude," she whispered. For an instant she had the strength to run, but his hands reached out, catching her by the hips and forcing her to remain in place. She tried to push them away, but he held her firmly.

"For God's sake, I should have walked out," he said, more angry with himself than her. "You were only eighteen, but I didn't have the self-control to keep my hands off you. You chased me—you know that. It was almost a game with you. You invited me to kiss you, to make love to you, while only half knowing what it was about."

Her cheeks crimsoned at his words, in shameful awareness of the truth. His hands burned into her hips, reminding her that even now his touch could enflame her with desire.

"You were way too young for me." As if he read her thoughts, his hands tightened on her hips, drawing her fractionally closer to him. "I dated women and I still do. But you, even that young—resisting you was impossible. I kept reminding myself that I was the adult, the one who had the sense to not let things get out of hand."

"I went too far," she said with a sigh.

"Yeah, well. Looking at you that night just blew every circuit I had. Then, after, you almost dared me to marry you, and somehow that seemed like it would make it right. So I said yes. It did occur to me that maybe you didn't mean it or didn't know what you were saying. But not that you were trying to get back at me. I was the naïve one when it came to that."

His hands slid to her waist, holding her for a second while her pulse raced at the darkening light in his eyes. She was a willing prisoner of his touch, pliantly allowing herself to be drawn against him. The hardness of his muscular length supported her as she leaned on him.

Her dark head was tipped back to gaze at his face. The warmth of his breath fanned her cheeks. Beneath her hand, resting on his chest, she could feel the drum-beat of his heart in tempo with her own.

"The only thing that's changed in nine years," Rhyder spoke slowly, his eyes shifting their attention to her lips, "is that now you're a woman. Everything else is the same. You'd think after all this time I would find that I wouldn't want to make love to you. But I do."

"Rhyder, no—"

He covered her lips with his. She yielded, inviting the mind-shattering exploration of her mouth. He kissed her for spellbinding minutes, then moved with tingling ease to the sensitive lobe of her ear.

"Please, don't do this," Gina murmured. She lacked the willpower to resist something she enjoyed so much.

"You know you want me to," he answered complacently, certain now of the power he had over her.

"Pete or Justin could come in any minute," she protested.

"No, they won't." Rhyder brought his lips to the corner of her mouth. "The only meeting I had planned was between you and me."

Chapter Eight

Gina twisted slightly to elude the fire of his lips, her mind already dizzy from their warmth. "But you said—" she began, feeling bewildered.

"I said that I wanted to arrange a meeting for tonight. I didn't mention anyone attending it except you and me," Rhyder finished.

His caressing fingers pushed aside the open collar of her scarlet tunic as he sought the sensitive skin at the base of her neck. His light nibbling sent quivers through her flesh.

"That isn't fair," she protested, although her yearning for him made her voice breathless with surrender.

Her body was molded to his, and his nearness intensified the throbbing ache she felt. Rhyder caught her chin and lifted it to gaze deeply into her eyes.

"What is fair, Gina?" he demanded, his low voice raw with desire, its unspoken message quaking through her. "Was it fair for you to haunt me for nine years?"

"Oh, please." Still, her romantic heart wanted to believe it.

"Was it fair to me to see you again and never have the

chance to touch you to find out if the fire in my soul was for a ghost or a woman?"

"Quite a speech."

"I mean every word." His features were set in uncompromising lines. There would be no turning back for Rhyder, Gina knew.

The compelling blue of his eyes held her mesmerized while his hands unbuttoned the light tunic and slid it from her shoulders to fall to the floor at her feet. He stroked her bare arms in a way that was almost unbearably arousing.

"I remember how much I wanted to do this that night on the boat. And then . . . you gave me a second chance. I didn't say no that time." Exploring fingers left her arm to unhook her bra. The warm pressure of their bodies as they'd kissed kept the lace cups and straps where they were, even though he'd unhooked it with ease. Rhyder seemed to want to take his time about removing it totally, trailing a thumb along her spine. The sensuous caress played havoc with her senses. "I had to see you tonight. I couldn't wait any longer. If you hadn't come, I would have been at your apartment, battering down the door."

His hands moved deftly behind her back, and he bared her breasts, throwing the bra on the floor. Gina shivered, but not because she was cold. Just the opposite. His touch heated her bare skin.

He palmed her nipples. All she could do was sigh with pleasure, even though some part of her still wanted to protest.

Rhyder drew her onto her tiptoes, burying his mouth in the hollow of her throat. Sensual fire raced madly through her body.

"Quite a spell, Gina. I want you more than ever." As he bent her backward, the moistness of his mouth followed the curve of her breastbone.

But it was his magic that had Gina in a trance. Her arms were gliding to his neck to curl her fingers in the sexy blackness of his hair.

Rhyder swung her off her feet and into his arms. "You were once my wife, Gina," he stated huskily, looking down at her. "Now you're going to become my lover. Give me another night to change your mind. Just one night. You belong to me."

In her heart she knew he was right and let her lips tell him so when his dark head bent to claim them. His strength became a thing to glory in and not fight, even in token resistance.

Later, when the heady rapture was receding under a cold wave of reality, Gina shivered and would have slid away. Rhyder's arm reached out to curve around the nakedness of her slender waist and draw her back to the warming heat of his body.

"This time there aren't going to be any tears, Gina," he told her as he gently shaped her to his side, her head resting on his muscled shoulder.

A sensation of coolness awakened Gina the next morning. She turned to find Rhyder and nestle against his warmth, but he wasn't there. The inner radiance glowing in her eyes was dimmed by the discovery. She sat up, unable to shake the nightmarish feeling of dread that this had happened before.

Her clothes were neatly folded and laid across a chair back. Not where they had been left. She slipped from beneath the covers to dress hurriedly. As she started to slip the scarlet tunic over her head, she heard the sound of voices in another part of the apartment. For a moment, she was paralyzed by the chilling sensation of déjà vu.

Almost against her will, Gina was driven to the bedroom door leading to the outer hall, the thin tunic top clutched in her hands. Hesitating, she finally reached out with a trembling hand and opened the door a crack, just enough to let the voices filter through.

"I hope you know what you're doing." At the sound of Pete's voice, Gina's stomach did a sickening somersault.

"I know exactly what I'm doing," Rhyder assured him. There was a faint arrogance in his tone at being questioned. "You just stick to the legal end of this."

"From what you've told me about Justin and what I've seen for myself, I know he isn't going to like it," Pete replied, still unconvinced.

"He doesn't have to like it. He simply has to accept it, and he will," Rhyder said complacently.

"Aren't you being a little premature?" Pete's skepticism was clear. "You haven't even talked to Gina yet, or so you said."

"After last night, I think I can guarantee that her cooperation is assured." There was a smile in Rhyder's voice, but the sound of it didn't gladden Gina's heart. A tremor of agonizing pain quaked through her. "I called my father—well, I left him a message; he's in Bermuda with his fourth wife. But I wanted to tell him the news."

"My God, it isn't even final yet!" came the protest.

"It's only a matter of time and a few signatures on a piece of paper," said Rhyder, dismissing his friend's apprehensive words of caution.

"Yeah, right," Pete agreed in a disgruntled tone, adding, "I'll talk to you later."

A door closed, and Gina guessed that Pete had left the apartment. Quickly she shut the bedroom door, slowly releasing the doorknob so there would be no telltale click of the latch to betray that she had been listening. She walked quickly to the center of the room, her heart splintering at the cold, hard fact of Rhyder's betrayal.

Oh, he'd wanted her, all right, for two not very good

reasons: to satisfy the lust she still aroused, and to en-
trap her with the sure knowledge that she loved him.
He'd intended to persuade her to convince Justin to
agree to Rhyder's terms in the real estate transaction.

Footsteps approached the bedroom. Her back was to
the door, and she quickly pulled the scarlet tunic over
her head as the door opened. Gina felt his gaze rest on
her. For a split second she couldn't move, the sensation
was so caressing. She recovered and twisted the blouse
until it hung straight on her body, realizing then that
she'd forgotten to put on her bra.

He didn't seem to mind. His long strides eliminated
the distance between them with casual ease. She just
stood there, taken aback, as he boldly caressed her
breasts, bared to his touch under the flimsy material. As
if he owned her, she thought with numb fury. She was
about to push his hands away when he stopped and settled them firmly on her shoulders.

Then Rhyder bent his dark head to nuzzle the curve
of her neck. Gina breathed in deeply, closing her eyes
as she tried to brace herself against the evocative caress.

"I was hoping you'd still be in bed," Rhyder murmured against the pulsing vein in her neck.

"I'm glad I'm not," her voice trembled as he found a
sensitive point. "I've overslept as it is."

"It's barely nine o'clock." He turned her into his
arms. Gina's mind wanted to resist, but her body eagerly allowed him. The brilliant blue light in his eyes
weakened her resolve. "Still a decent hour to be in
bed."

"You're up," she pointed out, lowering her gaze to
the collar of his shirt, starkly white against his mahogany tan. "And dressed."

"Not willingly." His arms slid around her to draw her
close. "Pete stopped over early on some business," he
explained, and added, "I should've hung a Do Not

Disturb sign on the apartment door and we wouldn't be having this discussion."

"I'm glad you didn't hang out that sign." Her hands were resting on the muscled wall of his chest, keeping him a little bit away just to preserve what was left of her sanity.

Gina was achingly aware that if it hadn't been for Pete, she wouldn't have known about the way Rhyder intended to exploit her love for him. Whether it was an act of revenge or simply just the way he did business, she couldn't imagine. She really didn't know him, and she never had. But for the second time in her life, she had been about to make an utter fool of herself over him.

"Why?" He tipped his head back to have a better view of her face.

"Because I'm due in the office. I'm a working girl, remember?" Gina forced the brightness in her answer.

"To hell with the office!" Rhyder slid a hand up to cup her chin, lifting her gaze from its hypnotic study of his shirtfront.

His mouth closed over hers with a practiced ease, sensually persuasive as he tasted the sweetness of her lips. Almost against her will, she found herself responding to the flawless technique of his kiss. His arms circled her body and made her even weaker.

He was a master of the art of seduction, and Gina's reawakened love made her even more vulnerable to his skill. She fought through the waves of rapture breaking over her senses and surfaced from his kiss, breathing raggedly as she managed to put a few precious inches between them.

"I have to go to the office," she insisted, staring at his shirt pocket, aware of the uneven rise and fall of his chest.

One of his arms still clasped her waist while his other

hand rested on her rib cage, tantalizingly near the swell of her breast. His head was bent toward hers, his warm breath stirring the raven hair near her temples.

"Call and say you'll be late," Rhyder instructed in a voice husky with desire.

Gina trembled. "I can't do that." She lowered her lashes to hide the contradictory answer in her heart.

Sensing that her resolve was wavering, he lowered his head farther, lightly breathing into her ear and making her flesh tingle as he spoke. "Why not?"

His hand slid to cup the underside of her breast while his thumb began repeating a slow circle over her nipple. The smooth cheek against her face carried the musky fragrance of him mingled with expensive after-shave. The heady scent combined with the other erotic stimulants to nearly undermine Gina's will. The searing temptation was there to seek the hardness of his mouth.

With her last ounce of will, she dragged herself away from Rhyder, not stopping until she was several feet away.

"I doubt that my clients would understand the reason for my coming in late," she answered his question at last.

"So don't tell them." His low voice was caressing, reaching across the distance to continue his persuasion.

But Gina was far enough away to resist it, although she doubted she would have the determination to resist Rhyder if he followed words with actions.

"It isn't a question of telling them." She gathered up her things, got dressed all the way, then walked toward the door, unable to glance at the tousled covers on the bed or Rhyder. She was already too aware of the sensual undercurrents in the room. "They think their time is vitally important, especially considering what I bill per hour."

He didn't make any attempt to stop her when she walked through the door, only turned to follow.

"I can't cancel them simply because . . ." Gina hesitated over the words that would spell out the reason in stark black and white.

"Because I want to make love to you," Rhyder finished for her.

The self-conscious glance she tossed him over her shoulder caught the knowing glint in his eyes. A faint pink came into her cheeks at his easy boldness. He was confident of his power over her, and she had given him that power by letting him see the depth of her love last night.

No wonder he had been so sure when he'd talked to Pete that he could get her to do whatever he wanted. And he might have if she hadn't overheard the conversation.

"Yes, that's it," she admitted, her footsteps carrying her into the living room. She saw her briefcase almost instantly. "The reason is a bit selfish."

"Selfish," repeated Rhyder. His gaze never left her for an instant as she retrieved her briefcase. Now he was between her and the apartment door. "After nine years, I don't think it could be described as selfish."

"Maybe not," she conceded, just to get him out of her way for now. She felt a little dazed. As she started to walk past him, he caught at her free hand just above the wrist. She stopped, not because of any restraining pressure in his grip but because his touch had the power to control her emotions. Her heart rocketed under the glittering blue of his gaze.

"There are a lot of other attorneys in your firm, Gina. Let one of them handle the appointment that can't be cancelled," he suggested.

His gaze never left her green eyes as he lifted her left hand and turned its palm upward. She weakened even more at the sensuous caress of his male lips in its center. If it had been love instead of lust that prompted the compelling fire in his gaze, Gina would have agreed without an instant's hesitation.

But it wasn't. "I can't do that." She shook her head, fighting the sensations the hard tip of his tongue was arousing.

"If you were ill, someone would have to take over your clients. Or if there was a family emergency. And I'm your husband, Gina, in desperate need of you." Rhyder said it lightly, but with no less meaning as he turned her hand over and kissed the gold band on her third finger, the ring he had placed there.

"No!" But the gesture nearly made her forget why she was refusing him.

He pulled her to him as if he had lost patience with the gentle tactics that'd failed to get him what he wanted. He arched her against his hip, the hard muscles of his leg sliding between hers.

Then Rhyder's mouth closed over hers, parting her lips in hungry demand. Gina was lost to the exploding force of his passion. At her surrender, he let his caressing hands rove over her flesh, melting her as easily as a flame melts wax.

Although her submission was virtually complete, Gina didn't let go of her briefcase, clinging to it tenaciously as if it were her self-respect.

"Gina, call your office and tell them you won't be in—all day," Rhyder ordered against her throat.

Her head was tilted back and to the side, allowing him freer access to the pleasure points along her neck. She glimpsed the gold wedding band on her finger.

Ignoring his command, she asked, "Did you ever tell your parents about me?"

The unexpected question made him lift his dark head. A frown creased his tanned forehead; his eyes were suddenly alert.

"Of course I did," he answered, giving her a crooked smile. "That's a strange question. What made you ask?"

"I don't know," Gina breathed. "I guess I was wondering if I was a skeleton in your family closet."

His head dipped toward her parted lips. "No skeleton in our closet ever had such beautiful bones."

His mouth had barely touched hers when the phone rang. Rhyder cursed beneath his breath at the interruption. He didn't let go of her waist, drawing her to the telephone with him. He kept her firmly beside him as he picked up the receiver.

Gina was close enough to hear a soft Bermuda accent on the line. "Go ahead, sah. We have your party on the line now."

It was his father, she knew instantly, obviously calling from a hotel so swanky that guests didn't actually have to dial if they didn't want to. She remembered his comment to Pete that he had put a call through to the senior Owens. And she knew she didn't have the composure to listen to Rhyder relating the news that he was about to close the deal on the real estate Justin was selling.

Not when he would have to veil the words in sentences where she wasn't supposed to guess the part he was intending her to play in it. Firmly she began to slip from his hold.

"Hello, Dad," Rhyder said. "Hold the line a minute." He slid his hand down to cover the mouthpiece as he turned to Gina. "What are you doing?"

"I'm going to the office."

"I'd forgotten what a stubborn little witch you are." He smiled as he spoke, but he had shifted his mental focus to the call.

"I have work to do." Gina insisted on taking advantage of the fact that he was torn between the desire to speak to his father alone and to have her stay. She gestured at the receiver in his hand. "So do you."

He gave her a long, hard look, then nodded. "All

right, I'll see you tonight. I'll pick you up at your office."

"There's no need. I have my own car," she answered, only implying that she was agreeing to see him that night. In truth, she had no intention of it. She couldn't risk it.

As she started to turn away to make her escape, he caught her hand, saying, "If you're going to make me work all day at business, the least you can do is kiss me goodbye."

Hesitating, Gina pivoted back, pressing her lips to his for a warm but brief moment. It was more of a goodbye than he knew, and it tore at her heart. She moved quickly out of reach.

Rhyder chuckled softly. "You'll pay for that tonight," he said in warning at the briefness of her kiss. Then the smile faded from his eyes. "Seriously, Gina, we have a lot to talk about tonight as well as a lot of time to make up for."

Not the least on the list would be Justin and the terms of the sale, Gina guessed bitterly. She simply smiled wanly in response to his statement and moved hurriedly toward the door. Before she reached it, she heard Rhyder speaking into the telephone.

"Sorry to keep you waiting, Dad, but Gina was here . . . yes, she's just leaving."

The rest of the conversation was lost to Gina as she stepped into the hallway and closed the door. It wasn't until she was outside the building that she realized she had no means of transportation. Her car was still parked in the lot near her office.

She paused beside an outdoor phone booth, debating whether or not to call a taxi, before deciding that a brisk walk in the sharp September air was just what she needed to blow away the cobwebs spun by her emotions.

It was rather startling to hear the birds singing. She

felt so dead inside. A scattering of leaves on the maple trees was tinged with crimson. To most, it would have been a harbinger of autumn glory, another tourist attraction in Maine. But the blood red shade only reminded Gina of the deep wound in her heart.

When she arrived at the office, she felt somewhat better from the long walk. Her heartache hadn't been resolved, but her determination not to let Rhyder use her had been strengthened. During the day Justin phoned her twice, each time insisting it was urgent, but Gina didn't accept the calls.

She dismissed the urgency of his calls with the reasoning that Rhyder wouldn't approach him until he had his discussion with her. And he still didn't know the discussion would never take place.

A few minutes before five o'clock, Gina hurried from the office building. Despite her assurances to Rhyder that he didn't have to pick her up, she was half afraid he would be waiting for her. She made it to her car without anyone trying to stop her.

But she knew it wasn't over. There was still tonight. When she didn't arrive at his apartment, she knew Rhyder would call. And when she didn't answer the phone, which she wouldn't, he would come over.

Even if she did answer, Gina knew he would never accept her refusal to see him and would come to her apartment anyway. She would call the police then; there was no other choice. She didn't dare listen to him. Gina was too susceptible to his brand of persuasion.

Her plan was reasonable enough and would serve to keep her from any direct contact with Rhyder, but Gina didn't feel any sense of triumph when she arrived at her apartment building. She loved him still and wanted only his love in return, but to be used was more than her stiff-necked Yankee pride—a trait she had inherited from her grandfather—could bear.

Melancholy deadened her footsteps as she approached the door to her apartment and rummaged through her handbag for the key. She inserted it in the lock, turned it and pushed, but the door didn't budge. She tried it again with no success, then looked to make sure she hadn't accidentally stopped at the wrong door. In this building, the doors were nearly identical.

It was her apartment, but the key wouldn't work in the lock. She double-checked to be sure she had the right key. She did.

Puzzled, she retraced her steps to the front part of the building where the resident manager lived and knocked at that door. It opened a crack, a safety chain keeping it from opening all the way. Gina smiled politely at the housecoated woman peering at her.

"I'm sorry to disturb you, Mrs. Powell, but I can't seem to get my key to work. Could you use your passkey to let me into my apartment?"

The chain remained in place while the woman tipped back her head to peer at Gina through the half-moon lenses of her glasses, as if trying to place her. The pinched lines around her mouth softened slightly in recognition.

"Of course your key won't work," the elderly woman declared. "The man's already come to change the lock."

Gina arched a winged brow briefly in surprise. Then she sighed. She supposed there had been a burglary or two, and all the locks had been changed as a precaution.

The notice must have been slipped in her mailbox, but that she hadn't checked in several days. The only time she ever got important mail was the first of the month when the bills arrived. She had no close family since her grandfather died, and her friends generally e'ed her at work. Actual letters had pretty much gone the way of the dodo.

"Could I have the new set of keys?" she asked patiently.

"Why?" the woman wanted to know, straightening her hunched shoulders slightly.

"To get into my apartment, of course," Gina replied.

"T'wouldn't be any reason to give 'em to you. There's nothin' in it that belongs to you," Mrs. Powell declared.

"What?" An open frown of bewilderment made Gina's mouth turn down as she tried to fathom this mysterious conversation.

"Everything's packed and gone. There's nothin' left there that's yours," the woman repeated in a louder tone, as if Gina were deaf.

"Gone where?" Gina demanded.

"Well, dearie, you're the one who should know where. It's not my business." The woman nodded.

"Well, I don't know where," Gina answered, her patience receding. "If somebody took my things, it was without my permission. Would you mind letting me come in, Mrs. Powell, so I can call the police?"

"The police? Why should you want to call them?" The woman peered at her in a baffled way. "There was nothin' stolen. Your husband supervised the packin' of nearly everything himself."

"My husband?" Gina breathed in sharply. It all became suddenly very clear.

"Yes, your husband. You don't think I'd just let anybody into your apartment and take your things?" Mrs. Powell sniffed indignantly.

"Of course not," Gina said, her lips compressed.

Rhyder had been so confident that he had moved her out lock, stock, and barrel. A slow anger set in.

"I explained to your husband that you still had four months left on your lease and a month's notice was required before vacating," the woman continued. "He paid for the rest of the lease and added another month's rent in lieu of notice. He took care of everything for you."

"Yes, I can see that." Gina nodded grimly.

"If there's nothing else . . ." There was a meaningful pause as the woman silently indicated that all these pesky questions were a waste of her valuable time. Gina could hear a soap opera blaring from an unseen TV set.

"No. No, nothing else," Gina agreed after a second's hesitation. "I'm sorry to have troubled you, Mrs. Powell."

"That's quite all right." The door started to close, the chain slackening. It straightened again as the manager added as an afterthought, "And congratulations, too. You have a fine man there."

Gina didn't respond to that as she turned on her heel, her temper simmering. She was saving the scalding fury of her anger for Rhyder. Its impetus carried her swiftly to her car.

Chapter Nine

Cold rage filled her as Gina paused in front of Rhyder's apartment door. Her sharp, impatient knock echoed the pounding of her heart against her ribs. Within seconds the door swung open, and Rhyder was facing her. A smile of lazy charm spread across his rugged face.

"About time you got here," he declared warmly, reaching out to her to draw her inside. "I was about to send out a search party for you."

Closing the door, he started to pull her the rest of the way into his embrace. Gina resisted, her seething fury making her immune to his possessive touch.

"Just where did you think I might go?" The question came out in a low, accusing rush that slowly straightened the curve of his mouth. "You made absolutely sure I had nowhere else!"

A smiling gleam remained in the brilliant blue of his eyes, crinkling at the corners as he looked at her. The hands gripping her shoulders didn't force her nearer, nor did they let her go.

"Your eyes are so damn green. The last time I saw the

ocean that color, it was building to a storm," Rhyder commented. "Did you have a rough day?"

Gina counted to ten, enraged that he could pretend to be so dense. He wasn't fooling her for a second. He knew very well why she was angry.

"I want to know where my things are," she demanded. "And don't say you don't know what I'm talking about. I mean the things you took from my apartment."

"Your clothes are in the bedroom. There are some boxes of this, that, and the other in the spare room that I wasn't sure what you wanted to do with. And as far as the odds and ends of furniture, I had that stuff stored for the time being," Rhyder answered with leisurely ease.

"Who gave you the right to do anything with my things?" Gina challenged, incensed by his calm.

"So that's what you're so upset about." He smiled softly as he understood the cause of her anger. His hands began slowly massaging her shoulders and arms with a stroking motion while his gaze ran possessively over her face, a smoldering light of banked desire in the look. "I probably should have let you know," he conceded, "but I wanted to surprise you."

"Surprise me!" Gina choked on the audacity of the bland claim.

"It's been my experience that women take an eternity to sort and pack, let alone move. Then they take even longer when it's time to unpack. Experience gained from observing my mother and sister," he added, as if to assure her he had helped no other woman to move.

As if a family as rich as the Owenses ever did their own packing, she thought with silent fury. Let alone move out of their Back Bay mansion or any of the other stately homes they owned.

"I decided that if I told you I was having a moving company come, you'd be there fussing around, and it would take twice as long. Now it's all done, and you don't have to be concerned about it."

"Well, you can just call up your precious moving company and have everything moved back!" she stormed.

His gaze narrowed, a quietness stealing over him. "Were you planning to maintain a separate residence?"

"Yes, I was. A residence permanently separated from you!" Gina pulled away from his touch to emphasize her determination to have no part of him or his life.

Rhyder didn't try to reestablish physical contact with her, yet there remained a coiled watchfulness about him. The air seemed charged with invisible lightning that heightened the tension between them.

"I think you'd better explain that remark," he said in that dangerously quiet voice.

"I don't see what there is to explain," she retorted defiantly. "I thought it was perfectly clear. I am going to live in my apartment, and you are going to live wherever else you choose. Your high-handed tactics of canceling my lease and moving my things out simply aren't going to work."

"I told you"—a muscle was flexing in his neck—"I was trying to be considerate. I wanted us to have time together instead of spending half of it moving you here."

Gina wanted to smack him. "When did I ever say that I wanted to live with you?"

His expression hardened. "You didn't in so many words," he admitted, "but after last night I assumed that—"

"You assumed wrong!"

"Are you going to try to convince me now that you didn't want to stay with me last night? That I forced you to?" He stared at her with equal parts confusion and anger.

Her cheeks reddened. "No, I'm not! But I never in-

dicated that I wanted it to be a permanent arrange-
ment!"

"You're my wife!" Rhyder snapped. "That oughta
count for something. You belong to me!"

"Have you lost your mind? This is the USA, not me-
dieval England. I don't belong to anyone but myself!"
Hell would freeze over before she told him that he
could claim full title to something that she used to own:
her heart.

"Damn it," he muttered beneath his breath, "I knew I
should never have let you leave this morning."

The words were barely out before he made a move to
grip her wrist. She reacted too slowly to dodge his hand,
and Rhyder yanked her toward him. In defense, Gina's
arm swung, the flat of her hand connecting with his
cheek. The hard contact sent shock waves of pain
rolling through her arm.

Instantly the striking hand was seized and pinned
against the granite wall of his chest. His expression was
dark with anger.

"How many times do you think you can slap my face
and get away with it?" he snarled.

Gina strained and twisted to break free, but it was no
use. He shifted his grip and brought her closer—and
closer still—until her lips met his in a rough kiss.

It felt so good, so unbelievably good. Only Rhyder
could kiss like that, although she knew better than to
tell him so. He wouldn't want to hear about the compe-
tition, not that there were or had ever been any serious
contenders since him. There was something instinctive
and very male about his possessiveness, and she liked it.
The rigidity of her body—token resistance, really—just
melted away.

Sensing as much, Rhyder began to enjoy the spoils of
his victory, searching relentlessly for the sweetness of
her lips, plundering their softness. The sensual fire of his
kiss sparked a quivering response.

But for some reason, Gina's beleaguered brain and common sense kicked in. This felt good, but it wasn't going to end well. Before Gina found herself surrendering to his hungry demand for passion, she tried to push him back.

"Let me go!" She caught her breath, her voice low. "And don't start talking about technicalities. There is such a thing as marital rape." She stared him down, but he wouldn't look away.

"Damn you, Gina." He groaned long and loud. "You have a knack for making me despise myself for the way I feel, and half the time I'm only responding to your invitations."

"Let me go," she repeated, aware that he spoke the truth. He did, reluctantly.

Her senses were clamoring from the musky male scent enveloping her and the lingering sensation of his hard body pressed against hers. Rhyder raked a hand through his black hair and inclined his handsome head to study her.

"How, Gina?" he demanded in a husky pitch. "How do I let you go? I can't. Not yet."

No, her heart cried in pain, he couldn't let her go until he had accomplished his objective of buying the property on his terms, not Justin's. For that, he needed her. In the meantime he would have a grand old time satisfying his lust and driving her crazy with desire.

But that wasn't enough. To settle for sex and sex alone would literally break her.

Extreme tiredness washed through her. Gina fought it as she fought the emotional upsurge of her love for Rhyder. Both could too easily be turned into weapons against her.

"In case you haven't noticed, you're no longer in my arms."

"I noticed," she declared in a low voice to hide her weariness.

He held up his empty hands. "I can't hold you prisoner. But I want you to be mine. Is that such a bad thing?"

"Oh, no. I'm not yours, and I never will be," Gina continued to protest, deafening her ears to his seductive words.

Rhyder allowed her to move a foot away, but the metallic hardness of his gaze still unnerved her. "Wait. We have to talk this out. I admit I made a caveman move, but I meant well." The qualification was the first sign that her adamancy was gaining her ground.

"There's nothing to talk out," she said. "The only thing I want from you is to have my belongings returned to my apartment and to be left alone, so there's nothing to discuss."

"Yes, there is," returned Rhyder in a voice that was positive and unrelenting in its purpose. "We're going to talk about the way you've changed from what you were this morning and last night to the way you are now."

"It would be pointless." Exhaustion was setting in again. She was tired of constantly having to struggle to protect herself, mentally as well as physically.

"I disagree," he said flatly.

He probably had the strength to keep on arguing, but Gina didn't. He'd loved her too hard and too long and too well last night for her to want to do anything right now but fall asleep. In her own bed. In her own place. Her eyes beseeched him silently not to put her through this, although her pride kept her from saying so.

His searching gaze focused on her face and its expression of vulnerability and hurt. A slight frown creased his forehead.

"Gina . . ." Rhyder began, reaching out to her. She realized at that moment just how much she craved the comfort of his strong arms and just how unwise it would be to run to him.

A knock at the apartment door checked his movement. His frown changed to one of irritation at the in-

terruption. The second knock drew his impatient
glance, and Gina was released from his compelling
gaze, gaining the respite she needed to reestablish the
firmness of her stand. Rhyder sensed the change immediately, the line of his jaw hardening.

He let his hands drop to his sides. "We aren't finished," he stated sharply, and left Gina to walk to the
door.

A silent feeling of apprehension made her shiver.
Her skin felt chilled all over, and she rubbed her arms
with her hands to warm them, but it didn't do much
good.

Her senses were following Rhyder, listening to his
footsteps and the sound of the door opening. The
blood froze in her veins when she heard him say hello
to Justin.

"What do you want?" Rhyder's clipped tone made it
plain that Justin wasn't welcome.

Gina met the harshly accusing look Justin gave her
over Rhyder's shoulder. He didn't seem at all surprised
to see her there. Gina went pale. This was one more
complication she didn't need.

"I was told," Justin stated coldly, his gaze slicing to
Rhyder, "that I could find Gina here."

Seconds ticked by in charged silence as Rhyder stood
in the doorway, blocking Justin's entrance. Slowly, like
an uncoiling spring, Rhyder stepped to the side.

"Yes, she's here," he agreed, stating the obvious since
he knew Justin could see Gina standing in the foyer of
the living room. "Would you like to speak to her?"

"Please," Justin answered stiffly, and walked into the
apartment.

As Rhyder closed the door, he looked at Gina's white
face, then at Justin, whose attention was darting between
the two. Rhyder's mouth curved into an aloof smile.

"I was about to fix Gina a drink. Would you like one,
Justin?"

The other man was on the point of refusing when he glanced at Gina and changed his mind. "Scotch and water," he said, accepting the offer.

Gina stared blankly at Rhyder, surprised that he had invited Justin in and offered him a drink. An inner sense told her that Rhyder really wanted Justin to leave as soon as he could, not welcoming the interruption from a man he possibly regarded as a rival. But he'd been courteous enough.

Her gaze searched his impassive expression for a reason, but Rhyder barely glanced at her as he walked by her into the living room and to the small bar located at the far end.

Her attention was forced to refocus on Justin. With her nerves stretched thin, Gina made a futile attempt to smile, wondering if she could pull off acting as if everything was fine.

"I've been trying to reach you all day." Justin's low voice held a note of accusation. "Couldn't get you on your BlackBerry or at the office. Or anywhere else. So did you turn off your cell phone or did the battery die on you?"

"Um, yeah," Gina said, not really answering either question, "I'm sorry I missed your calls, but I was tied up most of the day."

His brown eyes glowered their disbelief. "I see," Justin said grimly. "You were so busy you couldn't even spare five minutes to check in, is that what you're saying? Couldn't use someone else's cell? Or drop a couple of quarters into a pay phone?"

"Nope." Rigidly clinging to her lie, Gina turned to enter the beige living room.

"Aren't you going to ask how I found out you were here?" Justin snapped.

His nosiness and his self-righteous irritability were getting on her very, very strained nerves. But Gina just didn't want to deal with any more macho behavior from either man at the moment. Expecting Justin to become her ally and stand beside her against Rhyder clearly wasn't going to happen. That unvoiced hope vanished at his silent condemnation.

"How did you find out, Justin?" Gina asked the question he had prompted with icy calm.

"I went to your apartment. That old lady who manages the building told me you'd moved out. Your husband"—he underlined the word—"had moved your things."

"I thought that was how you learned I was here," she responded evenly.

"I couldn't believe it was true," Justin muttered in a bitter breath. "I kept telling myself that the stupid old cow made a mistake. I had to come to see for myself if you'd gone back to him."

"And now you're here." Gina lifted her chin, her face pale and proud, as she prompted him to say what was in his expression.

"And I see." His mouth tightened.

Gina knew that she had deliberately let him believe she had gone back to Rhyder, both by her words and her actions. But she couldn't let him go on thinking that way.

"Appearances are deceptive." Her explanation had a legal ring to it, but she was too tired to come up with a graceful phrase. Or one that would magically soothe his great, big, male ego. "I know how it seems to you, Justin, but it isn't true."

"Are you saying that you haven't gone back to Rhyder?" he asked warily.

As she opened her mouth to state unequivocally that she hadn't, Rhyder's tall shape entered her side vision, and he was answering the question before she had the chance.

"That was under discussion when you arrived, Justin. Scotch and water." He offered a squat glass to Justin, cubes of ice glistening in the pale gold liquid. The glass in his other hand he extended to Gina, the glittering light in his eyes holding her gaze. "My wife's moods are as changeable as the ocean. Our reconciliation is barely twenty-four hours old, and already it's in jeopardy."

His words hung suspended in the air, carrying the shock potential of a high-voltage wire. Automatically Justin had accepted the drink offered him, but he didn't say thanks, preoccupied by Rhyder's deliberate hint that he and Gina had shared at least one night's worth of "reconciliation."

A red flush of shame and anger rose in Gina's cheeks. She couldn't deny the truth, and Ryder knew it. Again she was subjected to a harsh glare of condemnation from Justin. Her failure to deny Rhyder's implication spoke as loudly as if she had confirmed it.

A blaze of temper, barely controlled, must have flashed in her eyes, because Rhyder's gaze narrowed faintly in warning. He grasped her hand and curled her resisting fingers around the cold glass.

"I don't want it," she said.

"Drink it anyway," Rhyder ordered. "It will help settle your nerves." He released the hand he had forced to hold the glass and slipped an arm possessively around her waist. He seemed unconcerned that Gina might fling the contents of the glass in his face. Strangely, she found she couldn't do it, although she wanted to. "Have a seat, Justin," Rhyder said as he led Gina to the sofa and maneuvered her to sit beside him.

Hesitating, Justin lifted his glass, downing a large swallow of his drink as if he really needed the reviving jolt of liquor. Then he walked to an armchair near the sofa and sat down, his sullen gaze sweeping over both of them.

"Gina's things are here," Justin said. His tone seemed to ask for the reason why.

"Only temporarily," Gina answered.

"Yes, they are here," Rhyder asserted, making it sound as if they would never leave. He waved a hand. "Lots and lots of boxes. She doesn't travel light, I can tell you that." Gina flashed him an angry look.

Justin stared at the cubes floating in his glass. "You should have told me, Gina," he said grimly, "instead of letting me believe that you hated the guy."

The guy in question didn't seem to like that comment. "You know, our relationship was stormy from the beginning," Rhyder responded when Gina failed to find her voice, "with equal amounts of anger and passion in between the dormant periods. You happen to be seeing us in an angry moment right now."

"Gina had said you weren't married, that the two of you were divorced." Justin seemed prepared for Rhyder's answer.

He shrugged. "A slight exaggeration. We'd been separated for several years, so it was only natural that she should think along those lines."

"And I still do!" Gina snapped, irritated by the way they were conversing as if she weren't actually there.

Rhyder glanced down at her, his features set in uncompromising lines. He didn't miss the glint of mutiny in her eyes. "That's something we will discuss in private."

She wanted to claim that being alone with him wouldn't matter, wouldn't affect her ultimate decision, but she was afraid it would. She had to look away from the masculine features, so hard and angular, that she had come to love more deeply than the eighteen-year-old girl had ever loved. Tears burned the back of her eyes.

Rhyder's fingers closed around the hand holding her drink and lifted it to carry the glass to her lips. "Drink it," he ordered quietly, sensing how near her nerves were to total collapse.

For an instant Gina resisted the command, but the

silent presence of his strength finally had her obeying. The drink burned her throat, made her choke in its fire, but at least the true cause of her glistening tears was disguised in her reaction. She could only hope that Rhyder hadn't guessed the reason for her shakiness.

"What about my property, Rhyder?" Justin broke the silence when Gina had recovered. "Are you still interested in it?"

Gina could almost see Rhyder withdraw behind an emotionless mask that revealed nothing. She waited, feeling the tension build inside of her.

"That depends," he answered noncommittally.

"On what?" Justin persisted.

"On some other related matters." Rhyder explained nothing, but Gina knew exactly what he had left unsaid.

An encompassing hurt scraped over her nerve ends that the liquor didn't assuage. Despite that, she decided to let Rhyder know she was aware of his plans to use her, to put it bluntly, in his dealings with Justin.

"What he means, Justin"—she kept her voice rigidly controlled—"is that it depends on me and what I decide. Isn't that correct, Rhyder?" She all but dared him to deny it.

He studied her for a silent second in aloof contemplation, a dark eyebrow rising ever so slightly.

"Good point, Gina." He directed his next words to Justin. "My answer will depend on her decision," Rhyder said calmly.

She hadn't expected him to admit it. He had so carefully avoided giving any indication that he wanted more from Gina than to have her live with him as his wife. Perhaps Rhyder had finally realized that she wasn't so easily fooled.

Justin exhaled a heavy breath and drained his glass, setting it on the table with an air of finality. He rose to his feet, his measured gaze turned to Rhyder. "How long do I have to wait for your answer?"

"Gina will give me her final answer tonight, one way or the other." Rhyder straightened. "So you'll have mine in the morning."

Justin nodded. "Since I have a personal as well as a business stake in the outcome, I'd better leave now. Don't want to delay the process," he concluded.

As he turned to leave, Gina realized that she was about to lose her chance to make a safe escape from Rhyder's apartment. She had made her decision. Rhyder knew what it was, but he hoped to change it. And Gina wasn't sure she could shield her heart against his persuasive sensuality.

She rose quickly from the sofa, setting her glass on a table, and took a step after Justin. His name became lodged in her throat as Rhyder's hands gripped the soft flesh of her arms and drew her shoulders back to his chest.

"Stay." The one word was quietly spoken near her ear, his warm breath gently stirring her hair.

Gina's resolve vanished. She let Rhyder hold her there as Justin paused by the door to glance back. The dull look in his brown eyes seemed to concede the victory to Rhyder. Momentarily caught in the spell of his touch, Gina couldn't deny it.

When the door closed, his hands slid down to her forearms, curling them across the front of her waist as he curved her more fully against him. His mouth sought the sensitive nape of her neck, sending quivers of desire over her skin. His caress had the power to seduce her will, and she strained her neck away, pushing herself free.

"Why did you do it?" she demanded breathlessly, her hands pressed against her rapidly fluttering stomach.

"Do what?" Rhyder asked her, seeking to draw her into his embrace again.

But Gina managed to stay out of embracing range. Her green eyes were rounded and wary. "Why did you invite Justin in? Why did you have to involve him directly in this?" She bombarded him with questions to keep him at a distance, the protective words rushing from her lips. "And why the aren't-we-all-civilized pose? You were courteous, but you didn't mean it. Not for a second."

"Sorry," he said curtly. "Were you expecting a brawl? Don't tell me you wanted to see us fight over you."

"No, of course not!" Gina retorted, knowing he had deliberately twisted her question.

"Good!" Rhyder snapped. "Because it would have been pointless. The woman always ends up choosing the man she wants regardless of who wins or loses. Fighting over you wouldn't have influenced your choice."

"You're right," Gina conceded tightly. "And you know my decision. You aren't going to change my mind. You're wasting your time trying."

"Why, Gina?" Now it was Rhyder who demanded answers, intimidating her with the force of his personality. "Why are you telling me no after coming to me so willingly last night?"

She searched wildly for an answer. "Did it ever occur to you that I might not want to be with you? I'm not that eighteen-year-old girl who fell in love with you. She's just a memory, not a real person."

"I didn't say you were her. And I wasn't holding a memory in my arms last night." Rhyder dismissed the suggestion swiftly.

"Maybe after sleeping with you, I figured out that I preferred Justin," Gina said desperately.

Although Rhyder didn't move, he seemed to loom nearer, a muscle leaping uncontrollably in his jaw. The atmosphere was electrified as Rhyder controlled his anger with an effort.

"If I believed you meant that"—his voice vibrated deep in his throat, harsh and raw—"I think I'd . . ."

He didn't finish the rest. He didn't need to. Gina could almost feel his rage. Shivering, she knew she had provoked him without thought of the consequences.

"Does it matter whether something happened last night or nine years ago?" she asked quietly. "It still doesn't change the fact that I want to be free of you."

"Why?" Rhyder demanded again.

"Because"—her dark head moved despairingly to the side—"I just don't want to spend the rest of my life with you. You have to let me go." The heartbreak would be unendurable. She knew perfectly well that he didn't love her, no matter what he said or how expertly he handled her in bed.

Frustration swept across Rhyder's features as he tried to find something to argue with in her words and failed. He breathed in deeply, utterly unwilling to accept her statement.

"So that's that, huh?" he questioned at last, low and impatient.

"Yes." Gina held her breath, praying that her misery might be at an end.

Rhyder pivoted away. "Why? Why? Why?" Drawn through clenched teeth, the words weren't directed at Gina. They were an angry demand to the fates.

A knock at the door made Gina jump. Her gaze flew to Rhyder, who had reacted with the same degree of surprise. She didn't want another interruption. He was about to let her go. She sensed that and didn't want the moment prolonged. Time was working against her.

Another knock, more impatient than the first, got him moving. Swearing beneath his breath, Rhyder strode toward the door.

He swung the door open, controlled violence in his movement. His arm was braced against the door frame to block the entrance. Gina knew that if Justin had returned, he wouldn't get inside this time.

Chapter Ten

With one glance at the person in the hall, Rhyder flung the door open and walked away. His action stunned Gina until she saw an equally surprised Pete following in his wake.

"Don't say hello. See if I care. I'd be happier with a drink," Pete said with a short, bewildered laugh. Then he noticed Gina and smiled. "I didn't think you'd be here—which just shows that a celebration is definitely in order."

"Save it, Pete," Rhyder snapped as he walked to the bar.

"W-what?" Pete cocked his sandy head, only that instant picking up the electrical tension crackling around Rhyder.

"There's nothing to celebrate," Rhyder said nastily. "Unless you want to toast the fact that you were right."

"You mean—" Pete looked at Gina, his eyes widening as he observed the pinched lines of strain in her pale face. He hesitated, reluctant to say the obvious.

"Gina has said no." Rhyder finished it, his voice taut.

Already in the living room, Pete virtually dropped into the same armchair Justin had chosen. He showed no elation whatsoever at being right. Something more like grim resignation, Gina thought. Pete reached into the inner pocket of his jacket and pulled out a sheaf of papers.

"And I just spent the whole day running all over half the state of Maine for nothing," he sighed, and tossed the papers on the table a few feet in front of the chair.

Rhyder walked from the bar and handed him the drink he had mixed, glancing briefly at the papers. "Then you got it?" he commented.

"Yes." Pete nodded glumly. "All signed, sealed, and legal."

Gina's gaze darted from one to the other, faintly puzzled by their exchange. Rhyder flicked a look at her, the raking glance taking in the questioning look in her green eyes. He moved to the sofa.

"You might as well sit down, Gina," he said crisply.

Numbly she moved to a chair next to Pete's. "What are you talking about?"

Pete met her eyes reluctantly. "I had the annulment ruling officially voided. Your marriage to Rhyder legally exists on a technicality. I thought the two of you had patched things up," he explained, implying that he knew about last night.

"No. Guess you didn't get the memo." Gina lowered her gaze, feeling the heat warming her cheeks.

"Someone should have warned me. Or called. I do have a cell phone. It even works." Pete sipped absently at his drink. "Rhyder was so positive."

"I changed my mind," she muttered. "It's my prerogative."

"Do you mind if I ask why?" The lenses of his glasses intensified the gentle light in Pete's eyes when he looked at her.

Rhyder answered the question with harsh flatness. "Gina can't stand the thought of living with me for the rest of her life."

"Okay. I don't have to know why. That's a valid reason. You wouldn't be my choice, either." Pete tried to make a joke of it, but nobody laughed.

Leaning forward on the sofa cushion, Rhyder rested his elbows on his knees, his hands clasped loosely in front of him. He stared at them, tiredness etched in the curve of his broad shoulders and the slightly bowed neck.

"What's the next move, Pete?" he asked dispiritedly.

His tone suggested that he didn't really care, and the question was asked because the world wouldn't stop to let him off. Gina knew the feeling. She felt it more intensely than Rhyder did because she loved him. Nothing like good old unrequited love to ruin a nice party.

"Well"—Pete breathed in deeply, held it for a split second as he glanced hesitantly at Gina, and let it out—"I don't suppose you would agree to a few months' trial period to see if the two of you could make the marriage work?"

"No!" Gina rejected the idea almost violently, then added on a more controlled note, "All I want is for Rhyder to let me go and to send my things back to my apartment."

"Your things?" A sandy eyebrow lifted above the frames of Pete's glasses.

"Yes." She nodded. "Rhyder canceled the lease on my apartment today and had everything moved here." For some reason, she couldn't summon up her righteous anger over it a second time. Gina just sighed and folded her hands together.

"Holy cow!" Pete sat back in his chair staring at Rhyder, amazed at his audacity. "You really did anticipate her decision, didn't you?"

"I thought I had cause," Rhyder muttered, rising impatiently to his feet and rubbing the back of his neck. "I should have guessed that some other guy was in the picture. Justin. Don't know what she sees in him, but for every garbage pail there's a cover, as our housekeeper used to say—"

"Leave him out of this!" Gina protested angrily. "He has nothing to do with what happened, and anyway, if you expected me to become a nun or something—"

"Time out," Pete interrupted, his hands making a T. "Nuns, garbage—please stop, you two."

"Oh, shut up!" Gina cried. "Both of you just shut up!"

Pete shook his head. "I wish I didn't have to referee this. But here goes. Shouting at each other isn't going to help. Calling names is counterproductive."

Rhyder turned his back on both of them, moving to the far side of the room and the bar. His snide remark about Justin still stung, but Gina pressed her lips together.

Glancing from one to the other, Pete smiled briefly in satisfaction. "Good. Now, let's start tackling this situation one step at a time. The immediate problem is your apartment, Gina. I'll go over first thing tomorrow morning, talk to the manager—what's his name, by the way?"

"Her name," Gina muttered, "is Mrs. Powell. And fifty bucks would buy her a very nice new housecoat."

"Point taken. Okay, I bribe her, have the lease reinstated, get Rhyder's check back, and everything will be straightened out."

"Thanks," Gina said.

"Then I'll have your belongings moved back. In the meantime, you'll have to get a motel room for the night or stay with a friend. Agreed?"

"Motel room." No way was Gina going to explain this situation to an inquisitive girlfriend. She needed time to think. She was achingly aware of Rhyder slowly pacing the confines of the living room.

"The next order of business would be the separation papers." Pete took a PalmPilot from an inside pocket of his jacket. His head was bent as he started to make notes on the little screen. He flicked a quick, confirming look at Gina over the top frame of his glasses. "I presume you'll be the one filing for divorce?"

Her heart constricted as she nodded again. "Yes."

"No!" Rhyder barked, stopping near her chair.

"On what grounds?" Pete continued.

"I don't know." Gina shook her head, her pulse racing as she tried to ignore Rhyder. "Incompatibility, I suppose." She shrugged.

"*You* are not filing for a divorce," Rhyder stated.

His agitation and his arrogance were driving her crazy. Gina stood up. When she was seated, his height advantage was simply too overpowering. "Then *you* file!" she retorted. "It doesn't matter to me."

"I'm not giving you a divorce!" he snapped.

Frozen by his declaration, Gina didn't shrug off the hands that reached to take her by the shoulders, none too gently.

"You're not getting rid of me as easily as you did nine years ago." His warning was a promise. "There will be no divorce."

Pete held up a hand. "Whoa. News flash: women have rights. Film at eleven."

"Shut up, Pete."

"Everybody keeps telling me that." Pete took off his glasses and polished them thoroughly on a bright silk handkerchief he took from his pocket.

Gina knew it was a lawyer's trick to force attention his way, and she almost smiled.

"Rhyder," Pete continued, "you know as well as I do that you can't force her to stay married to you. Yeah, you can drag your feet, waste money on harassing motions to delay the inevitable, cook up sob stories to tell the judge, but I'll tell you right now, Rhyder, none of it will fly in court."

"I don't care."

"Don't be a jackass, pal. Do you think she's going to go to jail or something? You might, if the judge gets tired of looking at you, especially if he or she finds out that you lied under oath. Maybe not. The annulment thing is ancient history. And intent is more important than a legal technicality as far as that's concerned."

"No divorce," Rhyder said grimly. "And no more out of you."

Pete threw up his hands. "Okay, don't listen. I'm not getting paid for this abuse."

Tears welled in Gina's eyes, shimmering with emerald brilliance. The sight softened something inside of Rhyder. He brought her to his chest, although her hands raised instinctively to press against the solid flesh in protest.

His head bent near her ear, his face partially buried in the soft raven hair. Gina had to close her eyes. His nearness evoked only longing.

"You're my wife, Gina," Rhyder murmured. "I'm not letting you go."

The torture of loving him and having to deny the love was revealed in her expression. She didn't try to hide it because she knew Rhyder couldn't see it. Pete did. Closing his notebook, he settled back in his chair as Gina found the strength to twist free.

"Whether or not you take Pete's advice, I'm filing for a divorce, Rhyder." Gina repeated the statement to reassure herself of her intentions. She kept her face averted from Rhyder until she felt a semblance of control return.

"I'll fight it."

"Let's not be hasty, Rhyder." Pete tipped his head to one side in a considering gesture and felt the thrust of Rhyder's gaze.

"You are my lawyer, Pete," Rhyder said loudly, "and I'm paying you to contest any action Gina takes in the divorce courts."

In a voice too soft for Rhyder, who went on talking, to hear, Pete said, "I don't need the money, and I won't do it." Gina looked his way and managed a wan smile this time.

"If and when I want your advice, I'll ask for it," Rhyder concluded.

"I'm just suggesting that I think we should sit down and discuss this rationally instead of continually getting sidetracked by emotions," Pete replied, letting the outburst slide over him. "I'm sure Gina agrees with me, don't you?"

"Yes," she said shakily.

Turning away, Rhyder seemed to disassociate himself from the talk. Hands twisted in her lap, Gina sat on the edge of her chair.

"What were you thinking of in terms of a divorce settlement?" Pete asked.

"I want a divorce, nothing more," Gina insisted huskily.

Rhyder exhaled a short, contemptuous breath. "That's a first."

His obnoxious comment prompted an instant retort. "I never wanted any money from you before. You wanted to pay it to get the marriage over with, and I took it because I basically didn't know any better. I never thought it would come back to haunt me like this. Want it back? I make enough money to repay you ten times over, Rhyder."

"No."

"The court will probably award you a token settlement," Pete commented, and sighed. "It could have all been very simple."

"It won't be," Rhyder snapped. "Whether there's a settlement involved or not, I'm fighting the divorce."

"I was referring to the fact that it would have been simpler if it hadn't been for your reconciliation, however brief it was," Pete explained, quietly studying

Rhyder's back. "It would have been a matter of mere paperwork."

But Gina was troubled by Rhyder's adamant insistence that he would contest any action to dissolve their marriage. "Why are you doing this?" she demanded desperately. "I'm only asking to be free of you, nothing more. Why? Tell me why."

"Your move, Rhyder." Pete's tone was crisp. "Gina is being more than cooperative. Tell us why you aren't."

"Damn it, Pete! You know the answer to that!" Rhyder pivoted to face his friend, obviously angry that the question had been asked.

Her shoulders drooped slightly as Gina sighed, "So do I."

Pete eyed her curiously. "If you do, then why did you ask?"

"Because"—she lifted her chin, but her gaze remained on the whitened knuckles of Rhyder's clenched hands—"I thought that under the circumstances Rhyder would have given up his plans to use me to get the property."

"What property?" Rhyder's voice was ominously soft.

"You know very well what property." She flashed him a look of irritation.

"Would you mind telling me?" Pete glanced from one to the other, settling finally on Gina.

"Justin's property, of course," she answered tightly.

"*What?*" Rhyder's voice was taut with angry astonishment.

Pete's sandy head lifted up, a thoughtful look in his eyes as he studied her defiant expression. "What were his plans?"

"I'm sure he discussed it with you," Gina retorted in a caustic tone.

A sound started to come from Rhyder, almost a growl, but Pete flicked him a silencing look and returned the focus of his attention to Gina.

"No, I don't believe he did," he replied calmly. "Would you fill me in?"

"He was hoping to charm me into persuading Justin to sell on his terms." Her lips were compressed for an instant. "Now, I suppose he's going to make it a condition before he'll agree to the divorce."

"Of all the—" Rhyder's explosion was halted by Pete's upraised hand.

"Are you sure about this?" Pete studied her intently.

"Yes, I'm sure." Gina wished she wasn't. "He admitted it when Justin was here a half an hour ago."

"That's a lie!" Rhyder said.

Gina flinched at his angry disclaimer and continued, "It's true. You told Justin your decision to buy the property would depend on me," she reminded him coldly. "Besides, I overheard you talking to Pete this morning."

"What's that got to do with it?" Pete asked in surprise.

"Have you forgotten?" she retorted bitterly. "Rhyder told you he could practically guarantee my cooperation, regardless of whether Justin liked it or not. He even called his father to give him the news that he was about to get the property on his terms, even though he hadn't talked to me."

"And you thought—" Pete began, a smile widening his mouth.

"Never mind!" Rhyder snapped the interruption. "Give me the land contract proposal Gina drew up."

The smile didn't fade as Pete reached for the briefcase resting against his chair. Opening it, he leafed through the papers and handed a stapled set to Rhyder. Gina watched, waiting for the tanned fingers to tear the papers in two now that Rhyder realized she couldn't be coerced, persuaded, or in any way made to agree to his scheme.

Her green eyes widened in confusion as she saw him

affix his signature to the proposal. Immediately he thrust the papers and pen toward Pete.

"Witness it," he ordered curtly. When it was done he shoved it into Gina's hands. "Here's your precious agreement, accepted, signed and witnessed—on Justin's terms!"

"I—" She lifted her gaze to Rhyder's face. "I don't understand." It didn't make sense.

"I'm not surprised," Rhyder growled. "The conversation you overheard this morning between me and Pete was about having the annulment officially overturned. I knew Justin wanted you, and he wouldn't be happy to find that you'd come back to me. As for the call to my father, he knew about us and that I'd met you again and realized I wanted you for my wife. The news I was referring to had nothing to do with the property. It was to tell him we'd been reconciled."

She looked from Pete to Rhyder in disbelief. "No," she protested, but he sounded so convincing.

"And a few moments ago with Justin," he continued without acknowledging her protest, "I did say that my decision about the property would depend on you. If you didn't come back to me, I wasn't buying the land. Because if I couldn't have you, I didn't want to set foot in Maine again for business or any other reason."

Gina's fingers closed around the agreement, unconsciously crumbling it into a ball. She wanted desperately to believe what he was saying.

"Why did you want me back, Rhyder?" she breathed, searching his tense face.

"For just one reason, Gina," he said bitterly. "I love you."

"You never said so. You only said you wanted me."

"Protecting myself. Because if you'd only known how much—" he said and stopped. "That's all. It's always been because I love you."

Her heart gave a leap of joy, no longer afraid to believe him. The deep abiding love she felt blazed in her eyes, but Rhyder didn't seem to see it.

"Come on, Gina," Pete prodded softly. "Tell him you love him so I can break out the bottle of champagne!"

A tremulous smile curved her lips. "Do you remember what you told Justin?" Her voice was barely above a whisper, trembling with emotion. "You said our relationship was equal parts anger and passion. It's true. Even when I hated you, I loved you, Rhyder."

The arrogance seemed to leave him along with the bitterness. His hand reached out to tentatively trace the line of her temple. Her dark lashes fluttered in response to the caress.

In the next instant his arms were around her, and his mouth hungrily possessed her lips. Gina returned the insatiable need with all the pent-up longing in her heart. Neither heard the explosive pop of the champagne cork or the fizzy sound of it being poured into a trio of glasses.

Pete smiled, picked up one of the glasses, and quietly left the room. The champagne would be flat when Gina and Rhyder finally drank their toast.

VALLEY OF THE VAPORS

Chapter One

"You gave Kevin Jamieson permission to marry me?" Tisha Caldwell asked incredulously. "What century are you living in?" She brushed back her long hair over one shoulder and gave her father an are-you-crazy look.

"You really weren't listening, Tisha. I told him I didn't mind if he asked you to marry him. I'm not even sure if he was serious." His reply was tense.

"Same difference, as far as I'm concerned," she finished, not attempting to disguise her annoyance.

They stared at each other, two forceful personalities, each trying to make the other give in first. Richard Caldwell was a tall man with a muscular physique that hadn't changed much since his college days. The years had only added character to his already handsome face and a few dignified streaks of gray to his dark hair.

Tisha Caldwell didn't have her father's striking good looks. Her oval face was only ordinarily attractive. But when animated by laughter or strong emotion, as now, she was compellingly beautiful. She had inherited her father's volatile personality and stubborn independence, though, qualities that brought out the beauty in her often.

"Anyway, Kevin seemed to be sounding me out on the subject, so I answered. That's all there was to it," Richard Caldwell retorted sharply. "Obviously I can't just hand you over to the potential husband of my choice, although sometimes I wish I could. Nice if you could drive someone else crazy for a change."

"Dad!" Tisha wanted to howl with frustration. Didn't he get what she was talking about?

"Kevin Jamieson is going to be somebody some day. He's focused and he's intelligent. Which is a lot more than I can say for some of the guys you go out with."

"That's for sure," Tisha agreed fervently. "I get the feeling when he kisses me good night, he runs home to take a shower and cool off."

Her father shook his head. "That's more than I needed to know, Tish. And there's nothing wrong with a little self-control." He pointed a finger toward her. "When you're out with Kevin, you don't come in looking like you've been pawed by some oversexed beast."

Her hands doubled up into fists. "You make me so angry I could scream," was her muttered answer. "Am I allowed to have a life? Do you have to make remarks like that just because once or twice I came in with my hair kind of messy?"

"And your shirt on inside out. And hickeys on your neck. That's high school stuff, Tish. The guys you date don't have to leave teeth marks on you. They don't own you. That's what I'm really saying, whether you want to hear it or not."

Tisha scowled. "Only a couple of the guys I've gone out with have ever stepped out of line."

"Well, that's two too many," he said, his brown eyes snapping with anger as he stared into the stormy sea green ones of his daughter. "I just don't like it. It shows no respect for you, especially when they drop you off without coming in to say hello. I don't like the way they dodge me."

"I'm twenty-one, Dad," Tisha sighed in exasperation. "Old enough to vote, drink, join the army, and make my own mistakes."

"Tell me about it," he grumbled.

"Stop treating me like a child, okay? I get to decide whether I want my dates to come in."

"Are you ashamed of them?"

"No! But I really don't think you have to meet them all."

"Believe me, it's not that I want to. But I can't help thinking that you could do better."

"Guess what. It's actually none of your business."

"If you live under my roof, I get to have an opinion. I can't control you and I don't want to. But you can't fault a man for being protective of his daughter."

Tisha fell silent for a moment, understanding what he was getting at. "I can defend myself if it comes to that."

"No woman can defend herself against the superior strength of a man," he scoffed with an authoritative ring of personal knowledge in his voice. "A young guy who's boozed up and looking for trouble—well, you know as well as I do what can happen."

"Is having a good time ever allowed, Dad? Didn't you down a few beers in your day? Or maybe it was mead. I forget that you grew up in the Dark Ages, when men were men and women sat in towers with spinning wheels."

"Skip the sarcasm."

"Don't run my life for me. That father-knows-best attitude is so over. So you can cut it out," she said.

"It's time it made a nostalgic comeback," Richard Caldwell muttered. He was about to expound further when the doorbell rang.

Tisha darted a baleful glance at him. "I suppose you told Kevin to come round this afternoon," she said. "So what's next? He hands me a sparkly, stupid little ring and you beam with satisfaction?" She dropped her voice to a low pitch in a perfect imitation of him. " 'Take her, son, she's a handful, but she's all yours.' "

Her father was silent. Tisha looked at him with growing alarm.

"This isn't happening. If he did buy a ring, I'll throw it in his face."

"You keep a civil tongue in your head, girl!" His finger waved angrily in the direction of her back as Tisha stomped around the room divider to the foyer, heading for the front door.

With an impatient hand she swept her dark auburn, nearly waist-length hair behind her back as she flung the door open, ready to lash out at the man she expected to see on the stoop. The woman standing there arched an inquisitive glance when Tisha's mouth snapped shut in a grim line. A bemused smile tilted the corners of the woman's mouth.

"I have the feeling I should come back another time." Her brown eyes were warm with laughter.

Tisha stepped away from the door, allowing the woman to enter. Light lines around her eyes and the faint wrinkles on her forehead and throat indicated that she was somewhat older than a first glance might suggest. Her short, feather-cut dark hair had a dramatic streak of white that called attention to her delicate features. The effect was quite sexy.

Tisha, still fuming, stalked back around the divider and left the slender woman standing just inside the door.

"It's only Blanche." She answered her father's unasked question before he could scold her for being rude. Tisha wasn't sure whether she was sorry or glad that it wasn't Kevin as she sank into the cushions of the flowered sofa.

A muscle in Richard's jaw jumped, signaling that his anger, like Tisha's, wasn't far below the surface, and she braced herself for his reply. "You will address your aunt as your aunt and not some acquaintance," her father growled. "No reason on God's green earth that you can't show respect for your elders. I didn't raise you to act like this."

"Oh, Richard. If she calls me Aunt Blanche, I'll clobber both of you!" But amusement was clear in the sternly voiced reprimand as Blanche Caldwell walked around the divider.

In her designer jeans and a beautiful antique Mexican blouse hand-embroidered with flowers and curlicues, Blanche was the picture of Southwestern chic. Unmindful of her brother's quelling look, Blanche Caldwell covered the short distance that separated them and planted a quick kiss on his cheek.

"And I'm delighted to see you, too, Richard," she said dryly.

"I'm glad you're here." He shifted his position slightly so his gaze could take in his sister and his daughter. "I'm trying to talk some sense into this girl's head, and she won't listen to me."

"Sense!" Tisha snickered, waving a hand airily in her father's direction. "He thinks I should get married just because he's tired of worrying about me."

"Does he have any particular man in mind?" Blanche asked archly.

"Yeah, Kevin Jamieson. Who gives me the creeps."

"I am not trying to force you to marry Kevin Jamieson!" her father shouted.

"What do you call it, then?" she demanded.

"Do you see what I mean?" Richard Caldwell turned to his sister, his hands raised in a frustrated, beseeching gesture for understanding. "She deliberately twists everything around, puts words in my mouth, and makes me sound like a control freak."

Blanche shot her niece a conspiratorial wink.

"Basically, all I said was that Kevin's got what it takes

to succeed and he's a good guy. She could do a whole hell of a lot worse."

"No matter who *I* picked to marry, Dad, you wouldn't be able to stand him. You'd find something wrong with him even if it was only the color of his eyes." Now it was Tisha who turned to Blanche. "He doesn't believe a woman is capable of knowing what or who is good for her. Like it's his responsibility to interfere in my life!"

"Considering the hell-raisers you go out with, it's no wonder that I feel the need to step in once in a while," he replied quickly. "Most of your dates aren't keepers."

"They don't have to be," Tisha retorted. "If you had your way, I wouldn't date anybody until you found the man you wanted me to marry," Tisha retorted. "If and when that happens, it's going to be my choice, not yours. Why won't you accept the fact that I'm an adult?"

"Because you don't act like one!"

"Only because you don't let me." She leaned forward to emphasize her next words. "When we sit down to a meal, you still ask if I washed my hands. I'm not a child!"

Blanche Caldwell had been watching the interchange silently, her gaze shifting from one to the other like a spectator at a tennis match.

"Oh, Richard, you don't do that, do you?" She laughed softly.

He looked momentarily disgruntled. "Well, maybe once or twice," he mumbled. "You get in the habit as a parent after a while. It's a reflex."

"Then it's a habit you have to break," Tisha demanded.

"Okay, okay. But that's a small thing. We're getting away from the topic of this conversation," her father stated, shifting his weight from one foot to the other.

"No, we are not!" Tisha said angrily. "We're talking about the way you're trying to run my life! The way you keep trying to dictate what I wear, who I see and where I go!"

"I'm your father."

"That doesn't give you the right to invade my privacy. Like I said, let me make my own mistakes!" Her green eyes opened wide, and her thick, dark lashes didn't veil her wrath.

"My house, my rules. I have *some* say."

"There is a solution," Tisha stated coldly. "Maybe I should just move out."

"Think it over, young lady." His anger seemed to subside, replaced by a practical persuasiveness. Tisha wasn't buying it, either way.

"You aren't earning enough money to live on your own," he continued, "and I still control the small trust fund your mother set up for you until you're twenty-five. Without that income, you couldn't get by, not on what you make."

"Is that your idea of how to teach me to be independent? I'd almost rather starve to death than to live under this roof where you can order me around!" she cried out bitterly.

"I'm not going to let you talk so disrespectfully to me. I have my pride, just like you do." His face was being drawn into grimmer and sterner lines as he made a superhuman effort to control his temper.

"Oh, please. Next you'll be sending me to my room!" For all her outward show of defiance, she did respect her father, and she felt bad about fighting with him in front of Aunt Blanche. But Tisha couldn't seem to stop.

"Patricia Jo Caldwell, it's just too damn bad that physical punishment went out of style around the time you were born," he growled. "In my day—"

A laughing sigh from Blanche dissolved the crackling tension in the air between father and daughter. "Oh, shut up, Richard. You ran faster than anybody when Daddy went for his belt back in the day. You'd

never lay a hand on anyone in anger, and we all know it."
Her gaze twinkled sympathetically toward her brother,
then moved to her niece with a warm, understanding
light in the depths of her eyes.

A disgusted frown marred his handsome face.
"Tisha's too darn headstrong for her own good."

"So were you, as I remember," Blanche said.

"If her mother was alive, maybe she could reason
with her. I'm only trying to do what I feel is best."

"But what about what I feel, Dad?" Tisha demanded,
the mention of her mother dulling the sharpness in her
voice.

"If you'd listen once in a while instead of arguing all
the time," Richard Caldwell began, only to close his
mouth on the rest of the statement. "You never were
one to take advice. You always had to find out for yourself whether the fire was hot."

"It could be a case of like father, like daughter,"
Blanche suggested quietly.

"Hell, no!" Tisha declared, rising to her feet. "I'm
not like him and I never will be."

"Where are you going?" demanded Richard Caldwell.

"To my room, because *I*"—she added unmistakable
emphasis to the word—"want to go there. And if Kevin
calls, you get to tell him I don't want to marry him—"

"Now, wait just a damn minute!"

"And you can tell him I never want to see him again!"

"I never said you had to!" Frustration mixed with
anger laced his reply.

Tisha paused in the doorway, half turning to look
over her shoulder at her father. Her back was still ram-
rod straight, but some of the storminess had left her sea
green eyes.

"No, Dad, you never order me to do anything," she
agreed grimly. "It's always all about what *you* think is
best for me. If you let Kevin believe that I had anything

other than the most casual interest in him, you get to explain why that isn't so. To him. I don't want to hear another word on the subject. You're pretty good at mind games, you know."

"What did I do that was so wrong?" he demanded, but with a hint of coaxing charm in his voice as he managed a conciliatory smile. "You haven't really given Kevin a chance. In time, you may find that I'm right about him."

The look in her eyes shadowed her wistful smile. "You won't give up, will you? I mean it, Dad. If I ever marry, and I'm beginning to seriously doubt that I'll ever want to, it will be to someone I choose, and you'll have nothing to say about it."

"Don't talk like that." A frown creased his forehead. "Of course you're going to get married."

"Is that the picture in your head? Me in a long white gown going down the aisle on your arm? Snagging a husband isn't at the top of my priorities list, if you really want to know."

He didn't reply. For a moment he looked almost defeated. Almost.

Tisha lifted a brow and shot him a mocking look. "Aunt Blanche didn't bother with all that. She concentrated on her happiness and her career. I respect that. And you don't even try to dictate to her."

This time Tisha didn't give her father an opportunity to reply as she stepped into the hallway that led to her room, knowing this was the moment to end the argument. Blanche's laughter followed her, as did her father's sputtering anger.

A few seconds after Tisha had entered her room, there was a light rap on the door. "Come in, Blanche," she called.

The older woman's face wore a smile of half-humorous understanding when she walked into the room. Tisha's lightning-quick temper had settled down, but a rebellious fire still glowed in her eyes.

"I'd say I was sorry," Tisha spoke, "but it wouldn't be entirely sincere. Dad just gets my back up in the worst way sometimes. He's good at it—well, you know that. You've known him a lot longer than I have."

Her aunt nodded. "There are times when Richard can be overbearingly male," Blanche said. "A case of too many females pandering to his ego in the past."

"Including me," Tisha sighed, picking up a jacket tossed over a chair and walking across the bold orange-and-gold patterned carpet to hang it in her wardrobe. The decor of the room was a reflection of her own gregarious personality, sunny and bright with striking splashes of color. "When I was growing up, he was Mr. Everything—strong, and powerful, loving and kind, handsome but rugged, blah blah. I used to dream of meeting a man just like him." A wry smile appeared on her face. "I'm glad I never did! Now I understand why Mom and Dad used to fight so much."

"As I recall," her aunt said idly, wandering into an alcove that had been remodeled to serve as a small studio for Tisha, "those arguments between Lenore and your father always ended in laughter and kisses. An ordinary woman couldn't have brought him the happiness he knew with your mother. Richard couldn't dominate her. That's why he loved her."

"Well, I wish he'd stop trying to dominate me."

Blanche smiled. "I don't believe he'll ever succeed at it. You're too much like your father and your mother."

"Why can't he see that? Why can't he accept that I know my own mind?"

"There are two reasons for that, Tish. First and foremost, reformed rogues always make the strictest dads. And my brother sowed a lot of wild oats before he met Lenore." She paused to watch the impact of her words on her niece and continued when Tish nodded. "Secondly, losing your mother when you were only fourteen meant that Richard became incredibly protective of you. That's only natural, even though I can see it drives you crazy. Richard knows he can't take your mother's place, but he does hover. He really wants to be involved with you, more so than if your mother was alive. It's not enough to have an aunt that only shows up when it suits her."

"Oh, Blanche!" A radiant smile immediately lit up Tisha's face. "Aunt Blanche, I mean. You always seem to know just what to say, and you're so easy to talk to. You really help me keep things in perspective."

"I'm glad I can be helpful once in a while."

"You are," Tisha said. "More than you know. Um, now tell me, what got you out of Hot Springs and made you drive all the way to Little Rock? I'm sure you didn't come to act as a referee for me and my father."

"I'm using the excuse that I came to pick up art supplies." There was a smile teasing the corners of her mouth. "But if you really want to know, I was feeling a little guilty. It's been too long since I saw my family— you and Richard. I tend to lose track of time."

"We didn't give you much of a welcome." Tisha's reply held a note of chagrin.

"I hope I haven't been gone so long that I require trumpet fanfares and red carpets." Blanche laughed easily. As if to turn the conversation away from herself, the slender woman turned to the array of paintings haphazardly placed about the alcove. "Your father indicated that you were well on your way to becoming a starving artist. He does think you're talented," she added quickly, "but he doesn't think you'll ever make any money at it."

"That is unfortunately true," Tisha sighed, walking over to stand beside her aunt, "at least in the paintings that I do for my own satisfaction. I'm slowly coming to the conclusion that I'm commercially adequate but not artistically unique. My brush doesn't have the stroke of genius that yours does."

"That's a very sweet thing to say, but I wouldn't call myself a genius."

"You're too modest."

Blanche studied a nostalgic still life depicting an old butter churn sitting in the corner of a wooden porch where sunflowers bobbed their golden heads above the railing.

"There's nothing wrong with being a commercial artist, Tisha. What have you been selling?"

"Some greeting cards and calendar scenes. A few ads. But a lot of small businesses do their own with Photoshop and Illustrator now." She frowned. "Dad was right, you know. I'm not earning enough money to live on. No matter how much I'd like to have a place of my own, I would still be dependent on my father's benevolence."

With a frustrated sigh, she pushed her long hair behind her ear. The silken tresses caught the sunlight streaming in the window, transforming the deep auburn into a fiery golden-red shade.

"Sometimes I think he wishes I'd been a boy," Tisha declared. Her voice vibrated with emotion. "He wouldn't hover if I was—he'd probably encourage me to do whatever I wanted. But the way he talks, it's like he expects me to be chained to some stove, flipping pancakes for Mr. Right and a pack of junior Rights. I've got more ambition than that."

"I don't doubt it." Blanche smiled a little sadly. "That was a big issue when I was your age. And there was a generation of male dinosaurs in Congress and everywhere else who didn't get it. Took a while for them to die off or just give up."

"Well, there's one left." Tisha waved vaguely in the direction of the rest of the house. "Richard Rex. The sole survivor of the Jurassic Era. Don't get in his way."

"Your dad's not that bad, Tish." Blanche laughed.

"But men who grew up in the West do tend to be a little more traditional about a lot of things."

"The word is reactionary." Tisha sniffed.

"Fair enough. I can't argue with that." Blanche picked up another small still life and admired it. "But who is this Kevin guy? My brother seems to really like him, and Richard's a good judge of character."

"Well, I don't want him in charge of my love life," Tisha replied. "Kevin's okay, but he reminds me too much of my dad. He wants me to listen to all his advice, not that I ask for it, and he actually thinks he knows something about art. He doesn't. Basically, I just wasn't as impressed by him as my dad was. And Kevin acts like he's doing me this huge favor when he asks me for a date."

"Sounds like he's trying too hard. But you've got a chip on your shoulder," Blanche scolded her mildly. "He might be a little intimidated by you, did you ever think of that?"

"I don't want a man who's intimidated by me."

"Men are more insecure than you might think," Blanche pointed out. "And he's young and so are you."

Tisha shrugged. "Kevin just isn't the one."

"You aren't trying to tell me that there haven't been a few boys you've liked, are you?"

A sheepish grin spread over Tisha's face as she realized how irritable and superior she had sounded. "Actually, there've been more than a few," she admitted, "but I've never fooled myself into believing that I was in love with any of them. That's probably why I never protested much when Dad kicked up a fuss about this one or that one not being good enough for his darling daughter. But he went too far when he decided Kevin was."

"All the same, Richard is concerned about your happiness, although I do agree that he's not exactly tactful about it," her aunt said. "Now that he knows how totally you oppose this Kevin, he'll back down."

"He'll find someone else," Tisha wailed. Her aunt put a finger to her lips. "I'm not going to be quiet about it, Blanche! I mean, I love my dad, but I just can't live with him. As long as I do, he's going to attempt to manage my life. Sometimes I feel like giving up painting and just getting a job. Working nine to five won't kill me."

"No, it won't. Most artists have to do other things to make ends meet. But I have another idea that might work," Blanche told her, turning back to look at more of her niece's paintings. "You could move to Hot Springs and live with me."

"Seriously?" Tisha breathed, unable to believe that she had heard correctly. Blanche Caldwell was famously protective of her privacy and solitude.

"Yes." Her aunt nodded, meeting Tisha's questioning gaze with calm assurance. "If you want a career in art, you're going to need time and space to focus on that. You shouldn't have to give up your dream this early in life. After all, you're not married and you don't have children and you are responsible only to yourself right now. Seize the day, Tisha."

"But what will Dad say?"

"Do you really care? Just do what you want to do and don't think twice. He won't argue with me, especially since he's likely to think of me as a chaperone." Blanche laughed, a deep, throaty sound to match her low-pitched voice.

"What about . . . I mean . . . will I interfere with your work?" asked Tisha, blurting out the thought that was uppermost in her mind.

"I do enjoy being alone, and I choose to live that way." There was a faint smile in the otherwise serious face. "Solitude—well, that's an ingrained state of mind for me by now. I could paint in the middle of the busiest intersection and never notice the traffic. But I think I might enjoy having a fellow artist staying with me, especially since she's my niece."

"What can I say?" Tisha cried, elated by the sudden turn of events that couldn't help but meet with her father's approval. In spite of all their arguments, she didn't want to alienate her father by openly rebelling and leaving home, as if that were the only possible way to resolve the differences between them.

"If you'd like to stay with me, then say yes. It's as simple as that. I'll handle your father," Blanche assured her. "Of course, your social life will probably suffer until you meet some new people."

"If you mean dating, I need a break from all that. Just about everyone I've hung out with lately seems immature and self-centered."

Blanche patted Tisha's hand. "Honey, it could be time for an older man. They treat you right. Remind me to introduce you to my neighbor."

It was Tisha's turn to laugh.

"Do I sound too wicked?" Blanche asked anxiously.

"No. Go ahead and introduce me. But I'm not going to tell Dad"—she grinned—"or he'll never let me stay with you."

"Well, he'd never tell you if he was fooling around, but he's likely to keep right on insisting that his daughter be a good little girl," her aunt declared with a decided twinkle in her eye. "Not that I'm advocating that you have an affair. Aunts have rules, too, although we're not nearly as straitlaced as parents."

"What does that mean?" Tisha teased. "That the porch light goes on twenty minutes after my date drives up to bring me home instead of Dad's usual five minutes?"

"Something like that." Blanche laughed, squeezing her niece's hand lightly before releasing it. "Now I have to go convince your father that it's his idea for you to come stay with me."

Chapter Two

Two days later, Tisha was en route to her aunt's house outside of Hot Springs, Arkansas. Her vintage Mustang, a miracle of restoration that owed a lot to the dry Arkansas climate, was jammed with clothes, paints, canvases, and every other personal possession she couldn't bear to leave behind. The lightness of her heart had nothing to do with getting out from under her father's dominating thumb. It was a result of his loving farewell that almost made Tisha wish she weren't leaving. Almost.

Autumn was beginning to make its vivid mark on the forested Ozark hills, splashing gold and scarlet on the leaves of the trees. Only the pines remained forever green as a direct contrast to the autumn hues. The sun shone brightly in a milky blue sky, but there was a nip in the wind that blew from the north.

Tisha had been to her aunt's house only twice since Blanche had moved into it less than a year ago, but her memory of the route through the back roads didn't fail her. She slowed her blue car to a stop at a tree-lined intersection, remembering the way the winding crossroad snaked up the mountain, its almost immediate curve blocking the view of oncoming traffic. Not that there was any and her aunt's house wasn't that far away. She pulled into the intersection without turning her blinker on.

Just as she completed the turn, an expensive foreign sports car came roaring around the curve, taking more than its share of her side of the road. There was no place for her to go to avoid it. The hillside fell steeply away on her side. Only skillful maneuvering by the other driver saved them from a head-on collision, but he clipped her front bumper as he swerved by.

For a split second after she braked to a stop, Tisha sat frozen behind the wheel, paralyzed by the near miss that had left her unharmed but shaken. Not as if this car had airbags or four-wheel-drive or anything. She didn't have the margin for error that the other car did.

Slowly she unclenched her white fingers from their death grip on the wheel, a trembling rage taking possession of her at the reckless driver who could have got them both killed. The white sports car had stopped near the crossroads.

Tisha bounded out of the Mustang, the sunlight setting her hair afire to match the anger burning in her green eyes. Her long legs got her quickly down the slight incline to the other car and the man just stepping out of it.

She let him have it. "Idiot! Jerk! What were you doing coming around that corner so fast? You could have got us both killed!" Tisha shouted. "Didn't you realize there was an intersection on the other side of the curve? Just because you drive a fancy freakin' sports car doesn't give you the automatic right-of-way! You were on my side of the road! People like you shouldn't be allowed behind the wheel!"

Tisha was five foot six, but she had to tilt her head back to look into the face of the man who was easily two inches over six feet tall. His strong features were set in a serious expression, but his brown eyes gave the impression that he was smiling at her. Her heart began beating double time, an aftereffect of the accident, no doubt.

"If you can run that fast and yell at me like that, I guess you weren't hurt." His deep, husky voice was very sexy, but Tisha was too incensed to notice.

"No thanks to you!" she retorted, shaking her head with a fury that sent her hair flying about her shoulders. "You must have been doing seventy when you came around that bend!"

"No way," he said complacently, "or I never would have been able to avoid hitting you head-on."

"If you hadn't been going so fast and on my side of the road, you wouldn't have hit me at all," Tisha reminded him curtly.

"Hard to say. I mean, this is essentially a private road used only by the people who live on the mountain. I didn't expect to meet anyone." His gaze was moving leisurely over the snug blue jeans and cropped tee she was wearing.

She bridled visibly at his once-over—and his arrogant statement. "That's no excuse for reckless driving!"

"You're quite right, Red," he agreed smoothly, reaching out to capture her elbow with a darkly tanned hand. "Let's go see what damage I've done to your car."

He had turned her half around before Tisha realized what was happening, and she quickly jerked her arm free, not missing the mocking gleam in his eyes.

Just one look at him—he had sandy brown hair streaked blond by the sun and a ruggedly handsome face—was all she needed. Obviously he was a man accustomed to charming his way out of situations. He would soon find that she wasn't easily charmed. She put on her coldest expression as she fell into step beside him.

"Classic Mustang, huh?" He named the year and

model before they got close to it. "Had it long? It's in great condition."

"Not anymore," she snapped.

"Looks like you have it pretty well packed," he commented as he walked past it to examine the front. "Are you moving somewhere around here?"

"That's my business," she replied with what she thought was cutting sarcasm, but his mouth twitched in amusement.

He was really quite insufferable, Tisha thought as she watched him inspect the damage to her car.

"Can you pop the hood?"

"Sure."

He was wearing an expensive brown suede jacket that showed off his muscular shoulders. A still-pissed-off part of her hoped that he would get engine grease on it, which would serve him right. She reached through the open window, releasing the lever that opened the hood, straightening as he bent over to look inside. The rest of him was lean and long, she noticed with unwilling interest.

His blondish brown hair was thick and inclined to wave, but its waywardness seemed to suit the slightly untamed look about him. There was a suggestion of a cleft in his strong chin and the rest of his features were just as masculine and just as sexy.

Tisha judged him to be in his early thirties. With no wedding ring on his finger, if that was anything to go by.

"There doesn't seem to be any damage, except to your bumper," he announced, closing the hood of her car. His brown eyes had a knowing look when he met her gaze as if he knew he had been subjected to her scrutiny. "A good body shop should be able to take care of it. If you're going to be in the area, I can give you the name of a local guy I trust."

"Oh, a personal recommendation. Well, the way you

drive, that just doesn't surprise me," she murmured sweetly.

"There have been one or two occasions when I've had him do work for me," the man admitted without really admitting anything.

"I'll bet there have," she said acidly. "Do you get a commission for all the business you direct his way?"

His gaze narrowed slightly, sending her pulse leaping with an unknown fear. "As you put it earlier, Red, that's my business," he replied, giving her a smile she couldn't really read.

Tisha chose to ignore his rebuke. "That's the second time you've called me that," she said sharply. "My name isn't Red, just so you know."

"It isn't?" He made a point of looking at her hair, coppery bright by the sun. "What is your name?" At the closed expression stealing over her face, he added quietly, "For the benefit of my insurance company, of course."

Tisha hesitated, wishing she didn't have to tell this arrogant stranger anything about herself. Of course, they would have to exchange insurance information before too long, but the idea rankled her.

"Patricia Caldwell," she said grudgingly.

"Patricia," he repeated, letting the name roll slowly out of his mouth as though he were savoring the sound of it. "What a nice, old-fashioned name."

He just looked at her in a way that was extremely unnerving, but Tisha refused to submit to the feeling of magnetic attraction. She guessed that most women would be fascinated by his smile.

"Whatever. My friends call me Tisha," she said coldly, "but you're not my friend."

"I guess not," he said, widening his eyes. "But I'm going to call you Tisha anyway. It's strong and it fits you."

"If you say so. Apparently there's no stopping you

from doing whatever you want," Tisha replied. Her chin lifted to a haughty angle. "Give me a few minutes to think of a way to annoy you in return. I'm pretty good at it when I want to be."

He laughed heartily. "Okay, Tisha," he said. You present an interesting challenge—"

"Shall we dispense with the personal comments and get down to the problem at hand, namely the damage to my car?" Tisha requested sarcastically. "I'll need the name and policy number of your insurance company."

One side of his mouth twitched again with ill-concealed amusement, but he reached inside his jacket pocket and withdrew a leather-bound memo pad and a pen. He took a small card from one of its flat pockets—she hadn't assumed he had his policy number memorized, even though he was a terrible driver, and she figured the insurance information would be on it. It was. She watched the quick, sure strokes of his pen as he jotted something on the card and gave it to her.

"I added my name and phone number in case you need to contact me," he said.

Unwillingly Tisha glanced at it, the bold slashes spelling out the name Roarke Madison over the printed insurance information.

"Now you know all about me," he said with a smirk.

"What a thrill. All I care about is getting my car repaired," she flashed.

Her sharp tone didn't seem to ruffle him. "It would be a good idea to get that bumper taken care of as soon as possible. The dent impacts that front tire."

"I'm quite capable of seeing that it gets fixed."

He shrugged one shoulder. "My offer still stands. Let me give you the name of a reputable body shop. I'd hate to see you get taken."

"What you mean is that you wouldn't like to see your insurance company get taken or your friend lose some business."

There was a small silence as the man named Roarke Madison slowly walked from the damaged front bumper, ignored Tisha as he went by, and stopped behind her to lean a hand on the roof of the car.

"The repairs shouldn't cost all that much," he said as she turned around to face him. He was watching her with an insolent look that she found annoying. "Do I look as if I need what my supposed share of the take would be?"

She didn't reply but admitted to herself that money was probably the least of his worries. There was a definite look of affluence about him, but it only annoyed her even more.

"I really wouldn't know." She wanted to make it clear that she wasn't interested in his financial status—or in him. "Since my dealings will be with your insurance company, not you, I couldn't care less."

"Is that right?" The mockery in his voice made it a taunt.

"Yes."

He said nothing more, and something inside Tisha snapped. She wanted to get to her aunt's, she wanted this weird little conversation to come to an end, and most of all, she wanted to know what he wanted from her. "What do you expect me to do, bow down or something? Obviously your car is worth more than my car, but—" Outrage flamed in the look she tossed at him. "You really take the cake. Are you always so disgustingly sure of yourself?"

If Tisha thought that a dose of freezing scorn would keep him at bay, she was wrong. "You know," he said quietly, "I figured you were shook up, even if you didn't want to admit it. And I said it was my fault—"

"Don't give yourself any medals, pal," she interrupted him. "It *was* your fault."

He continued on as if she hadn't said a word. "But I

have no intention of letting you keep taking these cheap shots at me."

Tisha discovered his arms were on either side of her, pinning her against the car, and his face was uncomfortably close to hers. Her mouth was suddenly very dry.

"What are you doing?" she demanded, hating the nervousness that had crept into her voice as she molded her body against the metal frame of the car.

"Being an obnoxious alpha male. That's what you think I am, right?" He backed off, a humorless smile on his face.

"Yeah," was her defiant reply. She stood up straight, folding her arms across her chest. It would be fun to kick him where it counted, but the road was deserted and she had a feeling he could resist any blow. And it wasn't as if he had actually done anything besides get a little too close for a few seconds. *Do not rationalize bad behavior,* she told herself sternly.

She remembered that her cell phone had slipped down under her seat about an hour ago, and there was no way she was going to bend over and retrieve it with him looking on.

The minor accident hadn't delayed her long enough to make her aunt worry, but Tisha longed to make a connection, if only to give her a reason to get away from the high-and-mighty Roarke Madison.

"Mind if I point something out, Tisha?"

"Not like I have a choice."

"You're pretty sure of yourself, too, for what it's worth."

"What's that supposed to mean?"

His gaze moved to her lips, slightly parted by her apprehension. "I don't know what card games you've played, but in the ones I know, a king takes a queen every time. You might do well to remember that," he mocked.

He walked away to his own car, surprising Tisha more than a little. She was prepared to fight off another unwelcome move. A metallic click broke her concentration. She glanced instinctively in the direction of the sound, startled to see his car door swinging open, and still wary.

"Gotta go." His eyes were laughing at her disbelieving expression. "You have the information you need. Nice to meet you."

Tisha snapped out of it and slid behind the wheel of her car, grateful to make her escape and not caring about anything else. She didn't waste a backward look as she put the car in gear and accelerated around the curve and out of sight.

A few minutes later Tisha was turning her car into the pillared breezeway of her aunt's house. The house was perched on a hillside overlooking a verdant valley to the south. Clad in unfinished, rustic cedar, the structure blended well with its setting, although its clerestory windows gave an indication of the house's totally modern interior.

There was no sign of Blanche as Tisha parked the car and climbed out. She started to reach into the backseat for some of her things when the sound of a stone rolling in the gravel turned her back around. A black-and-white-spotted goat was staring at her, little nubbins of horns beginning to appear on its head, and a hint of a beard beneath his chin.

She smiled at it. "Where did you come from?"

The goat shook its head a little aggressively, and Tisha noticed the intimidating look in his eyes. He probably thought that she was trespassing on his turf. Even though his horns weren't fully formed, she didn't want to be butted.

Careful not to make any sudden movement that

might antagonize him, she reached into the open window of her car and sounded the horn. She didn't take her eyes off the goat when she heard the front door open.

"Friend of yours, Aunt Blanche?" she asked hesitantly.

"You've met my gardener." Blanche laughed.

At the sound of her aunt's voice, the goat turned his head from Tisha, emitting a stuttering *baaah.*

"Get over it, Gruff," Blanche instructed. "Tisha's come to stay with us. Run along or I'll have you stuffed."

As though he understood every word, the goat cast one brief glance in Tisha's direction before wandering off.

"Don't goats eat everything?" Tisha asked. She gave her aunt a look that said she plainly doubted her sanity. "Are you sure it's a good idea to give him the run of the place?"

"I don't have much of a yard." Blanche shrugged, but there was an unmistakable twinkle in her eyes. "I needed something to keep the weeds down, though, so I got Gruff. He thinks he's a watchdog as well."

"He did an excellent job of convincing me that he was." Tisha stared after the goat, now contentedly munching some grass near the fence. "What did you call him? Gruff? It's a very good name for him."

"Billy was a bit too trite." Blanche smiled. "I guess Billy Goat Gruff isn't much better, but he's a very useful pet. He's quite affectionate at times."

There was doubt in the second look Tisha gave the goat. "I hope that includes me."

"Once he gets to know you, you'll be able to come and go as you please," her aunt assured her. "The very fact that he's ignoring you now means he's accepted you. Sometimes he simply hangs around when I have visitors, peering into the windows and lurking around corners. He rather unnerves them."

"He's the right pet for an eccentric artist, then," Tisha teased.

"Do you think so?" Blanche asked in an amused voice. "You're probably right. Well, shall we get your car unloaded and your things moved in? I've rearranged my studio so you can have part of it to work in."

"You didn't need to do that," Tisha protested.

"I have plenty of room for myself," her aunt insisted as she opened the rear door and dragged out a heavy suitcase. "I see you brought your brick collection."

"Give me that," Tisha said, laughing. "Those are books, not bricks."

"No, I can manage. How did Richard take your leaving?"

"He wasn't happy about it. More like resigned. He said it was the best solution." A wistful expression crossed Tisha's face. "The house must seem awfully empty to him now. Not to mention lonely."

"Don't go feeling sorry for him. You would be leaving home sooner or later, and he knows it. It's just as well that he gets used to it now. Besides, living alone isn't so bad. I ought to know."

"I'm not considering moving back," Tisha declared. "It would only be a matter of days before Dad and I would be fighting over something. I just hope I won't be in your way too much."

"You won't. If I thought you might, I would never have invited you." Blanche smiled reassuringly as she opened the door of her house for her niece to enter. "How was the drive here?"

Tisha frowned as she dragged another heavy suitcase inside. "Don't ask!"

"What happened?" Blanche laughed. "Did you take a wrong turn and get lost on the mountain roads?"

"I almost wish I had. A car sideswiped me at that intersection at the bottom of the hill. Some stupid guy was speeding around the curve on my side of the road.

He narrowly missed hitting me head-on. I was lucky to get away with a little dent on the front bumper."

"You weren't hurt, were you?" Blanche asked anxiously. Tisha shook her head. "That's a relief," Blanche sighed. "I wish that hadn't happened on your first day here."

"It's over. The car can be fixed. I just didn't see him coming." Tisha was determined not to think about her run-in with Roarke Madison, but she couldn't shake the annoying feeling that she had come out second best in their exchange.

Blanche propped an interior door open with the suitcase she was lugging, ready to go back for more. "I thought you might like the south bedroom. There's a great view from the window of the valley and our mountain."

It was the middle of the afternoon before Tisha was completely unpacked and had arranged her things in some kind of temporary order. She walked into the living room and sank wearily into the plump cushions of the amber-colored sofa. At almost the same instant her aunt appeared in the doorway of the kitchen carrying a tray of cool drinks and cookies.

"All done?" she inquired. "I was just coming in to suggest you take a break. How does iced tea and peanut butter cookies sound?"

"Yummy," Tisha replied, reaching for two cookies first and then a frosted glass. "Everything has been put somewhere, although I'm sure I'll change things around later."

"Moving is always a hassle," Blanche agreed as the front doorbell rang.

Tisha sipped at her drink as her aunt went to the door. The cool, sweet tea was deliciously refreshing as it slipped down her throat. She rubbed the back of her neck, stretching her shoulders to ease the ache of her muscles from all the bending, stooping, and lifting. The murmur of voices at the door registered only vaguely until she heard Blanche say in a cheery voice, "Come on in. I want you to meet my niece."

Then Tisha turned, curious to meet the visitor. Her automatic smile froze in place as she stared at the man beside her aunt. His expression was coolly composed, while she felt as if the sofa had just been pulled out from under her.

"You!" she gasped with disbelieving anger.

"Have you two met?" Blanche stared from one to the other in confused surprise.

A smile ticked the corners of Roarke Madison's mouth. "You might say we ran into each other."

"You ran into me," Tisha corrected quickly.

"So I did," he agreed, then turned to Blanche to explain, "I was the one who put the dent in her bumper."

"It was sheer luck that he didn't kill me," Tisha retorted, sending him a malevolent glance.

"I see," her aunt murmured, but her lips were compressed as though she was attempting to conceal a smile. "I assume that you exchanged names and all that. I'll skip the introductions."

"I'd already guessed that she was your niece," Roarke said calmly. "But I didn't find out her name until I started calling her Red. That really seemed to annoy her."

"My hair is auburn, for your information," Tisha said, not willing to let him tease her in front of her aunt. "And I didn't find out that you were a reckless driver until you mentioned the frequent flyer rate you get at the body shop."

"Yes." He smiled, not the least bit upset by her sarcasm. "The guy's good."

"Roarke is also my neighbor," Blanche said, her tone holding an unspoken message that Tisha didn't get at first. "Remember? I said I wanted to introduce you to him."

With sickening swiftness, Tisha remembered. He was the older man her aunt had mentioned. Oh, geez. Vivid color flowed into her cheeks, and she was temporarily at a loss to reply. Worse, she felt him studying her face with amused speculation.

"While I was in town, I stopped in at the body shop to make an appointment for you," Roarke informed Tisha, moving leisurely to take a chair opposite her. "You can bring the car in tomorrow."

"Call and cancel it," she answered coldly. "I told you I would make my own arrangements."

"Don't be silly, Tisha," Blanche intervened. "They're always booked up, and they're the best place for miles around. If Roarke managed to get you an appointment, keep it."

Tisha shot a fiery glance at the man, expecting to hear him get his two cents in again, but he remained silent. How much easier it would have been to let her temper fly if he had attempted to persuade her to agree.

"I seem to have no choice," she said, belatedly aware of how ungracious she must sound.

To her surprise, he didn't comment on it, just took out the same leather-bound memo pad and gave her the name and the address of the repair shop. He had the self-satisfied air of a man who'd done the right thing and had no more interest in the matter.

She couldn't exactly complain about that.

"If you're going into town tomorrow, I think I will, too," Blanche declared, setting her glass on a coaster. "It's been weeks since I've had a thermal bath and massage. I'd better call now to make an appointment. What about you, Tish? The spas here are quite good, and the thermal baths are extraordinarily relaxing. Shall I make an appointment for you?"

Tisha's head moved in polite refusal. "Another time."

Her aunt rose with lithe grace. "While I'm on the phone, why don't you get Roarke a glass of iced tea?" Blanche suggested, moving toward the studio and the telephone.

Tisha was quite willing to escape the subtle intensity of his brown eyes and the masculine presence that permeated the room. She got up and left him there, but the sound of unhurried footsteps behind her made her frown. She felt rather than saw him pause in the doorway, his lanky build filling the frame. The kitchen was new to her, and she opened three cupboard doors in quick succession without finding the glassware.

"This is it," Roarke said, walking immediately to the correct cupboard.

"You know your way around very well, don't you?" Tisha said, watching as he removed the pitcher of tea from the refrigerator and filled a container from the ice-maker.

His gaze slid over her as if he were physically touching her. "Fairly well."

"Do you come here often?" She deliberately made her voice as neutral as possible.

"What do you really want to know? Whether I'm fooling around with your aunt?" His candor caught her by surprise. The thought hadn't consciously crossed her mind. "Blanche is terrific. Very talented woman."

"She's at least ten years older than you!" She didn't want to look outraged but realized that she probably did.

"Is that a crime? Being older?"

"No," Tisha said. His questions seemed designed to trip her up, and she felt a little safer with a one-word answer.

"Well, your aunt mentioned your strict upbringing, your overprotective father and all that. That has to have affected how you perceive relationships." His tone was patronizing, insufferably so. Just what was or had been going on between him and Blanche? Tisha suddenly, desperately wanted to know.

"She had no right to be talking about me to you!" The amused way he was looking at her made Tisha feel like an inexperienced teenager. "I'm not exactly ignorant when it comes to sex and sexual relationships."

"Oh. Care to share?"

"You are totally out of line. That is strictly my business!" She doubted that her burst of bravado would convince Roarke Madison of anything.

He permitted himself an even more out of line inspection of her, pausing for a fraction of a second on the quick rise and fall of her breasts beneath her white tee before his gaze continued over her waist, the gentle swell of her hips, and down her long, slender legs.

"That's strange," he murmured, his knowing eyes returning to the heightened color of her face. "You look relatively innocent. You're right—I really was out of line. On second thought—"

"Don't bother!" Tisha snapped. "You can keep all your thoughts to yourself."

"For a sweet young thing, you talk tough." His tongue was very definitely in cheek as he met her murderous glance. "Being polite to you is going to be a challenge. But I like challenges."

"Do you?" she asked sweetly. "How's this for a challenge? I hardly know you but I already hate you. A lot."

"That'll do for a start." Roarke smiled, flashing white teeth in a smile that seemed genuine enough. "But it might have been more interesting if you'd despised me. More dramatic, too."

"Okay, then, I despise you," Tisha declared, infuriated by his glib replies—and the sure knowledge that she was being teased. "And you can save your interest for someone who appreciates it, like Blanche."

"Your aunt and I are friends. Nothing more," he said complacently.

"Really?" Tisha murmured. "That isn't the impression you gave me a moment ago."

"Just trying to get a rise out of you."

He was sure as hell making her blood pressure rise the way he was looking at her. She deliberately ignored the seductive note in his voice, focusing instead on a comeback.

"I see. And it's because of your friendship"—she paused, so her emphasis on the last word could sink in—"that you know your way around her house so well."

"The truth is much more plausible than that." He was actually grinning at her now. "I designed it."

Tisha felt as though she had just been dropped into ice water. "What do you mean?"

"I'm an architect. I not only developed the plans and did the blueprints, I also supervised the construction. Exterior and interior."

"I didn't know that," she faltered.

"You didn't ask. You assumed." A brown eyebrow lifted mockingly. "I had you going, didn't I?"

"How nice. You wanted to make a fool of me," Tisha said. "Now I feel better." She really did hate him, she decided. He was as unpredictable as the billy goat chomping weeds outside.

"Hey, I had a good reason. You're very beautiful when you're angry." He straightened negligently away from the support of the counter. "I guess I couldn't resist striking the match that would set you on fire."

Blanche appeared in the kitchen doorway before Tisha could think of a suitably cutting retort. "What are you two talking about?" Her gaze shifted from the indifferent satisfaction on Roarke Madison's face to Tisha's obvious annoyance. "Is this a private war, or can anyone join in?"

"We were just discussing all the hearts that Tisha broke," Roarke answered.

His calm statement drew a puzzled frown. There had been absolutely no discussion regarding the romantic aspects of her life. "What? Aunt Blanche, tell him to shut up," she found herself saying, wondering what the hell else her aunt had seen fit to tell this guy.

If Roarke Madison was an example of an older man's surefire charm, she wanted no part of it. His teasing only reinforced the age difference between them, and he seemed to think she wasn't grown up enough to play his game on his level. She didn't care if he was rich and successful and had a cool car; he was still obnoxious.

"I doubt that Kevin was overjoyed at your leaving," Blanche reminded her.

"I heard he wanted to marry you. How did you manage to talk him out of it?" Roarke inquired.

Her astounded look made him smile. Now she knew how thoroughly her aunt had discussed her. Maybe Blanche thought it was harmless to gossip about a guy Tisha hadn't liked much, but Tisha still wished that her aunt hadn't.

"I told him that I wasn't the marrying kind and if I was, I wouldn't choose him," Tisha answered bluntly. The truth was that she had been very apologetic when she had last seen Kevin. But she'd had to make things clear.

"Not very tactful, but I imagine he got the point." Blanche laughed easily.

"So you have decided that marriage isn't for you." Roarke ignored her reference to Kevin to pursue the first statement.

"I imagine that's about the only view you and I have in common," she murmured with arch sweetness. "Or am I wrong to assume that you're a confirmed bachelor?"

"Oh, I'm a bachelor," he assured her with laughter lurking in his voice. "I can't exactly admit to being a confirmed one, though."

"This looks as if it's going to be an interesting conversation." Blanche's eyes sparkled as she looked from one to the other. "Let's go back into the living room where I can relax and enjoy the fireworks."

Tisha turned, wanting to stalk out of the kitchen like a teenager, but her destination was her own bedroom. Roarke Madison had outmatched her. And he was about to do it again: she hadn't counted on his long, easy strides overtaking her before she reached the kitchen door. His hand claimed her arm, and her skin tingled beneath his touch, sending a sensual fire racing through her.

"Are you retreating before the battle has begun?" he murmured in a low, silky voice.

Tisha shook off his hand and marched into the living room. So he thought she was giving up without a fight . . . she wasn't going to give him that satisfaction.

"You know," she began, "I shouldn't have assumed that you were a confirmed bachelor." Kind of a lame lead-in to the verbal assault she planned, but she had to start somewhere, Tisha thought. "There's no such thing."

"How did you come to that conclusion?" An indulgent light flashed into his eyes as he settled in the same chair as before.

"Well, no man is immune to the power of a woman," Tisha declared with an expressive movement of her shoulders. "The Bible is full of such stories—Samson and Delilah, David and Bathsheba, Esther and King Ahasuerus. A woman always brings a man to his knees." She stared into the brown eyes, almost trapped again by the intensity of his gaze. "Don't you agree?"

Score the next point for Roarke, she thought despairingly. He would refuse to be trapped into any admission.

"I couldn't say," he replied at last. "I don't even remember the last time I picked up a Bible. I must have been a kid, but you know—I cut Sunday school every chance I got. Go on, though. Your viewpoint is very enlightening."

"What I'm saying is obvious. When a man proposes, he's the one who gets down on his knees, not the other way around." Her voice was close to a purr—the purr of a cat toying with a mouse. Tisha noticed the surreptitious glance Blanche gave Roarke before she hid her smile behind the iced tea glass.

"That's a gesture of respect," Roarke replied, "but we men never do bow our heads."

"We let you keep a little of your pride." Tisha smiled sweetly. "After all, if we wanted complete subservience, we'd buy a pet."

"That's generous of you." He chuckled. "It's amazing how you've managed to convince yourself that you're doing a man a favor by marrying him. But come to think of it, the benefits are all on the man's side."

"How do you figure that?" She wasn't prepared for this particular argument.

"For example, if a woman doesn't work outside the house, then for the price of food, clothing, shelter, a second car and so forth, a man gets a housekeeper, a laundrymaid, a cook, a seamstress, a dishwasher, a mother of his children, a babysitter, a nurse, an errand runner, and a bed partner. The wife also becomes a tax deduction. There are many advantages to marriage," he concluded with a pseudo-serious expression.

"But—wait a minute—" Tisha sputtered, unable to put her frustration into words.

"I believe in looking at things logically and realistically." Roarke smiled blandly. "You can't deny that those are facts."

"Unfortunately, you're right!" she raged, glaring at him. "But if you believe that's how it should be, you're wrong. In case you haven't heard, women do have rights. And careers."

"But they still earn less than men in many professions, and there still are glass ceilings in most major corporations. Oh, maybe you never heard of the concept. You're the artistic type."

"Somehow the idea of you as a defender of womankind is a little weird. I think you're just using the issue to bait me again."

"Again? I don't remember doing it before. Anyway, you started this discussion." He shrugged, the lines deepening around his mouth. "If you don't like the heat, stay out of the . . . oh, hell. I don't dare say kitchen."

She couldn't win. No matter what she said or did around Roarke Madison, Tisha knew she couldn't win. She left the room.

Chapter Three

"So tell me all about Roarke Madison." Tisha took her eyes from the road long enough to glance at Blanche. "He thinks he's hot stuff. I can't imagine why."

"Interested in my neighbor, hmm?" the woman's teasing voice answered. "After the way you stalked out of the room yesterday and then refused to let his name enter any conversation, I was beginning to wonder."

"I'm not interested in him the way you mean." Tisha's fingers tightened on the steering wheel, wishing it were his throat. "It's simply intelligent to find out all you can about a potential enemy."

"That's a little dramatic, isn't it?"

"Maybe, maybe not," Tisha said. After yesterday's discussion she wasn't inclined to give him the benefit of the doubt.

"You got the wrong impression about Roarke, I think," Blanche said. "He's a very considerate neighbor as well as a very talented architect. I'll grant you, with his looks and his money, there are any number of women who'd love to get closer, but he just doesn't seem to be a womanizer."

"How do you know that?" One of those questions

that gave away too much about the person who asked it. Tisha wished she hadn't asked it. She didn't want to seem to care too much about what Roarke did.

"My hairdresser," Blanche said simply. "The grapevine in an area like this is pretty reliable. If he were a womanizer, we'd all know."

"Okay, I guess it's not the kind of news that the *New York Times* would put on the front page," Tisha said.

"But it would be news around here," Blanche insisted. "I think he honestly does respect women."

"Then how do you explain his disgusting statement about wives?" Tisha demanded.

"You did rather invite that, you know. And I don't know what the Bible stories you mentioned had to do with your argument. David and Bathsheba weren't married, you know. At least not to each other," she added hastily. "But I thought he took your digs at the male sex good-naturedly enough. There was a certain amount of truth in both your observations."

"Like a lot of men, he secretly thinks that women belong at home and in the kitchen." An unhappy sigh followed her words as she made the turn onto the highway.

"Don't dismiss the importance of being a wife and mother," Blanche scolded gently. "It's a valid choice and a rewarding one."

"I can't believe that you, of all women, would say that!" Tisha declared, her voice sharpening in surprise.

"What do you mean?" her aunt inquired with a half laugh.

"Well, you have a successful career and you live alone. You seem really happy, Blanche. Do the math. No man equals no aggravation."

"Do you know why I never married, Tish?" asked Blanche suddenly.

"Guess you never felt the need or desire to." Tisha shrugged.

"There were a couple of times when I considered it very seriously." Blanche met her niece's curious look. "But I was intelligent enough to realize that I didn't want the responsibility of a family."

"Not every man wants a family," Tisha pointed out.

"Well, the men who don't—hey, ever hear a woman say she wanted a baby so bad that she married one? I wasn't cut out to pick up anyone's socks or argue about what time someone came home or put up with a lot of demands. I had work I loved and still do, and I wanted to concentrate on that."

"I hear you."

"But I don't regret my decision and, given the chance, I wouldn't change it. You see, Tisha, it's an individual thing that has nothing to do with being a man or a woman."

"What are you saying? That you're the exception to prove the rule?" Tisha's voice held no sharpness or cynicism. Her tone was quietly serious.

"You know, I've never known what that means."

Tisha laughed. "Me neither. It's just something people say."

"Anyway, what I was getting at is that very few people can make that kind of commitment to their career."

"Can I?"

"Do you live to paint?" Blanche asked softly, her passion for her work very clear in her voice. "Is art the ultimate goal?"

The ultimate goal? Tisha didn't think she knew what her ultimate goal was. She didn't have her aunt's unique talent, a fact she recognized. Blanche's sweeping landscapes of the Southwestern states, where she'd spent her formative years as an artist, her still lifes of the bleached bones she'd found in its deserts, and her depictions of the rugged beauty of its arid land had brought her a measure of fame and the money to live independently.

Without that, Tisha wouldn't find the fulfillment that Blanche knew.

She answered her aunt's question hesitantly but truthfully. "Painting isn't the be-all and end-all for me, but I really like doing it. I'd like to earn a living that way, but I doubt that it's going to be easy."

"The right partner in life can make it easy. Painting can combine very well with married life."

"Are you talking about finding someone who'll pay the bills so I don't have to be a starving artist? Now you sound like my father," Tisha accused, softening her words with a smile. "Trying to marry me off for my own good."

"Only to the man you love."

"If he exists." Her laughter added the exclamation point. "It would be terrible if all I met were the Roarke Madisons of this world."

"I wouldn't eliminate Roarke as a romantic possibility. I'm certain your failure to fall at his feet has piqued his interest, and you aren't indifferent to him either."

"He dented my fender. That got my attention, sure."

"There's more to it than that."

Tisha wrinkled her nose in distaste. "He brings out the worst in me."

"Maybe it's a defense mechanism to keep from being attracted to him," her aunt chided.

"Amateur psychology, hmm? Then I have to say he has a lord-and-master complex. Not interested. I want to live my life on my own terms." The defiant tilt of her chin accented the swanlike column of her throat.

"You wouldn't be happy with someone you could walk all over. Besides, a little mastery can be a lot of fun," her aunt said wickedly.

"Blanche! You're shocking me."

"I don't think so."

Tisha just grinned. "I won't tell Dad, don't worry."

She shot a glance at her aunt's composed profile. "Are you really trying to pair me off with Roarke?"

"He's my neighbor. I don't want you to hate him. It would be much more peaceful if the two of you were friends," Blanche suggested.

There was that twinkle again. "You're a sly one, Aunty Blanche. Tell you what, I'll agree to this much," Tisha said. "I won't pick a fight with him."

"That's a beginning." Blanche smiled, glancing out the windows at the cluster of buildings. "You can let me out at this corner. Bath House Row is only a block away."

After dropping her aunt at the corner, Tisha continued through the business district to the repair shop. As she pulled into the drive, the first thing she saw was Roarke Madison's white sports car. Her lips compressed into a tight line as she parked her Mustang and walked into the office.

"Right on time," Roarke murmured, straightening from his leaning position against a side wall.

"What are you doing here?" Tisha demanded, forgetting completely her just-made promise to not pick fights with him.

"The damage wasn't only to your car," he said with that hint of laughter in his eyes. "Among other things, I cracked a headlight. They've just finished with mine."

"I see," she said grimly, wondering why she had thought he was there to see her. A man in greasy overalls walked into the room, and she turned her attention to him.

"Hi, Mac," Roarke greeted him. "This is Tisha Caldwell."

The man's gaze moved admiringly over Tisha before he spoke to Roarke. "Now I understand why you ran into her."

A rush of embarrassment colored her cheeks, but

she quickly subdued it. "Here are the keys to my car. It's the blue Mustang."

"It'll be ready in a couple of hours," the man named Mac replied as he accepted the keys, misinterpreting the glitter in her green eyes when she glanced at Roarke. When he turned to leave, Tisha heard the muttered aside he directed at Roarke. "You sure know how to pick them. She's better than the one before and younger, too."

"Are your conquests always common knowledge?" Tisha hissed the instant they were alone.

"Do you classify yourself as one of my conquests?" A lock of sun-bleached hair waved rakishly over his forehead as he inclined his head toward her.

"No."

A pleasant smile appeared on his face. "I guess I should've told the man that you hated me. He wouldn't have believed it."

"Why not? Somebody has to hate you. Might as well be me."

"Yes, oh queen. But what difference does it make what the peasants think?"

It shouldn't have made any difference, Tisha admitted to herself as she recognized the underlying question in his wisecrack. "The mechanic just sounded like he knew a little too much about me. I didn't know that I was going to be a hot topic around Hot Springs. You people must be hard up for gossip."

She noticed that whenever he attempted to hide a smile, the cleft in his chin became more pronounced.

"You're new here. You're pretty. You're noticed," he mocked.

"Well, that's just wonderful," she said with saccharine sweetness. "But it doesn't mean I hop into bed with every man I meet."

"Neither do I," he murmured lazily. "But then I'm not gay."

"Ha ha. Then maybe you'll get lucky with some unsuspecting woman."

He certainly wasn't gay, she thought, troubled by the seductive way his eyes moved over her face. Her heart skipped a beat at the almost physical caress.

"I haven't been to bed with you," Roarke drawled, adding softly and with deliberate provocation, "yet."

"Oh, please." Instantly ticked off by that comment, Tisha turned around and marched out the door.

But those long, superior strides caught up with her in seconds, and a hand closed over her arm, jerking her to a halt. "Where are you going?" his laughing voice asked her.

"Anywhere away from you!" she retorted, her head thrown back to glare at his ruggedly handsome face.

"I was striking matches again. I apologize." The force of his masculine charm was focused directly on her.

He definitely had the advantage, in more ways than one. "Apology not accepted," Tisha declared, trying to twist her arm free of his hold gracefully. "Now, let me go!"

"I promise not to bait you any more," he coaxed, ignoring her efforts to get loose as he held her easily.

"You irritate me just by breathing!" she hissed.

"Well, I'm not going to die to prove that I'm sorry." Roarke smiled. "Let's call a truce. After all, we are on neutral ground."

"Are we? I think it's more like a DMZ!" Her eyes flashed up at him before she turned her head away, her toes tapping out a war beat on the pavement.

"How did you intend to pass the time waiting for your car?" he asked.

"Not with you!" Tisha declared, refusing to succumb to the persuasive sound of his voice. "I'm going to do some sketching. Now, will you please let go of my arm?"

He finally did. "That's right, you're an artist, aren't you? Like your aunt."

"Hardly," she corrected automatically. "Blanche is an artist. I dabble in art."

"And I thought I was in the company of a budding genius. You do have the temperament of one," Roarke said.

"That artistic temperament stuff is pure bull. And my aunt is about the most good-natured person I know."

"Blanche had to be as independent as you are or she wouldn't have succeeded on her own. And she's a warm and sensitive woman, undoubtedly the side she shows to her family."

"That's the way it should be." Too late Tisha remembered that she didn't want to get started with him. She rationalized her response by telling herself that he had deliberately provoked her, which was not wholly true.

"To get back to my original question, where are you going to do your sketching?"

"I thought I'd catch a taxi or bus downtown," she replied in a less abrasive tone.

"Get your sketch pad and whatever else you need and I'll give you a ride," he ordered, a bland smile on his face.

Tisha prickled at the way he expected her to obey. "If I accept your offer, will you leave me alone then?"

"I'll consider it."

"No, not 'consider it,' do it."

"Okay. I solemnly promise to do whatever you want."

"Then you can drive me there," Tisha gave in.

"Careful!" he called after her as she started to walk to her car, "or you might sound too eager for my company."

"That'll be the day!" she shot back.

Minutes later Tisha was inside his car, hugging herself close to the door to keep as much distance between them as was possible. But Roarke seemed to pay no notice as he pulled out into the sparse traffic on the street.

"Do you know much about Hot Springs?" he asked.

"I've been here before." Tisha shrugged, sweeping a strand of her hair over her shoulder in a gesture of indifference.

"Which doesn't mean anything," he concluded. "You've lived in Little Rock all your life, haven't you?"

"Yes," she replied. One clipped monosyllable would have to do. He didn't need to hear the story of her life.

"And like most people you never bothered to explore what was in your own backyard, am I right?" He darted her a knowing look.

"If you mean that when Dad and I took our vacations, did we come here, then the answer is no," Tisha said. "We usually went west or south."

"Then you actually know very little about Hot Springs," Roarke persisted.

"It has hot springs." A quick glance out the window took in Arlington Park, which signaled the beginning of Bath House Row. "You can let me out here."

Instead of pulling up at the corner, Roarke maneuvered his car into a parking space. Before Tisha could gather her things and escape, he was out of the car, had put coins in the meter, and was at her elbow.

"Thank you for the lift, Mr. Madison." She knew even as she said the words that she couldn't dismiss him so easily.

He looked down at her, mischief gleaming in his dark eyes. "I wouldn't be doing my duty as a resident if I didn't impart a little of the city's illustrious history to you."

Through gritted teeth, she said, "You just won't take no for an answer, will you?"

He gave her a lazy glance and smiled. "I don't believe you would think very much of me if I did."

For a moment Tisha was startled by his answer. She had the odd feeling that his remark was true. Blanche had said that Tisha wouldn't respect a man she could walk over. Yet, paradoxically, she resented being dominated. It was the last thought that roused her from her silence.

"I don't like to do things because someone else thinks they're good for me," she said coldly.

"Does anyone?" Roarke murmured. The light flashed to WALK, and he ushered her unceremoniously across the street. "Of course, the redeeming side to that is that sometimes it's the only way we find out if we like something."

Tisha studied the strength in his jawline, the chiseled cheekbones and nose, passed over the faint cleft in his jutting chin, hesitated a second on the sensual line of his mouth before looking into his eyes.

"You still can't let yourself agree with me, can you?" Roarke said softly.

"Um—"

He launched into the guided tour before she got further than that. All things considered, it was a relief to Tisha.

"The Indians called this place the Valley of the Vapors. This ground was sacred to all tribes. They came here in peace to bathe their sick and wounded in the springs. I mentioned earlier that we were on neutral ground. I'm willing to declare a temporary truce if you are."

It was an offer of compromise that wasn't really a compromise, but there was a humorous lift to her mouth. "What a choice!" Tisha murmured. "If I don't willingly agree to have you guide me around, you're going to do it anyway."

"Something like that." Roarke chuckled complacently. For the first time since they had met, her answering smile was one of genuine amusement, and it brought a sparkling glitter to her eyes.

"Pass the peace pipe, then," she sighed.

"Since I don't have one, will a handshake do?"

The firm pressure of the large hand closing over hers sent a pleasant rush of warmth through her bloodstream. And the sensation remained even after he released her hand. A slow, captivating smile spread over his face. Its dazzling brilliance warmed her even more as she turned in response to the guiding pressure of his hand on her back.

"We'll walk along the promenade first," Roarke announced in a low voice that seemed to vibrate around her. "Just to set the mood for the early history."

He had shortened his athletic strides to match hers as they walked the paved pathway toward the tree-covered mountain rising in the heart of the city.

"You must tell me everything about Hot Springs," Tisha commanded in a playful taunt.

"I said I'd do whatever you wanted, didn't I? Okay. All the Indians knew about the springs and their stories of their restorative powers were passed from tribe to tribe," Roarke began. "Although in modern times we have brochures."

Tisha laughed. "Which is where you got all this information."

"Mostly. Anyway, it's believed that these tales sent Ponce de León on his search for the Fountain of Youth, but unfortunately he never traveled far enough inland to find it. Therefore the first European to view the steaming valley of the vapors was the Spanish gold seeker Hernando de Soto, guided here by friendly Indians." A huge rock blocked their path, and Tisha stopped when Roarke did. "The plaque on this tufa rock commemorates de Soto's arrival here in 1541."

Then he led her around the rock to the steps leading

up the hillside to a wide, tree-sheltered brick walk scattered with benches and tables.

"But it was La Salle who came here in 1682," he went on, "and claimed the territory for France. If you remember your American history, the territory was given to Spain, then returned to France again in the secret treaty of Madrid in 1801. Subsequently Napoleon sold it to the United States as part of the Louisiana Purchase. President Jefferson, who initiated the purchase, sent two scientists here the following year to find out more about the hot water that flowed from the mountain."

"You said it was called the Valley of the Vapors. Why aren't there any vapors now?"

"Because, of the forty-seven original springs, only two have been left open for display purposes. The rest have been channeled into an underground reservoir where they're piped into the various bathhouses," he explained. "The city of Hot Springs is set in the middle of a national park. An Act of Congress in 1832 set aside the entire area, but later amended it to allow the town to grow around it." His hand moved to her elbow to guide her toward a set of steps. "The display springs are below us."

Back against the side of the mountain were two clear pools of steaming water set among rocks much like the large one Tisha had seen at the beginning of their walk. It was a peaceful, sylvan setting, a miniature glade behind the row of commercial bathhouses. Her fingers dipped quickly in and out of the hot water pool.

"The temperature of the water averages a hundred and forty-three degrees Fahrenheit as it flows out of the mountain." Roarke smiled.

"What makes it so hot?"

"There are several theories about that, none of which have been proven. All the thermal water from the hot springs shows radium emanation, which is believed to be the cause of the heat."

"Do you glow in the dark after a dip?"

"Not as far as I know."

"Hmm. Fascinating, isn't it?"

"I'm glad you're not too stubborn to admit it," he commented, looking into the tranquil depths of her sea green eyes.

Startled by the moment of intimacy, Tisha changed the subject with a quick question. "Is there more?"

"The history of Hot Springs would fill a book. All I did was give you the general highlights. This was the temporary headquarters of the state government during the Civil War. The city was the termination point of the legendary Diamond Jo Railroad. We'll skip the part about this being a favorite resort of the notorious Al Capone." He stretched out his hand toward her. "Come on, let's walk some more."

Tisha didn't think twice about accepting his hand, or about leaving it there as they retraced their way back up the steps to the quiet mountainside promenade. A squirrel scampered along the brick railing beside them, stopping every now and then to sit on his haunches and chatter at them.

"I think he's doing a little begging," Roarke chuckled. "The small critters around here are quite tame."

"Next time I'll remember to bring something," Tisha promised the persistent squirrel.

He followed them for several more yards before he finally decided there would be no handout and raced back the way he had come.

The pair continued past two older men seated at a concrete table, engrossed in a killer game of checkers.

"Would you like to sit down for a while?" Roarke motioned toward a bench on the side of the walk near the mountain.

Tisha slid onto the bench in silent acceptance, placing her bag and sketch pad on the table. She felt sublimely content. The traffic on the street beyond and below them was muffled by the lush foliage of the trees, just beginning the transformation from summer to fall. She watched with idle contentment as Roarke reached behind them to pluck a late-blooming buttercup and twirl it in his fingers. Then his dark gaze moved over to her face to study it with silent thoroughness.

"I wonder if you like men," he mused.

She gave him a puzzled look. One corner of his mouth lifted in a smile as he noticed her confusion.

"I think we'd better find out," Roarke murmured, reaching out with one hand to tilt her chin while he held the buttercup beneath it. The clear skin of her throat reflected the luminous yellow color of the wildflower. "Umm, that was a very positive reaction!"

"No, no—that's supposed to determine whether I like butter. Very scientific."

There was no coyness in her eyes as she met his gaze and remembered the game she had played as a child.

"What about you?" she teased easily, putting her hand over his to move the buttercup under his chin.

"I love butter, but the doc says I shouldn't. Men over thirty have to watch their cholesterol." He smiled, and Tisha became suddenly conscious of how close his face was to hers, and the way his gaze was resting on her mouth. "So what does the buttercup say?" he asked.

"Too much beard!"

She fought off a slight breathlessness as she removed her hand from the warmth of his and put a safe distance between them. "It's all right," she declared airily. "A little stubble is very attractive. Nice and scratchy." She wanted—really wanted—to run her hand along his jaw, but she stopped herself.

"Glad to hear it," he said quietly, a trace of sensuality in his smile.

Tisha drew her foot onto the bench and wrapped her arms around her knee to study the scenery.

"It's very peaceful here, isn't it?"

"I actually think you're enjoying my company," Roarke joked.

"I can be pleasant when I want to." That was as far as she wanted to go—being pleasant. Right now she was far too physically aware of him.

"Not to mention beautiful."

"Oh, stop it."

"Are you afraid of compliments?"

Her eyes widened at his question. "No. I just don't trust them. Or you."

"Hmm. But I am trustworthy."

"Prove it," was all Tisha said. She didn't know why she felt the need to challenge him.

"Okay. Have dinner with me Friday night."

Tisha recoiled slightly. "Why?"

"Why do you think?" he countered. "It's a test of my character. Not to mention there are some pretty good restaurants. Hot Springs wants to be your vacation destination."

"You really did memorize the Chamber of Commerce brochures, didn't you?"

"Look, Tisha, I'd like to take you out. That's about all there is to it."

"You sure?"

"At the moment, maybe not. You don't have to be so damn prickly all the time."

"Oh, excuse me," she said in a chilly voice. "Are you suffering because you haven't been able to conquer me?"

"Actually, no. You think a lot of yourself, don't you?"

If he could read her mind, Tisha thought, he would see that the exact opposite was true.

"I'm not some desperate college kid looking to get laid, Tisha. I'm a grown man. Does that bother you?"

"No, not at all." She tried to sound confident, but her voice shook. "But I do think your invitation isn't all that innocent. You're used to women falling into your bed at warp speed, aren't you?"

"I wish," he said wryly.

"I can figure out how it works." She raised her voice to a girlish squeal. "'Oo! Roarke Madison, you big hunky architect with the long, low car. Oo! Take me in your arms.'"

"How'd you know?" he grinned. "I get that all the time."

Tisha scowled. "Okay, I was exaggerating, but I don't think it's all that far from the truth."

"So you're afraid of the wine and candlelight routine, is that it?"

"I don't want to be seduced."

"The thought did occur to me," he admitted.

"Then we'll simply forget you made the invitation," Tisha declared, reaching stiffly forward to gather her bag and sketch pad.

He looked at her with infuriating calm. "If we're going out Friday, when should I pick you up?"

Exasperation furrowed her forehead as she glanced back at him. "Didn't you hear what I said? I'm not going!"

"Why? Since you specifically said that you don't want to be seduced, do you think I'm going to drag you under the tablecloth and have my wicked way with you?" he inquired with a satirical quirk of his brow. "I don't really believe all that nonsense you've been spouting."

"Well, I do!" she cried angrily.

"Give me a break. Why are you so afraid to go out with me?"

"I'm not!"

"Good. I'll pick you up at seven." Roarke rose lazily to his feet and gave her a mocking salute before walking away. Tisha's mouth was still working to find the words to protest even after he was too far away to hear.

Chapter Four

For three days she tried to come up with plausible reasons to cancel her date with Roarke Madison. A half dozen times, she reached for the phone, but backed away, knowing how he would poke holes in her weak excuses. Blanche was no help at all, believing Tish had accepted the date in an effort to make peace with her neighbor. Her aunt had been so delighted by her concession that Tisha had been left with no recourse except to go.

Roarke arrived precisely at seven o'clock, but Tisha was deliberately not ready. A half an hour later she walked into the living room, knowing full well that the shimmering dress she'd chosen accented the color of her eyes, sparkling now with the light of battle. It had taken nearly three-quarters of an hour just to coil her long hair on top of her head. The style was sophisticated, and she hoped it made her look less young. If nothing else, the numerous bobby pins that kept it in place would keep him from running his fingers through her hair. He was quite capable of making a move like that.

"I was beginning to think you were going to stand me

up." Roarke rose to his feet, impeccably dressed in a dark evening suit. Unhurried steps brought him to her side where he towered over her, dark eyes sweeping her in insolent appraisal.

"Now, why would you think such a thing?" Tisha asked sweetly.

His finger touched one of her jade earrings and sent it swinging as he replied in a husky murmur meant for her alone.

"Maybe it's that little pulse jumping in your throat. I don't think you're quite as poised as you look." For Blanche's benefit, he spoke louder. "We'd better be going."

Tisha turned to say good night to her aunt. It was difficult not to pull away from the hand that held her elbow.

"We won't be late, Blanche," she promised, brushing the woman's cheek with her lips.

"You two enjoy yourselves." Then with a wink at Tisha, she added in a teasing whisper, "Remember, twenty minutes and the porch light comes on!"

The color on Tisha's cheeks wasn't caused by blusher as she darted a speaking glance at her escort. "No need for that tonight." She knew there would be no lingering farewells outside the door.

"What was that about?" Roarke asked as he opened the car door for her minutes later.

"A family joke." She didn't meet his glittering eyes as she made sure her long dress was out of the way so he could close the door.

A golden sunset had painted the western sky with amber and cream colors, and Tisha pretended to be studying it when Roarke slipped behind the wheel.

"You don't think we're going to be reluctant to say good night when the evening is over?" he asked. "I've had my share of porch lights turned on by impatient parents. But that was a while ago."

"What? No shotguns?" she asked sarcastically.

"No, no shotguns." With a flick of the wrist, he started the motor and reversed out of the drive.

Tisha folded her hands primly in her lap. "I hope they'll hold our dinner reservation."

"I took the precaution of making it for eight o'clock," Roarke replied, a suppressed smile deepening the lines around his nose and mouth. "In case you took your time about dressing."

He seemed to anticipate her every move, she thought crossly. "You're probably more accustomed to women undressing for you, aren't you?"

"You could call it Madison's Law." He was definitely laughing at her attempts to belittle him. "What goes on must come off."

"Well, you didn't see fit to tell me where we were going," Tisha announced. "It's difficult choosing what to wear when I didn't know if we were going to a hamburger joint or a steak house."

"Obviously you realized I can afford the best."

"Don't brag."

"Sorry. Just thought I'd point out that I can do better than the boys you're accustomed to dating." His glance slid over her sophisticated attire. "I hope all that hair on top of your head doesn't give you a headache."

"Only you can do that," she retorted.

"I see. Well, you look great. Beautiful dress. And I like the high heels."

"They're not easy to walk in," she admitted. "But I promise I won't stumble. Don't want to embarrass you."

"The thought never entered my mind." His voice was as dry as the wind blowing off the Mojave Desert.

There was an odd quality to his voice that Tisha had never noticed before. It was that more than his warning that made her sit in silence for the rest of the drive. As usual, Roarke Madison's way with words made her edgy.

He seemed prepared to match fire with fire, and no holding back just because she was his date.

In the restaurant parking lot, Tisha deliberately stepped out of the car before Roarke could walk around to open the door for her. He caught up with her around the passenger side, but en route he bumped into the parking valet, a smirking kid in a red vest that was too big for him. Roarke gave him a five and the keys.

Big shot, Tisha thought. How easy it was for him to buy a little respect.

His eyes narrowed fractionally when he saw her standing there with a challenging look in her eyes.

"My, my. Aren't we independent. You look a little like the Statue of Liberty in that pose and that green dress," he declared.

"Thanks a lot," she said indignantly. Roarke only grinned, obviously pleased by his attempt at wit. The best thing to do was ignore him, although that wasn't going to be easy at a table for two.

The swish of her long dress had a regally haughty sound as Tisha swept ahead of him. Unfortunately her high heels made speed impossible, and Roarke was soon even with her, smiling at the disdainful expression on her face.

He moved ahead, opening the door and stepping through it, leaving Tisha to grab for the handle before it slammed in her face. Her cheeks were flushed with anger when she caught up with him inside.

Brown eyes flicked over her briefly, but long enough for Tisha to receive his message—she had wanted it this way. Before she could say anything, the host appeared and led them to their table. He was a handsome young man who informed them that his name was Brad along the way—the name du jour for all handsome young men, Tisha thought. She wondered why she wasn't out at a bar with a pack of Brads right now. But no. She had something to prove to Roarke.

They were barely seated when the cocktail waitress appeared. "A dry martini," Roarke ordered, completely ignoring Tisha and forcing the waitress to ask her preference.

"A strawberry daiquiri, please." Tisha instantly regretted the little-girl sound of her request, but she wasn't going to change it. She had no need to impress Roarke a second longer, because when it came right down to it, he wasn't worth impressing.

The look she shot at him was deflected by the shield of his menu. She opened her own and looked at it without really reading it. Fighting back her temper, Tisha set her menu on the table.

"Are we having fun yet?" she hissed.

Roarke lowered his menu to glance at her. "I'm not. How about you?"

"You might as well take me home, because I'm not going to put up with this." She moved her chair away from the table and started to get up.

"Sit down," he ordered, then repeated it in a more forceful tone. "Sit down or I'll sit you down. I'm not going to let you storm out of here. Bad manners."

And Tisha knew he was hateful enough to do just that. She leaned back in her seat and watched with indignation as he smiled slowly.

"As if you had any," she murmured. For all his relaxed air, she had the impression of a cougar, sleek and golden, waiting to pounce on his prey.

"If you don't want to act like a lady, I have no intention of being a gentleman," Roarke replied. "It's up to you whether we continue this war of insults or enjoy each other's company."

"It's impossible to enjoy your company," she spat.

His mouth tightened fractionally before he relaxed

it into a mocking smile. "Do you deny that our truce the other afternoon was pleasant?"

The waitress arrived with their drinks, giving Tisha an opportunity to think about her answer before she replied. Her fingers closed around the stem of the glass as she made a pretense of studying it.

"I won't deny that the afternoon was kinda fun," she agreed, flashing him a defiant look that was at odds with her reply. "You were a pretty good tour guide. But you overdid the charm."

"If you felt that way, why did you agree to go out with me tonight?" Amusement glinted in the look he bestowed on her.

"I didn't agree," Tisha reminded him. "You tricked me into accepting."

"Do you mean a mere man maneuvered an intelligent female like you into going out with him?"

Unsure of how to reply, she tapped her fingers on the laminated menu, then stopped when she realized he was looking at her.

"Nervous? I get the feeling you think men aren't worth the trouble," he concluded wryly.

"No. Men are wonderful. You, however, are trouble. Mostly because you seem to think you're perfect."

"Would you like me better if I was more humble?"

Tisha shook her head. "I don't think you could even come close to faking humility, Roarke."

"You have quite a vocabulary," Roarke chuckled. "And you always manage to pick the right word that will turn a compliment into an insult."

"How perceptive of you to notice." Her finely drawn brows arched mockingly.

"Shall we order now?" he inquired, picking up his menu again. "You might like the flaming shish kebab. It would match your temper."

"What will you be having? The bass? It doesn't say whether it's largemouth or not."

He ignored the obvious jab. "As a matter of fact, I think I'll have the shish kebab. I'm feeling carnivorous."

The meal was a disaster. Tisha ended up ordering a steak, but the succulently juicy cut of beef had no taste for her. She could have been chewing leather and wouldn't have noticed. Her only thought was to get the meal over with and return to her aunt's. She said a polite no to the server offering after-dinner coffee and then was forced to sit at the table while Roarke drank his.

"Are we ready to go now?" she demanded impatiently when he finally placed the empty cup in its saucer.

"I believe so." He smiled, and signaled to the waiter for their bill.

There were more moments of waiting while the man returned with the charge slip for Roarke to sign before he rose from his chair. Tisha walked swiftly toward the exit door, eager to be gone, but his fingers closed over the soft flesh of her upper arm and slowed her down.

"There's a small dance floor on the other side of the restaurant area. I thought we'd spend an hour or two there."

Her neck stiffened at his words as she glared up at him. "And if I insist that you take me home?"

"Ah, but you won't, will you?" He looked down with arrogant sureness. "You wouldn't want to deprive me of your vibrant company. Or should I have said volatile?"

"You should have said unwilling," she answered sharply, but didn't resist when he turned her away from the door and down the hallway to a dimly lit room. If he brought her home too early, she would have to discuss the evening with Blanche, and that was the last thing Tisha wanted to do. The second this date from hell was over, she was going to fling herself into the pillows to think it over in solitude.

Just why she could find him so sexy and so annoying at the same time was a puzzle that was worth figuring out. And she wanted to do it without one well-meant word of advice from anyone.

So she let Roarke lead her on.

The room was crowded with couples gathered around small tables illuminated by flickering amber candles. The atmosphere was intimate and sophisticated, and her shimmering dress drew admiring looks from the men and the women. For the first time that night, Tisha was glad she'd dressed up. Roarke walked with her to a small circular table. A combo was playing a selection of slow ballads from a raised platform in one corner of the room.

"Shall we dance?" Roarke asked after he had ordered their drinks.

What else could he say, she thought, but the line made her feel as if she was in a movie. "That's what we came here for, isn't it?"

"I have a feeling you're going to walk all over my feet," he murmured as they rose from the table together to traverse the short distance to the dance floor.

Tisha didn't tell him not to worry. She had no intention of getting that close to him. The hand that closed over hers seemed unnaturally warm compared to the icy temperature of her fingers. Her other hand wasn't so much resting on his shoulder as pushing against it.

She surrendered somewhat unwillingly to the pressure of his hand at the back of her waist, firmly guiding her into matching his steps. Tisha didn't look up into his face. That was just too romantic.

His arm tightened around her waist. "Relax," he said softly. The hand holding hers tightened, too, as he folded his arm around hers and drew it against the hardness of his chest. The action brought her closer to him . . . too close. She was thankful when the music ended and Roarke was compelled to release her.

At their table, he seemed disinclined to continue the conversation as he leaned back in his chair to study Tisha in quiet contemplation. She took a tentative sip of the drink she didn't want, then replaced it on its coaster. The small band was playing an upbeat tune. She tried to enjoy it, but she found the growing silence of her escort was too unnerving.

Fiddling with her swizzle stick, she glanced around, then at him. "You can't want to dance with me again," she declared, "so why don't we leave?"

"I think we should stay."

"Why?" Exasperation tinged the one-word question. "We can't just sit at this table and stare at each other."

The band had switched again to a slower ballad, and Roarke was standing beside her chair, pulling her to her feet. The arm around her waist kept her at his side until they reached the dance floor.

Once there, he turned her into his arms so quickly that she didn't realize what was happening until she discovered both his hands were linked together in the small of her back, molding her hips against his muscular thighs. Her own hands were ineffectually pressed against his chest to hold some part of her body away from him.

Tisha's fingers folded into tight fists as she fought the impulse to beat at his chest in an effort to be free. She lowered her head, staring at his white shirt, determined to endure the embrace without making a scene.

But she began to like it. The spread of his fingers on her back burned through the flimsy material of her dress. A liquid fire shot through her as his hands caressed the sides of her hips and Roarke drew her against the hardness of his body.

The exploring touch became a bit too daring, and Tisha could not stop herself from whispering, "Stop it!"

At the same time, she reached down to put his hands back on her waist. Instantly she realized her mistake. Without the leverage of her hands against his chest, he completed the embrace with one hand between her shoulders, bringing her against his chest.

"I don't like to dance this way," she told his collar while her fingers dug into the expensive material of his jacket sleeves.

"Why not?" he asked, nuzzling her ear.

"Because I'm a well-brought-up girl with old-fashioned morals," she muttered sarcastically. "I don't like embracing in public."

There was no escaping his touch. She could feel just about every muscle he had—he was strong—and an answering weakness in her own body.

"Don't be embarrassed," Roarke murmured. "Nobody is watching us."

The warmth of his breath played along her neck. "I don't care!" She tilted her head back to stop the trail of fire on her sensitive skin. Big mistake.

"Are you afraid of an unexpected kiss?" he taunted her. His lazy, half-closed eyes were focused on her lips.

"There's no such thing. A girl always expects to be kissed. It's only the where and the when she doesn't know," Tisha answered.

"We must answer those two questions, then." Warmly and briefly his mouth touched hers; then he was once again looking down at her, watching the hot color steal over her cheeks.

"Was that the best you could do?" she asked, surprised to find her breathing was shallow and uneven.

The glinting humor in his eyes took in the other dancers around them. "Under these circumstances, yeah," he answered smoothly.

"I didn't realize discretion was one of your virtues."

"I didn't know you thought I had any."

Right now, if she had to be absolutely honest, virtue

was the last thing on her mind. Just for a few precious
seconds, she gave in to the sheer sensuality of his embrace and the slow music that enveloped them and
made the world seem to disappear.

But the instant the song ended, Tisha wrenched herself free of his unresisting arms. She had just seated
herself in her chair when Roarke arrived at their table.
Instead of sitting down, he stood beside her chair and
touched her shoulder, smiling when she shrank away.

"I thought you wanted to leave, Tisha."

She was too overwhelmed by the sensations still rock-
eting through her body to answer politely. Keeping him
at a distance, physically and emotionally, was only going
to get harder. Tisha rose to her feet and didn't look at
him directly. She didn't want to take any chances that
he might change his mind.

The moon was a silver cartwheel in the dark sky,
sprinkled with silver stars that winked down at her as
she stared out the car window, determined to ignore
the man behind the wheel. Her skin still seemed to tingle with the memory of her body pressed against his. It
was a disquieting sensation.

"Guess I'm getting the silent treatment now," Roarke
said. "I don't know what to think, Tisha. Mind if I ask
what's going on?"

She answered in a tightly controlled voice. "I'm
tired. All I want to do is get home."

"It's been an exhausting evening," he agreed.

"It had its moments."

A low chuckle sounded from his side of the car.
"Well, that's not a rave review, but it's not a total slam.
Thanks."

"Interpret it any way you want to," she snapped.

"You'll fight me with your last breath, won't you?" he
murmured softly.

"You won't last that long."

Tall pines on either side of the country road blocked out the moonlight. Tisha watched the high beams light up the turn that led to Blanche's.

"As the song says, when an irresistible object meets up with an immovable one, something has to give," Roarke chuckled again.

"I suppose you classify yourself as an irresistible object." She hooted. "I have news for you. The strong, masterful type turns my stomach."

"From what Blanche tells me, that's a pretty good description of your father. Is that true?" he asked.

"You and Blanche seem to have spent a lot of time discussing me before I got here."

"She really loves you, Tisha. And I was curious, I admit it."

"The word is nosy."

"I saw your picture on her mantel, she told me you were an artist, and I was intrigued. I thought you were beautiful and"—he held up a hand before she could respond to that—"I apologize in advance for saying so. You made it clear that you don't like compliments."

"Well, I do take after my dad in that respect. He thinks being charming is a waste of time." Tisha gave Roarke a scathing look that was useless in the dim interior of the car.

"Don't women tend to marry men who resemble their fathers?" Roarke teased. "Guess that puts me out of the running."

"Huh?" His comment startled her. "How did we get from do-you-want-an-appetizer to talking about marriage?"

"Uh, I don't know," he said carefully.

Her muscles tensed as a quiver of apprehension attacked her. She had heard that theory before. As a child and teenager she had subscribed to it, thinking there could be nothing more wonderful than to marry a man as masculine and unconquerable as her father. Of course, that was before she had to put up with his controlling behavior for the last few years.

"That might be true for some women, I guess, but not me."

"Why?"

"Because the man I marry has to respect me as an individual and not tell me what to do as if I didn't have any sense of my own. He'll not only have to love me, but he'll have to trust me, too, and not . . . not . . ." Her hand waved through the air as she searched for the right word to complete her thought.

"And not turn on porch lights," Roarke supplied.

"Yeah." She nodded sharply, her hand returning to her lap. "Meaning that he shouldn't feel the need to check up on me."

"Is that the way your father treated your mother?"

Tisha sat very still. Of all the arguments between her parents, there had not been one triggered by jealousy or mistrust that she could remember. Their love for each other had been very strong and displayed in many ways.

"No, he never doubted her," she answered quietly.

"Your mother must have toed the line."

"My mother?" Tisha laughed. "She loved a good time just as much as Dad, but they had their good times together. She was as stubborn as he was, though—they argued a lot. But it never got bitter. I remember they would be in the middle of some heated debate and one or the other would burst into laughter and it would be all over. They had a one-in-a-million marriage."

"When did you lose your mother?"

"I was fourteen."

"Your father must have taken it very hard."

"He did. He wandered around the house like a lost soul for a long time," Tisha admitted. "Dad and I were very close after Mom died. But these last three years"—

she shuddered, remembering some of their unresolved quarrels—"he's been impossible to live with."

"Daddy's little girl grew up on him, and very beautifully, too," Roarke commented. "He sounds like he's afraid some good-for-nothing guy is going to take advantage of you, just because you're young. No doubt that's why he wants to get you married and out of temptation's path."

Another compliment, more speculation on her personal life, and advice she didn't need. Tisha sighed and snapped out of her reverie. She was going to have to have a talk with Blanche.

A light in the window of her aunt's home shone in welcome as she realized they were parked in the drive. She scolded herself severely for dropping her guard even for a minute. Roarke didn't need to know anything more about her past.

"One thing for sure, my father would never let me go out with a wolf like you," she declared, her hand reaching for the door handle.

"Wolf? Do people still say that?"

"He does."

"So I'm the Big Bad, huh?"

She shrugged. "You don't scare me." Tisha clasped the handle, but a second before she opened the door his fingers closed over her wrist.

"Not so fast!" His dark face was very close to hers, causing Tisha to draw back against her seat. "No self-respecting wolf would let a gorgeous woman like you get away without a good night kiss."

There was a drumbeat in her ears that she finally recognized as the pounding of her blood. "What a ridiculous line," she snapped, but her mouth felt unusually dry.

"That's right," he agreed smoothly. "But I got your attention. Do you or don't you want to kiss me?"

Tisha looked at him wide-eyed, noting the sexy

gleam in his shadowed eyes, and all rational thought fled. The fight went out of her. She wanted to say yes. She wanted him.

"Yes," she whispered.

"What did you say?"

"You heard me, Roarke."

His hand closed over her chin, lifting it to receive his kiss. It was deep and lingering, but also tender. The lack of force made it all the more potent and difficult to resist. When his mouth finally left hers, Tisha felt he had burned his brand into the softness of her lips. She exhaled a quivering breath.

So much for self-control. Roarke Madison got past every defense she had with unnerving ease. "Now may I go?" She was surprised that she was still able to talk.

His face was still close enough for her to see the deep smiling grooves around his mouth. In answer, he reached down and pulled the handle, opening the door. The interior light came on, glimmering on the golden streaks in his dark hair while Tisha slipped out of her seat and quickly slammed the door.

Billy Goat Gruff was between her and the house, but she scurried past. It wasn't the goat watching her that made her legs tremble, but the man in the car.

Since she'd started to date, Tisha had been kissed often, sometimes by boys experienced enough to arouse her a little. But their clumsy fumbling often missed the mark.

Right now she was feeling the white-hot heat of awakened desire. What was worse, it had been Roarke's kiss that had generated that discovery. And Tisha had always thought herself somewhat immune to just lust, too ruled by her mind to be betrayed by her senses. Not anymore.

Chapter Five

Tisha shifted her brush to her other hand and flexed the tense fingers that had been gripping it. Her shoulders sagged as she studied the half-finished painting. It didn't seem to matter what she did today, nothing turned out right.

"Problems?" Blanche asked, the heavy sigh from Tisha drawing her attention.

"Yes, a lack of talent," Tisha declared disgustedly.

Blanche laid her own brush down and, wiping her hands on a rag, walked over to her niece's side of the studio. Reaching into the pocket of her smock, she took out a package of mints and offered Tisha one.

"No thanks," Tisha said.

Blanche put a hand on her shoulder. "What's wrong?" she asked.

Tisha blew out an exasperated breath. "This bouquet is all wrong. It looks as if I'd stuck the violets on a straight line. I did the same thing with the daffodils earlier." Her shoulders moved in a deprecating shrug. "I can't do anything right today. I know what I'm doing wrong, but I can't correct it."

"You can't just learn what your mistakes are, Tish, or

you end up only learning mistakes and making them. Discover the right things you do so you can do them more often."

"Blanche, you're great." The scowl left Tisha's face, replaced by a rueful smile. "How do you come up with all those pearls of wisdom?"

"Common sense and experience." Blanche smiled, flicking back the natural white streak in her hair that had fallen forward over her dark brow. "Experience also tells me that you're tense about something. Sometimes tension can stimulate creativity, but in your case it's only causing frustration."

"What's your suggestion?" asked Tisha.

"Let's take the rest of the afternoon off." Blanche's brown eyes glanced at the skylight and the windows, continuing from ceiling to floor. "The light has gone anyway."

Tisha's own gaze shifted to the windows. Through the panes, she saw the rolling dove gray clouds that blotted out the early afternoon sun. The tops of the pines were gently swaying, yet there was nothing threatening about the clouds. But the good light was gone, as Blanche had said. Her aunt had returned to her easel and was busy cleaning up her brushes.

Tisha followed suit. All her effort had been wasted. Nothing she had done was good enough to sell or even give away. All because of the face that kept dancing in front of her eyes, the handsome, very masculine face with golden brown hair and velvet-dark eyes. It would have been so much better if she hadn't gone out with him the night before. She should have said no in the first place, or chickened out. Now she had to deal with the discovery that he had the ability to sexually arouse her.

"Tisha. Tisha, are you listening to me?"

With a start, she realized Blanche had been speaking

to her. "I'm sorry, I was daydreaming. What did you say?"

"I asked if you'd ever been to the Crater of Diamonds," her aunt repeated, a curious frown marking her forehead.

"No. A bunch of us were going to go once just for something to do, but we never got around to it. Why?"

"I thought we might drive over there this afternoon."

"To hunt for diamonds?" Tisha laughed a little, not quite able to visualize her creative aunt digging in the dirt.

"We could," Blanche agreed with a knowing smile. "But I was thinking of doing some character sketches. So I'd actually be working. No guilt."

"You're allowed to get out of the studio once in a while. That's nothing to feel guilty about," Tisha said.

"If you say so. I'm prone to thinking I shouldn't do this and that, and then I go right ahead and do it anyway."

Tisha nodded. If Blanche could feel guilty over trifles like that, she wasn't going to bring up the subject of her aunt's giving so much information about her to Roarke. Not now, anyway.

"I know what you mean." Tisha wanted to get out herself, eager to be distracted from her obsessing over Roarke Madison.

"Everyone has a bad day now and then. Don't let it get you down," her aunt said. The soothing tone was prompted by the desperate ring in Tisha's voice.

And Tisha could hardly correct her. Blanche liked Roarke and wouldn't understand Tisha's mixed feelings. She didn't even want to express her gratitude for the way her aunt hadn't asked any questions about last night, afraid she would slip up and blurt out the whole story, ending with that fabulous kiss.

"Don't change into anything too nice," Blanche called after her as Tisha started from the studio after straightening her things. "Diamond digging is all about getting grubby."

Tisha put on a pair of faded jeans and a scoop-neck top that was olive green. She secured her long hair with a scarf at the nape of her neck and then grabbed an equally faded denim jacket from her closet. She wandered outdoors to wait for her aunt.

It was midafternoon before Blanche turned her car down the graveled road carved out of a thick stand of pines. A light breeze whispered through the needles while an Indian summer sun peeped through a cloud and streamed down to lay golden bars on the ground. The stillness surrounding them was so profound that Tisha could almost imagine she and Blanche were the only humans for miles. The rows of cars in the parking lot came as something of a surprise.

After paying the entrance fee to the state park, they followed the path into the cleared, plowed area. Unlike the other visitors who carried hand tools of claw rakes, small scoops, and pans, Tisha and Blanche were armed with sketch pads and pencils. Scattered over the field on each side of the hill were people, on their own or whole families together, painstakingly sifting through the dark brown soil for diamonds.

Tisha reached down and picked up a piece of ruled paper, covered in a child's careful print. It looked like it had been there a while, so whoever had written it wasn't around. She hoped the kid had remembered all the facts and rewritten the paper at home. She glanced at the familiar information, appreciating the studious thoroughness and careful spelling of the young author.

Millions of years ago there were volcanic eruptions near an area covered by water. The sudden cooling of the molten rock by water caused a tremendous pressure that transformed carbon particles into precious diamonds and crystals.

The volcanic pipe, this source of the only diamonds found in their natural state on the North American continent, is beneath my sneakers even as I write.

Tisha smiled at the note of drama and read on.

It is an exhilarating sensation to actually stand on a diamond mine. The first discovery of diamonds in the 1900s started a rush that threatened to equal the California gold rush. But intrigue cloaked its past. Attempts to commercially mine the diamonds were met with frustration, mysterious fires, and even murder before the State of Arkansas finally purchased the Crater of Diamonds outside of Murfreesboro and turned it into a State Park. The End.

She folded the report and stuck it in her pocket. Blanche was already seated on the ground with the trunk of a tree for a backrest and her sketch pad propped on her knees. But Tisha was too caught up in the atmosphere of the place to settle down. Instead she wandered down a furrow in the field to where an elderly, gray-haired man was standing hip-deep in a pit he had dug. He was going through the soil, particle by particle, before discarding it on the growing mound beside him.

"Any luck?" Tisha called to him.

He glanced up, blue eyes shining above round smiling cheeks. "Nope!" he answered, tossing the panful of earth away and reaching into his pocket for a handkerchief to wipe his brow. "'Course, it would help if I knew what the heck I was looking for!"

"That would be my problem, too." Tisha laughed.

"They say if you find one, you can't mistake it for anything else but a diamond." He leaned back to rest a moment, obviously welcoming the break and the prospect of a friendly chat. "The problem is to remember that they don't just come in white. There's some that are tinted yellow, brown, pink, and tan. Not to mention they have black diamonds here, too. But when it's a case of finders, keepers, you can't resist looking. A person might find one."

"I suppose it's a question of whether Lady Luck is sitting on your shoulder or not." She smiled.

"When you realize that nearly all the people out here are amateurs, with maybe a little experience as rock hounds, luck plays an important part." He nodded in agreement. "But somebody is always finding one."

"I hope today you're that somebody."

"The fun is in the looking." He picked up his shovel.

Tisha wished him good luck and walked farther along the furrow, smiling as she found herself studying the ground in anticipation that a diamond crystal might be lying on the top. The diamond fever was contagious, she decided. Just as compelling was the memory of the man's face, roundly smiling and containing such a love of life. While it was still fresh, she found a comfortable rock to lean against and opened her sketchbook.

In her first attempt, she couldn't quite capture him and flipped to a fresh page. This time there was no hesitation in the strokes of her pencil as it flew across the paper. Adrenaline seemed to be pumping through her, accenting the exhilarating feeling that she was doing the best portrait she had ever done.

"That's excellent, Tisha!" Blanche exclaimed. While Tisha had been engrossed in her drawing, her aunt had walked silently to stand beside her. "You've captured Roarke exactly."

The tip of Tisha's pencil stopped in midstroke. The face staring back at her from the paper was Roarke Madison. His mouth was almost curved into a smile.

There was that lazy, arrogant look in his eyes. Just how she had turned a kindly old guy into him, she didn't know. Her stomach constricted into a sickening knot as Tisha realized what she had done.

Blanche paid no attention to her niece's silence as she began enumerating the successful qualities of the drawing. "That hint of a smile is such a great indication of his superb sense of humor. And you've caught the strength and determination in the jawline. I'm amazed, though, at the way you captured the self-assurance that's so much a part of his character."

"He's arrogant!" Tisha slammed the book shut and scrambled to her feet.

Blanche's brown eyes twinkled with amusement. "He does make your blood run hot, doesn't he?"

"No!" The denial was out before she realized her aunt was referring to her temper and not desire. Red flames swept into her cheeks. "I mean, yes, we rub each other the wrong way."

"The chemistry between two people can be compatible or combustible," her aunt said good-naturedly. "With you and Roarke, it's obviously the latter."

A heavy sigh shuddered through Tisha. "Combustible." That was an excellent word, she thought. She brushed back the tendrils of hair near her forehead and tried to seem calm. She succeeded in looking miserable.

"Don't be so glum," Blanche teased gently. "You can't help it if you don't like him."

Her troubled eyes turned to the older woman's face. For a moment Tisha hesitated; then the overwhelming need to confide in someone took over.

"Roarke Madison is everything I don't like in a man—arrogant, argumentative, domineering. Yet,"— Tisha swallowed nervously—"yet he makes me feel more like a woman than any other person I've dated."

There was a significant silence as Blanche studied

the embarrassed flush on her niece's face. "Are you saying that you find him sexually attractive?"

"It doesn't make any sense, I know." Tisha shifted uncomfortably, her fingers tightening on the sketch pad. "I don't like him or respect him. He seems to think that women shouldn't talk back, ever."

"That's rather a harsh judgment," Blanche murmured in an effort to placate her niece. "And I noticed you can hold your own around him. That argument you two had was quite entertaining."

"Maybe to someone watching it. Not if you were in the middle of it," Tisha said. "Aunt Blanche, he thinks being the Big Bad Wolf is more fun than anything. I get the feeling that he's one of those predatory males who charm you into letting your guard down, then rush in for the kill."

"Now you're being melodramatic. I think that's a bit much, don't you? That's not the Roarke I know."

He's not trying to get into your pants, that's why. Tisha didn't dare say that out loud. Blanche wasn't that open-minded—and her aunt was right about her being melodramatic.

"You've hardly had any time to get to know him," Blanche continued. "Aren't you afraid you're being too hasty in condemning him?" Before Tisha could voice her denial, Blanche went on hurriedly but calmly, "I'm not saying that you're wrong, honey. Your first meeting with him didn't go too well—he smacked into your car before you ever knew that he was my friend. You didn't trust him from the start, and I don't think that's changed."

"I think he would have made me bristle no matter how I met him," Tisha declared.

"That could be true." The older woman's speculative gaze rested on Tisha. "But it bothers you more to know he arouses you physically, doesn't it?"

Tisha's mouth tightened, and she didn't reply. The

subject made her uncomfortable, to say the least. She'd brought it up, though.

"I wish I knew what to tell you," Blanche sighed, putting a comforting arm around her niece's shoulders. "It's something you have to work out for yourself, I guess. What do you say we start for home now? We can stop along the way to eat and save us the trouble of fixing a meal tonight. I know a great little restaurant that serves delicious catfish and hush puppies."

"That sounds fine," Tisha agreed, trying to match her aunt's cheerful voice as they jointly turned to retrace their path to the parking lot.

"Looks like we're going to get some rain after all." Blanche studied the overcast sky, now a menacing shade of turbulent gray. "I don't know which I dislike more, driving after dark or driving in the rain."

"We don't have to stop to eat. It wouldn't be too much trouble to cook something at home," Tisha said.

"We need the night out," Blanche insisted. "Besides, I think the rain will hold off until later this evening, and there's lots of time before the sun goes down."

On the drive back, it seemed as though her forecast was going to be correct, but when they walked out of the restaurant, it was into a downpour. Blanche willingly accepted Tisha's offer to drive the few miles to the house.

Although the sun wasn't officially down, the black clouds made it appear as dark as night. The rapid lashing back and forth of the windshield wipers couldn't keep up with the onslaught of the heavy rain. Tisha was glad when they reached the lane leading to home.

"Do you think we dare stop at the mailbox to pick up our mail?" Blanche asked.

"I don't see why not," Tisha answered. "The road is firm, so we're not likely to get stuck. I can pull over close enough so all you have to do is roll down the window to reach the box."

"I was expecting some important letters," her aunt murmured. "You know that important is a code word for check, right?"

Tisha smiled.

"I haven't forgotten my starving artist days, and I never let them sit in the box overnight."

"It's no problem. We'll stop," Tisha assured her as the car headlights picked out the mailboxes by the side of the road, and Tisha slowed the car to a stop beside the first one.

The wind drove the rain inside the car as Blanche hurriedly rolled the window down and stretched her arm out to retrieve the mail, then quickly rolled the window up before she was completely drenched.

"Whew!" She laughed as she shook the water off her exposed arm. "Let's get home where it's warm and dry."

Thunder rumbled ominously overhead as Tisha maneuvered the car into the garage, thankful they had left the doors open, even if it was an invitation to burglars.

"I'm going to have to change out of this blouse," Blanche said after they had entered the house through the connecting garage door. "Why don't you get some hot coffee going?" She lifted the damp garment away from her skin and laughed. "It's unbelievable I could get so soaked when I only had the window down for a few seconds."

Tisha was already filling the coffeemaker with water. Her shoulders were stiff from the strain of peering through the driving sheets of water.

"Hurry up and change," she instructed her aunt, "or I'll drink this whole pot myself!"

A quarter of an hour later Tisha was snuggled up in the armchair in the living room, a fresh cup of coffee beside her as she listened to the rain hammering at the window while lightning flashed outside. Blanche had changed clothes and was sitting on the couch going through the mail.

"Oh, dear!" Blanche murmured suddenly.

Tisha glanced over and saw her staring at a fairly large package. "Is something wrong?"

"That stupid mailman put this package in the wrong box," Blanche sighed impatiently. "It's Roarke's, and he put it in my box instead of his."

"You can give it to him the next time you see him, can't you?"

Her aunt nibbled anxiously at her bottom lip. "I can, yes," she admitted. "Except the other night when he came to pick you up . . . well, honey, I was talking to him, and he mentioned that he had some plans he was supposed to have done by Monday, but he couldn't finish them because he was waiting for information on a new product. He was hoping it would come today. And now the mailman's given it to me."

"That's not your fault." Tisha couldn't muster any sympathy for Roarke's problem.

"No, but I know he needs it before he can finish. Would you mind running it up to—no, never mind." Blanche shook her head firmly without finishing the question. "I'll take it up to him."

"That's silly. You don't have to run that up to him in this storm."

"I know he needs it. And I know what it's like to try to finish something and not have the necessary tools or materials," her aunt insisted, rising to her feet.

"You're really going to take it up to him tonight, aren't you?" Tisha shook her head incredulously. "As much as you hate driving in this kind of weather?"

"I know how you feel about him, Tish," her aunt said as she reached into the closet for her raincoat and umbrella, "but he is my neighbor and a friend. He would do the same for me, regardless of what you think about him."

Tisha scowled as she realized she wasn't going to be able to persuade her aunt to change her mind. And her conscience wouldn't allow her to let Blanche drive in this kind of weather. As independent and self-sufficient as her aunt was, there were a few things that unnerved her when she got behind the wheel. Two were operative at the moment: a raging thunderstorm and the dark.

"If I can't talk you out of it," she said, reluctantly getting to her feet, "then I'll take it for you, Blanche."

"That isn't necessary."

"I think it is," Tisha asserted. "Now, put your coat back in the closet and give me the umbrella."

"I'll ride along with you."

"There's no need for both of us to go out in this storm." She bypassed the denim jacket that matched her jeans in favor of her water-repellent windbreaker hanging beside it in the closet. "You stay home and save me a cup of coffee."

"Are you sure you don't mind?" Blanche asked anxiously.

"I don't mind," Tisha breathed in exasperation, and slipped the jacket over her shoulders. "Where's the package?"

"Here." Blanche pushed it into her hands. "And, Tish . . ."

"Yes?" Tisha paused before walking through the kitchen to the connecting garage door.

"Roarke's house is something of a showplace. It would be worth putting up with his company for a few minutes just to see it." Blanche didn't allow time for Tisha to reply as she added, "Drive carefully."

Tisha thought to herself that the house would have to be pretty fantastic for her to stay. In her present frame of mind, she didn't want to be alone with Roarke. Her attitude toward him was much too ambivalent.

Until she was able to control or understand her feelings, the less she saw of him, the better.

The heavy downpour forced her to keep the Mustang at a crawling pace, but it handled well on the narrow road. She negotiated the quarter of a mile to Roarke's house, nearly missing the shrub-bordered driveway, her headlights catching it at the last minute. The rain was creating miniature rivers in the graveled road while the towering pines seemed like high walls closing in on the car.

Tisha hadn't realized the house was set so far back from the road. Tension closed her grip on the wheel, and she knew her knuckles were white. At last a light pierced the gloom, a beacon in the midst of a storm. She parked the car and switched off the engine. It took some tricky maneuvering to open the umbrella as she climbed out of the car and dashed through the puddles and driving rain to the overhang. The package was tucked under her jacket in an attempt to protect it from the downpour.

Impatiently she pushed the doorbell. With the growling thunder it was impossible to hear if it was ringing inside. The wind was beginning to beat the rain in about her legs, so Tisha grasped the large brass knocker and hammered it against the door. In seconds it was opened with Roarke framed in the doorway, wearing a cream pullover sweater and jeans that were faded in all the right places.

"Tisha?" His surprise was obvious as he peered under the umbrella. "I thought only ducks were out in this kind of weather."

"Quack, quack," she said sarcastically, fumbling under her jacket for the package.

"Okay, it was a dopey comment, but you're never at a loss for an answer, are you?" Roarke chuckled. His hand reached out to touch her shoulder and draw her into the shelter of the house. "You caught me by surprise. I didn't think you'd miss my company so much that you'd come out on a night like this."

He had automatically taken the umbrella from her, closing it and setting it against the wall, where a puddle of water formed almost immediately beneath it.

"I didn't come to see you," Tisha said bluntly. The package was free of her jacket folds, and she held it out to him. "This was put in Blanche's mailbox by mistake. She thought you would need it, so I ran it up here for her."

The door behind her was already closed. She would have preferred to hand him the package and run. After taking the thing and glancing at it briefly, he tossed it on a walnut table.

"Thanks for bringing it by, I'd been waiting for it. Blanche probably remembered." He smiled. "Let me take your jacket."

"I'm not staying." She backed away as he stepped forward to help her remove it. "I only came to give you the package. I'll leave now."

"You can come in by the fire and dry your clothes. I don't think your aunt will miss you if you stay for a few minutes."

"No, thank you," she repeated coldly. "I'll just get wet again when I go back out to the car."

"I just made cocoa. Sure you wouldn't like a cup?" he offered.

"No, I wouldn't."

"Mini-marshmallows on top," he said seductively. "Floating. Melting."

"Quit it."

"No. I insist." Once again his hand closed over her arm before she could elude him. "It wouldn't be neighborly to refuse my offer of hospitality in return for you driving through that storm to deliver the package."

"I really . . ." The protest died away as Tisha sensed

that she wasn't going to win the argument. "Very well, I'll have one cup. Then I'm going to leave."

"One cup," he said with a nod. He pointed to her right. "The living room is in there. I have a good fire going. You can dry out a bit while you drink your hot chocolate. By the way, we do offer a whipped cream option as well. So what'll it be, marshmallows or—"

"Whipped cream, please," she requested, moving away from him the instant he released her arm.

"Go on ahead. I'll bring the cocoa in a minute."

Hesitantly Tisha went the way he'd pointed, slowly walking through the opening he had indicated. Without his presence to distract her, she took in her surroundings, glancing back at the marbled foyer with its white tile floor and light walnut-paneled walls. Then her feet touched the thick, soft pile of a carpet, and she looked ahead.

A carved wooden banister set off the three steps down to a sunken living room carpeted in a vibrant shade of dark blue. Floor-to-ceiling curtains of nubby white covered almost one entire wall while the rest of the walls alternated between walnut paneling and areas of cream white.

Golden flames leaped behind an artisanal wrought-iron screen in front of the white stone fireplace in the center of an inside wall. Tisha moved to the middle of the room, fascinated by the artistic perfection of its interior. A large sofa covered in white velour faced the fireplace. The whiteness of its cushions was accented by large pillows in the same bold shade of blue as the carpet beneath her feet. On either side of the fireplace, facing the sofa, were two large blue-striped chairs flanked by occasional tables that gleamed brightly with the reflected light from the fire.

Blanche had told her Roarke's house was a showplace, but Tisha had expected something ostentatious.

Certainly nothing as cozy and inviting as this room was. The luxury was implied, not brazenly displayed.

"Take your jacket off and sit down."

She turned with a start to see Roarke standing at the top of the steps.

"If you want more light, there's a dial on the wall by the fireplace." He motioned with his head since he held a cup in each hand.

That was when she noticed the indirect lighting in the ceiling above. Now its dimness suggested an intimacy that Tisha felt the need to dispel, so she walked to the dial and brightened things up.

"Nice room," she commented in a tight voice. The adjective really wasn't enough to describe the glorious space and its welcoming comforts, but it was all she felt like saying.

"Thank you," he replied, accepting her compliment with a brief nod, but Tisha couldn't find any arrogance in the gesture. "You can move the chair closer to the fire if you like."

"It's all right," she assured him nervously as she slipped her arms out of her windbreaker and sat down on the edge of one of the blue-striped chairs. She started to lay the jacket across her lap.

"Let me hang that up for you," Roarke offered, setting her cup of cocoa on the table beside her.

Reluctantly Tisha gave it up. It was damp, and although it wasn't dripping water, she knew the logical thing to do was to put it somewhere where it could dry without getting something else wet in the process. She watched Roarke as he carried her jacket up the few steps before disappearing in the foyer. In seconds he was back. His presence seemed to complete the room, adding the vitality it lacked on its own. As he reclined his lean body on the couch, Tisha picked up her cup, concentrating on the swirling cream floating on top rather than meeting his gaze.

The silence began to grow. She swallowed nervously, the crackling of the fire adding to the tension in the air. Somehow she had to speak—about anything.

"Blanche told me your home was beautiful, but I never expected anything like this."

"What did you have in mind?" Roarke asked dryly.

Tisha glanced over at him, trying to read the veiled expression in his brown eyes. He seemed quite relaxed, yet there was tenseness there, too.

"I suppose I thought it would be . . . more showy," she replied, trying to sound casual.

"Showy as in gaudy? Or showy as in meant to impress?" He winked at her.

"I really don't know. I didn't think about it that much." Tisha shrugged, feeling annoyed that he had put her on the defensive. "Probably if I had, I would have expected a sofa that turned into a bed at the flick of a switch while the lights dimmed and soft music filled the room."

"How James Bond. Sounds like a perfect setting for a seduction scene."

"Something like that," she agreed, "but this"—she gave an expressive movement of her hand—"is much more subtle, although I'm sure it accomplishes the same purpose."

"Isn't it strange?" Roarke murmured. "I always looked on this as my home."

The bland comment curled Tisha's fingers as she carried the cup to her mouth. She heard the edge in his words and knew she deserved it. The hot liquid burned her throat as she tried to drain the cup dry so she could leave. She started when Roarke got to his feet in a lithe movement.

"Come on," he ordered. "I want to show you the rest of my home."

"Another time," she said quickly, setting her cup down and rising to her feet.

"No," Roarke said firmly, his tall form blocking her way to the steps. Tisha had no doubt he would try to stop her from leaving. "I want your impression to be complete."

She took a deep breath. "Very well."

"After you." His outstretched hand signaled her to precede him down the hall branching off from the living room.

Tisha complied, her shoulders squared as she led the way. A few feet into the hall were two doors directly opposite each other. Roarke opened the one on the right first, turning on the light switch to reveal a blue and green bathroom. Then he moved to the opposite side of the hall and opened the other door.

"This was meant to be the spare bedroom," he explained, turning on the light and waiting for Tisha to enter the room. "But I use it as an office and drafting studio."

She looked around for a state-of-the-art computer system—he had to have one—and saw two, the monitors glowing faintly in the half light. Shelves covered one wall with a desk and leather chair in front of them. An old-fashioned drafting table and stool occupied one corner while the rest of the furniture consisted of a leather sofa and a matching recliner. It all had a masculine, businesslike air.

Roarke didn't wait for a comment from Tisha as he led her out of the room to the door at the end of the hall. This time he offered no explanation as he opened the door and flicked on the light switch. As Tisha stepped in she realized why. This was the master bedroom—Roarke's bedroom.

There was the same thick blue carpeting on the floor, but this room was dominated by a large bed covered in a spread of shimmering Thai silk. Tisha found it difficult to swallow as her gaze remained riveted to the inviting expanse of the bed and the lustrous, otherworldly blue of the bedcoverings. She was painfully conscious of Roarke standing beside her.

"It's very nice," she said abruptly, turning on her heel to escape.

Her pace didn't slow up until she was in the relative safety of the living room. She glanced back at Roarke. From the look on his face, it was clear he knew instinctively that being in his bedroom made her nervous. He was a wolf. Big. And bad.

"I'd better be going now," she declared.

"You haven't seen the kitchen yet," he reminded her with a big, bad smile. "All women are interested in kitchens, aren't they?"

"Show me the kitchen, then," Tisha snapped.

The marble tile of the foyer led into the modern kitchen, spacious and efficient. The blue theme of the rest of the house appeared again in the small yellow and blue bouquets on the handpainted Provence tiles. Nice touch. Tisha was drawn to the homey essence of the room and even admired the custom-color fridge and restaurant-grade stove, but she refused to let it win her.

"Yup. Very nice." The coolness in her voice didn't seem to bother him.

"Glad you like it," Roarke said. He moved back in the entrance hall where he retrieved her windbreaker from the closet. "Please thank Blanche for me. I really did need what was in that package this weekend."

"I will." Tisha nodded, slipping on her jacket and reaching for the umbrella sitting in the corner. She tilted her head back to meet the measured look of his eyes. "And thank you for showing me around."

He reached around her and opened the door as if he was in a hurry to be rid of her. "My pleasure."

A stab of lightning illuminated the night as Tisha hurried out the door, more anxious to leave than he was to have her go.

Chapter Six

The puddles were deeper and the rain was still pouring down. If anything, the storm had increased in intensity as Tisha waded through the running water to her car. When she opened the door and ducked inside, she noticed the headlights of her car shining through the downpour. Just barely shining, which was why she hadn't seen them in her mad dash through the rain. Then they flickered and went out. Groaning aloud, she tossed the umbrella on the floor beside her and turned the key in the ignition switch. Nothing. Only the click of the key and no answering response from the engine.

Her hands clutched the steering wheel, and she rested her head against it. The battery was dead. She had left the lights on and discovered one of the major disadvantages of a classic car: they didn't go off automatically. That meant she had to go back and ask Roarke for help. And that thought didn't appeal to her at all.

With the protection of the umbrella over her head, Tisha sloshed back to the house and banged the knocker against the oak door. This time she didn't have to wait as long for Roarke to answer the door.

"I left the lights on, and my battery is dead," she announced as the door swung open. "Can you give me a jump?"

He stared at her for a brief moment. "I'll get my car out of the garage." Tisha nodded and started to turn away. "Wait," Roarke called her back. "There's no sense getting drenched trying to start it tonight. I'll give you a ride home and bring your car back in the morning."

Tisha started to argue, then changed her mind. "Okay. My shoes are wet. I'll meet you by the garage door," she said, avoiding the suggestion to come in that he seemed about to make.

She arrived at the double doors just as Roarke began raising them from inside. In seconds she was out of the rain, folding up her umbrella and climbing in the passenger side of the white car. She huddled in her corner while he reversed the car out of the garage and turned it down the lane. Lightning jagged across the sky, followed immediately by rolling thunder.

"Well?" Tisha muttered, glancing his way. "Aren't you going to say something about my stupidity?"

"Why should I?" His head turned briefly toward her. "You didn't leave your lights on deliberately. It was an honest mistake."

"But a stupid one," she said, more annoyed with herself than he was willing to be.

"We all make them. That's what makes us human." The words were barely out when they were followed by a muffled "Damn!"

Tisha pushed herself up in her seat, then felt the application of brakes and glanced ahead. Through the downpour, she could see the reason he swore. A large pine tree had fallen across the road, taking two smaller trees with it.

"Can you move them?" she whispered as she stared at the formidable barrier in the road.

"You can't be serious! Do I look like Superman?"

"Maybe we can push them out of the way," Tisha said, and fumbled for the handle of the door.

"Forget it," Roarke barked. He slipped the gearshift into reverse and backed to a wider section of the road and turned the car around.

"Where are you going?" she asked.

"Back to the house," he answered. "Where else? You'll have to stay the night."

"No way."

"The road is blocked. We don't have any choice."

"Oh, yes, we do," Tisha declared as the lights of the house came into view.

"What brilliant suggestion do you have this time?" He turned the car into the garage and switched off the engine as he brought his gaze around to her.

Her hand closed over the door handle and opened the door. "I'll walk home," she declared, scurrying out of the car before the arm that was reaching out for her could stop her.

She fumbled with the umbrella catch while her feet carried her swiftly out of the garage and into the storm. The answering slam of his car door only made her hurry more while the rain began drenching her hair and face.

"Tisha!" Footsteps sloshed through the rain after her. "Tisha, come back here!"

"I'm going home!" she cried.

Then the umbrella was taken from her hands as Roarke pulled her around. The sloppy ground made her stumble.

"I don't know what's going on with you, but I'm not going to let you walk home!" He gave her a slight shake. "Now, be sensible!"

"I am being sensible." She knew she was going to have a hard time convincing him of that the way she was carrying on. "I'm not going to stay in that house with you."

"Damn it, Tisha!" Water was pouring down both their faces, making spikes of their lashes and streaming down their necks. "I didn't put that tree in the road! You're acting as if I'd engineered the whole thing."

"It isn't so very far to my aunt's house. I've walked farther," she insisted.

"What happens if a tree falls on top of you, or you get hit by lightning?" he demanded.

"I wouldn't know by that point because I'd be dead, right?"

"Okay," he said, striving to sound calm. "For some reason, you have gone crazy. But I still have to answer to Blanche. So you're staying here tonight. Got that?"

"Absolutely not. You'd have to tie me up."

"Don't tempt me." He grinned—and she smacked him. He stood his ground, not even rubbing his reddened cheek.

"You deserved that," she said tightly.

"Maybe I did. But just tell me why you won't stay. You—ah—don't like the way I make cocoa? The carpet clashes with the drapes? What?"

"I just don't want to be alone with you."

He brushed the streaming water out of his eyes. "No need to play the trembling virgin. I didn't plan to ravish you, Tisha."

If her own temper hadn't been driving her, Tisha would have seen the building anger in Roarke's face. She would have noticed the tightening of the muscles in his jaw instead of the slick darkness of his rain-soaked hair. The look in his eyes made her heart race, getting up to tempo with the hammering rain.

"You know I wouldn't lay a hand on you," he muttered savagely. "And you know that I won't let you walk through a storm like this. So what the hell is this really all about?"

She couldn't tell him why or how he seemed more

dangerous than the violent weather when she didn't really know that herself. Especially when he reached out and took her in his arms for a soggy but mind-bendingly passionate kiss. She could fall in love with him without thinking twice. And that was the last thing she wanted to do.

"Roarke, let me go." It was a weak plea, almost lost in the crash of lightning, and Tisha couldn't tell the difference between the rolling thunder and the pounding of her heart.

The denim material of her jeans was plastered against her legs, sapping them of strength with cold dampness, but the crush of his body against her was sending out heat waves. Yet the violent assault of the elements was nothing compared to the effect his embrace was having on her senses. In the midst of the storm, they were isolated from it.

Her lips moved to breathe his name again as she stared into the darkly burning eyes. A hand touched her cheek, pushing back the dark streaks of wet hair that had escaped her scarf before the fingers curled around the back of her neck and Roarke drew her head upward to meet the mouth descending toward hers.

Hungrily Tisha accepted his fierce possession. A tentative response was not enough for the flaming ecstasy that consumed her. She responded to him, body and soul. There was nothing tantalizing about his kiss this time. He took her mouth with sensuous mastery. A desire to be closer to the straining muscles of his body sent her fingers around the buttons of his jacket, releasing them so she could feel for herself the throbbing of his heart. The rain seemed to increase the musky scent of his skin as Tisha twined her arms around him to force herself closer.

With a low moan Roarke wrenched his mouth away from hers and buried it in her neck, running a trailing fire along the pulsating vein in her throat. She trembled violently, understanding the driving need he felt for her because it was burning inside her, too.

"Roarke," she murmured achingly, turning her head to seek the hollow of his throat above the crew neck of his sweater.

But the movement of ultimate submission was rejected with a strength that left her stunned as he thrust her away from him. Rain glistened on her lips, still swollen from the sensual pressure of his kiss. She couldn't believe the coldness in his eyes as he glared across the distance that now separated them.

He'd kissed her just to show her who was boss, she realized. He didn't feel blazing desire; he hadn't thought that was the kiss to end all kisses. She'd been dumb enough to instantly read more into it, make it romantic . . . make it loving. Tisha swallowed her hurt and her pride with a racking sob and turned to flee.

"You aren't leaving!" His hand brought her up short again.

"After . . . after that, you expect me to stay!" Her voice pierced the night like the cry of a cornered animal.

"It was just a kiss. I don't expect anything. But you're staying!" Roarke snapped.

She'd been right. Tisha swung at him, and he dodged her, then regained his grip with ease. "You're soaking wet. Let's get in the house before you catch pneumonia."

"No!"

"Tisha, you're just not rational. And I'm going to catch pneumonia if I stay out here one minute more. Therefore, I am now in charge. And you are coming inside if I have to carry you over my shoulder, caveman style."

He tried to scoop her up, but this time she fought him like a wildcat, kicking at him, flailing her arm about his head until he caught it in a viselike hold.

While aiming blows at his legs, she tried to gnaw on his hand. Finally he gave up, while she tried to catch her breath. "I think it's time to try something else, don't you?" he said conversationally.

He rushed forward and picked her up by the waist, carrying her under his arm like a sack of potatoes to the house. The insults she strung together went unheeded, as did her struggles. Roarke didn't put her down until they were in the foyer and the door was shut behind them.

Her eyes were smoldering as she faced him, her fists rigidly clenched at her sides. He was between her and the door, and Tisha knew she couldn't get by. Except for the water trickling from his sodden clothes onto the floor, he looked as unruffled as if he had just walked in from the kitchen; whereas she was panting from her exertions to be free.

"You're crazy!" she spat at him. "Wait until Aunt Blanche hears about this!"

"Call her right now," he said mildly. "There's the phone."

She made a mad dash for it and poked in her aunt's number with a shaky finger . . . until she realized that the line was dead.

"You knew I couldn't!"

"Actually, Tish, I didn't," he said coldly. "None of this is my fault. I didn't topple the tree, call down the lightning, or make it rain."

"You kissed me," she said accusingly.

"Guilty on that score. I enjoyed it. How about you?"

"Don't try to distract me," Tisha said indignantly. "You—you wouldn't let me leave, and you brought me into—"

"Into my lair. Grrr. Guilty on that score, too." Roarke shrugged and slipped off his jacket. "Give me your windbreaker."

Tisha stared at him defiantly, and Roarke took a step

toward her. She hesitated only briefly before angrily ripping the wet windbreaker from her back and throwing it at him. The thin knit top was clinging to her like a second skin, accenting the rapid rise and fall of her breasts beneath the scooped neckline.

"Into the kitchen," he ordered.

Tisha stalked into the room, knowing Roarke was only one step behind her. She stopped at the table, her fingers closing over the back of a chair as she watched him walk to a cupboard and take out a bottle of whiskey and two glasses. The door leading to the garage was to her left. She could see it out of the corner of her eye and edged slightly toward it.

His back was still turned to her as he snapped, "Don't try it!"

"Try what?" Her gaze was innocent when he turned around.

The line of his mouth mocked her. "You'd never make it to the garage door, and don't tell me that's not what you were planning, because we both know it was." He poured a shot of single malt into each glass, then emptied his in one swallow before picking up the other and walking over to her. "Drink this."

Roarke held the glass out to her, but she pushed it away, seeing the liquid slosh out of the glass onto the floor. The muscles in his jaw were working fiercely.

"Somebody ought to take you over their knee," he muttered.

"Do you always talk to women like that?"

"Only the howling lunatics. They don't listen to reason."

"Your behavior hasn't been exactly reasonable. That caveman routine was the last straw. And to think I let you dance with me. The civilized exterior had me fooled. I really didn't know what you were like underneath."

His eyes narrowed. "I think you still don't know. Would you like to find out?"

She kept her gaze boldly riveted to his, her head tilted back defiantly. "If you come near me, I'll scratch your eyes out," she vowed.

"There goes my brilliant career," he chuckled, his dark blond head cocking arrogantly at her puny attempt to threaten him.

"What's the matter? Don't you think I could do it?"

"I think you'd try," Roarke admitted, walking over to set the mostly empty glass on the counter. "But don't worry, the only thing I'm interested in is getting out of these wet clothes."

"Don't let me stop you."

"I don't intend to." His gaze lazily moved to her. "Come on, you're going with me."

"Where?" Tisha took a hasty step away from him.

"To my bedroom," he answered flatly. "That's where I keep my clothes. You need to get out of those wet things, too."

"Into what? Your bed?" she taunted him.

"That's where I do my ravishing," he replied complacently. "Virgins wait in the line on the left, all others go right."

"Very funny. I'm not going."

"Do you want me to pick you up and carry you there?"

Tisha refused to let him tease her. She was jumpy as a cat. The combined effects of the powerful electrical storm and that incredible, unexpected kiss—then their crazy tussle in the garage, not to mention his alarming male aura—had her mind in a whirl as it was.

"I want you to stop trying to bully me. I want you to quit ordering me around. I want you to leave me alone!" she cried.

"Will you stop behaving like an outraged female? All I did was kiss you, and I don't even know why!"

"You don't?"

"No! Because you were there, I guess. And now you're here—and you're making me crazy! Just accept the fact that you have to spend the night whether you want to or not!" he roared.

Tisha was unprepared for the quick movement of his arm as he reached out and pulled her away from the chair. Before she could attempt to struggle free of the hold on her arm, he was pushing her away and ahead of him out of the kitchen door, through the foyer, and into the living room. The hands on her shoulders continued to propel her down the hallway to the door at the end. When she forced him to reach around her to open the door, she tried to bolt past him, but he caught her around the waist and flung her into the room.

She turned to face him, hands clenched and up, her legs apart. She moved hastily backward as he walked down the stairs, but he paid no attention to her poised kickboxing stance, and she felt a little foolish. He walked to the other side of the room.

"The bathroom is through that door behind you," he drawled, peeling off his sweater and shirt as he opened a set of folding closet doors. "A good hot shower will drive the dampness out of your bones."

"What are you going to do?" Tisha ventured in a guarded tone.

"The same thing." He glanced over his shoulder. "Only I'll be in the spare bathroom."

Sinewy muscles rippled over his broad naked chest as he turned toward her, a pair of dry slacks over one arm. A shiver trembled over her as he came nearer, but again he went past her to a tall chest of drawers.

"There's clean towels hanging inside," he said. "I don't have any shower caps, but your hair is already wet, so I don't suppose it makes any difference. And here." A pair of cranberry silk pajamas were thrust in her hands as he walked by. "They'll be too big, but at least they'll be dry."

"You wear them." She tried to hand them back to him.

"I don't mean to shock you, Red"—he smiled without amusement—"but I don't wear pajamas in bed. Those were a gift from someone who didn't know that. Now, go and take your shower."

She colored furiously. "I don't want to take a shower. I don't want your clothes. And I don't intend to go to bed!"

Roarke stopped and turned back to her, his jaw set in an uncompromising line. "Let's get something straight. You're going to take a shower if I have to strip you and shove you in there myself. And unless you want to walk around in a skimpy bath towel, you're going to wear those pajamas. Lastly, you're going to go to bed. No more arguments."

With his decree ringing in the air, he walked over to a smaller chest and took out a pillow and some blankets.

"What are you doing?" she demanded.

"Since I'm going to be sleeping on the couch, I thought I might like some covers," he answered shortly before a wicked glint appeared in his eyes. "Or were you going to offer to share the bed with me?"

"Absolutely not!" Tisha declared vehemently.

"Selfish," Roarke taunted. "I could make you sleep on the couch, you know."

"You're not going to make me do anything."

"Guess not." He waved her away. "Go and take your shower before you catch cold."

"I hope you get pneumonia and die!" she called after him as his long strides carried him up the steps to the hallway door.

"Thanks. You sleep well, too. G'night." The door closed with a finality that left Tisha with the impression that Roarke was glad to get her out of his sight. For a moment she stood there, the silence of the room closing in around her, muffling the growls of thunder outside the window. A shuddering chill quivered over her as the dampness of her clothes began to seep into her bones. However reluctantly, she had to admit that the tingling spray of a hot shower would feel good.

With the pajamas still clutched in her hand, Tisha walked into the bathroom, locking the door behind her. For several minutes she stood motionless under the pounding spray as it beat out the emotions that had strained her nerves to the breaking point. When she finally stepped out of the shower stall and toweled herself dry, she was feeling a little more human.

And a little more vulnerable to a certain very sexy man.

Going through the motions of hanging up her wet clothes, she told herself she was glad he had essentially rejected her. If anyone had tried to tell her that she could feel such lust for a man she didn't like, she would have called them a liar, but her own actions had proved her wrong. No matter how hard she tried, she couldn't wholly blame Roarke for the emotional storm that had broken open in the middle of the actual one.

She wrapped her long hair in a towel and piled it on top of her head as she reached for the pajama top. The silk felt cool and slippery against her skin, but the sleeves hung far below her fingertips. It took some time to roll them up to a point where her hands were free. With the buttons buttoned, the ends of the pajama shirt stopped a few inches above her knees. One glance at the pants and Tisha knew they were miles too long and too big around the waist, so she simply folded them back up and laid them on the counter.

Unlocking the door, she reentered the bedroom and walked to the bed, giving the lustrous Thai silk of the spread that covered it an absentminded pat. Roarke did have incredibly good taste.

She felt a little guilty for liking his things, liking his house. She picked a spot near the edge of the bed and sat in a cross-legged position with her back to the door. Unwrapping the towel from her head, she began vigorously rubbing her long hair dry.

A knock on the door was followed immediately by Roarke calling out, "Are you decent?"

"What do you want?"

But the door opened without an answer, and Roarke walked in. He still wore only a pair of jeans, but they were older than the pair he'd had on before. The light, faded color accented the deep tan of his chest. Tisha watched him from over her shoulder as he walked in.

"I brought you some cocoa to help you relax and get some sleep." His face wore an inscrutable expression as his dark eyes flicked over Tisha.

"Thoughtful of you," she said, turning away from him to continue rubbing her hair with the towel.

"There'll be a crew out in the morning to clear the road, and the phone line's already back up. I called Blanche to let her know I was putting you up for the night," he continued.

"I could have done that myself."

"I think the operative phrase is 'thank you.'"

"Thank you." Reluctant gratitude edged her voice.

"Do you want this cocoa or not?"

She could tell that he was still standing right where he'd stopped. It would have been quite simple to walk over and take the cup from him, but she didn't care to meet the indifference of his gaze.

"You can put it on the bedside table. I'll drink it later," she replied, keeping her head averted as she heard his footsteps moving down the stairs toward the bed. Through her long hair, she saw him walk by her without a glance. When he turned to retrace his steps, she asked, "Is there a comb I can use to get these tangles out of my hair?"

"There's probably one in the medicine cabinet."

"Thanks," she said shortly, uncurling a long leg from beneath her to slip off the bed.

She was halfway to the bathroom when his voice barked out at her. "Where's the bottoms of those pajamas?"

Tisha stopped and glanced back at him, surprised at the restrained fury on his face. "They were too big." She shrugged.

"Put them on," Roarke ordered.

"I told you they were too big!" she repeated, bristling at his bossy tone.

"And I told you to put them on. What are you trying to do—look like a sex kitten?" he jeered.

"Meow, meow," she said, adding a descriptive word for him that would've scorched his ears if she'd said it loud enough for him to hear. She glared at the tall figure standing at the steps. "The last thing I would try to do is entice you," she snapped. "I told you they were too big for me, but don't take my word for it."

Spinning around, she stalked into the bathroom and slammed the door, grabbing the bottom half of the pajamas from the counter. Fighting the long legs, she finally managed to draw the waist around her chest while her feet wiggled through the material to touch the furry carpet. She shuffled over to the door and swung it open.

"See what I mean?" she demanded, looking from Roarke to the baggy pajama pants crumpled around her feet.

"Roll up the cuffs," he growled.

"Fine." A sweetly mocking smile curved her mouth. "What do I do about the waistline? You're not exactly a size ten!"

"Improvise."

"How? And what's wrong with wearing only the top? It nearly comes to my knees. What's so indecent about that?"

Tisha took two angry strides in his direction. On the third the material tangled about her feet and catapulted her forward. Her arms reached out ahead of her to break the fall, but her hands encountered Roarke's arms and chest as he tried to catch her. Off-balance, they both tumbled to the floor, Roarke's body acting as a cushion as Tisha fell on top of him.

"Are you hurt?" he asked, gently rolling her off him onto the carpeted floor.

"No," she gasped, momentarily winded by the shock of the fall. "No thanks to you."

"Was I supposed to let you dive headfirst onto the floor?" he muttered.

"You shouldn't have made me put on these stupid pajama bottoms," she retorted, suddenly conscious of the heat of his body against hers. "I told you they were too big, but you wouldn't listen to me."

"Guilty, guilty, guilty," Roarke declared angrily, reaching over her to place his hand on the floor and lever himself upright.

His arm accidentally brushed her breast. Tisha drew in her breath at the intimate contact. That jellylike weakness spread through her bones as he turned his enigmatic gaze on her. He was propped inches above her, his bared chest with its curling dark hairs close enough to caress. The desire to touch him came dangerously near the surface, and Tisha turned her head away, a solitary tear trickling out of the corner of her eye.

"Tisha—"

"Oh, go away and leave me alone!" Her voice crackled slightly on the last word.

His fingers closed over her chin and forced her head

around to where he could see the angry fire blazing in her eyes.

"I can't stand this," she said hoarsely.

"Tish, Tish—what are you talking about? I still don't understand what happened."

"Neither do I."

His gaze was focused on her parted, trembling lips. She brought up her hands to ward him off. The instant her fingers touched the burning hardness of his naked chest, Tisha knew her body was going to betray her again. When his mouth closed over hers, she succumbed to the rapturous fire that swept through her veins. The hands that had moved to resist him twined themselves around his neck while his hands trailed down to her waist, deftly arching her toward him.

Her nerves were attuned to every rippling muscle of his body as they responded to his searching caress. It was a seduction of the senses, in which she knew nothing but the ecstasy of his touch. An almost silent sound of feminine bliss came from her throat as he pushed the pajama top away from her shoulder and treated her skin to erotic little nips. Then his mouth sought out the hollow of her throat.

"You're a witch," he murmured against her lips, then moved to nibble her earlobe. "A beautiful rainy day witch."

Tisha moved protestingly beneath him, her breath stolen by his ceaseless caresses yet needing the fire of his lips against hers. Her hand began a sensuous exploration of his back and shoulders, their nakedness inflaming her desire. His mouth moved over hers, lingering for precious seconds before he raised his head, his hands closing over her arms and pulling them away.

In one fluid movement, Roarke was on his feet, grasping her hands to pull her to his side, leaving the oversized pajama bottoms on the floor. The lashes of her rounded green eyes raised, and she looked at him, afraid of the cold rejection of before, but this time finding smoldering fires that threatened to blaze again.

"Do you have any idea what you do to a man?" he asked. His fingers closed over her shoulders, holding her in front of him while keeping her safely away.

Tisha was still trembling from the shock waves he had produced and could only look at him numbly. With one part of her mind, she seemed to sense the effort he was making to control his emotions.

"Drink your cocoa and go to bed."

"Hey . . . I'm not five years old, Roarke."

"I know that." A finger lightly touched her lips as he walked determinedly toward the door. He stopped midway up the steps and looked back. "When I leave, put the chair under the doorknob. There isn't any lock."

"I trust you," she whispered.

"Thanks," he answered dryly, "but at the moment I don't trust myself, so do as I say."

"Yes, Roarke." Tisha nodded, surprised by her own meekness.

"Another thing"—his gaze moved possessively over her—"there's no need to bother wearing the rest of those pajamas. I already know what you look like without them."

She smiled shyly, not wanting him to leave, but afraid to have him stay. "Good night."

"Good night, Tisha."

"Sleep well."

"More than likely I'll go quietly out of my mind." A lazy smile moved across his face as he opened the door. "And don't forget about the chair."

"I won't," she promised. But she did. Somehow she knew it wouldn't be necessary.

Chapter Seven

Tisha rolled over on her stomach, burying her head in the pillow to fight off the wake-up call of her conscious mind. A deliciously warm sensation of contentment was enveloping her, and she didn't want to break its spell. An eyelid flickered open, and she focused on the cranberry silk material covering her arm.

The events of the night before came back to her in a vivid rush. Roarke had aroused her sexual curiosity and her passion, then had left without satisfying either. Was she glad? She blinked open both eyes as she shifted onto her back and stared at the sunlight sifting through the curtains. Yes, she decided, she was glad. There was no doubt in her mind Roarke wanted her. Physically. Whether there was anything more to it, she didn't know.

A little sigh escaped her lips at the unanswerable question. For the moment she didn't want to try to figure out the whys and wherefores. There was time enough for that later. At the moment she wanted only to find Roarke, to see if the bright light of day would change her reactions toward him and vice versa.

A little reluctantly she slipped out from under the covers and padded into the bathroom. Her clothes from the night before were dry, and she hurriedly put them on. It took several minutes to untangle her hair, and the static electricity in it kept it from lying neatly about her shoulders the way she wanted it to. The scarf that had held it back was wrinkled from last night's drenching. A search of her pockets revealed a pair of hair elastics, and Tisha divided her hair into pigtails.

Softly humming a happy tune, she hurried from the bedroom, listening and looking for a sign of Roarke. An overhead light shone from the open doorway of his den. She slowed her steps as she neared it. When she glanced into the room, she saw Roarke slouched over the drafting table, his head cradled in his arms and a blanket thrown over his shoulders. She stopped humming and walked quietly into the room.

She felt a compelling urge to push back the wayward strand of light brown hair that had fallen over his forehead. In sleep he looked less formidable and, if possible, even sexier. As her hand closed over the railing to guide her up the steps, Tisha saw him move. The carpet had muffled the sound of her footsteps, and she knew he couldn't have heard her enter. Still he wakened, propping his hands up with his elbows while they wearily rubbed his face. Any moment now he would notice her presence in the room.

"Good morning," Tisha greeted him brightly.

He turned a scowling face toward her.

"Is it?" he mumbled testily as he stiffly moved his protesting shoulders.

"It's not raining," she added hesitantly.

But he seemed not to hear her. His large hand rubbed his mouth and chin. "I don't suppose you've made any coffee," he grumbled.

"I just got up."

"Well, go and make some."

The fragile bubble of happiness burst. Except for one frowning glance, he hadn't even looked at her.

"Yes, master. I will make coffee." Her sarcasm seemed to be lost on him. "But only because I would like a cup," she declared icily. "If you want one, you can come out to the kitchen and get it!"

She left the room, but not as quietly as she had entered. A few slammed cupboard doors later, she'd filled the coffeemaker with water, found the coffee, turned the thing on, and was sitting stiffly in a chair listening to the bubbling sound.

The coffeemaker heaved its last dying sigh when Roarke entered the kitchen. Without looking directly at him, Tisha noticed he had shaved, restored his hair to some semblance of order, and donned a linen shirt instead of a tee over his jeans.

"The coffee's done," she announced, rising to pour herself a cup and carrying it over to the table, but she didn't offer to pour him one.

"Do you want juice, toast, or anything?" he asked.

"No, thank you," she answered coldly.

"Well, don't bite my head off," Roarke shot back.

"Don't snap at me, then." She darted him an angry glance. "Just because you sat up all night working instead of going to sleep doesn't give you the right to take it out on me."

His gaze pierced the air between them. "The couch happens to be five and a half feet long. My driver's license says I'm six feet two. You try sleeping in those circumstances."

"It's not my fault." She shrugged airily.

"As I recall, you were sleeping in the only available bed," he pointed out, leaning against the kitchen counter while he sipped at the steaming coffee in his cup.

"You could have—"

"I could have what?" he asked quietly.

Tisha rose hastily to her feet, hot color washing over her cheeks as she moved past him to refill her cup. "You could have slept in the bed, and I could have taken the couch," she finished.

He set his cup on the counter and reached out to halt Tisha in front of him. That feeling of sensual hyperawareness returned as his eyes wandered over her.

"Or I could have slept in the bed with you," Roarke murmured.

"I didn't say that," she breathed.

His hands moved to her waist, drawing her closer to him. "But I could have stayed with you, couldn't I?"

A thrill of longing quivered through her at the husky, caressing quality in his voice. Her head bowed in mute affirmation of his statement.

"And if I had," Roarke went on, "this morning you would have been trying to find a way to attach strings."

A cold chill touched her heart. "Is that why you didn't?" she demanded, tossing her head back with injured pride. "Because you were afraid I would turn into a clinging female?"

"Whoa." He held up the hand that wasn't holding the coffee cup. "Don't go crazy on me again, okay?" he said. "Once was enough. I think I know why you did, though. I got too close—and I'm way out of your league."

"What's that supposed to mean?"

"You're inexperienced."

"Since you prefer experience," she said, ticked off by his casual dismissal of her, "why did you bother to kiss me? Were you just making sure you hadn't lost the knack?"

"No." Roarke shook his head gently. "When a female becomes all soft and yielding beneath his touch, a man's reaction is instinctive. And for all that you have a smart mouth, Red, you're a very desirable woman."

"At least you don't find me totally objectionable," she snapped.

"I don't find you objectionable," he assured her calmly. "The truth is the exact opposite."

"You're talking in circles. I don't understand anything you're saying," she cried. "One minute you say I'm too naïve for you, and in the next you imply that you want me. Can't you make up your mind?"

"Yes, I can." His tone became more intimate. "But what about you? How do you feel toward me?"

"At the moment . . . I hate you."

"Okay. Clear enough. Well, that's a start."

"What?"

"I don't think you really hate me, Tisha. You're confused. Maybe we both are." His hand moved in a suggestive caress over her hip. "Yes, last night you would have allowed me to make love to you."

A sigh broke from her lips as the anger dissolved away. Her troubled eyes sought his face, a helpless whirl of dismay in her own expression.

"It's crazy, isn't it?" she murmured. "I hate you and I—" The rest of the sentence became stuck in her throat.

"Careful," Roarke warned. The teasing glint left his eyes. His hands automatically tightened, drawing her to him until the muscles of his thighs met the contact of her softer, feminine form. "I might hold you to any admission you make."

Tisha wasn't sure what that admission would have been. Love couldn't happen this quickly, or allow her to feel such burning antagonism toward him.

"In one way or another, Roarke," she spoke softly, "we're a combustible combination."

"I couldn't agree with you more."

The smile on his face amplified the satisfaction in his eyes as his hands moved up her back, pulling her against him while his mouth started another fire against hers. The contact was tenderly possessive and intimate, and ended too soon. But the comforting warmth of his arms held her against him as he nuzzled her hair.

"Good morning, Tisha. I don't believe I've said that yet, have I?" he murmured.

"No." She smiled against his chest, no longer caring about her ambivalent reactions to him. She tilted her head back to look at him. "Are you always such a grouchy old bear when you get up in the morning?"

"Only when I've had a girl running around half-naked in my bedroom the night before." He grinned. The look in his eyes turned her legs to rubber.

There was a click of a door latch, and Tisha felt Roarke stiffen beside her. With a curious turn of her head, she glanced toward the door connecting the kitchen with the garage. Shock held her motionless for a full second.

"Dad!" Her voice was a guilty squeak as she wrenched herself from Roarke's arms. She stared into the cold fury of her father's face, but he looked only at the man beside her. "What are you doing here?" she gasped.

His eyes shot her a look of chilling disgust, and Tisha knew with scary certainty exactly what he was thinking. Red flames of embarrassment scalded her cheeks.

"Dad, it's not what you think," she rushed. "I had to stay last night because there was a tree blocking the road and . . . and I couldn't walk home in that storm."

"That's funny," he murmured sarcastically. "There wasn't any tree in the road when I drove up here."

The challenge in his eyes was unmistakable as he glared at Roarke, who was still leaning calmly against the counter, his gaze frankly meeting the open hostility of her father's.

"A road crew was supposed to clear it this morning." Her hand moved nervously around her throat. "They . . . they must have already done it."

Blanche appeared in the doorway, her sympathetic

eyes seeking Tisha out immediately. "I'm sorry, honey," she murmured. "He arrived this morning. I couldn't stop him." Her hands were upraised in a helpless gesture.

"Your name is Madison, isn't it?" Richard Caldwell demanded, and Roarke only nodded in reply. "Patricia, I want you to drive Blanche back to the house."

"Dad, stop this!" she cried. "You're acting like some Victorian father. All you need is a shotgun! Nothing happened last night. Roarke, explain to him!"

"Yes," her father challenged, "I'm sure that intimate little scene I witnessed when I walked in was only a demonstration of your brotherly affection for my daughter!"

"It wasn't intimate!" Tisha protested. "He was only holding me in his arms."

"I told you to leave!" The thread holding her father's temper snapped.

"No!" She planted herself firmly in his path. "Not until you accept our explanation."

"I don't need your explanation! I knew what had been going on when I walked into the room!"

"For heaven's sake, Dad, I'm your daughter. Won't you listen to me?" Despair and frustration made her voice tremble. Then her mouth turned down in a grim line. "Or is it because I'm your daughter? Because you know what you would have done, back in the day?"

A glimmer of guilt flickered across his face before he quickly squelched it. "You don't know what you're talking about!" he blustered. "And don't try to sidetrack me."

"I'm not trying to sidetrack you. I'm trying to keep you from making a fool of yourself and me!"

Richard Caldwell stared at her for a long minute, resisting the plea in her tear-filled green eyes. His hard gaze drifted toward Roarke, who was still quietly watching the proceedings.

"Mr. Madison and I are going to have a private talk," her father declared in a controlled tone. "I want you to get in your car and go home with Blanche."

"I can't. The battery is dead," Tisha retorted, maintaining her mutinous stand in front of him.

"Then take my car!" he snapped.

She folded her arms and continued to glare at the tall, dark-haired man. "I'm supposed to be the wronged party in this farce. Surely I'm entitled to listen to this 'private conversation'?"

"You'd only get hysterical," he stated forcefully.

"Oooh!" The angry sound was ripped from her throat. "You're the one who can't discuss things intelligently! You weren't even here last night, yet you're so positive you know everything that happened!"

"I will not tolerate your sass any longer!" her father exploded. "You will leave this house now!"

"Now who's hysterical? Actually, you could be bordering on homicidal! I am not leaving you here alone with Roarke!" Tisha exclaimed, raising her voice to match the level of her father's.

There was a slight sound of movement behind her; then a hand was touching her waist. "I'm capable of fighting my own battles, Red," Roarke drawled in an amused tone.

"I was beginning to think you were the type that hid behind the nearest female," Richard Caldwell jeered.

Over her shoulder, Tisha saw the sudden narrowing of Roarke's eyes, although his expression remained outwardly bland. From her own experience, she knew Roarke was a formidable opponent. She had never been able to get the better of him, even though there were times when she thought she had.

"I appreciate your concern for your daughter, Mr. Caldwell," Roarke replied with amazing calm. His glance slid down to Tisha with a reassuring glint in the depths of his brown eyes. "And I quite agree that it will be difficult to discuss this rationally with her here."

She gasped at the ease with which he switched sides. "I am not leaving!"

"Go on." He gave her a little shove. "Take Blanche home. I'm certain your father and I can come to an understanding."

This time she turned her rebellious stand to him, tilting her head back to glare at him defiantly. "I won't go."

"Do what your dad says," Roarke stated in a very quiet and very firm tone.

"And if I don't, what will you do—pick me up and carry me out to the car?" Her voice trailed away on the last word. The look in his eyes reminded her of last night when he had unceremoniously carried her into the house.

"If necessary," he murmured.

Tisha was defeated and she knew it. One glance at her father saw the glimmer of respect in his eyes at the authoritative tone of Roarke's voice. He would probably applaud as Roarke carried her bodily out of the house if she continued to resist.

The fury was divided equally between the two men. "I think both of you are high-handed, arrogant jerks! I'm leaving, but it's because I can't stand the sight of either of you!"

She marched out of the kitchen with her aunt trailing quietly along in her wake. At her father's car, she paused, then walked around to the passenger's side.

"You drive, Blanche," she commanded tightly. "I'm so mad I'd probably run us into a tree."

Her aunt nodded and got behind the wheel. In silence she started the car and turned it down the lane. Hot tears of frustration scalded Tisha's cheeks.

"I've never been so humiliated in all my life," she

muttered. "Why did Dad have to show up? Why is he always ready to believe the worst?"

"He missed you, Tisha," her aunt murmured softly. "He drove up to spend the day with you."

"Well, I wish he hadn't come. I never want to see him again!" she declared angrily. Her shoulders sagged in defeat. "I didn't mean that. He's my father and I love him," she sighed, brushing the tears from her face. "But why can't he trust me?"

"It isn't you so much that he doesn't trust. It's Roarke." A small smile flitted across her aunt's mouth. "Let's face it, if Roarke had been sixty years old and pudgy and balding, your father would have never jumped to the conclusions that he did. And if he walked in, as you said, and found you in Roarke's arms, you can't blame him for thinking the obvious. You have to remember your father is a man who was used to getting his way with women. He most likely imagined Roarke doing the same thing with you."

A wave of shame washed over her. Only Tisha, and Roarke, too, knew how close her father's accusations had come to being the truth. He must have picked up on the guilt in her voice. Without meaning to, she'd made her explanation a lot less believable.

"If only that tree hadn't blown down last night," Tisha sighed, and made a sulky face. "And it's too bad the road crew cleared it away this morning."

"If only I hadn't sent you up there last night with that package," Blanche reminded her dryly. "I was the one who insisted that it had to be taken up last night."

"Oh, Blanche, I don't blame you."

"I know you don't." Blanche smiled, parking the car in front of her house. "I left the coffee on."

"I hope it's strong and black," Tisha declared, opening her car door and stepping out, "because I could sure use it!"

Inside the house, Blanche poured them each a cup

of coffee and carried it to the kitchen table where they sat in silent commiseration. Then Tisha sank her head in her hands and groaned.

"After what's happened, I don't imagine Dad will let me stay here."

"You're twenty-one," Blanche reminded her.

"Doesn't matter. He controls my trust fund."

"You could get a job."

"Sure, Blanche. Minimum wage. I can't live on it."

"You're being defeatist."

"Dad'll probably pack me up and take me home where he can keep me under lock and key. If I thought he intimidated my dates before, it will be nothing compared to what he'll do now," she said with a resigned shake of her head.

"You don't have to leave," Blanche assured her firmly. "No matter what my brother says, you're welcome to stay."

"Thanks." Tisha smiled, her gaze straying out the window. "What do you suppose he's going to do to Roarke?"

"I doubt that he'll do anything to him," her aunt said wryly.

"I wish I knew what was going on up there."

"We'll soon find out," Blanche stated.

It was over an hour later before they heard the sound of Tisha's car coming up the drive. She exchanged a sympathetic glance with her aunt as she prepared to meet her father. When he walked into the kitchen, there was a very satisfied smile on his face. He rubbed his hands together as if he had just successfully completed a very difficult mission.

"Is there any coffee left?" he asked cheerfully.

Tisha had expected anything but affability. A puzzled frown creased her forehead as she watched him pour himself a cup of coffee and carry it to the table where she and Blanche were sitting.

"You're a very lucky little lady." He nodded at her as he straddled a chair at the end of the table. The sun winked over the silver wings of his hair near the temples.

"What do you mean?" Tisha asked warily.

"Roarke Madison has agreed to do the right thing by you," he announced smugly, taking a cautious sip of the scalding liquid.

Her back stiffened at his words. "What do you mean by the right thing?"

"He's agreed to marry you, of course."

"Oh, my God!" Stunned disbelief held her motionless. "You can't be serious!"

"You're damned right I'm serious," he declared. "You can get the blood tests and the marriage license this week."

"No!" Tisha cried. "No, no, no! I'm not going to marry him!" She jumped to her feet.

"You most certainly are."

"I hardly know him," she protested with a desperate cry. "As a matter of fact, I'm not even sure I like him!"

"Well, you spent the night together."

"I spent the night at his house, but not with him. Dad, this is the twenty-first century. There are coed dorms. Roommates of the opposite sex share apartments. It is possible for a man and a woman to enjoy each other's company and—"

"From what I understand, there was a little too much enjoying going on."

"What did he tell you?"

"Actually, there was no reason to discuss the exact details of what happened last night," he said in a level voice. "As soon as I discovered his intentions toward you were honorable, there wasn't any need to go into any of that."

"This is like that old episode of *Gunsmoke*," Blanche said brightly. "I think it was called 'Honorable

Intentions.' The mail-order bride accidentally spent the night with the preacher, and in the morning they had to—"

"Aunt Blanche, this is my life, not a TV show! And *Gunsmoke* went off the air before I was born!"

"So it did, honey."

Richard Caldwell seemed amused by the exchange. Tisha had a feeling that he was remembering the same show.

"His intentions were honorable," Tisha repeated. "Do you mean Roarke does want to marry me?"

"I persuaded him that he should."

"This is insane. I don't believe a word you're saying."

"Well, he agreed to it, my darling daughter." Richard shifted his position. "The man is intelligent. He understood that I wanted to protect my daughter's reputation. And of course, he had to protect his against the possibility of scandal."

"What scandal? Men are allowed to have sex with women without marrying them, you know—"

"So you did."

"I didn't say that! And you just can't make me marry him. He's intelligent enough to know that. I think he was humoring you, Dad."

Richard Caldwell shook his head. "I know when someone's shining me on. Raising you was an education in lie detection."

"Richard! You shouldn't talk about your daughter like that. She might not have told the truth every time she came in late, but she's a good girl."

"And now she's got a good man to take care of her. Very personable fella, already established in a lucrative career and doing well, from what I was able to determine."

Tisha fell silent. She knew Roarke had done his utmost to get on her father's good side—she just knew it.

"You could do much worse. Kevin would never have

been able to handle you, but I think Madison will be able to keep you in line," her father asserted. There was a sparkle of fire in his eyes when he looked at her. "When I walked in that kitchen, you were very willingly in his arms, and he had just kissed you, too. You may not be in love with him now, but with a man like that, it will come in time."

"No," she breathed helplessly, "I am not going to marry him!"

"We can discuss it later when you're calmer." He set his cup on the table and rose from his chair. "Now, if you'll excuse me, I'm going to have to start making arrangements to be free this week. That's one of the blessings of being your own boss. In cases of emergency, you can delegate."

"I don't believe it," Tisha murmured, sinking into her chair as her father walked from the room. "How could Roarke agree to this?"

"I'm as surprised as you are," confessed Blanche.

"Dad's gone off the deep end."

"I think you're right. That storm last night seems to have shorted the wiring in everyone's brain. I can't focus on my work at all."

Tisha remembered the incredible kiss and everything else that had happened between her and Roarke. "I know exactly what you mean, Blanche. I think you're right."

"It's very odd. I mean, none of us were hit by lightning, but we do seem to be acting like we were."

"Especially Dad," Tisha muttered. "He's in for a rude awakening."

"Let him down gently, honey. We still haven't spoken to Roarke, but I'm sure there's a reasonable explanation."

Tisha shook her head. "And it probably involves a lot of wishful thinking."

"At the very least, it sounds like Roarke didn't disagree to this . . . marriage," her aunt said hesitantly. "I know he's very attracted to you, physically, anyway. I was wondering . . . have you fallen in love with him?"

"Me? In love with Roarke?" In spite of all the indignation Tisha put in her voice, it trembled with uncertainty. "Never!" she added firmly, somewhat afraid to examine her emotions. She rose quickly to her feet again. "I have to speak to Dad. I have to make him understand how crazy this is. I'm not going to marry Roarke!"

Chapter Eight

For the rest of the morning and the better part of the afternoon, Tisha argued and pleaded with her father. Neither tears nor logic nor anger could persuade him to change his mind. He was fixated on the idea of Roarke marrying her. She stormed into the studio where Blanche had discreetly retreated to allow them privacy.

"Please, go and keep Dad occupied," Tisha pleaded, her frustration in her voice. "I have to call Roarke, and I don't want Dad accidentally picking up the phone and finding out."

Blanche immediately set down her brush and began wiping her hands on a rag. "No luck?" she asked sympathetically. The grim expression on her niece's face provided a wordless answer. "Roarke's number is in the address book by the phone."

Tisha waved a thanks to her departing aunt and walked to the studio phone. She dialed the number and listened impatiently to the rings that went unanswered. She was ready to slam down the receiver when she heard Roarke's voice.

"Where have you been?" she demanded angrily.

"Who is this? Tisha?"

"Yes. Your bride-to-be. I understand my father threw in five magic cows and a spinning wheel franchise."

He laughed. "Pretty funny."

"Not if you're me," she snapped.

"Yes, of course." There was dry amusement in his voice. "Well, hi. Sorry I didn't know it was you right away."

"Especially considering we're about to tie the knot."

"Right."

"I can't wait to ditch you at the altar, Roarke."

"Now I'm sure it's you. Who else would be that rude to me? As to where I've been, I work for a living, you know."

"Quick question, honeybunch—what the hell did you tell him?"

"Long story."

"Then I haven't got time for it," Tisha retorted. The husky, mocking sound of his voice added more fuel for her fiery temper. "Dad might find out any minute that I'm calling you."

"After what he already suspects, what harm is there in a phone call?"

"Just shut up and listen. Dad's always in bed by ten o'clock. I want you to meet me at eleven sharp down at the end of the lane. Got that?"

"Yes—"

She cut in on the rest of his words, "I'll see you there," and hung up.

Tisha stayed clear of her father until the evening meal, where she maintained an icy coolness. She tossed a barbed remark his way now and then, just to let him know she still did not accept his edict of marriage. But nothing shattered his calm resolve. He was positive that interfering in her life was the right thing to do. By the time she and Blanche had cleared the table and her father had retreated to the living room, she was beginning to consider running away.

Roarke was the key to the solution, she decided, immersing her hands in the dishwater. Between the two of them, they would come up with a way out of this mess.

Her gaze wandered idly to the window above the sink. With a start, Tisha recognized the white sports car pulling to a stop in front of the house. A glance at the clock told her it was only a few minutes past seven o'clock. Surely Roarke hadn't misunderstood her. She had said eleven, not seven.

The dish in her hand slid back into the water as she reached for the towel in her aunt's hand. "It's Roarke! He's here now!" she exclaimed in a panicked whisper.

Blanche frowned. "I thought you said you were going to meet him at eleven."

"That's what I told him." Only the excess water was wiped from her hands. "I have to stop him before Dad sees him!"

Before she was halfway across the kitchen, the doorbell rang. Richard Caldwell was already at the front door by the time Tisha reached the kitchen archway. She stopped in its frame, poised to take flight as she watched the calm, almost friendly way the two men greeted each other. Her heart was lodged somewhere in the vicinity of her throat, pulsing wildly at the sight of the tall man exchanging pleasantries with her father.

"I hope you don't mind me dropping in," he was saying in a composed voice. His brown eyes glanced at Tisha. "I wanted to speak to your daughter. May I see her alone?"

Her father followed his gaze to Tisha, a triumphant gleam lighting the depths of his eyes. "I have no objection."

"Would your sister's studio be all right?" Roarke inquired with careful politeness that grated on Tisha's already raw nerves.

"Certainly," her father agreed.

If Tisha hadn't wanted so badly to see Roarke and put an end to this talk of a marriage between them, she would have refused outright to see him. As it was, she was forced to lead the way to the studio.

The instant the door was closed behind them, she turned on Roarke with a vengeance. "I told you to meet me at eleven o'clock!" she hissed.

"You didn't think I was going to fall into that trap, did you?" he said coldly.

"Huh?" She stiffened at his tone, staring up at him with a confused frown. "What trap?"

"I expected something more original from you, Red." One hand was hooked in the belt loop of his jeans as his gaze moved over her slender body, ignoring the bewildered expression in her eyes.

"What are you talking about?"

His slight smile gave her the fleeting hope that he was kidding, but his next words dashed that. "I wonder how many men have been trapped into marriage after spending a night with a girl, however innocently, while the outraged father appears on the doorstep in the morning."

With a gasp of dismay, Tisha realized he thought she had planned the whole thing. "You don't think that I—" she rushed. "You can't believe that I engineered this! I swear to you I had no idea my father would be coming to visit me today. I never intended any of this to happen. Roarke, you've got to believe me!"

"Tisha"—a sardonic glint appeared in his eyes—"if I thought for one moment that you'd arranged this, I would wring your neck."

She gasped—and then she saw the suppressed laughter in his eyes.

"Had you going, didn't I?"

"This is no time to be joking!"

"I only wanted you to see how it might look from my point of view," he said.

"I swear, I was beginning to think you were as delusional as my father."

"That's a pretty strong word."

"Roarke, I can't get him to stop talking about this marriage."

"That's one of the reasons I got here early."

Tisha crossed her arms over her chest. "What do you mean?"

"If I'd met you at eleven as you wanted, in some dark lane, and if your father had found out, how do you think he would've interpreted it?" Roarke demanded. "There's no reason to get him more worked up. I'm trying to calm him down."

Tisha couldn't meet the force of his gaze. There was too much truth in his statement for her to shrug it off, and he knew it.

"This way," he went on, "coming to the house, keeping everything open and aboveboard, he may be persuaded to trust us."

"But we can't just agree to whatever he wants. What good is it going to do to have him trust us," she pointed out, "if we can't get him to change his mind about this ridiculous marriage idea?"

Roarke sighed. "Look, I agree, he's being a little obsessive."

"A little? I'd say a lot."

"The stress of your leaving home really got to him. He's a man—he's not going to admit that he's lonely. Or that the idea of his only daughter leaving home scares him to death."

"What are you saying?"

"You can't expect someone like your father to make an about-face overnight. You have to change his mind by degrees."

"In other words, it will take several small miracles instead of one large one," she murmured.

"Something like that," Roarke agreed.

"And how do you propose to begin?" The tilt to her head challenged him to come up with an answer. "Are you going to mention an imaginary wife to convince him you'd be committing bigamy if you married me now?"

"That's rather drastic," he answered with a dry smile. "I had thought we might convince him that we want to extend our engagement, just for starters."

"And in those few months, he'll see how incompatible we are," Tisha concluded for him. "Won't work."

"Why not?"

"You don't know my father." She grimaced. "He's like a bulldog. Once he gets hold of an idea, he won't let go."

"I'm sure he'll put your happiness first."

"I'm not." She shook her head grimly and slumped against a stool. "He thinks you can handle me. That's what I mean when I say he's delusional."

Roarke grinned. "He could be right about that point, though."

A quick glance in his direction caught the look of amusement her words aroused, a look that ignited her temper.

"This is all your fault anyway," she declared. "If you and Dad hadn't conspired between you to make me leave this morning, we wouldn't be in this pickle. Why did you let him bully you into agreeing to marry me?"

"I didn't really do that. I just let him talk. He needed to, Tisha. And he's not the kind of guy who's ever going to go to a therapist and say, 'Hey, I'm hurting.'"

"That doesn't qualify you to solve his problems. Definite conflict of interest there, since I seem to be the biggest problem."

"Yeah, you are," Roarke answered calmly.

"Oh-kay. I'm glad we can agree on that. Am I your biggest problem, too?"

"Well, I do feel guilty about what happened."

"Why?" she flared. "There was nothing to be guilty

about! Nothing happened! If you'd backed me up when I was trying to convince him of that, he might have believed us!"

"You're right. Physically nothing happened except a torrid love scene that never reached a climax." His gaze roamed over her, producing again the sensation that he was touching her. "But in my mind, let's say that it didn't end with kisses, little girl."

"Stop . . . stop calling me that," she replied tartly. "I'm not a little girl."

"No, you're not." Roarke's hand caught a long strand of her hair. He let it spin through his fingers, then fall across her breasts. "You're very much a woman, even if you are young and not exactly experienced. But you have great instincts, as you proved last night."

"We're . . . er . . . getting off the track," Tisha stammered, turning away from him while taking a quick step to put some distance between them.

His hands settled around her waist in a provocative caress. "I don't think so." He nuzzled her hair, following it as it flowed down her neck to her shoulders.

"Don't do that," she protested weakly, trying to move away, only to have him hold her tighter against him.

"Why not?" he said. "We're engaged, in a manner of speaking. We should enjoy some of the pleasures that go along with it."

Tisha gulped quickly for air as her resistance started to melt. She twisted in his arms, trying to use her body as a wedge to halt his searching lips.

"You forget we're trying to find a way out of this engagement."

"Are we?"

She saw his lazy, half-closed look dwelling on her mouth, and she moistened it nervously with the tip of her tongue. An imperceptible movement of his head signaled his intention to taste the parted sweetness of her lips.

"Roarke—" she began, only to be silenced quite effectively by his kiss.

She turned the rest of the way into his arms, not sure if it was by her design or his. Her fingers were slowly inching their way toward his neck to yield completely to his embrace when there was a rap on the door followed immediately by the turning of the knob.

Tisha knew even before she broke away from Roarke's kiss that it would be her father in the doorway. She was right.

"Hi, Dad. What's up?" *Give me a gold star for fake nonchalance*, she thought. *My father's losing his mind, and I'm engaged all of a sudden to a guy who's so sexy I'm losing mine.*

"I was going to see if you two wanted some coffee." He grinned.

Tisha attempted to struggle out of Roarke's arms without appearing to do so, but he held her easily in their circle.

"Maybe later." And her father closed the door.

"That was not helpful," Tisha said, pushing Roarke away. "It's not going to be easy to convince him that we don't want to get married if he keeps catching us in clinches. Why did you have to do that? I can't marry you! I just can't!"

"How was I to know your father was going to walk in?" Roarke shrugged indifferently. "So he saw us. So what?"

"Is that all you can say?" she asked. "Here I am trying to figure out a way to get out of this mess while all you're doing is trying to find a way to take advantage of it! You're—you're—" She searched wildly for the right word.

"Self-centered," he offered.

"Yes!"

"Arrogant."

"That too."

"Crazy about you."

"Oh, shut up, Roarke. What are we going to do?"

"I don't really know. Your temper kind of complicates things."

She put her hands on her hips and stood with arms akimbo. "What? I'm not following you."

"Well, if I do marry you—and I'm not saying that I will—"

"What?" she said again, really incensed.

"Do you think I want a screaming shrew of a wife hanging around my neck for the rest of my life?" he asked, studying her with a bland look. "Although I'll admit it would be a novelty to marry someone with a split personality."

"I don't know what you're talking about," Tisha muttered.

"You're always so ready to hurl insults at me. Self-centered, arrogant, et cetera."

"Those were your words, not mine."

"But you think they describe me pretty well. Yet you're always so ready to respond to my advances. Have you ever wondered why?"

"It's strictly an animal attraction." Feeling a little ashamed of how easily she flew off the handle, she reminded herself to stick to the subject under discussion. "That's all there is to it. Sorry. I'm not going to marry you."

"You don't have to. But do you have an alternative suggestion to the one I made?"

"Sure. Running away."

"Doesn't solve anything," Roarke reminded her quietly.

"It would eliminate you as my husband," she retorted.

"And what about your father?"

"What about him?"

"Are you prepared for the estrangement your running away would bring? He's kind of fragile right now.

It may be hard for you to see him that way, but it's clear to me."

"Look, Roarke, I think it's great that you're willing to listen to him rant, but you shouldn't encourage his fantasy of marrying me off."

"I'm not going to encourage you running away, either. Once the bond of love and trust has been broken, it's difficult to go back. You two fight and argue now, but isn't that better than silence?"

Tisha shifted uncomfortably. She didn't need Roarke to tell her that her father was only doing what he thought was best for her. Running away would break his heart. Except for Blanche, she was the only family he had left. He loved her as much as she loved him, if not more.

A pain-filled sigh shuddered through her. "I don't know what to do. I love my father, but I can't marry someone just because he wants me to."

The hands that touched her shoulders conveyed none of the intimacy of before. Their contact was friendly and consoling as though they wanted to guide her through a dark passage into the light. She raised her eyes to his understanding smile.

"I may not have any right to ask you this, Tisha, but would you leave this to me?" Roarke asked gently. "Would you trust me to find the solution that will make us both happy?"

She searched the warm brown eyes, soft like velvet with its hidden resilience. He wanted to make sure there was a way out of this difficult situation as much as she did, one that would cause all three of them the least amount of pain, she reminded herself. There was no ulterior motive to his request. What one could there be?

"Yes," she murmured, "I trust you."

"Good." He winked as if to laugh at the seriousness in her voice. "Leave everything to me. No more arguments with your father. Say and do nothing that will make him more stubborn. The more you try to convince him that he's wrong, the more certain he'll become that he's right. Okay?"

"Okay," she repeated, surprised that he had coaxed a smile out of her. She had thought there was nothing left to smile about. "I bet you regret not letting me walk home last night."

"If I'd thought for one second that you had an outraged father waiting in the wings," he chuckled, "I would have carried you home. And I would've gotten some sleep last night, too, instead of stiff muscles."

"The next time something like this happens to you, put the girl on the couch and sleep in your own bed," she teased.

"There won't be any next time," he said firmly, but an enigmatic expression darkened his eyes. "Let's take your father up on his offer of coffee before he comes back to find out what we're doing now." His hand touched her elbow. "And remember, leave everything to me."

"I will, Roarke," she promised, and wondered why she felt so secure in the hands of a man she professed not to like.

During the next few days, Tisha began to wonder if she hadn't made a mistake in trusting Roarke to calm her father down and help him get a grip. Richard wouldn't stop talking about the marriage, and he'd persuaded a friend at the county courthouse to give him the forms for the blood tests and the license.

Forms she was not going to fill out.

She saw no point in allowing her father to believe that the impossible was going to happen. More importantly, she hated reinforcing the idea that she could be handed over to another man, as if she were a piece of property. He might be clutching at straws, emotionally speaking, but she couldn't change reality to suit him.

She knew she was right, but panic was beginning to

set in. Even Blanche, whom she had considered an ally, seemed to be taking the wrong side sometimes. Whenever they'd found a few minutes to talk privately, her aunt had bugged her with questions concerning Tisha's feelings for Roarke. Was she sure she didn't care for him? Did the physical attraction go deeper?

Tisha was beginning to wonder herself. If Roarke was going to put his foot down and tell Richard that he couldn't force things, he just couldn't.

Slowly she trudged along the faint animal path through the forested hillside. Her father was off on some mysterious errand this afternoon, and Tisha had hoped to find Roarke at home. She'd walked through the woods to confuse Blanche about her destination, a route that was longer than if she had followed the road. When she'd finally reached his house, it was to find Roarke gone. She'd assumed he'd be there and hadn't called; she didn't know why. She just wasn't thinking straight. Her useless hike had succeeded only in making her tired and irritable and more depressed.

Billy Goat Gruff lifted his head when she entered the clearing below her aunt's house. After a passing glance her way, he lowered his head to tear at the grass, accustomed now to her comings and goings. With a slight change of direction, Tisha headed for the kitchen door, glumly wondering how she could see Roarke tonight.

When she reached the side entrance, she glanced through the windowpane of the door and saw Roarke sitting at the kitchen table with Blanche. The troubled expression on his face stopped her hand as it reached for the knob. It was eavesdropping, she knew, but she paused anyway to listen.

"Are you positive she said she was just going for a walk?" Roarke asked.

"Yes," her aunt said patiently, a solemn expression on her usually animated face. "Besides, her car is still here and so are her clothes. I know she hasn't run away."

Tisha wasn't certain what she thought she was going to hear, perhaps some comment that would reveal they were all conspiring to get her to marry Roarke, but they seemed to be only concerned with her whereabouts. With a resigned sigh, she opened the door and walked in.

"There you are!" Blanche rose quickly to her feet, a forced smile of brightness on her face. "We were wondering where you'd gone."

"First I considered throwing myself off the steepest cliff, but I couldn't find one," said Tisha. "Then I thought about getting lost in the woods, but I kept ending up in somebody's backyard. So here I am," she finished bitterly.

"Don't joke about things like that," her aunt murmured, a worried frown lining her forehead.

"I'm sorry, Blanche," Tisha sighed wearily. "Chalk it up to paranoia. I'm developing quite a case of it. Sometimes I think people are talking about me behind my back." She darted a resentful glance at Roarke, who was watching her closely. "So how are you?"

"Doing okay," he answered casually. His gaze followed Tisha as she walked to the counter and poured a cup of coffee. "Grab a chair and sit down."

"I don't feel like it." The combination of her own strain and his unruffled demeanor bugged her. She was nervous; why wasn't he?

She intercepted the look he sent Blanche, who immediately turned to leave. "You two would probably like to be alone. I'll go and play with my paints for a while."

As soon as she heard the studio door close behind her aunt, Tisha turned toward Roarke, her green eyes blazing.

"Well? Have you talked to Richard? He doesn't seem any less fixated on the idea of a hurry-up wedding."

"I know," he answered, calmly meeting the challenge of her gaze.

"If you know, why aren't you doing something about it?" she demanded.

Very slowly, he uncoiled his long body from the chair and walked over to the counter where she stood. "The world hasn't come to an end." The sunlight glinted on the bronze streaks in his hair.

"Not yet," she retorted bitterly. "I'm beginning to wonder if you have any plan at all to rescue us from this disaster."

"I thought you were going to trust me." The gentleness in his voice reached out to soothe her.

"I was." Her own voice was very low, barely squeezing through the painful lump in her throat.

"That's the past tense. Does that mean you don't trust me anymore?"

Tisha looked up at him, her chin trembling as she tried to hold back the misery that was welling to the top. "I don't know anymore."

"Hey." His head tilted down as she lowered her chin to escape his searching eyes. Not even the teasing reassurance of his voice could raise it again. "What happened to you? I miss getting my chops busted. I don't think I could handle it if you admit that you don't know everything."

"Well, I don't know everything," she admitted, breathing in deeply and rapidly to hold back the tears. In spite of all her efforts, one tear slipped from her lashes and trickled down her cheek.

"You're crying," Roarke said gently.

"You're darned right I'm crying!" she flared, as more tears followed the first. "And if you were any kind of a man, you'd offer me your shoulder instead of standing there looking so righteous!"

"I didn't think you'd want my shoulder," he mused softly, reaching out to draw her into his arms. The beat of his heart was oddly reassuring as he cradled her against his chest. His head was bowed near her forehead. "Of course, on the other hand, I didn't realize you would give in to tears," he murmured. "Go ahead and cry, Tisha. It's about time you did."

She needed no more encouragement than that to weep freely, sparing only a fleeting thought that she was getting his shirt wet as she huddled closer to him. When her sobs had subsided to hiccups, Roarke offered her his handkerchief, wiping the excess tears off her cheeks himself. Her head stayed nestled against his chest.

"Feel better?"

"Yes." Her answer was accompanied by a tiny shake of her head. "Hold me, please," she requested, knowing that when she left the shelter of his arms that lonely feeling would descend on her.

"Sure." She could feel him smile against her hair while his hold tightened reassuringly around her.

"I walked up to your house to find you," she said after a few minutes of silence.

"And I came down here to see you," Roarke returned. One arm was removed so he could reach his hand into his pocket. "I have something I wanted to give you."

In the next minute, he was holding a glittering diamond solitaire ring in front of her. The size of it drew a gasp of delight from her as the sunlight was caught by its cut surface and reflected a rainbow of colors.

"Is it real?" she whispered.

"Would I give you a fake?" he said. "I don't like to have my chops busted that much. Yeah, it's real. Touch it. It won't disappear."

Her initial elation faded. "No," she said firmly, moving against the back of his arm as he brought the ring closer. "That's an engagement ring. It's beautiful, but—"

"Your father expects you to have one."

"Exactly. He expects a wedding, too," Tisha reminded him none too gently.

"This is about you and me. It doesn't have anything

to do with him or what he wants. Trust me. Tisha. Please."

The warmth of his gaze rested on her face as she glanced warily at him. "I'll take it," she said. "But I'm going to give it back to you as soon as this whole thing is over."

Roarke slipped the ring on her finger. "You can give it back if you want to, or keep it as a souvenir."

"That wouldn't be right." The ring was a perfect fit, if a little snug, and she couldn't help admiring the way it sparkled when her hand moved. "You shouldn't have bought something so expensive. What if I lose it?"

"I had it made a little small to make it harder to get off your finger in case you threw it at me during a temper tantrum," he said.

"I wouldn't do that," she murmured, self-consciously moving out of his arms.

"Oh, yes, you would." He grinned.

"Roarke . . ." A worried frown swept away the glow that had been on her face. "What are we going to do about Daddy?"

"Leave everything to me."

"Yes, but—"

"No buts. I'll take care of everything. It will all work out for the best."

"I wish I knew what you were going to do," she sighed.

"Right now I'm going home—and you, stop worrying." He touched the tip of her nose and moved toward the door. "Tell Blanche thanks for the coffee."

"When will I see you?"

He stopped at the door and turned around. His gaze moved over her in a touching caress that quickened her heartbeat.

"Tomorrow."

Chapter Nine

By two-thirty the following afternoon, there was no sign of Roarke. Somehow Tisha had received the impression that when he had said he would see her tomorrow, he had meant in the afternoon. She had been clinging to the slim hope that he would arrive before her father returned from another mysterious errand, but she could hear her father greeting Blanche as he came in the door and knew that if Roarke did come now, there would be little chance to see him alone.

She wished now she had been more persistent yesterday in finding out how he intended to postpone the wedding. Twenty-four hours ago, she had trusted him. She had let his charm persuade her to leave all the details to him. Today she scolded herself for being so foolish. It was her life, and she had a right to know what was going on.

The diamond on her finger sparkled brilliantly in the sunlight streaming through the skylight of the studio. A shudder quivered down her spine at the implications of marriage the ring carried. She allowed herself to imagine their wedding day for a few minutes—but the white-lace-and-promises scene dissolved into a depressing premonition of him standing her up at the altar. Well, she had said she couldn't wait to do exactly that to him.

It made no sense. They hardly knew each other, and they shouldn't even be thinking about marriage. Yet he had gone and given her a very expensive ring and insisted it had nothing to do with her father's temporary obsession. She hoped it was temporary.

"What's the little bride-to-be doing today? Working?"

At the sound of her father's voice, Tisha turned from her blank canvas. His handsome, smiling face was peering around the studio door, looking very much like a grown-up boy who had a secret he was bursting to tell. A sad smile was all she could manage to return.

"Come on in, Dad," she said, a little afraid to show any emotion. "I'm not really doing anything."

"No, you come here. I have something I want to show you," he insisted.

Tisha wanted to refuse, but there wasn't any point in doing so. Reluctantly she followed him as he led her to her room, not really interested in whatever it was he had to show her.

"Couldn't work today, huh?" he inquired gently.

"No."

"Don't be so dejected. It's only prewedding nerves," he assured her, opening the door to her room.

"Please, Dad, I don't want to talk about it." The tension that was pounding at the back of her head put a sharp edge to her voice.

"I bought you a present." A gesture of his hand drew her attention to the box on the bed. "I hope you like it."

Tisha stared at it in a kind of frozen silence. The shape of it indicated a dress. She bit into her lower lip, knowing that if she opened it and saw a wedding dress, she would scream.

"Go on, open it," he prodded her gently.

With trembling fingers, she slowly pulled the string off the box, trying to summon the courage to lift off the top cardboard. After an apprehensive glance at her father, she removed the top and swept aside the tissue paper. Her eyelids fluttered down, and she saw the white material of a dress. Summoning up a little more spirit, she unfolded it and held it up against her, the long, filmy sleeves trailing over her arm.

"It's very pretty, Daddy. Thank you," she murmured, her lips gently touching his shaven cheek. He had actually gone and chosen a wedding dress—she would never wear it. She had no intention of continuing this charade. But right now, she knew that losing her temper was probably the worst thing to do. She could talk to Roarke later, discuss what to do with Blanche—her father was obviously not rational.

But there was so much love shining in his eyes when he looked at her that a lump rose in her throat. He caught at her hand and looked down at it as if he, too, needed a moment to control his emotions. Pushing the empty box to the back of the bed, he sat down and patted the cover beside him.

"Sit down, Tish. I think it's time you and I had a little talk."

Carefully she laid the dress over the foot of the bed and joined him near the edge. Some of her apprehension returned as she tried to anticipate what he wanted to talk about.

He gazed tenderly into her face, a small smile lifting the corners of his mouth. "I can't remember the last time that I told you how very much I love you. Maybe it's something that parents don't often tell their children. It's taken for granted, I suppose. But I wanted to say it out loud. I wanted you to know how very much you mean to me."

Tears sprang to her eyes. "Oh, Daddy, I love you, too," Tisha whispered as she reached out, put an arm around his shoulder, and tightened it in an affectionate hug.

"After you were born and your mother and I found out she couldn't have any more children, she felt that she'd let me down by not giving me a son. I don't believe I ever convinced her that I was satisfied with the beautiful child of our love. Oh, I did want a son—every man does. But you were never second best, honey," her father assured her, his hand stroking the head that rested against his shoulder. "If I could have traded you in for a boy the minute you were born, I wouldn't have done it. Do you believe me?"

"Yes." The simple answer erased the worried frown on his face.

"I want you to be happy, but sometimes I know I've gone about it in all the wrong ways. There were many times when I should have been more understanding, but I'd never been a parent before."

"I wouldn't have traded you for anyone." Tisha hadn't felt so close to her father in years. She couldn't even bring herself to be angry over his insistence that she marry Roarke. Given time, he'd give up the strange notion and get back to being himself again: stubborn, macho, and overprotective. But not obsessive. And not irrational. She had to agree with Roarke that her father's mental stress had been triggered by her abrupt departure from his home.

"These last few days," he went on, "I've had several opportunities to talk to Roarke. He's very concerned that I'm rushing you into something you aren't prepared for."

Unconsciously Tisha held her breath. Was this the moment? Was this when her father would agree to the long engagement that Roarke suggested?

"Last Sunday, my temper ruled my judgment," he went on. "You'd been on my mind, night and day. I wasn't sleeping much, could hardly eat—and when I got up here and saw you with him . . . well, I lost it. Big-time. And I'm sorry about that. But after talking to him and realizing how much he wants you to be happy, I know he'll be a better husband for you than I had a right to expect."

Her heart plunged to the pit of her stomach. Roarke's let-me-handle-this approach hadn't worked. In her father's mind, the wedding was not going to be postponed.

"Are you very angry with me for making all the arrangements for the wedding without consulting you?" her father asked gently.

"No," she answered truthfully. What did she care about a ceremony that was never going to take place?

"When your mother and I were married, we had a big, fancy wedding," he told her. "She was an only child, too, but her parents insisted on making a production of it, every great-aunt and uncle and fourth cousin was invited. The celebration lasted all day and probably all night, but we slipped away before it was over."

He paused, his eyes taking on a faraway look as if he were reliving the precious memory of that day.

Some seconds later, he continued, his voice low and unbelievably tender, "When we'd driven some distance, I remember Lenore said she wished the ceremony had never happened. I was stunned at first because I thought she was regretting marrying me. Then she explained that she felt our love was a precious blessing from God, a private, beautiful emotion that wasn't meant to be flaunted.

"There were tears in her eyes when she told me that she wished it could have been only the two of us standing in front of the altar without all the bridesmaids and groomsmen around, only the two of us exchanging our holy vows in God's house. We happened to be driving through a small town when she told me this. I saw a church with the lights on, and we stopped. We made our vows a second time in front of a simple altar with rows of empty pews behind us. We loved each other, Tisha, more than words can ever say."

His voice cracked as he took her face in his hands and stared into it, a poignant sadness in his eyes.

"And that is why, my darling, darling daughter," he murmured tightly, "your wedding to Roarke is going to be so simple. Not because I want to hide anything or make it a hurry-up affair. It was the second time that we pledged our love that your mother and I treasured. For you I want it to be the first, with no other memory to detract from it."

She turned her face in his hands, pressing a kiss against his palm, a conflicting tide of emotions swamping her. How could she tell him that she couldn't go through with the ceremony he planned?

"I never realized completely how much you loved my mother." Her soft voice was still smothered in his hand.

"She loved me, too," he whispered, gathering her against his chest. "Seeing you with Roarke this last week has reminded me of it so vividly. Whenever he's around you hardly take your eyes off of him. You're constantly sending little messages to him the way Lenore used to do with me. I bet you didn't think your old dad noticed things like that, did you?" She could feel him smile against her forehead and frowned. "I realized last night that the biggest reason you don't want to marry him, or say you don't want to marry him, is because of the speed at which it's all happening, as if the two of you had done something to be ashamed of last weekend. I know you didn't."

"What?"

"You've never told me serious lies, honey, and you didn't when you told me nothing had happened. I've already seen for myself that Roarke respects you too much to have taken advantage of the situation. I know it's terribly old-fashioned to say that I'm glad you waited, but I am. Do you remember a couple of weeks ago?" He chuckled, and gently held her away from him. "It seems longer than that. But you told me that I would never approve of the man you married, that I would find something wrong with him. You were wrong. Roarke might even be too good for you, but I doubt it. You couldn't have made a better choice if you'd searched the whole world. I'm not only going to have a daughter I adore, but a son-in-law, too. A father couldn't be any luckier than that."

Tisha could only stare at him in dumb amazement. None of this was happening to her. She was overwhelmed. There seemed to be no arguments left. Her mind refused to think.

Her father glanced down at his watch and shook his head wryly. "Here I've been rambling on and paying no attention to the time."

"It doesn't matter what time it is."

"Well, I know you were working on something in the studio. But I was hoping you'd want to try the dress on to see if it fits."

She stood up, resigned to that much, but she had a dejected look on her face. If only Roarke was here to talk to her dad—and to reassure her. She wanted very much to see him and reveal her father's new stand. She picked up the dress and fingered the material of the flared skirt.

"Well . . . okay. Why not?" she said hesitantly.

"I can always take it back, Tisha. I have to tell you, the saleslady and the other customers sure looked at me funny. Guess it's not every day that a dad walks in and buys a dress for his daughter, especially if she's not with him. But it's not like you could get married in slacks, right?" He smiled.

Tisha nodded. "Right."

He turned his back to her as she changed into the dress. Her mind kept flitting back over her father's words. His expression of love for her moved her even as it seemed to trap her.

If she did come to love Roarke, they would be together if and when they decided that was what they wanted. Her father would undoubtedly be very happy to hear them exchange solemn vows, but those vows had to mean something. A real marriage ceremony wouldn't be—couldn't be—something they would do just to humor him.

Tisha stepped back from the mirror to stare at her reflection. Tension had produced a starry, ethereal quality in her face. Nerves had knotted her stomach until she wanted to press her hands against it to relieve the pain. The dress was pretty, and it fit her well enough. But it was not what she would have chosen. Well, she would have to twirl around and pretend she liked it for now. But Tisha kept right on praying silently that Roarke could come up with a solution for their latest crisis.

"You can turn around now," she said.

He did. "You look beautiful, Patricia," he said with intense sincerity.

She nodded at his compliment, feeling more and more uneasy. At least he hadn't bought her a veil. "I think—I think I'll take it off now, though."

"Okay, honey."

She changed back into the clothes she'd had on before, and they sat and talked about nothing at all for a very long time.

As the next few weeks dragged on, her father showed no sign of going home to Little Rock. She couldn't bring herself to return the wedding dress or tell him that what he wanted most wasn't going to happen.

Roarke spent a fair amount of time with Richard, talking to the older man with a patience she admired—

from afar. She wasn't included in the conversations and had to trust what he chose to tell her about her father. But Roarke had had to be on site for the development of an office park he'd designed, and he left early and came back late. His reassurances were comforting, but he didn't seem to know any more than she did how to resolve the situation.

Even Blanche hadn't had much luck, as kind as she was, with getting her brother to listen to her. She'd retreated to her studio, maintaining a dignified silence. How long her aunt planned to keep that up, Tisha didn't know.

No one seemed able to confront Richard Caldwell with the plain, unvarnished truth of the matter: his daughter and Roarke had no plans to get married.

Discouraged by the lack of progress, and her dad's general air of cheerful obliviousness to her real feelings, Tisha fled the house one day and headed into Hot Springs. She stopped at the first church she saw, a white frame building with a tall steeple that seemed to pierce the sky. The weathervane, she noticed, was an angel, aimlessly swinging from east to west and back again.

Tisha felt as if she was being pushed around in the same way, by forces beyond her control, with no way out.

She tried the front door, expecting it to be locked, but it wasn't. The interior of the old church was cool and dim. But the sunbeams coming through the stained glass windows cast patterns of color on the aisles and pews. Tisha was heartened by the sight and slid into a pew, happy to have the place to herself.

Thinking in churches was something she'd always liked to do. She liked them better this way, without the shuffling, or the what-page-are-we-on commotion over the hymnals and prayer books, or the complaining of fretful children.

She'd been sitting in silence for over an hour when

she heard the door to the church open. Tisha bowed her head, pretending to pray. She didn't want to chat with a tourist or be greeted by a fellow worshipper. She closed her eyes, feeling a little guilty about not actually being here to worship.

Since the church was empty, she assumed the new arrival would have a look around and leave quickly, or perhaps slide into a distant pew and not disturb her. But she heard footsteps come down the aisle and stop at her pew. Then whoever it was sat down at the very end.

She couldn't pretend she hadn't heard. Tisha opened her eyes and looked around, prepared to say a polite hello and leave as soon as it didn't seem rude to do so. Then she realized that she was looking at Roarke.

He turned to her. "Come here often? Sorry. Corny line but I couldn't resist. I happened to see your car, so I came in. You okay?"

"I guess so," she said softly. She scooted over to him.

He put an arm around her shoulders. "It's okay to cuddle in church. God won't mind. And we have the place to ourselves."

"Yup."

They sat in silence for a few minutes, and then Roarke spoke. "Tisha, I don't know what to do about your dad. I thought he'd give up on his crazy notion, but he hasn't."

"And he isn't going to any time soon. I told you he was a bulldog."

"You were right." He took her hand and looked at the gorgeous ring. "Maybe I shouldn't have given you this. Do you want me to take it back?"

The warmth of his hand holding hers was deeply comforting. The diamond caught a colored sunbeam and flashed fire for a moment.

"No," she whispered. "You said you didn't give it to

me because of my dad—you said it was about you and me."

"That's right."

Tisha settled against his chest, looking up into the high recessed space over the altar where the light was brightest. "I take it you don't go around handing out engagement rings to all the girls."

"No, I don't. Just you."

She was silent for a while longer. "Do you think we—"

"We should wait," he said firmly. "We should drive your dad back to Little Rock and give ourselves some breathing room. This won't work any other way. I'll have to tell them that. I've been putting it off, but that's not doing him any good."

She nodded, hot tears squeezing out from under her lashes.

"And it's not doing us any good. I want there to be an 'us,' Tisha, more than I can say. And I don't really care how long it takes."

"I do," she whispered.

He gave her shoulders a squeeze. "Say that again. I like the sound of it."

"I do," she said. The words echoed in the empty church.

"I hear you. Loud and clear. Listen, Tish. When and if you decide on your own whether you want to marry me—do you think you'd like to be married here?"

The unexpected question startled her into sitting up. She looked into his eyes and knew at that moment what she wanted.

Not only to belong to him physically, but mentally as well. Not by any legal act, but because she wanted to be. She wanted to share his life, have his children, grow old in his arms.

She stared at the diamond in her engagement ring, sparkling with multicolored light, imagining a plain gold wedding band beside it. That was what she wanted—the rainbow and the moon—and both were equally out of reach without Roarke's love.

"I love you, Tisha. And I'm willing to wait for as long as it takes."

"Why?" she said tremulously.

"Why do I love you? That's a long list."

She burrowed into his muscular side, not wanting him to see her tears. "Go ahead."

"You're just what I had in mind. But I didn't know it until I met you, Tisha. Fiery. Talented. Kind to squirrels. Patient with your dad. I think you've got it all. Did I say sexy?"

Her laugh was muffled by having her face against his shirt. "Don't say that in church. It just sounds so weird."

"Sorry." He tousled her hair, messing it up. "Let's go. I think we need to get this relationship started. Beginning with getting your dad back to Little Rock."

"Yeah. I'll do it."

Roarke shook his head. "We'll do it. Together. Okay with you?"

She sat up and kissed him passionately.

Several months later . . .

"By the authority vested in me, I now pronounce you man and wife. You may kiss the bride," the minister prompted.

Her lashes fluttered down to close her eyes. Roarke gently turned her to face him. There was no ardor in his kiss, none of the warmth that she usually felt. His touch was cool and controlled as though he was obliged to carry out the minister's instruction. The face he turned toward her was serious and a little guarded.

It seemed only seconds later that he was bustling her away from her father and the few celebrants gathered in the pews. Tisha felt an odd sense of loss, wishing she had a flock of bridesmaids to keep her spirits up and a bunch of happy groomsmen to rock the party afterward.

But they had decided to keep the wedding small. Tisha cast her mind back to her father's description of how he had exchanged vows with her mother, quietly and meaningfully, in a nearly empty church. She had hoped for the same feeling of rightness in making her promises today, but she felt . . . almost nothing.

The months leading up to this moment had seemed like a happy dream. She and Roarke had made the most of their time together, and he'd done everything he could to convince her of his love.

Their love, she reminded herself. She did love him. The emptiness she felt right now would pass. Call it post-wedding blues or something like that. It was probably just as common as being on cloud nine.

Walking quietly, Blanche appeared to escort her down the church steps to his car.

He waited for her, hands folded in front of him, looking just as serious. Blanche fluttered around, insisting on taking pictures with her new digital camera, arranging a cousin here and a friend there, and telling everyone to smile until Tisha wanted to scream.

Sooner than she thought, the picture taking was over, and Roarke assisted her into the car. Blanche—bless her, Tisha thought—stood by her brother, her arm through his.

"Richard Caldwell, you never looked prouder," Tisha heard her aunt say.

Roarke got in on the driver's side, waved to the guests with something resembling enthusiasm, and shot her an inquiring look before turning the key in the ignition. "Well, we're married now."

"So we are."

"You don't look any too happy about it."

"Drive," she said.

Chapter Ten

"I like being married to you," Roarke said calmly. "So far."

Tisha didn't respond.

"Not feeling talkative, huh?"

"No. Not really." What could she possibly say? *I feel so let down, but I don't know why. But thanks for marrying me. Nice of you.* The great big rush of emotion she'd expected to feel just wasn't happening. She thought back to that magical afternoon when he'd found her in the church alone.

Just the two of them, together by chance. They'd realized at nearly the same moment that it wasn't by chance at all. And that they really did love each other.

Tisha looked out the window, but the direction of the light hid the road and the land they drove through, showing only her face reflected in the glass. Her eyes were huge and thoughtful.

It had seemed best to wait, but the intervening months had passed a little too quickly somehow. Between Roarke's latest assignments and her own preoccupied state, she'd grown more uneasy, not sure if she was, after all was said and done, marrying Roarke to please her father. Certainly Richard Caldwell had come to terms with the fact that his beloved daughter was no longer living under his roof, and he'd given their engagement his blessing.

But whether she—or they—had done the right thing, Tisha couldn't say.

"Want to talk about what's bothering you?"

She shook her head.

"Okay. I'll just get us to the hotel, and we can take things from there."

His tone was brisk. Businesslike. Unromantic. But Tisha hardly knew what she ought to expect from him. The last thing she wanted to do was ask if he felt as disappointed as she did. Unless she was just plain afraid. They'd rehearsed the ceremony, even mouthed the vows, but going through the real thing was very different. *As long as you both shall live* suddenly seemed like a very, very long time.

Tisha had dutifully kissed her new husband and turned around to look at the teary-eyed celebrants. They seemed to feel more than she did. Not a good sign.

Roarke turned the car into the parking lot of the hotel. It was a very nice hotel, but at the moment it was the last place on earth she wanted to be.

"I didn't realize the hotel was this close," she said.

"We could drive around in circles for a while if you'd like. Got the jitters?" His glance mocked the apprehension in her voice. "But we have to go in sooner or later. We have reservations for the honeymoon suite. So would you rather order in or eat at the hotel restaurant?"

"Neither. I'm not hungry," she avowed, not finding any humor in his statement.

"We'll have a drink first. Maybe some of the shock of becoming Mrs. Madison will wear off and your appetite will return. You see"—Roarke grinned as he pulled into a space—"it's already beginning. Whenever you start insulting me, I know things are back to normal."

There wasn't any "normal" anymore, Tisha thought as she watched Roarke get out of the car and walk around to open her door. She took the hand he reached out and got out a little awkwardly, hoping no one was looking. She felt unbelievably conspicuous wearing white everything.

"Your fingers are freezing. I have a jacket in the back if you want to warm up."

Wearing his jacket—too big in a nice way and smelling pleasantly of him—just seemed too intimate.

"No thanks."

"Okay. Be cold." His voice was suddenly edgy.

"I'm not trying to be cold, Roarke. I just don't want to wear your jacket." She paid no heed to the troubled look in his eyes. "Just leave me alone, okay?"

"What does that mean? Are you planning to sleep in the car?"

She looked around the parking lot, grateful that there was no one around. "No. Don't be ridiculous."

Roarke sighed. "Tisha, if you want to take things slowly, I understand."

"I guess I do," she said in a whisper. She no longer felt cold. In fact, her whole body was pulsating with a wild heat at the thought of what might happen once they were behind closed doors.

"We don't have to spend the night here. I would like to eat, though, even if you don't. There's nothing at the house, and I don't suppose you want to traipse around a supermarket in a bridal gown."

"No, I don't." Tisha shook her head firmly. "I mean, I planned to change here, but now I don't want to—be here."

"Okay. I'm getting that. But I think the most logical thing to do is to return to my house—oops, sorry, our house—when we've eaten. Do you agree?" He seemed suddenly disinclined to argue with her, and Tisha was glad. His sly questions were beginning to make her far more edgy and irrational than she already was.

"So what I'll do is have the bellboy take these suitcases up to our suite, and you can change. I'll wait for you down in the lobby. And I'll just cover the cost if you decide you don't want to stay the night here."

"That's fine." She nodded.

Despite her nervousness, Tisha ordered food just to be polite. She didn't know if her appetite had really returned or whether she took such a long time over each course to prolong the inevitable moment when they would be alone.

The silence between them was neither comfortable nor uneasy, broken occasionally by idle comments to avoid any building tension. After a second cup of coffee following dessert, Tisha knew she had lingered as long as possible.

Roarke did, too. He motioned for the waitress to bring their bill. "Are you ready?" It was a polite question, since he knew the answer. "Let's go home."

The intimate darkness of night had descended outside with only a few stars shimmering in the distance. The moon was new, a pale sickle turned down low. Tisha stopped at the bottom of the steps, noticing the magnum of champagne on ice and the two stemmed glasses on the tray beside it.

"How did that get here?" she demanded. He glanced over his shoulder, his gaze following her pointing finger to the champagne.

"I gave your dad a call to let him know we wouldn't be staying at the hotel. It's from him."

"Good idea," she said. "Guess he had to cancel the brass band he hired to play in the hotel lobby."

Roarke looked surprised. "He didn't mention that."

"I'm kidding."

"Oh. Well, he had the champagne delivered here instead to celebrate our wedding night. There's no sense in letting it go to waste. Why don't you open it up while I put your things in the other room?"

Tisha didn't know if she had the strength to wrestle a champagne cork out of the bottle or the enthusiasm for drinking it. But Roarke didn't wait for a reply to his suggestion and resumed his course to the bedroom, the suitcases under his arm. Tisha walked to the couch, staring distractedly at the wine bottle and the pair of glasses. Her imagination filled in the seduction scene: she and Roarke in front of the cozy fire, sipping champagne. How romantic . . . if she happened to be in a romantic mood, which she wasn't. She was still staring at the bottle when he walked back into the room.

"Haven't you opened it?" he asked unnecessarily.

"I don't know how." She swallowed nervously, avoiding the couch in favor of a chair.

Covertly she watched as he uncorked the bottle and poured the first rush of bubbling foam into one of the glasses. He filled it up the rest of the way and handed it to her without a word.

"I don't want any," she answered shortly.

He shrugged and took a sip. "Suit yourself."

With a casualness Tisha wished she had, he removed his suit jacket and loosened his tie before settling down on the couch. When he picked up a newspaper and began leafing through the sports section, she couldn't make up her mind if he was ignoring her deliberately or whether her presence didn't bother him at all. The last was a sharp jolt to her ego.

"How can you sit there and read?" Tisha exclaimed in exasperation. "Isn't there something you can do?"

"Like what?" He folded one side of the paper back so he could look at her.

"Like talk to me."

The newspaper was raised to block out his face. "Somehow I never expected to spend my wedding night talking."

"And I never expected to spend it watching my husband check out how the Razorbacks are doing."

He rattled the newspaper but stayed behind it.

"So how are they doing?" she persisted.

Roarke finally looked over the top of the sports section. "I really don't care. But you called me your husband. That's a start."

Tisha swallowed hard. Her mouth was awfully dry, and she wouldn't have minded a sip of the cold champagne. "I didn't mean to start anything," she said nervously.

"Let me know when you do," he said, winking. He set the newspaper aside and picked up his glass, sipping it slowly. "I don't mind waiting, though."

"Are you trying to make me less nervous?"

Roarke grinned. "Maybe."

"Won't work." He was teasing her, that was all, she told herself as she searched his face to be sure she was right.

"Will you stop making fun of me?" she muttered, biting her lip as she turned toward the fire.

"You're too nervous," he declared. "Why don't you reconsider and have a glass of champagne?"

The grate of ice against the bottle was followed by the sound of liquid being poured into a glass. Then Roarke was beside her holding out the partially filled glass.

"Shall we drink a toast to the happy bride and groom?" he suggested mockingly.

She watched him sip his own drink. His amusement

at the whole situation irritated her more than his indifference.

"I'd rather not," she said in a low, trembling voice.

Tish swallowed almost the entire contents of the glass, her fingers gripping the stem so tightly that with the slightest addition of pressure it would have snapped.

"This is good wine. It's meant to be sipped, not gulped," he chided. Rebelliously Tisha swallowed the rest and glared at him, longing to throw the empty glass into the fireplace just for the hell of it.

"Whatever you do," he murmured, correctly interpreting the gleam in her eyes, "please don't throw that glass at the fireplace. It would take you forever to get all the splintered particles out of the carpet."

"What makes you think I would try?" she demanded, tossing her head back.

"You're the woman of the house now. Keeping it clean is usually the wife's job." Roarke smirked, leisurely moving away from her.

"You'd like that, wouldn't you? She said. "We"—that word just stuck in her throat—"you can hire a housekeeper."

"Expensive, but probably worth it. You don't strike me as the Martha Stewart type," he murmured.

"Well, no. I don't know how to use a glue gun, and I'm not a convicted felon."

"My kind of girl."

Tisha set her glass down. "Let's get one thing straight, Roarke—I'm not your girl and I never will be."

"No," he said, his expression entirely serious. "You're my wife. And that means a whole hell of a lot more to me than it seems to mean to you."

"That's right!" Tisha stormed. "Right now it doesn't, not at all!"

"Tisha, what do you want?" he asked quietly, his eyes narrowing ever so slightly as he looked at her.

She sat up straight and looked at him with all the pride she could summon up. "To be left alone." With an imperious turn, she rose and started for the hallway, finding it impossible to continue fielding his comments.

"Where are you going?" Roarke asked with a bland show of interest.

"To bed," she tossed over her shoulder.

"It's a little early, isn't it?"

"It's only nine o'clock," she agreed, "but I have to unpack and shower."

"It has been a rather hectic, nerve-racking day," he admitted. "It probably wouldn't hurt to turn in early."

"For once we agree," she murmured sarcastically, and hurried down the hall before he could reply in kind.

Her suitcases were sitting on the floor at the foot of the bed. She had no intention of unpacking them since she was determined not to remain very long in the house. The line of her mouth tightened grimly as she searched through the cases for her pajamas. It was just too bad that she'd left that task up to Blanche. Her aunt had packed only a slinky nightgown that was going to cling suggestively.

Taking it, a blue robe, and the cosmetics with the makeup remover, Tisha scurried into the bathroom adjoining the master bedroom, trying very hard not to recall the last time she had been in there. She was going to remove every last molecule of makeup and mascara and look as unsexy as possible.

At least she wouldn't have to wear Roarke's pajamas this time, she thought wryly as she stepped into the shower stall to adjust the water temperature.

A quarter of an hour later, she was dressed in her nightgown and had slipped on the covering robe before opening the door into the bedroom. As she stepped into the room, she saw Roarke standing on the other side of the bed, unbuttoning his shirt.

"What are you doing here?" Tisha breathed, her eyes widening as he removed his shirt.

"I decided you had the right idea about making it an early night," he returned smoothly.

"You're not sleeping in here?" It was meant to be a statement, but the uncertainty in her voice made it a question.

One brow was raised in mockery before he turned to sit on the bed, his back to her. "I'm not about to spend another night trying to sleep on the couch."

"Well, I will, then, because I am not going to share a bed with you!" Tisha declared, moving hurriedly toward the door, afraid at any moment to feel Roarke's hand on her arm.

A glance over her shoulder as she opened the door into the hall revealed that he was still sitting on the bed, now removing his shoes. Worst of all, she felt disappointed that he hadn't tried to make her stay. Some weak part of her wanted her objection to be swept aside.

Inside the study, Tisha stared at the couch, realizing she had forgotten to get any pillows or blankets, but reluctant to return to the room where Roarke was in case she gave in to any last-minute persuasions. Sleep was impossible anyway, she decided, walking aimlessly about the room.

An audio system was enclosed in a glass-fronted cabinet on the far side of the room. Leafing through the CDs stacked next to it, she chose one and put it on to play. She returned to curl onto the couch as violins cried a melancholy tune.

Perfect. Nice and dismal and definitely unromantic. Drawing her knees up to her chest, she cradled her chin on them and listened to the sad melodies that expressed her mixed feelings better than she could say.

A shadow fell across the steps. Her muscles stiffened as she raised her head to stare at Roarke. Her pulse was beating wildly in her throat at the implacably calm expression on his face.

"What are you doing here?" she demanded in a wary tone.

His dark eyes swept over her before he mounted the steps and walked toward the wailing speakers.

"I'm not going to stay awake tonight listening to lonely violins," he answered, pressing the power button of the audio system to off.

She was sure that he could hear the pounding of her heart in the ensuing silence. She tried to appear as calm and in control as Roarke did.

"Would you bring me a pillow and some blankets?" she requested icily.

"No."

His reply was spoken so quietly that at first Tisha didn't realize what he had said. When it did sink in, she unconsciously tilted her chin at a defiant angle.

"What do you mean?"

"I mean that you won't need them," Roarke answered, still standing in the shadowy corner near the audio system where it was difficult to see his face.

"Why?" Have you decided to sleep here instead?" she asked, maintaining a hostile façade with a concerted effort.

Slowly his footsteps eliminated the distance between them until he was standing in front of her, the sexy look in his eyes holding hers captive.

"No. And neither are you."

There was an agitated shake of her head. "I'm not spending the night with you." Her voice trembled, making her words uncertain.

"Yes, you are," Roarke answered smoothly, reaching down to draw her to her feet. "So stop arguing."

Tisha tried to pull away from his grip. "No, I'm not! I don't want to!" There was panic in her voice.

"I think you do." One corner of his mouth quirked in a smile. "Don't try to pretend that you don't want me as much as I want you." He smoothly picked her up and carried her in his arms down the steps, through the door into the hall.

"Put me down!" she gasped, uselessly kicking her feet in the air while one arm was pinned by her own body against his chest and the other was restrained by Roarke. "What's up with this king-of-the-apes routine?"

"Me Roarke. You Tisha. Tonight's the night, babe."

"Ohhh . . ." She didn't know whether to laugh or cry. But his direct approach had some very definite advantages, like not having to think.

The bedroom door was open, and Roarke carried her in, closing it with his foot. Out of the corner of her eye, Tisha saw the bed, its covers turned down, and she wiggled against the firmness of his hold.

"Stop it! Put me down!" Her cry was softer as he carried her down the steps. "And I don't mean on the bed, either! This isn't fair!"

With an amused sigh, he set her on her feet, his hands still holding her arms at her sides. "There's only one way to silence you, isn't there?" He smiled.

And he pulled her hard against his chest, melting her reluctance with a conquering kiss. For a moment, Tisha was able to resist the assault on her senses, but he was much too determined and persuasive—if dragging a woman around like a caveman could be called persuasion, strictly speaking. But she couldn't hid her passionate response.

Betrayed by my own body, she thought with a surrendering sigh. She slipped her arms around his neck, no longer fighting his attempts to mold her closer as she gave herself up to the rapture and fire of his touch. While his mouth sensually explored her neck and the hollow of her throat, she yielded happily when his hands slipped the robe from her shoulders.

As his fingers touched the shoulder strap of her nightgown, Tisha knew there was no turning back. And there was exultant gladness in knowing she didn't want to either.

"Roarke," she whispered. The ache for him was in her voice. "I want you to know I love you."

"I guessed that all along," he murmured against her mouth.

"Roarke—"

"You talk too much," he declared, lifting her again into his arms and carrying her to the bed, his mouth effectively shutting off any more attempts at conversation.

Later in the night he turned to her again, and this time Tisha offered no token resistance to his desire. There was none of the pain of before as he aroused her to the ultimate fulfillment, again and again.

When the morning sunlight awakened her, she slipped quietly from the bed, glancing briefly at Roarke, sound asleep, as she picked up the robe from the floor to hide her nakedness. The bliss that had so tenderly enveloped her last night was gone, replaced by yesterday's odd, disoriented sensation that none of this had happened, that she wasn't really married, and pretty soon she was going to wake up and look around at reality.

Staring out the window, Tisha tried to figure out just what was going on with her. At the muffled sound of covers being thrown back, she turned from the window, her gaze hungrily seeking the masculine figure in the bed. He was awake, lazily watching her with a dark light in his eyes that immediately sent an answering rush of fire through her blood. But Tisha determinedly tilted her chin.

"Good morning," she greeted him coolly.

Roarke propped himself upright on one elbow, arching a brow as he searched her face. "Good morning," he returned, his eyes narrowing slightly. "We must have had a cold front move in during the night."

She ignored his innuendo. "I'm going to make some coffee. If you want any, you can come out to the kitchen and get it."

To get from the window to the steps leading to the door, Tisha had to go by the bed. Even though she was prepared for some movement from him to prevent her, she still wasn't able to elude the hand that closed over her wrist.

"What's the matter with you?" he demanded. The covers shifted farther, revealing the bareness of his muscular, tanned chest while she fought the intoxication of his touch.

"I don't want any morning romp in the bed, so let go of my arm," she answered sarcastically.

He did, then gave her a disbelieving frown and raked a hand through his tousled light brown hair. "What happened to the loving woman I held in my arms last night?"

"Last night might have been a mistake." There was a tremor in her voice. "I just don't know, Roarke. When I get too close to you, I can't think very well."

He pulled her onto the bed beside him, his eyes narrowing as he searched her face. Tisha lay rigidly beside him, not fighting or attempting to escape.

"What is it? Are you regretting what happened between us last night?" Roarke muttered.

"Maybe." The vague answer struck out at him more effectively than her hands. "I don't know why I feel the way I do."

"For God's sake, why don't you just stop second-guessing everything and relax? We have a lifetime to get used to the idea of being married."

"Maybe that's it. The lifetime part," Tisha said unhappily.

She saw his baffled irritation vanish in less than a second. The anger went out of Roarke's eyes as he threw back his head and laughed. Her breath was caught by the engaging smile on his face when he brought a tender gaze back to her face.

"That's what's bothering you, isn't it?" he murmured, the smouldering fires in his eyes making her heart race. "You are young. A lot younger than I am. Sometimes I forget that."

"Sometimes I think you kind of took advantage of that," she snapped, swallowing back the longing that rose in her throat.

Yes, I did. I know a good thing when I see it, and I know a beautiful woman when I see one, and I wanted you from the second I saw you. We waited to get married, just like you wanted. So you can't really say I took advantage of the situation. But I really enjoyed taking advantage of you last night."

She whomped him with a pillow just to get the look of self-satisfaction off his handsome face. "Shut up! You're awful!"

"Why is it awful to make love to my wife—who enjoyed it very much? Didn't she?" His lips followed her jawline in a feathery caress.

"Don't change the subject!" She forced herself to remain immobile even as he found the pulsing cord in her neck.

"I will if I want to. So listen up. I love you, I wanted to marry you, I want some day to feel our children growing inside you, and it's you I want to see in the rocking chair beside me when we've both grown old together. Do you call that taking advantage, Tisha?"

She couldn't hold back a sob of pleasure at his tender and unmistakable declaration of love.

"But I want to be sure you love me." His fingers

traced the line of her mouth. "I thought a long engagement would give you time to think things through. And the day I gave you the ring, I was certain beyond any doubt that you loved me. So if you just changed your mind on that"—he fell back into the pillows—"um, I don't know what to say."

"I do love you, Roarke. I knew I did that day when we met at the church. But not yesterday during the ceremony," she murmured, not even aware that her hands were sliding over his bare chest. "I just couldn't believe that you loved me. That it was real."

"Well, you can stop doubting it," he ordered. "I don't say what I don't mean. Love, cherish, honor—yeah, that's what I vowed to do for you for the rest of your life. And I meant it."

"I think," she whispered, brushing her lips teasingly against his while a mischievous light of happiness sparked in her eyes, "that you may have to spend the rest of your life proving it to me."

"It will be my pleasure," Roarke answered. His arms brought her closer in his embrace. "I hope you're not going to make that coffee now."

"What coffee?" Tisha smiled, meeting his lips eagerly as his head moved down to hers.

Don't miss
TRY TO RESIST ME,
available now from Zebra . . .

There was Sin, larger than life, filling the archway to the bedroom. Clad only in a pair of ripped denims, he walked into the kitchen. The hard, muscled chest looked deceptively lean—and she felt a flash of delight at seeing his bare skin, nice and brown, broken only by the V-shaped pattern of dark chest hairs.

His steel-and-silver hair was uncombed, its thickness in sexy disarray. A deep sleep had softened the rugged cut of his features, but his eyes were alert as he took in the look of shock on Mara's face.

"Good morning." His greeting sounded so natural that it made her wonder if she had her days mixed up. Was it Saturday? No, it definitely was Friday.

"What are you doing here?" she recovered enough to demand, then said, "I didn't see your car outside."

"You didn't look. My car is there, parked alongside of the cottage," Sin informed her, regarding her with lazy interest.

That explained it, Mara realized. Since she'd walked instead of driving, her angle of approach to the cottage hadn't given her a glimpse of the far side where his car was.

"Then you're the one who turned the thermostat up and made coffee," she concluded, relieved that it hadn't been an oversight on her part.

"I must be," he agreed, "unless there's a ghost haunting the cottage that you didn't tell me about." His mouth curved into a half grin. "Did you think you'd lost it?"

"I . . . I had a lot of things on my mind," Mara faltered in her own defense. "Adam's been sick with a cold all week. He's better now. So it was possible I might have overlooked a few things Monday."

"Not you," he said lightly. "You're Miss Perfect."

"Why are you here?" His comment annoyed her. "It isn't Saturday."

"I decided at the last minute to come up a day early. Is that all right?" Sin asked, knowing that he didn't have to ask her permission. "I don't recall reading any restriction in the lease that said I couldn't use the cottage seven days a week."

"Of course there wasn't," Mara retorted impatiently. "But you could have let me know you were changing your routine."

"I told you it was a last-minute decision. I didn't think you'd appreciate a phone call in the wee hours of the morning."

"Um, no." He had a point there, Mara thought.

"And it was well after midnight when I decided to drive up here a day early," Sin continued.

Mara doubted that he'd been alone at that hour of the night. That thought prompted another: maybe he hadn't made the journey alone either. She looked beyond Sin to the bedroom and glimpsed the sleep-rumpled brown satin sheets.

Sin followed the direction of her look and her thoughts. "There's no one with me, if that's what you're

wondering." Amusement edged the hard corners of his
mouth when her dark gaze flew back to him.

"You've been spending more and more of your week-
ends alone lately," Mara said. "Don't you get bored without anyone to entertain you?"

"Not yet but that's possible," he conceded dryly. "But
if it gets too dull around here, I can always argue with
you."

This conversation was going nowhere. Mara wondered why she hadn't just walked out the second she'd
seen him bare to the waist, lounging in the doorway
wearing only ripped jeans.

Scratch that thought. His physical charm was just
about irresistible. But he took obvious delight in laughing at her, no matter what she said or did. She turned
away and took out her annoyance on the items in the
grocery bag, not caring if she crushed the bread or
dented a can or two.

"I've had a long week, you know. Taking care of
Adam isn't easy work. And I don't feel like arguing with
you. Now or ever," she added tightly.

He studied her profile, noticing the strain etched in
her features but unable to guess that he was the cause
of most of it. Her eyes were large black smudges against
the ivory cream of her complexion. The line of her
finely drawn mouth was tense, her emotions rigidly contained.

Sin walked to where the coffeemaker was plugged in
only a few feet from her. Opening the cupboard door
above it, he took out two cups and set them on the
counter.

"Why don't you take a break for a few minutes, Mara,
and have a cup of coffee with me?" he suggested. "It's
fresh and hot. The groceries can wait until later."

Oh, how sweet. Well, he didn't have to pretend a so-
licitous concern for her well-being, because she wasn't

impressed. She flashed him an icy look as he filled the first cup.

"Forget it. I don't want coffee." The sharpness of her retort made his eyes widen.

He set the carafe back in the coffeemaker as a heavy silence filled the air, charging the atmosphere. His steady blue gaze stayed on her.

"No problem." His voice was low. "But I could use the caffeine. Gotta wake up, right?" He took a long sip from the cup he'd just filled.

Mara hesitated only an instant before answering coldly, "Go ahead." She continued unpacking the bag, her movements as brisk and rapid as she could make them without throwing things around. "But I don't need stimulating." The second the words were out of her mouth, she wished she hadn't said them.

"You sure about that?" Sin's voice changed subtly, a sensual quality entering it. "Makes a man want to prove you're a liar."

"Which says something about male arrogance, doesn't it?" Mara countered.

"Or female talent for provocative behavior," he said smoothly.

"I didn't mean it to sound so suggestive. I wasn't thinking—and, like I said, I'm tired." She clutched the loaf of bread in her hand, and she paused to pat it back to plumpness before realizing how silly she must look. She put the bread down and turned to confront him. "And I wasn't trying to be provocative."

"Whatever you say." Sin was closer to her than she had realized. She started to take a breath to make some reply when his hand touched her neck. His fingers began tracing the base of her throat, exploring its hollow, and all her muscles constricted. Mara's heartbeat was erratic, speeding up, then slowing down as his fingertips lingered or moved over her sensitive skin. Her gaze was locked with his and she had the sensation of being drawn into the blue depths of his eyes.

"I'll bet ice cream doesn't melt in your mouth," Sin declared in a soft, but very masculine voice that felt like a caress.

The straight line of his mouth never varied. There wasn't a hint of a smile. He seemed oddly detached, as if conducting some simple exercise that didn't require his concentration. His fingers began outlining the neckline of her blouse. At the point, they brushed the top of her breasts before encountering a button. Then they started their upward slant to the base of her throat.

"What do you . . . No, it doesn't melt." Her voice was soft, too, thanks to the state of sensual confusion she was in. "I eat it too fast."

No matter how she tried, the delicious daze wouldn't lift. Not as long as he was touching her, she realized. At first she had submitted to the caress of his fingers to prove it didn't affect her. Now that she knew better, she had to bring this sudden intimacy to a close.

Fighting the threatening sensation of weakness, Mara reached up and pushed his hand from her neck. Then she took a step away and turned her back to him, looking for a distraction. The loaf of bread was on the table where she'd left it. She grabbed it just for something to do.

"What's the matter?" Sin asked in a voice that said he knew.

"Nothing's the matter." Mara opened a cupboard door to put the bread away. She seemed to lack coordination. Her movements were jerky and out of synch. "Don't paw me like that, please. I'm not interested in sex for the sake of sex at this point in my life."

"Oh?" There was a lot of curiosity in the one-word question. "When do you think you will be?"

Instead of putting him on the spot, she'd tripped herself up. It was a question she couldn't answer and she knew she didn't dare try.

And here's
RANCH DRESSING,
available now from Zebra . . .

His voice was low and it was difficult to see his face in the shadowy dimness of the room. There weren't any lights on downstairs. What light there was came from the stairwell and outside. Yet Charley could feel the disturbing intensity of his gaze.

"Then what are you doing here?" Forced anger was her defense against him.

"After I had my steak dinner, I went to a bar. There was this drunk there . . ." His voice took on a different quality, gentle, almost caressing. "He kept singing 'Charley Is My Darling.' And I started wondering what I was doing in that bar when my Charley was here."

Her heart cried out for him, loving him all the more for saying such beautiful words, but it hurt, too. Charley turned her head away, closing her eyes tightly.

"You can skip the sweet talk, Shad." She fought for self-control.

"I'm telling you what I feel," he countered.

She tried to take the potency from his words with an accusation. "You've been drinking."

"Yes, I've been drinking," he admitted. As she started

to walk away from him, he caught her wrist and pulled her around. She was in his arms before she had a chance to resist. "But I'm not drunk."

"Let me go, Shad." She tried to twist out of his arms but they tightened around her, holding her fast. The warmth of his hands seemed to burn through the thin material of her robe.

"Wow!" He spoke under his breath as he became suddenly motionless. An exploring hand moved over her hip. "You don't have anything on under this."

Aware of the imprint his body was making on hers, her own senses echoed the aroused note in his voice. Yet she tried to resist it.

"Shad, don't," she protested.

But he merely groaned and rubbed his shaven cheek against hers, brushing her ear with his mouth. "It's no use, Charley. I've tried to stay away from you, but I can't."

His mouth rocked over her lips, persuading and cajoling, sensually nipping her lower lip until she was reeling. Restless male hands wandered over her back, caressing her. She was helpless against this loving attack.

"Do we have to deny ourselves?" Shad muttered thickly as her lips grazed along his jaw. "I don't see any reason to pretend I don't want you. Do you know what I mean?"

"Yes." The aching admission was torn from her throat, the ability to think lost. "I want you too . . . just as much."

It was the answer he had been waiting for as he swept her off her feet and into his arms. Her hands circled his neck while her mouth investigated the strong column of his throat, savoring the taste of him. He carried her to the couch and lowered her to the cushions while he sat on the edge facing her.

He leaned down to cover her parted lips with his mouth, his hard tongue taking total possession. Raw desire licked through her veins, a spreading fire that left none of her body untouched. His hands deftly loosened the buttons of her robe and pushed the material aside to expose her beautiful breasts.

Just as eagerly, her fingers tugged at his buttons. When the last one was unfastened, Shad yanked his shirt free out of his jeans. She moaned softly as she felt the heat of his flesh beneath her hands. Her fingers moved over his flexed and rippling muscles, excited and stimulated by this freedom to touch and caress.

Forsaking her lips, his mouth began a downward path. Delighted quivers ran over her skin as he explored the sensitive cord in her neck and left a kiss in the hollow of her throat. Her fingernails dug into his flesh when his mouth grazed her breast, its point hardening with desire, luring his attention to it. Charley shuddered with uninhibited longing under the arousing touch of his tongue.

When she was weak with need, he returned to soften her lips with his kisses. "Tell me you want me, Charley," he begged. "I want to hear you say it again."

"I want you, Shad," she whispered against his skin. "More than that, I love you."

"I want you more than I've ever wanted any other woman in my life," he told her roughly.

"Stay with me tonight, Shad," she murmured. "Tonight and tomorrow night and every night of my life. I don't want you to leave me."

"You know I can't promise that, Charley," he muttered, brushing his lips over her cheek.

She knew. Her arms curved more tightly around him, fusing the warmth of his bare flesh with her own. "Hold me," she whispered. "Don't ever let me go." Her eyes were tightly closed, but a tear squeezed its way through her lashes. It was followed by more until Shad tasted the salty moisture on her skin.

"Don't cry, Charley." She felt the roughness of his

callused hand on her cheek, wiping them away. "For God's sake, don't cry." His voice held no anger, only a kind of anguished regret.

"I can't help it." She honestly tried to check the flow of tears but it was unstoppable.

With a heavy sigh he eased his weight from her and sat up. She blinked and felt his hands closing her robe. Then he was leaning his elbows on his knees and raking his fingers through his hair to rub the back of his neck. Charley sat up, a hand unconsciously holding the front of her robe. She touched his shoulder, tentative, uncertain.

"Oh, Charley," he said, then turned to look at her. A dark, troubled light was in his eyes. "I swear to God I never meant to hurt you."

"I know," she murmured gently and a little sadly. "It isn't your fault. You didn't ask me to fall in love with you. Maybe if you had, I'd be able to hate you, but I don't."

She swung her feet to the floor and slowly walked to the stairs, leaving Shad sitting there alone on the couch. It was almost an hour later before she heard him come upstairs. He paused at the top of the stairs and Charley held her breath. Finally the door to his bedroom opened and closed. The tears started again.

Sleep eluded her. The hours that Charley didn't spend staring at the ceiling, she tossed and turned fitfully. By Wednesday morning the lack of rest began to paint faint shadows below her eyes. They didn't go unnoticed by her brother.

"You feeling okay, Charley?" he asked at the breakfast table that morning, studying her.

"I'm fine," she insisted.

"Well, you don't look so good," he concluded bluntly.

"Thanks," she snapped and paled under his scrutiny.

Gary's eyes narrowed suspiciously, but he made no comment. Charley knew that her brother probably guessed the cause of her sleeplessness, but there was nothing he could do about it.

When she crawled into bed that night, she expected it to be a repeat of the previous nights. She listened for the longest time, waiting for the sound of Shad's footsteps on the stairs. She dozed off without hearing, then awakened later and strained to hear sounds of him in the other bedroom—boots dropping on the floor, jeans flung across a chair. But there was nothing. Finally fatigue overtook her and she fell into a heavy sleep.

The buzz of the alarm clock was insistent, making her open her eyes despite her attempt to ignore it. She climbed wearily from the bed, irritated that the one time she'd managed to sleep, she had been forced to wake up. She dressed in her usual blue jeans and blouse and left the bedroom in a daze.

Charley barely glanced at the closed door of Shad's bedroom. She didn't know whether he was still sleeping or already downstairs. Not that it mattered, she told herself and entered the bathroom. With her face washed and her teeth brushed, she lost some of that drugged feeling.

At the bottom of the stairs, Charley was shocked to find Shad sleeping on the couch in the living room. Too tall for it, he was sprawled over the length of the cushions with his feet poking over the end of the armrest. From somewhere, he'd gotten a blanket, which was loosely draped over him. She couldn't imagine what he was doing sleeping on the couch. She walked over to waken him.

Her hand touched his shoulder and he stirred, frowning in his sleep. The second time Charley gripped his shoulder more firmly and called his name. "Shad. Shad, it's time to get up."

He shrugged off her hand but he opened his eyes. They focused slowly on Charley's face as she leaned over him. He gave her a slow smile.

"Good morning." His voice was husky with sleep, its drawl thicker.

"Good morning." She wanted to ask him what he was doing on the couch, but his hand reached out to capture one of hers and pull her onto the cushion beside him.

"Don't I get more of a greeting than that?" Shad mocked and put his hand behind her neck to bring her head down.

Charley stopped needing direction when she neared his mouth. Her lips settled into it naturally and moved in response to his sampling kiss. She was breathing fast when she finally straightened. He started to shift his position and winced from a cramped muscle. The discomfort made him take note of his improvised place to sleep. He seemed to register vague surprise when he figured out that he was on the couch.

"Why are you sleeping here?" Charley finally asked her question.

"The mood I was in last night, if I had gone upstairs, I would have ended up sleeping in your bed." There was impatience in his expression as his hands settled onto the toned muscles of her upper arms and began rubbing them absently.

"Oh, Shad." She trembled with the quick onrush of desire.

"Yeah, you should say, 'Oh, Shad.' I don't think you know what you're doing to me," he muttered. "At this rate, I'm going to be sleeping in the barn next, just to keep my hands off you."

Here's a look at Janet Dailey's
compelling new hardcover,
CALDER STORM,
available now from Kensington . . .

Trey hesitated, then headed in the opposite direction. Away from the dance area, people tended to gather in clusters or travel in twos and threes, making it easy for him to spot a solitary figure. There were few of those, and all male.

Then he spotted her coming his way, the neon light of a bar sign flashing over the sheen of her hair, and everything lifted inside him, his blood coursing hot and fast through his veins. His long striding walk lengthened even more, carrying him to her.

A smile broke across her lips. "You forgot to say which stage. There happens to be three of them."

The glistening curve of her lips and the sparkle of pleasure in her eyes acted like the pull of a magnet. When mixed with the pressures of waiting, wondering, and wanting, the combination pushed Trey into action.

His hands caught her by the waist and drew her to him even as he bent his head and covered her lips with a long, hard kiss, staking his claim to her. There was an instant of startled surprise that held her stiff and unresponsive, but it didn't last. It was the taste of her giving warmth that lingered when Trey lifted his head.

Through eyes half-lidded to conceal the blatant desire he felt, he studied her upturned face and the heightened interest in her returning gaze. He allowed a wedge of space between them, but didn't let go of her waist, his thumb registering the rapid beat of the pulse in her stomach. Its swiftness signaled that she had been equally unnerved by the kiss.

"I was just about convinced that I'd have to turn the town upside down to find you," he told her in a voice that had gone husky.

"It wouldn't have been a difficult task," Sloan murmured. "After all, you know where I'm staying."

"I forgot," Trey admitted with a crooked smile. "Which shows how thoroughly you've gotten to me."

She laughed softly, paused, then reached up, fingertips lightly brushing along a corner of his mouth. "You're all smeared with gloss."

He pressed his lips together and felt the slick coating, but it had no taste to it. "You use the unflavored kind, too." Automatically he wiped it off on the back of his hand. "My sister claims that a man should taste her and not some fruit."

"You have a sister?" Sloan asked, absorbing this personal bit of information about him. "Younger or older?"

"Younger." By less than two minutes, but Trey didn't bother to divulge that and have the conversation diverted into a discussion of the twin thing. Instead, he took note of the change in her attire—the bulky, multipocketed vest and tan pants replaced by a femininely cut tweed jacket and navy slacks. "You ditched the camera and changed clothes."

"The others were a bit grimy from all the arena dust." Her matter-of-fact answer made Trey wish that he had taken the extra time to swing by the motel, shower and change his own clothes, but he'd been too anxious to get here. A quick smile curved her lips, rife with self-mockery. "This is my first street dance," she said. "So I had to ask the desk clerk what to wear. He assured me it would be very casual."

"Your first street dance, is it? In that case it's ti. showed you what it's all about." Grinning, Trey shi..ed to the side and hooked an arm behind her waist, drawing her with him as he set out for the dance area.

"I should warn you," she said, slanting him a sideways glance, "I'm not much of a dancer."

His gaze skimmed her in frank appraisal. "I'm surprised. You have the grace of one." He guided her through a gap in the row of onlookers, then turned her into his arms, easily catching up her hand. The band was playing a slow song, which suited Trey just fine. "Don't worry about the steps," he told her with a lazy smile. "Dancing was invented solely to provide a man a good excuse to hold a woman in his arms."

A laugh came from low in her throat, all soft and rich with amusement. "Something tells me it was a woman who came up with the original idea. How else would she ever coax a man onto the dance floor?" she teased.

"And something tells me, you're probably right."

GREAT BOOKS, GREAT SAVINGS!

When You Visit Our Website:
www.kensingtonbooks.com
You Can Save Money Off The Retail Price Of Any Book You Purchase!

- All Your Favorite Kensington Authors
- New Releases & Timeless Classics
- Overnight Shipping Available
- eBooks Available For Many Titles
- All Major Credit Cards Accepted

Visit Us Today To Start Saving!
www.kensingtonbooks.com

All Orders Are Subject To Availability.
Shipping and Handling Charges Apply.
Offers and Prices Subject To Change Without Notice

By Best-selling Author
Fern Michaels